'Emylia was born to write detective fiction.'
—Veronica Henry, author of *The Impulse Purchase*

'An expertly plotted and hugely compelling murder mystery . . . Crime fans are in for a treat.'
—Lucy Clarke, author of *One of the Girls*

'Certain to win the hearts of Richard Osman and Agatha Christie fans.'
—Hannah Richell, author of *Secrets of the Tides*

'A big-hearted page-turner with twists you won't see coming and the best pair of amateur sleuths I've read in a long time. I loved it!'
—Lucy Diamond, author of *Anything Could Happen*

'My favourite new crime series.'
—Ginny Bell, author of *The Dover Café* series

'Irresistible, beautifully written, and hugely compelling . . . Kept me turning the pages for one more delicious chapter well into the night.'
—Rosie Walsh, author of *The Man Who Didn't Call*

'Gorgeous writing and a plot crammed with suspense, this is your perfect new crime series.'
—Kate Riordan, author of *The Heatwave*

'Beautifully written, gripping, and so atmospheric . . . One for fans of Richard Osman!'
—Emily Koch, author of *What July Knew*

'The mystery is perfectly paced and the characters vivid and true, inviting us to join in as fellow sleuths as we unravel the secrets of the past. I can't wait to return to Cornwall with Emylia Hall for the next adventure.'

—Emma Stonex, author of *The Lamplighters*

'A treat of a book: immersive, suspenseful, full of twists and turns . . . It's as captivating as a Cornish summer. I loved it.'

—Susan Fletcher, author of *Eve Green*

'*The Shell House Detectives* is a hug of a book that is transporting and full of love, with a humdinger of a mystery at its big heart.'

—Amanda Reynolds, author of *Close to Me*

'Captures the magic and beauty of Cornwall wrapped within a warm and engaging detective story. I loved it.'

—Rosanna Ley, author of *The Forever Garden*

'An intriguing mystery that perfectly captures how a seaside community is rocked by murder.'

—*The Sun*

'Mystery with heart! Fans of intriguing crime mysteries will adore this brand-new series, which is just crying out to become Sunday evening television.'

—*The People's Friend*

'Engaging and enjoyable.'

—*Daily Express*

THE
ROCKPOOL MURDER

THE ROCKPOOL MURDER

A SHELL HOUSE DETECTIVES MYSTERY

Emylia Hall

Text copyright © 2024 by Emylia Hall

Published by Thomas & Mercer, Seattle

www.apub.com

Amazon, the Amazon logo, and Thomas & Mercer are trademarks of Amazon.com, Inc., or its affiliates.

ISBN-13: 9781662505164
eISBN: 9781662505171

Cover design by The Brewster Project
Cover illustration by Handsome Frank Limited – Marianna Tomaselli

Printed in the United States of America

For my family

Prologue

There's no answer at first so he knocks again. After the night they've all had, it's no surprise that people are lying low, but it's a new day now – whether they like it or not.

Beyond the garden, the endless sea and sky are painted bands of sapphire: an unreal backdrop. It's dead calm out there, nothing stirring. Meanwhile, just steps away, the infinity pool glitters with the light of the already fierce sun; his head aches to look at it. Police tape wraps its untroubled waters as neatly as a gift.

Frustration roars inside of him. This time he knocks at the outhouse door with both hands: a hard, fast paradiddle. When he wipes his forehead, his palms come away glistening.

Across the snooker-baize lawn, Rockpool House is like a tall, iced cake. A shimmering all-white confection that looks good from a distance but inside is a mess. Flies crawling. Sticky trails of accusation. Tears puddling – but maybe not as many as people might think.

Still no response, so he tries once more.

The door opens easily.

Inside, the room is stifling; the windows shut fast. He's expecting the usual: old booze vapours and sweat and the faint hum of that eye-wateringly expensive aftershave from some place on Jermyn Street.

But instead, he gets the stench of a butcher's shop. One where the cuts don't shift as quick as they should, and the decks go unswabbed.

He blurts a wake-up call – then stops abruptly. He claps a hand to his mouth; retches.

It looks fake. A prank. A hoax. But maybe it always does?

Until yesterday, he'd never seen a dead body.

He backs away, nausea swilling in his gut. Then he turns and runs; as fast as he can, all the way back up to the house. His scream – a shrill falsetto – goes with him.

1

THE DAY BEFORE

'What do you think?' says Ally. 'Is this better here, or over in the corner?'

Sunita tilts her head, considering. 'Perfect where it is. It'll be the first one people see when they walk in.'

Ally steps back and smiles gratefully at Sunita. This will be her first solo show. While Ally's been making art for most of her life, until now her pieces haven't been found in galleries – apart from a single piece hanging here in the Bluebird for months on end. One is on the wall in a hospice in Truro; sea meeting sky in a blaze of colour. Another in a primary school, with windbreaks and sails and high-flying kites. But these were gifts, because Ally appreciated the fact that her work was wanted at all. Her vast seascape collages, made from litter-picked ocean plastics, aren't to everyone's tastes. From a distance they're all colour and light, the beauty of nature, but up close you see the detritus, the carelessness of human beings.

It was Jayden who talked Ally into accepting Sunita's offer to have a summer show at the Bluebird, Porthpella's one and only gallery and tea room. Jayden seems to be able to talk her into pretty much anything, though Gus thinks it works the other way round, too.

'You're going to have a full house for the private view,' says Sunita. 'Congratulations.'

'Oh, that's down to you, not me.'

'That's not true. People are curious. All these years you've been living here, and a lot of folk didn't even realise you were an artist.'

'Well . . .'

'And a detective,' twinkles Sunita. 'How goes that, anyway? I heard you and Jayden helped old Mr Wilcox find his heir last month. Stopped that beautiful house going to that no-good brother of his.'

Ally has lived in Porthpella for more than forty years, but it always amazes her how word travels; news, gossip, other people's business, flying across the dunes and over the village rooftops. Bill was always in the thick of it. As the local sergeant, he prided himself on knowing what was going on. And people gave him energy; every conversation or interaction was a vital shot in the arm. For Ally it's often the opposite. As happy as she is that a crowd will be coming to the gallery tomorrow, the thought is also overwhelming. She even asked Sunita if it was essential that the artist attend the opening. Sunita laughed, thinking she was joking. Then told her not to forget to write a speech. Now surely *Sunita* was joking.

'We've been fairly quiet lately,' says Ally. 'And Jayden's been busy getting the campsite up and running. They've done a wonderful job.'

'If they think they're busy now, wait until the school holidays hit. Jayden and Cat won't be able to take a breath until September.'

Which perhaps means Jayden won't be able to take a case, either. Ally is quite prepared for it to be a gentle summer for the Shell House Detectives.

Sunita puts her hands on her hips and surveys the space. The Bluebird isn't a big gallery, but the white walls give it a spacious feel, and Ally's collages pop.

'Okay, so it's looking great. Just those last two to go? Cup of tea, Ally? Or the iced version? This heat.'

'Iced tea would be lovely.'

Ally follows her through the arch to the tea room. It's near enough the end of the day, and Sunita has already flipped the 'Closed' sign. After the morning coffee crowd, then the lunchtime rush, it's been quiet this afternoon, the beach proving the greater draw. The temperature has been steadily climbing all week, and they are now, it seems, officially in a heatwave. Ally's daughter is always quick to offer her perspective: *You try summering here in Sydney, Mum. It's on fire. Literally.*

Ally's just sinking into a chair, wafting her linen shirt for air flow, when the door swings open. A woman steps inside.

'I know it says "Closed", but please tell me you're not really? I'm dying here,' she says.

But she looks like the opposite of someone on their last legs.

The woman takes off her floppy straw hat and beams. She has an American accent and a film star's smile. Long silver-blonde hair. The kind of figure that looks yoga-strong: long-limbed and taut. Ally reckons they're close in age – she's sixty-five – but that's probably where the similarities end.

'Then we're here to save you,' says Sunita. 'What'll it be?'

'God, really? You ladies. Thank you. Are you drinking iced tea? One of those, please. I'd go Long Island but I'm driving, and these lanes are already killing me.'

The woman slides into a chair, crossing her long legs. She runs her fingers through her sparkling hair.

'Where are you headed?' asks Ally.

'Rockpool House. You know it?'

'Of course.'

Everyone around here knows Rockpool House. Sitting high on the clifftop on the coast road out of Porthpella, it's an art deco masterpiece. With its clean white lines and curved face, it shimmers like a pearlescent shell. It was in the same family for decades but this spring the owners sold up, and in stepped Baz Carson, former lead singer of The Nick – The Nick being one of Gus's favourite bands of all time. Imagine his excitement when the rumours were confirmed: a rock star in residence at Rockpool.

'You've met Baz?' the woman asks, just as Sunita hands her a tall glass of iced tea.

'Oh no,' says Ally.

'Never,' says Sunita. 'Though I think I've seen his car.'

'He's become quite private. He wasn't always that way.' She smiles over the rim of her glass, but there's something sad there too. 'I've known him forever.'

Ally can feel a story coming: those last two pictures of hers can wait. But the woman's pointing through to the gallery space.

'I'm loving what I'm seeing. I thought in a place like this it'd be all cutesy seaside scenes.'

Then she's up and out of her seat, moving from collage to collage, glass in hand, as if she's already at the opening.

'Plastics. Now that's something. I bet Baz would love these.'

'You're looking at the artist,' says Sunita, nodding to Ally. 'Ally Bright.'

'Oh, beautiful.' The woman holds her hand out to each of them and they shake. 'I'm Tallulah Pearce. Pleasure to meet you.'

'Artist and private detective, I should say,' says Sunita with a wink. 'Isn't that right, Ally?'

Ally shakes her head. 'Occasional,' she says.

'Seriously?' Tallulah gives a delighted laugh. 'And now I feel like I'm back in Hollywood.'

'So, you're a friend of Baz's?' says Sunita.

'Yes, a friend. That's what we've become.' Tallulah gives a wistful smile. 'But once upon a time, Baz and I were in love. Forty-five years ago, we were everything to each other. Forgive the over-share, I'm emotional.'

'Oh wow,' says Sunita. 'You've got history.'

'History up the wazoo. And I haven't seen him in thirty years, so let's just say the stakes are high. Which is why I wish this iced tea had a little jazz in it. My big entrance. I'm nervous, girls.'

But Tallulah looks anything but nervous.

'Alright if I go freshen up?'

'Please,' says Sunita, gesturing to the loos.

As Tallulah disappears, Sunita grins at Ally. 'You've got a potential sale there. Imagine it, Baz Carson becomes a collector of the works of Ally Bright.'

Ally laughs. 'No, I can't imagine.'

Because what will probably happen is that the fabulous Tallulah Pearce will disappear behind the gates of Rockpool House, and they'll never see her again.

2

Baz Carson stands at the edge of his infinity pool looking out over every shade of blue. There's the chlorinated water at the tips of his toes, the salted stuff beyond – endless miles of it – and up above a sky of such pure cerulean that he wants to take a bite out of it; eat the whole lot up.

I earned this. Every damn inch of it. And that thought is all the high he needs these days.

Any moment now, Baz's nearest and dearest – or the closest thing to it – will be descending on Rockpool House for a party weekend like no other. He's turning seventy, and while once he would have thought that meant game over – wrinkly buttocks, zestless, basically waiting to do everyone a favour and die – Baz now knows better: he's in his prime. The doctor said as much last month, as he passed his MOT with flying colours. *Keep doing whatever you're doing*, was the only prescription.

And right now, he couldn't feel more alive. Vitality fizzes in him, from the tips of his fingers to his toes. If he were to dive into the pool, it'd be like a lightning strike.

At this exact moment, thousands of people are reading his words. Baz Carson unplugged. But there's nothing lo-fi about this memoir of his – it's electric. And it's lit up with his trademark honesty and integrity; life lessons worth listening to. It's a buzz, being the talk of the town again. Everyone knows he writes killer songs, but for his words to stand alone – without the beautiful noise of Davey's drums or Jimbo's bass (RIP) or Stu's keys (RIP) – that's something else.

It'll be a buzz, too, having everyone here this weekend. Not the hangers-on or the yes-men, but the inner circle. The people that are part of his story, for better or for worse.

Nicole and the kids; though Ruby and Jet haven't listened to anything he's had to say in, what, twenty years? That funny little Imogen, who he hardly knows at all. Davey and Rupert, the only ones left from the old days. Felix, Connie's boy. And Tallulah, flying in from LA. There are people missing – and he's thinking of Connie now, dear Connie – but such is life. And right now, Baz is feeling so damn good, nothing's going to take from that. No sad stuff.

They won't all like the book, this gang of his; they won't all like the things he has to say. But Baz has followed his instincts, and his instincts have never proven him wrong. The first draft that Felix turned in was as forgettable as a cup of tepid tea. Stupid idea to get a ghostwriter in the first place. But the boy took it well, the parting of ways. And anyone would say it's a better book for it.

More punch.

More truth.

That's rock and roll for you.

You don't get to seventy and start watering it down. You blaze, that's what you do. You blaze all the way to the finish.

Somewhere behind Baz a door opens: light footfall across the terrace. Probably the chef girl, Saffron, setting everything up ahead of the first guests arriving. Up above, a lone gull floats on a thermal; it drifts lazily, its wingspan wide and true.

This is living, thinks Baz. *And I'm going to keep on doing it forever.*

Try stopping me.

3

Unblocking toilets: not Jayden's favourite job, but it's about taking the rough with the smooth. At least that's what he tells himself as he rocks back on his heels and tries not to gag. And while they haven't had a lot of time to enjoy the smooth so far, there have been definite glimpses.

Like yesterday, when Jayden did a lap of the campsite just as the sky was filling with pink light. The air was thick with barbeques, and someone had a killer spice rub going on. People were gathered around fires, their music considerately low (he's always glad when he doesn't have to get his stern face on and be the fun police). An old man in beach shorts, lumbering along with a bucket full of dirty dishes, said *Evening, good sir* just as two pre-schoolers in onesies – up past their bedtime, good thing his daughter couldn't see them – sped by on scooters.

In that moment, Jayden felt like they'd made something special.

They'd planned to call it Halcyon Camping. A neat idea about joy and peace and holiday nostalgia. But then Cat said, 'I think it sounds a bit up itself,' to which Jayden replied, 'What, because it's Greek?'

'Because it's show-off Greek.'

And Jayden pictured his dad's face at that one; he'd passed on his love of Greek myth to him as a kid. 'Well, fine, what do you want to call it?'

So, Top Field Camping it was. 'Dad's idea,' said Cat. Which kind of says it all. It isn't that Jayden doesn't get on with his father-in-law, but it's been a little intense, living first in the farmhouse with Cat's parents, then in a cottage on their family farm, for coming up to two years now.

That mathematics doesn't quite make sense to Jayden, because it means it's nearly two years since they left Leeds: the city Jayden was born and raised in; fell in love and married in; worked in, too, as a police officer in the city centre. Two years since Jayden's partner Kieran was stabbed while on duty, and died in his arms, as a Saturday-night crowd surged around them. In that moment, everything changed. Cat said *let's start over*, and he knew that meant Cornwall. The far western corner, where her family had farmed for generations. She was pregnant then. And now Jasmine's growing up with sand between her toes and a campsite as her back garden. This is the life they're giving her. And while there are things Porthpella lacks – it's a very small pond; it's not the most diverse; there's no Leeds United – he can't deny the gifts.

This toilet though? Not a gift.

Jayden flushes once more for good measure, then peels off his rubber gloves, stows his bucket and plunger, and heads out into the late afternoon sunshine.

He's got used to the way the weather changes, living here. Clouds blowing in, and out again just as fast; sudden downpours then polished skies. But for the last week the mercury's been rising. The sky, and sea, set permanently to blue. Jayden loves this heat and so does Cat. Apart from anything else, it's good for business.

A young guy saunters towards him, a towel over his arm.

'Hey man.'

Jayden's memory quickly brings up the details: Felix from London, here in his camper. Plot 37. Arrived Thursday for four nights. Nice guy. Chatty.

'Hi, alright, Felix? How was your day?'

'Yeah, good. Great. This weather, man!'

Jayden's not sure what's brought Felix to Porthpella. He drives an old Bongo, but there are no surfboards or bikes lashed to it. Maybe he's a hiker? Or an artist? He looks the part, in a kind of cool, creative way.

'I had a crack at surfing. Beginner's lesson.'

'What, with Broady?'

Broady opened his long-awaited surf school at the start of the summer, running it out of a hut beside Hang Ten coffee shop. With his girlfriend, Saffron, working next door, the two of them have a good thing going on. The plan is to extend next season; Broady has a vision that's sustainable, all salvaged timber and upcycling. If he can pull it off, it'll be really something.

'That's it. Very patient with my floundering.' Felix raises his arms; stretches. 'And now I feel like I've been in a fight – and lost. Man, I'm unfit. But hey, it was what I needed. Nothing like going ten rounds with the sea to put things in perspective. S'pose you surf, living down here?'

'Not sure you could call it that,' says Jayden. 'I'm with you on the floundering. We've only been in Porthpella a couple of years, which round here is . . . nothing. Emmet vibes.'

'Emmet?'

'An old word for an ant. Otherwise known as a holidaymaker down here. Nice, huh?'

Felix laughs. 'Where were you before that? Before your status was, er, lowered?'

'Leeds.'

'Presumably not running campsites?'

'Police.'

And it's unusual for him to offer it so easily.

'Wow, okay. Big change. You ever miss it?' Felix waves an arm, takes in the blue sky, the big sea, the rolling sun-scorched fields. 'Stupid question probably.'

'You'd be surprised,' says Jayden. 'I haven't totally left it behind though. I do some detective work down here.'

'What, with the local force or . . . private?'

'Private. My friend and I set something up. Keeps us on our toes.'

And Jayden's willing to bet Felix is picturing a grizzled old ex-cop, the kind usually to be found bothering the golf courses of the Algarve or hunched at a bar, dourly pondering the cases that got away. Not Ally in her dune house. Not Fox.

Felix runs a hand through his hair, grins back. 'I better watch my step round here, then. No using all the hot water in the shower block. No disposable BBQs, right?'

'Yeah and watch the volume on your music. I've dealt a few ASBOs in my time.'

'You've got my number, there,' says Felix. 'I'm in the music business.'

'What, really?'

'Strictly on the sidelines. Journalist. But I did pack my Gibson. I'll keep the fingerpicking down.'

'You know Baz Carson lives in Porthpella now?' Even though the name didn't mean much to Jayden at first, he presumes Felix knows who he is.

'I did hear that, yeah.' Then, 'He's the reason I'm here.'

'You're writing about him?'

'No, it's pleasure, not business. Kind of. Well, duty. Maybe that's the right word.'

Jayden's about to tell him that his friend is catering Baz's party weekend when Felix abruptly changes tack.

'Anyway, mate, has the shop closed?'

'Technically. What do you need?'

'Just some milk.'

'I can sort you out. Come on.'

They stroll round to the office, a timber cabin that Cat's dad and his mate erected back in the spring; through the build Jayden hovered in the background, passing them tools every so often, making tea. It's not that Jayden's rubbish at DIY – anyone can watch a YouTube video and work it out, right? – but he knows that Cat's dad likes playing up his role. Just like Cliff built his daughter a doll's house once upon a time, now he's building her a campsite. And it is his land, so who's Jayden to complain?

They sell a few basics from the cabin – milk, local eggs, good coffee – but for anything else they point guests to Wenna and White Wave Stores, five minutes down the lane.

Jayden unlocks the door, Felix following behind him. As he goes to the fridge Jayden hears the ping of Felix's phone.

'Semi-skimmed or full-fat? Or oat milk?'

When Felix doesn't answer, Jayden turns.

He's staring at his phone, and his skin, which was pale to start with, is sheet-white. He swears under his breath, and for a second Jayden sees a flash of someone completely different.

Felix looks up sharply. 'Sorry. Just . . . people, eh? Erm . . .' He scratches his stubble. 'What did you ask me again?'

'The kind of milk you wanted.' Then, 'Everything okay?'

'Yeah.' Felix blinks. 'Yeah. Sorry. Semi-skimmed.'

Jayden passes him the carton and Felix takes it, his eyes still on his phone. He murmurs his thanks as he wanders out.

Jayden stands in the doorway watching Felix trudge slowly up the path in his flip-flops.

'That's a quid,' he says to himself. But it feels petty to yell after him. He'll catch him another time, when he's less distracted.

People, eh?

4

Saffron has driven past the gateway to Rockpool House plenty of times. She's seen it from the water too, a beacon on the clifftop, but she never thought she'd get to go inside. So far, it's proved a little surprising.

Electric gates and soaring views: check. Light-filled rooms and abstract paintings: check. But the kitchen is a long way from what she imagined. She'd been picturing shimmering granite work surfaces, a double oven and a vast American-style fridge. Bespoke and up to the minute, for sure. Instead, the vibe is pure eighties and shades of beige: totally functional, but a little worn and torn.

Saffron stands by the T-shaped island, putting the finishing touches to her canapés: smoked mackerel and whipped crème fraiche, lobster skewers, Cornish mozzarella and tomato toasts. Everything locally sourced. She chops chives, as fine as iron filings, and scatters them. *Almost done.*

She wouldn't normally take on a gig like this, because there's nowhere she'd rather be in the summer season than her own café, Hang Ten. But Porthpella's newest resident, Baz Carson, heard about her beachside cook-outs on the grapevine, and decided he wanted that flavour for his party weekend. Broady and the girls talked her into it, reckoning it could be the start of something big for her. But Saffron doesn't want big. In her café on the sand, surfboard stowed out back, she already has everything she ever dreamt of. The fact that the place was only possible because of a small inheritance from her mum is the sad part of the story, but Hang Ten is made of love – from every piece of timber in the walls to the micro-foam of her flat whites. Pure love.

But it takes money to keep it all going, and like everybody's lately, her basic costs have gone up. This Rockpool gig is too well paid to turn down.

And it is kind of fun, cheffing for a celebrity. Not that she'd heard of Baz Carson before this.

Spare no expense! was the brief. Followed by: *Make it authentically Cornish.* Seeing as Saffron is Porthpella born and bred, just like her mum before her – and her dad too, in fact, which she discovered last year thanks to Ally and Jayden – she figures that means she can cook anything she likes. Baz told her he's teetotal, but the wine cellar is fully stocked, there are several magnums of champagne, and a special birthday cocktail in the works. *If they want to keep on slowly killing themselves then that's on them*, he told her with a drawl.

Now, Saffron takes one of the vast serving platters and starts to lay out her canapés. It's not often she makes things this fiddly. Standard fare at Hang Ten is wedges of lemon drizzle and fat cookies, carrot cake and brownies – the best in West Cornwall, she's been told. When she runs one of her cook-outs down on the sand, the fire's going and it's all about massive vats of Sri Lankan curry, bursting with monkfish and sweet potato and ginger, and bowls of zesty coconut sambol on the side. Or paella by the bucketload – and that's what she's making for Baz's birthday night. She's not going to broadcast the party on Instagram – a private chef means keeping it private – but she'd like a few pictures for herself.

She's just lining up the shot, phone in hand, when she hears whistling and looks up. Baz swaggers into the kitchen, hands in the pockets of his shorts. He jumps up and takes a seat on the counter, nimble as an imp.

'You know that song? "Mellow Yellow". Donovan was mad about you, apparently. Which of course I understand, now that I've met you.'

Saffron doesn't get the joke – she presumes it's a joke anyway – but she's spent enough time in the service industry to know that sometimes you just smile and keep on keeping on.

He grins back at her, and the elfin vibe continues. His eyes sparkle like gems in his tanned face.

Before she took the job, Saffron looked him up. She watched videos from the early eighties, live at Knebworth and Earl's Court; Baz's hair skimmed his shoulders, his jeans were skin-tight, and onstage he snarled and prowled like a big cat. She wonders if her mum liked The Nick. Saffron still has her mum's vinyl collection, but she was always more into reggae and soul than rock. Still, she'd probably have thought it cool that Saffron is cheffing for a one-time rock star this weekend. Their biggest hit, 'You Do It For Me', was used on a major TV show a few years ago and, according to Baz, it topped the charts again as a result. Saffron doesn't watch much TV, so she wouldn't know.

'So, I'm going to give you a cheat sheet for the weekend,' he says. 'Listen up.'

When Baz hired her to cook for a group of nine – cook and serve and do drinks too – she'd wondered about bringing in some help, but he'd been fixed on the idea of an intimate gathering. *My mum was one of seven kids*, he said. *Which means, counting herself, my nan ran around after nine people every day of her life, near enough. Did it standing on her head.* So, with that logic, Saffron went with it. He didn't seem like he was being stingy.

'I want you to be part of things, Saffron, not hidden away below-stairs. So, you'll need to remember names. That goes a long way, a little thing like that: remembering a name.'

Saffron nods. Smiles. She's already got Baz's number: he likes to dispense advice. He also likes to say her name a lot. *Saffron, Saffron.*

'We've got Nicole. I'd better start there. We were married for twenty years. Divorced for the same. She's a live wire, Saffron. Get on her wrong side and you'll know about it. But she gave me my kids and my kids are everything to me.'

In Saffron's brief wanderings about the house, she hasn't seen any photographs of said kids though. Framed pictures of Baz onstage, sure. But none of family.

'Jet's a hell of a guitarist but he hides his light so far under his bushel it needs surgical extraction. No drive. None.' His eyes flash. 'I can tolerate pretty much anything, Saffron, but indolence, lethargy, bone-bloody-idleness? Not that. And it comes through in his playing. There's no heart. No feeling. It's like he doesn't care if that instrument's in his hands or not.'

'Jet's your son?'

'He is. And Ruby. My little Ruby. Not a lot of shine in that one anymore, and that breaks my heart. She's married to the most boring man in Surrey. Which is saying something.'

'Is Ruby a musician too?'

Baz barks with laughter. 'Oh no. Her daughter, Imogen, tinkles the ivories from time to time though.' He looks down at his hands, pulls at the skin at the edge of a nail. 'Or used to, anyway. I haven't seen her in a few years. We don't keep up.'

He claps his hands together.

'The good news is that Adrian, the boring husband – an accountant, nothing interests me less than numbers, Saffron – isn't here. The lack of invitation might have something to do with that,' he says with a chirrupy laugh. Then narrows his eyes. 'You think I'm harsh.'

'Not at all,' she says, 'it's your party.'

But she can't help wondering if Baz is this indiscreet with everyone.

'Then I've got my boys, Davey and Rupert. The only ones still standing from the old days, Saffron. I love Davey but he's a lost soul. I'm amazed his heart's still beating. Drinks, drugs, you name it. We all liked to party once upon a time, but when you get to a certain age it just doesn't work anymore does it? It's not, as you kids say, a good look.'

'They were in the band with you?'

'Davey was my drummer. He knew what he was doing back then. Never found his feet after we split though. Sad. You'd think Jet was his son, to see the pair of them. Inveterate underachievers.'

He shakes his head, looking thoughtful suddenly.

'And Rupert?'

'Rupert's the money man. Been with me since the start. I call him a necessary evil and he doesn't disagree. The best thing about Rupert? He takes care of everything, and I let him. Nothing bores me like money, Saffron. Maybe that's a rich man's privilege, to say I find dosh tedious, but I've never cared. Enough is as good as a feast. You won't miss Rupes: big voice, big guy. Looks like he should be hanging out at the Stock Exchange instead of on a Cornish clifftop.' Baz counts on his fingers. 'Alright, then we've got Felix. And we've got Tallulah.' He looks up sharply. 'You've heard about the book, have you?'

'The book?'

'My memoir. Hot off the press. There's a copy knocking about here if you want it. I'll stick my paw print in it for you and it might be worth a bob or two,' he says with a wink. 'They're all in the book. Nicole, the kids, Davey and Rupert. Some would call it a roasting, but I call it love. Tough love. But what's love without honesty?'

Saffron makes a mental note to get a copy of the book. It'll make for some interesting bedtime reading while she's staying at

Rockpool. Weird bedtime reading too, with the characters in it living and breathing all around her.

'Have your guests all read the book?'

Baz raises an eyebrow. 'You mean, are there going to be fireworks this weekend?' He winks. 'Put it this way, I won't need to order in any rockets or Catherine wheels. I'm joking. We're all grown-ups here, Saffron. And I'm the birthday boy. I can get away with anything, can't I?'

He jumps down from the counter.

'Felix, you'll like. A good guy. I gave him his start but then he ran with it. Made something of himself. I'm genuinely very proud of Felix. I wanted him to stay here but he's slumming it at some campsite. Can't think why.' Baz passes his hand across his mouth. 'There's always been a bit of friction between him and the kids, I guess. His mother, Connie, she was very dear to me. Well, it's all in the book.'

Like a key change in a song, something appears to shift in Baz. Saffron watches him as he moves to the window; his shoulders dropped.

'It's strange to you, I suppose. Putting all of your life on the page for anyone to read.'

'Not if you're famous to start with. Maybe you want to set the record straight.'

He turns. 'Set the record straight. I like that.' Then, 'I'm not really very famous, Saffron.'

'Okay, yeah. I've got to admit I hadn't heard of you before,' she says with a grin.

He bursts out laughing. 'But you'd heard the song, right? Everyone's heard the song.'

'I *think* I've heard the song.'

'You'll have heard the song. It's been good to me, that tune. Perpetual pay day.' He claps a hand on the counter. 'I wouldn't have this place without that song.'

'It's a great place.'

'Tallulah. Tallulah's the last guest. But don't go getting starry-eyed on me.'

'Why would I?'

'A hundred years ago Tallulah and I met in LA and fell in love. But life had different paths for us. Mine led back to Blighty and straight to The Nick, but hers never left California. But we reconnected. It was after Connie died. Tallulah seemed like the only one I could talk to. There was some of the old magic there still. She's flying in. First time I'll have seen her in . . . decades.'

'That's romantic,' says Saffron.

'Maybe there's a song in it, huh? Anyway, that's us. That's my tribe. They're all I've got, Saffron. Not one of them is perfect, but then who is?'

At that moment a buzzer sounds.

'The gate,' says Baz. 'The first arrival.' He looks at her, his face suddenly creased with doubt. In this very short time of knowing Baz, Saffron suspects it's an unfamiliar emotion to him. 'It is a good idea, isn't it? This party? I won't live to regret it?'

'A party is always a good idea.'

But as the buzzer sounds again – impatiently, raucously – and Baz heads out of the kitchen, Saffron feels a sudden sense of foreboding. It comes out of nowhere, as quick and powerful as a rip current. 'A party is always a good idea,' she repeats to herself. Only this time with less conviction.

5

Tallulah takes the lanes slowly. They freak her out, these tunnels of green, the way the briars scrape the sides of the hire car – *thank you, damage deposit* – then the sudden cresting of a hill and the ocean appearing like a splash zone on a roller coaster. Maybe she should close her eyes and throw up her arms and whoop. Or maybe not. She'd quite like to arrive at Baz's place in one piece.

People complain about driving in LA: the gridlock; the keeping a lid on the road rage because you never know if someone's packing (once she was cut up by a 4x4, and when she sounded the horn she got the wave of a pistol in reply). But she'd take it over these country lanes any day.

Tallulah is out of her comfort zone, just like Wendy said she would be. Wendy, her therapist with the pistachio-coloured Venice Beach bungalow, the rattan couch and the dachshund called Bobby McGee. When Tallulah told her that she was going to England to see Baz for the first time since that gig way back in the Nevada desert – what was that, thirty years ago? – Wendy leant forward in her chair. She knew it was going to be good.

And it was. Tallulah told the story with such equanimity too, sounding as balanced as a pair of scales: a true Libran.

She hadn't been pining for Baz all those years, because she wasn't the kind of woman to live her life in the shadow of what she'd lost. But Baz Carson was unequivocally The One: the relationship by which she'd measured all that followed. It wasn't quite first love, but almost. She'd been twenty-two. He was three years older. The English boy abroad, not an alien in New York but a stranger in LA. They'd met in a club on the Strip, and he didn't know that wasn't Tallulah's natural habitat, that she was, in fact, far happier hunkered round a beach fire in Malibu – before it became what it is now – or rocking in a hammock on the deck of her cabin in Topanga. That little A-frame that's been hers for five decades: remodelled, expanded, but still the same spot, with the croaking of frogs and yipping of coyotes and the smut and smog of the city a million miles away (or just over the hills).

Baz loved Topanga too, for a time. But he'd come to California to make his fortune, and although he'd found Tallulah – the length of her legs, the slide of her smile, who couldn't argue with that kind of luck? – he'd wanted the lights. He might be publishing a book called *Turn It Down: Living and Loving the Quiet Life*, but back in '79 Baz had wanted to say yes to everything – and he'd wanted to live loud. When he found that the Strip wasn't paved with any kind of gold, he'd put his guitar in its case and said he was homeward bound – holding out his hand as though all she had to do was take it and off they'd go. *London's where it's at, babe.* But Tallulah didn't want London. Or, more precisely, she didn't want to leave Topanga. Could a heart belong to a canyon? To a stretch of pebble-strewn beach and a forest-lined highway? To the electric sunsets and drifting eagles and horseback rides to the summit? Hers did.

So, they'd parted. They'd parted with tears and transcendental sex. They'd parted with promises. But then life got in the way of the promises.

'For you too?' Wendy said at that line.

'For me too.' When you were the one paying, you could afford a lie or two.

'Tell me about the gig in Nevada.'

23

'It was hot,' she said. 'They were loud. And incredible. Baz tried to set me up with his drummer. He was married by then. And famous.'

'And how did you feel about that?'

'Which part?'

'The drummer.'

'Not my type.'

Another lie. How ridiculous, the urge to save face. The truth is she slept with Davey Hart and woke up the next morning in a Vegas motel with a screaming hangover and a whole lot of self-hatred. She thought Baz would see them at breakfast at least – that she'd observe some shrapnel of desire, some flicker of jealousy in his eyes – but he never showed.

It was a watershed moment. *No more*, she said to herself.

But then, out of the blue, four and a half years ago – something like three decades after the concert, after the pointless drummer – a letter. Sent on a wing and a prayer to the house in the canyon. *Are you still there?* was the first line.

And of course she was. It was the place she said she'd never leave.

In his grief, Baz was softened. He was searching and spiritual. He wrote a lot about Connie, and Tallulah let this tap run and run. Then one day it sputtered. Stopped. And something else began.

Do you remember how crazy the frogs were at night? he wrote. *I went round shutting all the windows and you opened them all up again and said, 'Get used to the damn frogs, Baz.' I could have done, you know. Got used to the frogs.*

They were faithful correspondents, prolific too, their lines of connection fizzing back and forth across the Atlantic Ocean. She forgot he was famous – or used to be anyway. He was her boy with a guitar standing on the deck in his shorts, with his slow-tanning chest and wicked grin. He told her about the book he was writing,

24

and she even read bits of it. And then the invitation. *I'm turning seventy and I'd like you to be there.*

When Tallulah found out what an intimate gathering it was, a handful of people – family, really – at his new home at the westernmost tip of England, a crook of land called Cornwall, she took it as a sign. Not a party at an ostentatious London hotel, or a salty club in Soho, trying to capture the old days, but in the place where his life had settled into something different; stiller, softer.

It was an invitation to more, she was sure of it.

Her 'yes' was resounding, because at her age she'd learnt to take no prisoners.

Now, as the car lifts over the hill, she feels herself leaning back in her seat, resisting the drop; her fingers squeeze the wheel. Then she sees it, Rockpool House, lying ahead on the clifftop. Stately; curvaceous. Half lighthouse, half mansion; ice white and gleaming. Those sweet ladies back in the gallery talked about it with a whisper of awe, and now she gets why.

Tallulah considers herself immune to wealth, living where she does. She's not impressed by square footage or ocean frontage, because she's known too many assholes who've had plenty of both. But this first sighting of Baz's house speaks to something deep inside of her. She imagines Cupid crouched on the rooftop, shooting arrows with a sniper's accuracy.

What do you want from the trip? Wendy asked in their last session. Bobby McGee was stretched out at Tallulah's feet and the thick scent of the Venice canals drifted through the beaded curtain. For once Tallulah was moved to tell the whole truth and nothing but the truth. Such was her confidence; such was her joy.

I want everything, she said.

She presses the accelerator and shoots down the hill towards Rockpool, leaving all the lost years behind her once and for all.

6

Imogen sits in the window seat, feeling the burn of sunshine through the glass. Her mum told her to keep the blinds closed so it'll be cooler at night but there's no way she's going to block the view. And that's just one example of why they're incompatible roommates. A situation that sucks on multiple levels.

Uncle Jet gets his own room. He's in it now, probably sleeping off the hangover she could smell on him as he gave her a high-five earlier. *Yo Imo, what's up?*

Davey gets his own room. He arrived with his sticks, drawling, *Let the good times roll!* Imogen heard him playing on Grandad Baz's basement kit earlier, and even she could tell he was out of time.

Rupert gets his own room. In fact, he gets what Baz calls 'the cottage', a separate outhouse by the pool, but Rupert clearly thought it was a downgrade, the way he slammed down his case and said, *What am I, contagious?* To which Baz replied it was en-suite and something about his dodgy prostrate.

The American, Tallulah Pearce, gets her own room. She was the last to arrive and Imogen was watching then too. The way Tallulah threw her arms around Baz, Imogen reckons she'd much rather be sharing with him, though she couldn't tell if Baz feels the same. Imogen doesn't know her grandad well enough to read him, but she likes to think this weekend might change that.

Even the chef, Saffron – cool name; cool hair – gets her own room. All the way up in the attic, away from everyone – which she's probably glad of. Mum's already been bending Saffron's ear about dairy-free canapés, and Granny Nicole was loudly offended that Baz hadn't refurbished the kitchen ahead of their arrival. Saffron must think they're entitled idiots from London.

They are entitled idiots from London. Mostly.

And Imogen's no better, griping about sharing a room in a house that is, on the whole, pretty freaking fabulous – so long as you see past the tatty fixtures and fittings. But it's not the sharing bit, it's the Mum bit. *Girls together*, Ruby said to her, with an almost-hug. But then she went back to whatever she was doing on her phone. Scanning Rightmove or arguing with Dad, probably.

Consider yourself lucky, love. Felix is at a campsite down the road, Davey said to her with a wink earlier.

She's never met Felix, but she knows who he is, of course. She knows who everyone is. Imogen couldn't tell you the exact moment that she realised she'd been born into a complicated family, but the folklore has been fixed her whole life. Granny Nicole and Grandad Baz split when Imogen's mum was eighteen and Uncle Jet was sixteen. Baz moved in with Connie, who ran pottery classes from a converted garage in south-west London. He used to drink way too much, drugs too, but when he was with Connie he stopped all that. Only Baz wasn't *with her* with her. And, although it doesn't sound very fair to Imogen, Granny Nicole seemed to hate Connie all the more for that. Felix was the kid, caught in the crosshairs of this platonic romance; sandwiched between Ruby and Jet in age and therefore despised by both. By the time Imogen came along – thirteen years ago – Granny Nicole was ever-present but Grandad Baz was a dim and distant figure who she saw once or twice a year, or even less.

And now they're all here, together. Not Connie, she died a few years ago. If she was still on the scene this party would probably never have happened, as – according to Mum and Granny Nicole – Baz only had eyes for her. But everyone else who matters – that's how Baz put it on the invite; ouch for Dad – was invited.

From her spot high up in the window, Imogen sees a movement down by the swimming pool. It's Baz, doing what looks like a mixture of meditation and some martial art. Behind him the blue waters of the pool appear to meet the sea. Imogen checks her watch. Drinks on the terrace at six o'clock, that's what Baz said.

Should she change? Probably. Her t-shirt has a tuna mayo stain on it from their lunch at the motorway services. Cornwall is a long way from anywhere and maybe that's why Baz likes it. That's another thing Imogen wants to ask him this weekend. Why Cornwall? From the way Mum was grumbling about it, Imogen suspects it's something to do with Connie. But then Mum grumbles about everything.

She pulls her t-shirt off, dipping away from the window as she does. Rooting about in her bag, she pulls out a blue cotton dress. It's creased but pretty. Imogen doesn't usually do pretty, but suddenly she wants to make the effort for Grandad Baz. And, judging by her mum's packing, Ruby clearly has no plans to change out of her uniform of Breton tops and ankle-skimming chinos. It's mean, really, to make no effort.

Imogen moves to the mirror, smoothing her hands over the skirt. She turns to the side. She actually looks okay.

Her eye catches something then, in the reflection behind her. Someone's already hit the pool. Maybe it's her mum, thrashing out a grumpy crawl, or Tallulah slicing the water as elegantly as she does everything else. Imogen turns to look properly.

It's Grandad Baz, floating like a starfish.

Face down. Fully clothed. Surely he'll kick and flip any second?

For two, three seconds, Imogen watches – her breath held. Then she screams. 'Mum! Mummy!'

7

Saffron hears the scream before she sees its source. She sprints out into the hallway just as the girl, Imogen, comes clattering down the stairs. A confused-looking Jet is in her wake.

'Help! Someone help! He's in the pool!'

'What the hell is going on?' cries Nicole, suddenly appearing, swaying on her corked heels. Her face is an angry red. 'What's all this bloody commotion?'

'Baz,' sobs Imogen. 'Pool.'

Saffron's fast on her feet, hurtling across the terrace and the lawn. She immediately sees him, face down, drifting towards the outer edge.

Rupert and Davey have emerged carrying sticks, and at first Saffron thinks they're to help pull Baz out, but they're pool cues. The two men stand gaping, drinks in one hand, cues in the other; no use to anyone.

'Call an ambulance,' she says, as calmly as she can. 'Now!'

And Jet's already reaching for his phone.

Then Saffron dives in, splitting the water, three fast strokes and she's with him. She hooks her arm around Baz's neck and shoulders; kicks hard to draw him into the shallow end. As soon as she can touch the bottom, she turns him so he's floating on his back. Saffron tries not to look at his face: the slack jaw, the staring eyes.

There's a commotion at the side of the pool and someone is there, a shadow falling across her.

'Help me,' Saffron says, 'help me get him out.'

It's Davey, batting ineffectually at Baz's shoulders. There's crying somewhere behind: Imogen, probably. And a shriller note that maybe belongs to Nicole.

Realising there's no more help to be had, Saffron hauls herself out of the pool and reaches back down to Baz. With all her strength she tries to draw him out.

'Someone help me with him!' she cries again.

'I can't get hold of him,' Davey mumbles, his hands shaking. Rupert huffs and puffs as he tugs uselessly at Baz's sodden shirt. Jet steps in belatedly, his sunglasses slipping from his nose; and with surprising strength he helps tug him in.

Saffron falls back on to the paving, the weight of Baz immense now he's out of the water. She quickly rights herself and crouches over him. She tilts his head back and leans close.

He's not breathing.

She clamps her mouth to his and gives rescue breaths: one, two, three, four, five. Then she closes her hands, one on top of the other, and places them in the centre of his chest. She begins to press: up, down, up, down.

'The ambulance is on its way,' says a voice close to her. Jet? But Saffron keeps pressing. Counting. She hears the crunch of feet on gravel; a scream – a loud, long banshee wail.

Then a sharper lament from Nicole. 'Oh, for goodness' sake.'

Then Saffron's being crowded out, pushed sideways. She smells perfume – an expensively sweet and spiced scent. *Tallulah.*

Saffron drops back as Tallulah's hands take over. Slender, tanned fingers with chunky silver and turquoise rings. Hands criss-crossed; pumping. For all her emotion, Tallulah knows what she's doing.

'Stay with me, baby,' Tallulah sobs. 'Don't leave me. Not now. Please.'

Saffron rocks back on her heels. She looks to the group, wondering if they already know what she knows.

Imogen stands chewing her thumb, her mum close beside her. Nicole has her hands planted on her hips, her head held as high as a ship's figurehead. Jet is sunk on the grass, his shades back on. Rupert is slumped with his face in his hands, and Davey is leaning on his pool cue as if it's the only thing keeping him up.

'Please,' says Tallulah, her voice broken. 'Please, stay with me.'

Saffron drops her head. She wills the ambulance to hurry, just for someone else to take over. Just so that someone else – someone whose job it is and who knows how to say it – can tell Tallulah that Baz is gone.

8

Mullins watches the ambulance disappear through the iron gates of Rockpool House. Its siren is silent; no need to rush when you've a corpse onboard. He passes a hand across his slick forehead; juts his bottom lip and puffs air upward. Mullins isn't built for this hot summer sun, and high on the clifftop, against the dazzling backdrop of Baz Carson's house, it feels hotter than ever.

He turns back, gazing up at the smooth white lines of the house. It's enormous, with a front as rounded as the hull of a cruise ship. From the road it looks like it's been built so close to the cliff edge it could just steam on out into the bay – after dropping a hundred feet down, that is. But up close there's a run of lawn, trimmed as neat as a bowling green, and a silly great swimming pool. Tiers of terraces, with palm trees and exotic flowers. He's peeking behind the curtain, seeing how the other half live. Only it isn't really the other half, is it? It's the other 1 per cent probably. If that.

Mullins starts to walk back to the poolside, where a group of people are clustered in various states of disbelief and upset. It's his job to speak to each one of them. But yeah, okay, he's a little intimidated. A place like this, people like this, it's not his usual speed.

He'd heard a rumour that Saffron took a cheffing gig with Porthpella's resident celebrity. Nice work if you can get it. He hadn't expected to get a call-out to said celebrity's pad, only to find Saffron standing there, soaking wet from head to toe, the bloke dead at her feet. *I tried*, she said. *But it was too late*. And she looked so completely gutted that Mullins didn't know where to put himself. If he were a hugger – a hugger, and not a police officer – then he'd have got right in there. But he isn't. And he is. So, he didn't.

Right now, Saffron's inside with the girl who found Baz Carson floating in the pool; Saffron doing her 'being nice to people' thing. Mullins needs to speak to the girl – she's an important witness – but that can wait for a minute or two. He'll deal with the adults first.

A woman breaks from the group, then, and comes towards him. A glamorous granny, that's how he'd describe her; though that's probably un-PC, coming from a PC. In fact, she looks like a movie star. Hell, she could be a movie star, for all he knows. He's about to ask for her name and address but she speaks first.

'When are the CSIs getting here?'

Her voice is as tight as a jar lid and very American.

'Forensics? They're on their way.'

'Well, they better get here fast because . . . Baz was fighting fit. And he was a hell of a swimmer. Laps every day. He wouldn't just . . .' She stops, her eyes closing. She takes a long and careful breath. She looks, Mullins thinks, quite calm. But then she covers her face with both hands, and turns and walks briskly back up to the house.

Mullins hesitates, thinking about following. He can feel sweat pricking his forehead, and flicks it away.

'Oh, let her go,' says a woman, stepping forward. 'I'm Nicole Carson. His ex. Ruby and Jet over there are his children.'

She points to two thirty-somethings, sitting on the white wall beside the pool. The man's in black skinny jeans and a ripped t-shirt; slightly built and shaven-headed. He looks the part as a rock star's son. Maybe he's a rock star himself? Mullins isn't really into music, and definitely not the ancient stuff. Mick Jagger could be propping up the bar in The Wreckers and Mullins would think he was just another old-timer from the village. The woman though, Baz's daughter, there's nothing showbiz about her; she's like any of the upmarket mums that scurry round here in the summer, ignoring their kids.

Mullins turns his attention back to Nicole. She smiles stiffly. 'What do you need from us, Officer?'

He can see the streaks of her blonde highlights, as if someone's taken a paint brush to her head. Her jewellery is as shiny as a magpie's hoard: gold chains and a bright red jewel that shimmers like a sucked sweet. Her top plunges in a V-shape that he tries – and fails – not to register before fixing back on her heavily rimmed eyes. She must be the same age as his mum.

She is absolutely nothing like his mum.

'So, we, erm, need to establish what happened,' he says. 'Whether anyone saw anything.'

'Well, Tallulah's right about one thing. He's a strong swimmer.'

'You're the next of kin, madam?'

'I don't bloody know. We're divorced. I don't know what I am.'

'Heart attack,' says a voice from behind him. 'Has to be.'

Mullins turns to see a burly man stumbling on to the patio. The sun glints off his fat gold watch and he sucks up a drink, ice chinking. His forehead shines with sweat, much like Mullins's own right now.

'Sorry. I needed this. Shock. Terrible shock. Anyone else for a drink?'

'What's your relationship to the deceased?'

'Jesus, the deceased,' the man mutters. 'Manager: former. Friend: present. I'm Rupert Frost.'

Mullins scribbles in his notebook.

'We don't know it was a heart attack, Rupes,' says Nicole.

'What else? You don't just fall in your own pool. That or a stroke. My money's on the heart though. He said he was getting chest pains a while back. Thought it was indigestion. Maybe the writing was on the wall.'

'I don't know anything about chest pains,' says Nicole. 'He was bragging to me that his doctor just gave him a gold star.'

When Mullins first arrived at the house, he took a good look at the body – he's getting better at that now: the bodies – and there were no signs of a struggle as far as he could see. No ruddy great knocks or cuts. But until he's gathered witness statements, until there's a post-mortem, they won't be ruling anything out.

'What's your name, sir?' he asks, noticing another man pressing closer. A guy with a shiny bald head and grey stubble. He looks like a Glastonbury version of Gus. His t-shirt says *The Grateful Dead* on it – which, given the circumstances, seems in bad taste.

'Davey Hart.'

'Relationship to Baz?'

'Bandmate. Old mucker. We went way back.' He blinks; looks shell-shocked. 'Grew up together, near enough. We've been through it all.'

'Listen,' pipes Rupert, 'here's the truth of it. There was a time when we'd have laughed if you'd have said Baz would make seventy. We'd have laughed if you said sixty, or fifty, the way he was going.'

But as Mullins looks around, no one's laughing now. 'And you're all staying at the house?' he says. 'Everyone here?'

'He was my best friend,' says Davey, his voice breaking.

Rupert makes a noise of disagreement. 'Baz didn't do best friends. He was a lone wolf, Davey boy. You know it and I know it.'

'He was.' Davey's voice is climbing now, catching the higher notes.

'Get it together, Davey,' says the guy sitting on the wall.

Jet. Is that even a real name?

'What, he's not allowed to show actual emotion? Some people did genuinely like Dad, believe it or not.'

This from Ruby, Baz's daughter. *No love lost between the siblings*, notes Mullins. Maybe no love lost between them and their father either, by the sound of it. *Intriguing.*

'And Imogen, the girl who spotted him, is your daughter?' he says to Ruby.

She tucks a strand of mousy hair behind her ear and takes a fast little breath. 'Yes. She's inside with the help.'

'The chef,' corrects Mullins. 'Saffron.'

Ruby stares at him. Snorts. 'Are you sure she's not the window cleaner?'

Mullins is wondering how to reply when a car speeds through the gates and crunches to a showy stop. DS Skinner. There's a moment's pause before his boss exits the car, but then Skinner covers the lawn in a few fast strides.

'I'm sorry for your loss,' he says, without aiming it at anyone in particular. 'Detective Sergeant Skinner, from the local force. I had a great deal of respect for Baz Carson. It's a tragedy.'

Mullins blinks. He's not sure he can remember the last time he heard Skinner use the word *tragedy*. Not when JP Sharpe was killed at Christmas, and that was murder. Nor when Larry Boscombe fell from the scaffolding of that newbuild on the road to St Ives. Nor when Mary Cummings, age ninety-one, lost her footing on the stairs. Where was Skinner and his talk of tragedy then?

'What happens next?' says Ruby, her arms tight across her chest.

'Baz's daughter,' Mullins says quietly to Skinner.

'We gather some information from you good people,' says Skinner. 'PC Mullins here will take statements. There'll be a postmortem. Toxicology. In the case of sudden death, it's standard procedure. As difficult as it is, please bear with us.'

'Toxicology?' Nicole laughs: a spiky, cruel laugh. Mullins sees Skinner catch it too. 'Haven't you read his memoir, Sergeant? Baz was clean and sober. Famously so.'

'It goes without saying,' says Skinner, 'but don't leave town.'

A snort comes from the wall. 'You people really say that?' says Jet.

Skinner turns to Mullins. 'Is everybody here?'

'His granddaughter saw him in the pool. Imogen Edwards. She's in the house. And . . .' He looks at his notebook. 'Tallulah Pearce. She's upset, Sarge. Charged off before I could speak to her.'

'Relation?'

'Old girlfriend.' He consults his notebook again. 'Flown over from LA for the first time in decades.'

'I think you need to talk to Tallulah Pearce. And then the child.' Skinner offers his most charming smile to Nicole – which isn't saying all that much. 'I'll keep an eye on things out here.'

So, Mullins traipses up the garden. To be honest, he's glad to get out of the sun.

9

As soon as Jayden hangs up the phone, he drives straight to The Shell House. The news will fill the newspapers when it breaks: *Rock star found dead in clifftop mansion swimming pool.* Speculation will be rife. It'll feel like a story, even if it's not.

What's he saying? Death is always a story. Death is always a shock – even the ones that are foreseen, anticipated, the quiet exits behind hospital curtains. Jayden thinks of his friend Kieran, stabbed while on duty in Leeds city centre. Dying on the street, as Jayden held him, talked to him, did everything he could. That moment is in him now, part of Jayden's DNA. And it's a big part of what brought him to Porthpella.

He wonders what brought Baz Carson to Porthpella.

He jumps out of the car and waves to Ally. She's standing on the shaded wooden veranda, a lead in her hand. Fox turns circles at her feet.

'Hello there,' she says, brightly. 'We're just heading out for a walk. Fox wants to get his paws wet and so do I.'

She stops, looks at him more thoroughly. She's good at people, Ally, even though she thinks she isn't. And she can read Jayden like a book.

'You've got a case,' she says.

He jogs up the steps. Delivers a quick knuckle-bump. As their hands touch, she laughs.

'Not exactly. But something's happened. Baz Carson, the guy at Rockpool? He's dead.'

Ally's face changes in an instant. 'But he can't be.'

'He drowned. Or . . . he was found floating in his swimming pool, anyway. I don't know the cause of death.'

Ally holds her hand to her mouth. She looks down the shimmering coastline; turquoise sea meeting sunlit cliffs. Around the next bay, you can catch a view of Rockpool House in the distance, just like you can see their campsite and the sturdy bulk of Cat's family farmhouse too.

'I met someone earlier,' she says, turning, 'someone who was going to his party. An American. A lovely woman. She was . . . so excited to see him. Oh Jayden, how terribly sad. When did he die? And how do you know?'

'Saffron told me. She's cheffing up there. Al, it was Saffron who pulled him from the pool.'

He'd phoned Saffron, wanting to book her for a cook-out at the campsite in the school holidays. He knew she was working so expected to leave a voicemail, but she answered. And Jayden could tell straight away that something was wrong.

'She was still in shock, I think. She said Mullins and Skinner were there.'

'Oh God, poor Saffron.'

In perfect unison they drop side by side on to the bench. Fox casts a mournful look at the lead in Ally's hand, then settles at Jayden's feet. Jayden rubs his ears. It was this little dog who grounded him after they found Lewis Pascoe lying at the foot of the cliffs back in spring last year. The case that started everything for them. Resigned now, Fox rests his head on his paws.

'So, what will happen now?' asks Ally.

'Witness statements. Post-mortem. It's a sudden death, but whether it's suspicious or not might not be clear straight away.'

'So you're saying it could be suspicious?'

'No idea. But Saffron said he was fully clothed. It was chaos afterwards, but she got the impression that no one saw anything. It was Baz's granddaughter who spotted him and raised the alarm.'

'Could he swim?'

'Every day, apparently.'

'He could have suffered a stroke. Or a heart attack.'

'Yes, he could,' says Jayden carefully.

Ally's husband Bill died two years ago from a heart attack, and while she often talks of him, she never goes into what happened the day he died.

'The police will be looking at medical records. And with someone like Baz, they'll probably fast-track the post-mortem. They won't want the media getting carried away.'

'Tallulah will be devastated,' says Ally. Then, 'The woman I met earlier.'

'One of our campers is connected too, you know. To Baz.'

'Who?'

'I think he's one of the party guests. Though he described it more as duty than pleasure. Nice guy. Music journalist called Felix.'

'Was he at the house when it happened?'

'I don't think so. He'd had a surf lesson with Broady and was crashing out, knackered.'

'Have you any idea how many people were there? At Rockpool, I mean.'

'Good question. I know it was a small group for the weekend. Maybe ten? Saffron said she was catering it on her own. But Al . . . you know what, I'd love to talk to Felix. He got this message on his phone when I was with him earlier and it was something serious, or shocking, or . . . I don't know. He was in the middle of talking to me and his face completely changed as he read it.'

'You think it's connected?'

'Possibly. Possibly not. Could have been anything, right? A message from a partner, something to do with work. It was too early to be news of Baz's death. When I called Saffron, maybe like an hour and a half later, it'd only just happened.'

Ally turns Fox's lead in her hands. 'But whatever the message was, it provoked an emotional reaction. After you spoke to Saffron, you didn't think to go and find this Felix?'

'I didn't think it was up to me to tell him. Saffron would have trusted that it wouldn't have gone any further. Except to you. Obviously, I was always going to tell you.'

Ally places a hand on his arm. 'Jayden, what about Gus? He's a huge fan of The Nick. You know how excited he was when Baz Carson bought Rockpool House. And he's been talking non-stop to me about his memoir that's coming out. I'd far rather we told Gus than he was caught off guard hearing it on the news.'

'Yeah, sure. Of course.' Then, 'Al, hold on. Did you say Baz was publishing a memoir?'

'It came out today. Gus was planning a trip to St Ives to buy a copy especially.'

Jayden's on his feet suddenly. 'Interesting timing, don't you think?'

Her eyes widen as the thought lands.

'If there's even a hint of foul play,' he says, 'it's worth a read, isn't it? If I was Skinner, I'd be buying a copy right now.'

'And what about if you were a Shell House Detective?'

Is there a way in for them? Jayden knows it's unlikely. The force will be feeling the extra pressure with a celebrity death; they'll be all over it. For a moment he imagines the atmosphere at the station right now: the evaluation of witness statements, the wait for Forensics, the theories already being mooted. He knows better than to get in the way of all that.

But a little bedtime reading never hurt anyone.

Or did it?

10

Gus is sitting in a deckchair out on the veranda of All Swell, in a patch of perfect shade. He's got a cool glass of beer in one hand, and a brand-new book in the other. Happy days. It's not just any book, either. Most of the time, Gus reads detective novels. Since he started writing his own, he's become a determined student of the genre, scouring every page for learning. *I've lost my innocence*, is how he put it in one of his navel-gazing letters to his old friends, Clive and Rich. *I'm an escapist no more.*

But in other regards, those same old mates consider him to be exactly that: a great escapist. At sixty-four, Gus thought he was more or less happily married, but at sixty-five he was made to realise the fallacy of this. Divorce was quick and painful, his ex, Mona, soon installed in a new riverside apartment with her new – not so new, it turned out – lover. Disillusioned, and more than a little lost, Gus rented a cottage by the sea for two months, taking up with a cruel mistress: the novel he'd always meant to write. And he's still here now, nearly a year and a half later. Not quite ready to tap out *The End* on either the book or his time in Porthpella. Depending on who you speak to round here (Jayden, Cat, Saffron, even Tim Mullins, probably) the main reason for this is his friendship with Ally Bright. But here's where Gus mumbles and shuffles his feet.

Gus takes another sip of amber nectar and sets down his glass. He runs his finger over the embossed lettering on the cover: *Turn It*

Down. In smaller letters beneath: *Living and Loving the Quiet Life.* Then, in the biggest letters of all: *Baz Carson.*

Baz. Lead singer and founder of The Nick. They only made two albums, but they were both corkers. When the first one came out, Gus was just finishing up at teacher training college: ready to step boldly into the world of geography teaching, strike out over that terrain with a Thermos by his side and his best anorak. Back then, he had a droopy moustache and hair he had to tuck behind his ears. What he'd give for that hair now – or any hair, frankly. Gus got his first teaching job at a comprehensive in an Oxfordshire dormitory town. His first car, a navy-blue Morris Minor, followed. As did his first long-term girlfriend, Carrie-Anne, a soft-voiced, brown-eyed beauty who, of course, he let slip away. And the soundtrack to all those firsts? Baz Carson and The Nick.

Gus is humming 'You Do It For Me' as he opens the cover and checks the dedication.

For Connie, of course. Love always.

Great tune, 'You Do It For Me'. That spine-tingling riff, killer drums from Davey Hart, and a chorus that's the ultimate earworm. It's the one that hit the charts back in the day, and even now it keeps popping up: on a film soundtrack, an advertisement for an online insurance broker, or as a sickly-sweet cover by a young folk-pop act. A couple of years ago a hit TV show used an acoustic version of it – Baz's voice so intimate you could feel every word, every syllable – and it jumped to the top of the charts again. Ever since, Gus has had a fantasy that the band will reform and play a secret gig down The Wreckers Arms. Or maybe just Baz: unplugged, up close. Because the really exciting thing is that Baz Carson now lives just outside of Porthpella, on the road that runs up past Cat and Jayden's.

Gus was in The Wreckers, in fact, when he heard the news; eavesdropping on the grizzly old blokes propping up the bar.

43

'It's a singer who's gone and taken it.'

'What, Beyoncé? Kylie? I'd drop round with a cup of sugar.'

'Baz Carson.'

'Never heard of him.'

'Yeah, you have. *Dum, da-da dum, da-da, dum-da . . . You do it for me, baby.*'

The penny dropped, the other guy joined in, and it was all Gus could do not to hurl back his pint and join in with the chorus. Instead, he said, 'Couldn't help overhearing, chaps. Baz Carson's moving to Porthpella?' And while a bar stool wasn't exactly proffered, Gus is considered enough of a regular to stand and chew the fat with from time to time. *I'm tolerated* – that's how he puts it in those letters of his – *which after thirty years of marriage is a familiar sensation.*

Then he went home and did a little desk research. Baz Carson was not just going to be Gus's neighbour – well, *ish* – but was also publishing a memoir that, according to his publisher, would be tell-all, high-octane, and as rousing as the chorus from 'You Do It For Me'.

Baz's detractors were less complimentary. As one particularly scathing blog put it: *So, Carson is going to tell his story, but is there anyone left to care?*

Well, Gus cares. Gus cares a great deal. Four boys from Northampton, defining a generation. Well, a year. A summer, maybe. But a summer that lives on in Gus's memory. And clearly Baz has done alright off it, with that hit topping the charts again so recently too. You'd need a bucketload of cash to buy Rockpool House. Only trouble with a house like that, you could disappear behind its gates and, well, disappear. Baz has been in residence – *fly the flag, for God's sake, you're rock royalty!* – for three months, and Gus hasn't clapped eyes on him once.

But Gus figures there's time. Maybe once the summer crowds have ebbed – crowds who are already flowing in, despite the schools not having broken up yet. Gus can picture crisp autumn days, sauntering along the empty beach with his hands in his pockets, or taking a turn about the village. *Morning Baz. Morning Gus.* Or, *Fancy a quick one at The Wreckers?*

Oh, Baz is clean and sober now, isn't he? That'd be a misstep.

So, *Coffee at Hang Ten?* Or, *Cheese scone at the Bluebird?* Or, *Bag of chips on the square?*

It wouldn't be the strangest thing, for two blokes of a similar age to fall into friendship in this little corner of the world.

Gus looks down the beach at this perfect view of his: gilded sand and sparkling water; the story-book island lighthouse; the horizon so hard and clean and bright, its perfect geometry stirring something in Gus's soul. No wonder Baz Carson wants to be in Porthpella. For all the things that Gus and Baz might not have in common – one a noted hellraiser turned teetotaller, the other a moderate all the way – they do share this place. And if he doesn't know it already, Baz will soon see that Porthpella is a little bit magical. Friendships have been founded on far less.

And, of course, there's the Saffron connection: Saffron, who Gus has come to count as a friend, is catering his weekend party. Gus is hungry for the stories. He'll be first in line for his coffee at Hang Ten on Monday morning. But then again, that's nothing new.

'Gus, hello there.'

And it's Ally. Ally in a sea-blue tunic, her hair glowing white in the early evening sun. Her cheeks have summer colour.

'Pull up a chair,' he says. 'It's reading hour.' And he holds up his book with a grin. He'll get her a glass. Or better still, dig out a bottle of cold white wine; see if he can't drum up some olives.

But the look on Ally's face stops him in his tracks.

11

Inside Rockpool House it's cool and quiet and very white: white tiles, white sofas, and glinting white chandeliers. Mullins checks behind him, feeling like he's trailing dusty footprints from the gravel drive; as if he's clouding the air just being here.

He can't see any sign of Saffron or Imogen. Or Tallulah.

'Hello?' he calls out. And silence sizzles back.

Mullins peers into the kitchen. It's a large, light-filled space, with French windows leading to the terrace. But the fixtures aren't as fancy as he imagined. Unless it's deliberately retro, in line with Baz's heyday? He sees the signs of Saffron at work: chopping boards, a knife, bunches of half-chopped herbs. Two platters of canapés are just sitting there on the counter. Mullins glances around. It'd be rude not to, wouldn't it? He snaffles one, and the flavour is like a sweet punch. He doesn't know what it is, but he knows he wants another. His fingers hover, moving like one of those grabbers in an amusement arcade, and he takes his pick. Then, because he's not stupid, he rearranges what's left. *Leave no trace.*

Mouth full, he moves back into the hallway. Mackerel pâté is it? But nothing like the stuff his mum scrapes on to her Hovis.

'Hello?' he calls again. 'Police!'

He tries for a calm and collected voice, because they've had enough of a shock, this lot. Tallulah Pearce's reaction seemed the most emotional of them all. Does someone here know more than they're letting on? *You never know with people*, thinks Mullins sagely. And at this stage, they're ruling nothing out.

He takes the stairs. If he, Mullins, was upset, he'd make for his bedroom – the same room he's had since he was a chubby five-year-old covering his wardrobe in football stickers. Sometimes when he peers out the window, looking down Ocean Drive and that same old view, bungalow on top of bungalow, he feels the years whisk away and he might as well be that kid again, tugging at the broken blind, thinking about what his mum is making for tea. Huffing on the pane and drawing smiley faces, watching out for his dad coming home.

This place, though, it's as sleek as you like. No football stickers or broken blinds, here. The staircase sweeps like a go-slow helter-skelter, and Mullins stands on the bend, looking back down. He's got a bird's-eye view of a framed photograph: four musicians onstage, shot from behind; a sea of people beyond. He wonders which one is Baz Carson – the singer? Guitarist? Mullins hasn't really done his homework, and why would he? Cornwall is stuffed to the gills with the rich and famous. On paper, anyway. Most of them buy houses, build houses, buy more houses, then disappear up-country for the other fifty weeks of the year. So, please excuse Mullins if he's not all that interested in Baz Carson.

Though, that said, people reckon Baz was properly living here, year round. Or, since he moved in three months ago, anyway. Was he that rare breed of rich person who not only wants to buy in Cornwall, but live in Cornwall 365? Mullins isn't going to be awarding any medals just yet; it's one thing making the right noises, and another following through. Though the following-through bit is kind of irrelevant now.

He pauses on the landing. One of the bedroom doors is wide open, and from this angle he can see a perfect square of sea through the window. It really is as if the house is a cruise ship. He moves closer and peers in; sees an open suitcase. There's a shiny-looking dress lying on the bed and a strong scent of perfume in the air. Mullins sees Baz Carson's face staring up at him from a book on the bedside table. So, what, the bloke was an author too?

'Are you looking for me?'

Mullins jumps. It's the glamorous granny – though he's really got to stop calling her that. Apart from anything else, it doesn't do her justice. She's wearing some sort of wide-legged, floaty, jumpsuit thing, and looks like nobody he's ever seen in real life.

'I am, yes. Tallulah Pearce?'

She nods. 'It's a wonderful view from here, isn't it? Baz wrote to me, said, "I'm giving you the best room, Tally. I want you to love it here like I love it here."'

Then she drifts to the window, one hand playing with a string of beads at her neck.

He wonders if she's taken something, because there's a strange sort of calmness to her now, compared to by the pool. Her white-blonde hair, her white outfit, this white room. Mullins finds it quite mesmerising; he feels like his eyelids might flutter and close and he could drop back on the bed at any second.

'We need to try and understand what happened,' he says, shaking himself. 'You arrived just as he was brought out of the pool. Is that right? Where were you before that?'

'Here, in my room. I heard a commotion. The girl screaming, everyone running to the pool. Never in my wildest dreams did I think . . .'

'Had you talked to Baz before that?'

'We greeted one another. We held one another. I hadn't seen him for thirty years. There was so much for us to say but . . . I thought we had forever to do it. I went to my room to settle in and freshen up.'

Her eyes swim with tears, and Mullins coughs. He's no good at this stuff. No good at all. Not with anyone, really, but he's really at sea with a person like this.

'And you flew in from America just today?'

'Heathrow, late last night. I drove down today. The lanes here are . . .' She shrugs. 'Well, I thought that was the trial. The tribulation. And when I saw Rockpool, I was so happy I'd made it in one piece.' She shakes her head, and her long hair swooshes. 'The irony of that.'

'Whereabouts in America do you live? I'll need your full address. And where you're staying here.'

'Well, I'm staying . . . here. But back home . . .' She draws a breath, slowly exhales. 'Back home I live at Laurel Heights, 374 Skyway, Topanga Canyon. California.'

Mullins scribbles it all down. 'And your relationship to Baz Carson?'

'Ah,' she says. 'Now that's a long story, Officer. And I'm not sure I've got the strength to tell it.'

'Friend?' offers Mullins.

'Yes, friend,' says Tallulah softly.

She turns back to the window. Says, 'Look at them all down there.'

Mullins goes to stand beside her, intrigued by her tone. This close, he's suddenly conscious of his pink cheeks; the sweat gathering in his pits. He focuses on the people on the terrace. They're much as he left them. The mismatched brother and sister are still on the wall. The skinny bald guy, Davey Hart, is waving his arms about. The manager bloke, Rupert, has his head together with Baz's ex. Meanwhile, Skinner appears to be handing out bottles of water, like he's a steward passing through a broken-down train.

'You'll catch them, won't you, Officer,' she says. 'Please promise me that.'

'Catch them?'

'Whoever killed Baz. Because it was one of those five people down there. At this stage in the investigation, don't rule anything out.'

And apart from the way her voice shakes with emotion, that last line could have been his.

Before speaking to Tallulah, if he had to put money on it, he'd have said Baz's death was natural causes. But there's something hypnotic about the woman's conviction.

'Can you think of any reason why someone would want to hurt him?'

Her eyes brim. 'Of course I can. He told me everything.'

She breaks down then; her shoulders shaking, her face buried in her hands.

Mullins doesn't know where to put himself. He edges back: one step, two. Then reaches out to touch her shoulder, like a nervous child patting a pony through the bars of a gate.

12

Ally watches Gus as he stares down at the cover of Baz's memoir.

'I can't believe it. I never even got the chance to . . . I mean look at him, Ally. He's in the prime of his life.'

And it certainly seems true. Baz Carson has gleaming blue eyes and a direct gaze; his lips lift in a half-smile. He wears a tight t-shirt, and his frame is sinewy, tanned. His arms are folded, a tangle of leather bracelets at his wrists. Altogether, he looks like a man with stories to tell.

'He did something like yoga but not yoga,' he says. 'It'll be in here. He swam every day. And he never touched a drop, Ally. Hadn't for years. Plus . . . he was seventy. What's seventy, these days? It's nothing.'

Gus looks at her, then, and his cheeks colour as he no doubt remembers her Bill. Bill, who died at sixty-six, that great big heart of his giving out. Some days she wakes and, for a fleeting moment, forgets, thinking she'll roll over and find his warm bulk beside her. *Morning, my love.*

'Ally,' he says, dismayed.

She waves her hand, says, 'Not at all.'

Awkwardness is infectious, and she's determined not to catch it. Not with Gus. She spent the days before Christmas worrying about the depth of her friendship with him, whether it might be coming to mean something else or if he might be misinterpreting it.

But things were righted on Tom Bawcock's Eve, and they went into the new year on just the right footing: neighbours in the dunes, often sharing a glass of something and a slice of conversation; each open in their gratitude for this unexpected friendship. There's been no boat-rocking since. And most of the time – *most of the time* – Ally thinks that's a good thing.

Now she tells him how it was Saffron who pulled Baz from the pool – who tried to save him.

'That poor girl. How is she?'

'Jayden said she was quite distressed. Of course she was. It was Baz's granddaughter, a child, who raised the alarm. By the time anyone got there, it was too late. He was floating face down, Jayden said. Fully clothed.'

'Unbelievable.' Then, 'So, he invited a whole houseful of people down and not one of them was around when he needed them. That's a kick in the teeth, that is.'

Ally doesn't reply. When does a sudden death become a suspicious death? Gus's cogs must be similarly whirring, because he suddenly asks, 'They're not saying there's more to it, are they?'

'I don't think they're saying anything yet. This is confidential, by the way, Gus. I should have said that at the start. Jayden happened to call Saffron about the next campsite cook-out and it'd just happened.'

'Gotcha. Of course.' Then, 'Fully clothed?'

Ally nods. 'Jayden thinks the timing is interesting. What with the book just out. Gus, what's it like to read, is it . . . incendiary?'

Is there a reason to kill?

'Well, I haven't got into it yet but I expect it'll be no holds barred. That's what publishers want these days, isn't it? A bit of drama? I should imagine everyone who's in it would have given it a read before it went to print.' Gus shakes his head. 'I can't get over it. Not Baz Carson.'

'I'm sorry, Gus.'

'Was Davey Hart up there? The drummer. My God, he's the only one of the four left. He'll be in pieces.'

And Ally thinks again of Tallulah. Tallulah, who she met for only five or ten minutes but who left an indelible impression. Her confidence, her friendliness, and her obvious affection for Baz. Did she get to the house in time? Did they even manage to see one another?

As much as Ally would like to talk more with Gus – here on the shaded deck, the extreme heat of the day just starting to drop – Fox will be pacing the boards back home. And Ally can't deny that the news of Baz's death has shaken her a little too. She wants to slip inside The Shell House. Be quiet, for a while; be still.

'Gus, I should be going. Fox will be wondering where on earth I've gone to.'

'Of course. Sure. You go.'

He looks disconsolate as he pats the cover of Baz's book. 'It sounds silly, but he's part of my life, is Baz Carson. So many of my memories are tied to his music.'

'Bill liked The Nick too,' says Ally.

'Of course he did. Bill had excellent taste.'

And the colour is suddenly high in Gus's cheeks again.

'I can't argue with that,' says Ally with a smile.

'You don't really think there was anything dodgy about it, do you?' he says. 'You and Jayden? Baz's death?'

And it's one of the many things Ally likes about Gus, that he has so fully embraced their roles as detectives.

'Impossible to say. But when the news breaks, we'll know if the police are treating it as suspicious.'

'I'd have loved to have met him, Al. I thought I had all the time in the world, what with him living just around the corner. If I'm honest, it would have been a dream come true.'

Gus's voice breaks and he looks down quickly. She rests her hand lightly on his shoulder.

'I know,' she says.

He looks up, puffs out his cheeks. 'Oh, how did it go? Hanging your stuff? I'm looking forward to tomorrow. It's a big night. A real milestone.'

'Don't say that. I'll panic.'

But what's so intimidating, really, about a roomful of people who are kind enough to want to come and see her pictures? Or is it the worry that no one will come (and what is the lesser evil for an introvert anyway)? Ally thinks again of Tallulah, and the generous way she looked at her work. How full of zest she was, as she set off for Rockpool and her reunion with Baz. Ally would like to tell her how sorry she is, but what Ally said to Sunita earlier still holds, perhaps now more than ever: she's certain they won't see Tallulah again.

'Gus,' she says, 'I should be getting back. Will you . . . be alright?'

'What, me? Oh, right as rain. It's a little close to home, that's all. You know what I mean.'

'I do.'

And they share a sad sort of smile.

Ally's just about to strike out on to the dune path when her phone rings its FaceTime ring. The only person who ever FaceTimes her is Evie, and right now it's the small hours of the morning in Australia. Ally digs inside her bag, a bolt of nerves rushing through her.

'Evie, are you okay?' she says in a rush, as her daughter's lovely face fills the screen.

'Mum. I'm fine.'

'The boys are okay?'

'We're all fine.'

Ally breathes a deep sigh of relief. She waves at Gus, gesturing to the phone, and he gives her a thumbs up. She sets off into the dunes.

'You're phoning very early, love.'

'That's because I woke up and realised something terrible.'

Ally's heart climbs into her mouth again. 'What?'

'That it's your show tomorrow and I haven't sent a card or flowers or anything.'

'Oh, Evie. Don't be so silly.'

But her daughter's face is so serious, and her voice is uneven when it comes again. 'That's the thing about living here. I'm so far away. I should be there for the show. The boys should be there for the show. We're your family, Mum.'

'Honestly, it's just a few pictures. It's really nothing new.'

'It is something new. It's a solo show.' Again, Evie's voice splinters. 'You've been doing amazingly, so amazingly since Dad.'

'Oh, Evie.'

Her daughter rubs her eyes. 'It's four a.m. here. I should go or I'll wake the boys. I just wanted to say sorry I'm not there. And good luck. Not that you need it. I love you.'

After Evie rings off, Ally stands for a moment. The pull towards her daughter is as strong as the tide; as physical as the sand shucking between her toes, the rush of seawater.

Then a message from Gus brings her back to the present: Will you and Jayden be lending your services if there is anything untoward? I reckon Skinner'd bite your arm off after JP Sharpe.

Then: I can't stop thinking about him. Baz I mean, not Skinner. I'm gutted.

And all the walk home, thoughts swirl in and out of Ally's mind: Evie waking in the middle of the night, on the other side of the world; the exhibition tomorrow; Baz Carson's body floating in a swimming pool just along the way. And Gus. How sad he looked. How she doesn't want him, of all people, to be gutted about anything.

13

'Dadatz!'

Jayden's daughter toddles down the hallway, her arms out-stretched. *Dadatz.* Jayden loves being called this. It's way cooler than just Daddy or Dada. He stoops to sweep her up and Jazzy presses her face against his. He kisses her cheeks, then pulls back slightly.

'Your nose, honey. It needs a good wipe. Where's Mummy?'

As he sets Jazzy back down, he takes her pudgy hand in his. 'Come on, let's get a tissue.'

'Tiss-oo.'

'That's right. Tissue. Otherwise known as basic hygiene, Jazz.' Then, 'Cat! Where you at?'

'I'm here,' his wife says, rounding the corner. She looks great, because she always looks great. A bikini top and board shorts, her long hair spilling over her shoulders.

It hasn't always been easy, since their daughter came along. Sixteen months of love like no other, no doubt. Have songs been written about this? They should be. Forget romance: fathers and daughters, that's where it's at. But, also, sixteen months of broken sleep; moving zombie-like through the day that follows. Which means tempers a little shorter, and perspectives a little . . . skewed. In the whirlwind of raising a child, it's easy to forget to pay atten-tion to each other.

'Hey, listen, are you good for putting Jazzy to bed? I'm thinking of getting a surf in.' Cat grins. 'Unless you want to instead?'

'I'm good. You go.'

Jayden is a terrible surfer, but it doesn't seem to affect his enjoyment. When conditions are right, he'll paddle out and fall in and call it a good time. Meanwhile Cat feels like she's got some making up to do after all the landlocked years. Since being back in Cornwall she's been a born-again surfer and loving every second. Jayden definitely prefers it to her sessions with a ripped personal trainer called Matt. She called time on those after the fifth go. *Too boring* was the verdict, but Jayden has never been quite sure if she was referring to the exercise, or the man himself. Some part of him still wonders if there was a bit more to it: he saw the way that guy looked at Cat, even if it wasn't returned.

'You go for it,' he says. 'Soak up the sunset. Looks like it's going to be another bobby dazzler.'

'Bobby dazzler. You've been hanging out with Ally too long.'

'Well, that's a little bit ageist.'

Cat is on board with the Shell House Detectives. Mostly. She likes that it makes him happy – when they first moved here, he was a long way from happy – but, on balance, she'd probably prefer it if he was all in on the campsite; if his 98 per cent campsite commitment was 110 per cent. Jayden thinks 98 per cent is pretty good, personally. And while he's loving the summer heat, and the bookings income, part of him is looking forward to his job list not including unblocking toilets or telling people to turn their music down or apologising that, yeah sorry, it is a bit of a walk to get down to the sand.

And when there's more time for detective work, too.

'Talking of Ally, I was just with her.'

She's moving towards the door, eager to get to the water. Just like he was eager to get to Ally after speaking to Saffron.

'Cat, this is hush-hush, it hasn't broken yet, but Baz Carson's dead.'

Jayden fills her in on the details, including the way his mind's starting to tick, just a little bit: a house full of people, Baz floating face down in the pool, and that book of his just published. Jayden's done some googling: *Baz Carson tells it like it is*, one review said, *and not everyone's going to like it.*

'But that's awful,' she says. 'He's hardly been here.'

As if the curtailing of Baz's enjoyment in Porthpella is the worst of it. It always amuses Jayden, his wife's belief that Cornwall is the fix for everything.

'You know that guy, Felix? Up in plot thirty-seven?'

'The green Transporter?'

'White Bongo.'

'Think so. Two dogs?'

'No dogs. He's on his own. Our kind of age. Londoner.'

She shakes her head. 'Anyway?'

'I was with him earlier, getting him some milk.'

'What, past hours?'

'Only just. And—'

'Jay, you can't let people take liberties. Once you start . . . there's no going back. We'll be at everyone's beck and call, 24/7.'

Jayden gestures to their daughter, who's currently trying to remove his flip-flop. '*Plus ça change*, babe.'

'Boundaries. We've got to have boundaries.'

'Anyway, turns out he's here for the party up at Rockpool House. He's a journalist. A friend of Baz's.'

Jayden rethinks this. How Felix said *pleasure, not business*, then corrected himself to say *duty*. But there must be some intimacy, if he's part of such a small group.

'I don't know if he knows yet. About Baz, I mean. I might check in on him later.'

'Boundaries, Jay?'

'It's common decency. You'd do the same.'

She narrows her eyes. 'Or have you got an ulterior motive here? Are you the benevolent campsite owner chatting to just another one of his guests or . . . is this a you-and-Ally thing?'

'A me-and-Ally thing?'

Cat's busy applying SPF to her lips when she stops suddenly, says, 'So, why's this guy staying with us and not up at the house, if he's close to Baz?'

'Now that's a good question.'

'I knew it. It's a you-and-Ally thing. But Jay, listen, a celebrity death? Don't . . .'

'Don't what?'

She sets her hands on his shoulders, turns those marine-blue eyes of hers on him.

'Don't go getting in the way of the police.'

'As if.'

'And don't harass the guests either.'

'Roger that.'

'Talking of guests, does the name Martin Radford mean anything to you?'

Immediately an image comes to Jayden's mind. A big guy in a sharp suit. Wide grin. Gallows humour. *Radders.*

'Yeah, it does. He was a DI. If it's the same guy. He's booked with us?'

'Someone called Keely Watson made the booking. But I saw Martin's name under the listed guests and recognised it. Plus, it's a Leeds postcode.'

Jayden can't really see Radders camping. He was always that little bit slick. He brought his own AeroPress in to make his coffee and had expensive taste in watches.

He says this to Cat and she grins. 'They're in a motorhome. Wanted to check the dimensions against the plot. It's a whopper.'

'Okay, that could be him, then. Does he know it's our place, do you think?'

Cat shrugs. 'Might be a coincidence. Or maybe he wants to look you up. Or headhunt you.'

Jayden laughs. 'Yeah, right.'

But as Cat heads out the door, he can't help wondering. Not least how to address him; if DI Martin Radford's on holiday and Jayden's in his flip-flops, does he still call him *sir?*

14

'You're sure I can't get your mum for you?' says Saffron.

Imogen shakes her head, her long fringe barely shifting. Saffron hasn't seen the girl's eyes yet, but she's pretty sure they're full of tears.

They're sitting on a bench at the side of the house, on a hidden patch of patio. There are big planters, each glazed in a spectrum of sea-blues; fat-leafed succulents burst from them like jungle flowers. It's a calm space, but Saffron feels anything but. Her heart's going like a drum.

She folds her arm around Imogen's shoulders, gives her a squeeze. Saffron can't believe that Imogen's mum hasn't made it her business to be here. Whatever Ruby's going through herself – and her dad did just die, Saffron must give her that – surely comforting Imogen is the most important thing.

'I knew as soon as I saw him,' she says, 'because he wasn't moving at all. He looked like a giant starfish, all splayed out.'

'And that's when you ran downstairs, wasn't it?'

'If I saw him sooner . . . Mum always says I move too slowly. Drag my feet. If I was there before . . .'

'You did all the right things.'

But Saffron has the same kind of 'ifs' running through her own mind. If she'd finished the canapés sooner. If she'd taken a tray of drinks out to the terrace. If she'd run faster, swum harder, hauled him to the side seconds quicker. Would it have made a difference?

Saffron had never given somebody mouth-to-mouth before. And for all her time at the beach and out on the water, she'd never seen anyone come close to drowning; for all that massive swell, surfers lifting and dropping, rocket-speed wipe-outs in churning water. Yet here, in this infinity pool that appears so totally serene – more of a landscaping feature than a place for real swimming – a man has died.

'Could he swim, your grandad?'

'Yeah, course.' Then, 'I think so. I don't actually know.' Imogen draws an arm across her face, wipes her nose on her t-shirt. 'I didn't really know him very well. It wasn't like I really saw him ever. This weekend was, like, super-rare.'

'Your mum and him didn't get on so well?'

'Understatement of the year.'

'You know what, we can still feel close to someone, even if we don't know them very well. Family's weird like that.'

But even as she says it, Saffron's not sure if she fully means it. This time a year ago, she had no idea who her dad was – and she was totally cool with that. But now, thanks to Ally and Jayden, she does know. They've even hung out a few times. And the fish she's cooking this weekend? He sorted it for her. But she's never called him Dad. *Hi Dad, bye Dad, thanks Dad.* Not once, even by mistake. A name like that is one you earn, not something you can just hook on the end of a line.

'I like his music,' Imogen says. 'He should have kept making it. Uncle Jet says he quit at the top because he was too afraid to fail. I don't know if it's true. Mum says Jet's no better. Worse, even. That his laziness is just a protective mechanism.' Imogen looks up. For the first time her fringe parts. Her eyes are as green as a cat's and just as wide. 'Mum and Uncle Jet don't really get on either.'

'But you're all here for the party weekend. That's nice. God, sorry, I mean . . .'

Imogen gives a tight little smile. Deadpans, 'It's a really great party so far, isn't it?'

Just then Mullins appears around the corner of the house, looking all hot and bothered.

'Aha,' he says, 'so this is where you're hiding.'

And Saffron groans inwardly and shoots him a warning look. *Don't stuff this one up, Mullins.*

'You okay?' he asks, settling on the bench next to Imogen. The girl nods, shifting slightly to make more room. Mullins is especially hefty in his uniform; his black vest, with all sorts of bells and whistles on it, feels over the top in these surroundings.

'I'm going to need to chat to you both about what happened,' he says. 'So we can build up a bit of a picture. Imogen, we'll need your mum here. What are you, about fifteen?'

'Thirteen,' says Imogen, looking pleased. 'But does it have to be my mum? She wasn't even there. It was Saffron who was there.'

Mullins nods. 'Fair enough. She's a responsible adult, is Saffron.'

And it's the classic time for Mullins to make a joke, but for once he doesn't.

'You alright with that, Saff?'

'Of course,' she says.

'Okay, then. So, Imogen, talk me through what happened. Try not to leave out any details. They might not seem important, but they may be. What were you doing just before you found your grandad?'

The girl knots her hands in her lap.

'I was just up in my room, keeping out of everyone's way, mostly. I was looking out the window and I saw Grandad Baz by the pool, doing stretches or yoga or something. Then I went to get

63

changed and the next time I looked . . . he was in the water. Not moving, Inspector.'

Saffron can't help smirking at the use of *Inspector*.

'So, did you see anyone else from the window? Anyone at all?'

Her fringe swings and her eyes fix on Mullins, with sudden surety. 'Anyone who'd want to murder him, you mean?'

The word is a shock, tripping so easily from Imogen's mouth.

'Erm, there's no obvious evidence of foul play,' he says. 'You don't need to worry about all that, Imogen. These are just questions for the coroner. They're the people who—'

'Oh,' she says. 'Oh. I thought someone must have killed him—'

'No one killed him, Imogen,' says Saffron.

'Oh. Oh good. Because I was going to say that if you're looking for anyone who'd want to kill Grandad, then just read his book, Inspector. Granny Nicole's hopping mad about it, and she said everybody else here would be too. Though they'd probably be too spineless to say anything. Her words not mine.'

And Saffron waits for Mullins to reassure Imogen again that she's not among murderers. But he's got his listening face on, and it's not one Saffron sees too often; the Mullins she knows is usually in broadcast mode. He flips to a new page in his notebook and something in her goes a little bit cold.

'Right, tell me more about this book,' he says.

15

With Jazzy tucked up cosy in bed, and Cat back from her surf, Jayden heads for his evening rounds of the campsite.

Normally, if there's the slightest lick of breeze it carries over the headland, stirring the hedgerows and flapping the canvas of the tents, but tonight the air is hot and still. Jayden moves with intention, his mind turning things over.

Multiple things.

Strange to think of his old and new worlds colliding. Jayden messaged an old mate from Radford's division, and he confirmed that, yep, the DI had taken leave for a week. Jayden imagines chatting to him by the shower blocks or giving him the Wi-Fi code on a scrap of paper. Weird. He can't help wondering if he's heard about his detective work down here. Jayden's proud of the cases he and Ally have cracked, but how would it look to someone like DI Martin Radford?

As he passes plot 19, he hears a lullaby carrying on the evening air. There's a baby on the campsite, maybe seven or eight months old. Jayden's seen him in his high chair at first light and bowling around on his playmat, his infectious laugh bubbling away. And Cat's clocked him too. She keeps saying how adorable he is.

What do you think? Cat said a couple of months ago. *Is it time?*

His wife is an only child. She grew up queen of the farm, recipient of all her parents' attention; she's someone who's always made friends easily, never short of a squad. But Jayden has a big sister and knows how much he loved it as a kid. Ella is the only other person in the world who knows what it was like to grow up in the house on Elton Road. To scour the pages of the *Racing Post* with their grandad John, who lived in Whitby, putting small-change bets on the horses with the coolest names. To swing in the hammock in the garden of their great-grandparents' house in Trini, bowls of melting Soursop ice cream in their laps, lips sweet with Solo cream soda. Jayden and his sister did everything together.

Despite his and Cat's happy upbringings, they each now seem to want the opposite.

Two years is a good gap, Cat said. *Just saying . . .*

And while they're not officially trying, they're not *not* trying.

But honestly, when Jayden pictures them as a family of four, he just can't see it. And when he can't picture something, it scares him a little. Right now, they're a triangle, the most powerful shape: three is a magic number. And Jazzy, they're so lucky with Jazzy. Why roll the dice again, when they already have the perfect daughter?

He wants to give his wife everything. But he's just not sure about another baby.

He's thinking about all this as he walks through the site – mostly because of that particular smile Cat gave him as he headed out. *Don't be long, Jay.* Her sea-wet hair running down her back, the flick of her narrow hips in her boardshorts. And yeah, okay, call him crazy but he's taking this walk slow. If Felix wants to talk it out, then Jayden's here for that. Even if it gets him in hot water back home.

Plot 37 is right at the top of the field and has the best view. Beyond the multicolours of their campsite, the sea unfolds all the way to the horizon. Sunset has been and gone, and the sky is deep purple. Felix's camper is in near-darkness and at first Jayden thinks no one's there. But then he sees the glow of light, and the shape of someone outside, sunk in a chair.

'Evening,' says Jayden.

Felix looks up. He seems to stare right through him.

'Hey, man,' he says, after a beat.

'I'm doing the rounds,' says Jayden, with a smile. 'Shutting down the wild parties. Making sure the kids are in bed. You know the drill.' Then, carefully, 'How's it going?'

'Yeah . . . it's going.' Felix runs a hand through his hair; flicks a glance at Jayden. 'I got some bad news, actually. That party I'm in town for . . . I think it's off.'

Jayden nods. 'I heard. I'm sorry.'

'Village gossip, or has it broken yet? When I last looked it hadn't.'

'The former.'

Felix hauls in a breath. 'It's a shock. I know I was glib before – the whole "duty" thing – but Baz and I . . . we go back a long way.'

Jayden feels a pang of sympathy. Sympathy mixed with curiosity. He wants to ask if the police have spoken to Felix yet, but he doesn't want to change the speed of things. So instead he tells him that he's sorry.

'Thanks.'

Jayden shows Felix the beer he brought him. 'You tried this yet? Local brew. Thought you'd like it.'

Felix shines his phone light on the label. '"Grommet"? Related to "emmet"?'

'Better, probably. It means a little kid surfer.' Jayden passes it over. 'I don't know if there's a term for us late-adopters.'

'That's kind,' says Felix. 'Cheers. Hey, hang on a sec.'

He hauls himself out of the deckchair and ducks inside the van. Suddenly they're pooled in a soft glow as Felix clicks on a lamp.

Jayden gets a glimpse of the inside of the Bongo. It's simple and functional – not like some of the vans here, with their Aladdin's cave interiors. All he can see is a guitar and a laptop. A small stack of books.

'Cultural exchange,' says Felix, coming back out with a grin and handing Jayden a can. 'This brewery's at the end of my road.'

'Ah thanks, but you don't have to do that.' He studies the label. 'Dalston? My cousin lives there.'

'Oh yeah, where?'

'Kingsland Road.'

'Small world.'

'You want to crack these together?' says Jayden.

Felix looks back at him, and Jayden knows he's weighing it up. He looks like he wants to say yes, but something's stopping him.

'I don't want to take up your time, but . . . yeah. Thanks.' Felix gestures to the deckchair then perches on the van step. 'Take a load off. I'm good here.'

They settle in their spots; there's the snap of ring pulls, the satisfying fizz. The camping field is in darkness now, but the sky above is lit by a not-quite-full moon. There are strings of fairy lights on several tents; silhouettes moving behind canvas. Voices have switched to murmur mode, with the odd unstoppable laugh.

'When the news about Baz breaks, you'll get the media down here,' says Felix. 'Peace over.'

Jayden has so many questions, but he figures Felix is going to tell him the answers on his own.

'Everyone's going to want me to write something.' Felix chews at a nail. 'I'm a journalist. I told you that, didn't I? I've known Baz since I was fifteen. He got me started. Opened a few doors. My first piece out of college was an interview with Jimmy Page.'

'Nice.'

'Nepotism at its finest.'

'How did you meet him? Baz, I mean.'

'Mum.'

Jayden wants to ask more about the connection between Felix's mum and Baz, but Felix is already moving on.

'You know he just published a book, right? *Turn It Down: Living and Loving the Quiet Life* by Baz Carson.' Before Jayden can answer, Felix gives a low laugh. Says, 'Course not. Sorry, I live in a bubble most of the time. The smallest of small worlds. So, his memoir came out today. Mum's in it. A lot.'

'Were they in a relationship?'

'They were never together,' he says, 'much to Baz's disappointment. But they were good friends. I make a brief appearance in the book as a spotty guitar-obsessed teenager who can't rub two words together in actual conversation but is pretty good at getting them down on paper. Obviously, Baz takes the credit for seeing my potential there, but hey, maybe he did.'

'So, he was kind of a mentor?'

'Kind of.' Felix sucks in a breath. 'I wrote part of a first draft with him, actually. He hired me as a ghostwriter. But he changed his mind and said he wanted it to be his voice and his voice only. So he paid me handsomely but sacked me.' He swigs his beer. 'Anyway. Tell me about leaving the police. Setting up here. That's a story I want to hear.'

How does Felix know there's a story? Maybe because he's a journalist. *Maybe the fumes are coming off me and they always will.*

'There was an incident – my partner was stabbed. After that, I needed to change something. Cat and I had a baby on the way. So, we came to Cornwall. This is my wife's family farm.' It sounds so simple, put like that. The turmoil, the conflict, the way his heart felt split in two: all that edited out. But from the look on Felix's face, he knows.

'I'm sorry, man.'

They sit for a moment. Overhead, bats dip and dive. The moon looks close enough to touch.

'I saw him,' says Felix. 'Yesterday. The day before his publication day. I thought he'd be surrounded by people, but he was on his own. We ended up having lunch.'

'How was he?'

'He was Baz. Bursting with life. Picture of health, as far as I could see.' Felix drums his fingers on the can. 'Though . . . I guess we never know what's going on inside.'

'My friend was hired as the chef for the weekend. She pulled him from the pool.'

'No, really? Is she okay?'

'Yeah, she's okay.'

Felix gives a low, humourless laugh. 'It figures that it should be her and not one of them. Everyone's right there and yet they're still useless. That should have been Baz's epilogue for the memoir: "Even when I was drowning you lot couldn't pull your finger out."'

The bitterness trips easily from Felix's tongue, and Jayden can't work out exactly who it's aimed at. But then Felix is wiping his arm across his eyes. His voice fractures as he says, 'Or maybe that's the point.'

'What do you mean?' says Jayden.

'Maybe they were all standing there. Watching him sink.'

Jayden lets Felix's words settle. Then asks, casually, 'So who are the other guests at Rockpool?'

16

Rupert lowers himself into a wicker chair and it creaks beneath him. The terrace is in near-darkness, but there's none of the cool air that he was hoping for; his clothes are sticking to him. He slugs from his glass of whisky, feeling hot and irritable. He skipped the fussy cocktails that Nicole made the pretty chef girl hand out and instead went straight for the bottle of single malt he brought with him. Thanks to Davey and Jet getting in on it too, there's not much left. *Chancers.*

Baz dead? He's surprised to find that he feels quite numb – and he's not sure how much the whisky has to do with that. The truth is, for all their long-standing relationship, they were never proper friends. Not really. Theirs was no meeting of minds, other than the fact that Rupert wanted to make money and The Nick – Baz, basically – delivered. But Baz never cared about the money; if he did, he might have had more respect for what Rupert did for him.

Not that Rupert is bothered about that. What's respect worth, really? It's an intangible asset.

He shifts in the chair. *Creak.*

Is it revolting of Rupert to rejoice in the fact that he's still standing when a comrade falls? He's only human – no spring chicken himself. And his instinct for survival has always been second to none.

Nicole: now there's another survivor.

After the police left – one no more than a clumsy school-boy, the other in a suit so shiny it looked wet – the valiant Nicole insisted dinner go ahead. *Didn't you hear the officers? No one leave town. So, we might as well have the evening Baz planned.* But few of them had the appetite for the crab linguine that was served. Only Rupert made the effort, clearing his plate and accepting seconds. His theory that everything goes downhill once you're outside of the M25 wasn't supported for once: the crab was delectable, and he told the chef girl as much. Potentially with too much gusto, as she looked at him like he'd said something inappropriate.

Well, none of them has the script for these circumstances, do they?

Now, snippets of the conversation at dinner flit about Rupert's mind like mosquitoes, and he bats them away. It feels good to be alone out here: whisky in glass; the quiet of the garden. But still the mosquitoes buzz and buzz.

'Baz got everything he wanted. A life lived well and then some. No one can take that away from him.' Davey. Teary to boot.

'The grim reaper's done a decent job.' That was Jet.

'He could have done so much more. So many squandered opportunities.' Nicole.

'Not least marriage to you, Mum.' Jet again.

'I always thought he'd make a comeback' was Rupert's own contribution. 'I was waiting for that call, every day for the last thirty years. "Rupes, get me back out there." I'd have done it too. Big time.'

'Baz wasn't into that. When he made his mind up, he didn't go changing it.' Davey again. 'And the Netflix show did it for him in the end.' Dear old Davey. Not a hint of sour grapes, either.

'Sales of the book are going to go stratospheric. It's almost like he planned it. Hey, Rupes, were you working on some kind of

secret PR plan, you and Baz? Talk about commitment to the cause.'
Jet. A goading glint in his eye, too.

To which Rupert shot back, 'That's bloody dark that is.'

'But true. Where's Imogen?' Ruby. Finally weighing in.

'She went up to her room to watch TV.' That was the pretty chef girl. And did Rupert detect judgement in that so-sweet voice of hers? Ruby wouldn't win mother of the year, but then Nicole wouldn't have either and that's history for you: it repeats.

'Tallulah Pearce is hiding herself away too.' Nicole. Undisguised venom. Nicole didn't care for attractive women, and ones who'd got history with Baz were the worst.

And on they went, back and forth, round and round, no one acknowledging the elephant in the room. No one had seen Baz die, had they? And the police had done plenty of scribbling in their notebooks about that.

Now, the strings of fairy lights that lace the terrace blur before Rupert's eyes. Further down the garden the swimming pool is spot-lit and the blue water, looming up out of the night, looks electric; a neon show, draped with police tape. Trust Baz to make a flash exit.

Rupert raises his glass to the sky above. 'Travel well, Barry Frederick Carson.' And the stars seem to burn back harder than ever.

'You getting sentimental, Rupes?'

Nicole.

'I'm bloody heartbroken,' he says.

She shakes her head. 'Been there, done that. I won't give him the satisfaction. Not again.'

Rupert looks at her. She's every bit as together as when she first got to Rockpool. No mascara streaks for Nicole. For a second, he imagines drawing her on to his lap, planting a kiss on her red-painted lips. But Nicole's never done it for him. Everyone said she was a gold-digger when she married Baz, but when he left her,

Rupert could see it wasn't just the money she missed – though she ended up with plenty of that. Strange how love can morph so easily into hate. Because Rupert is pretty sure that Nicole hates Baz, and has done for twenty years.

'How are the kids?' he asks.

'I can't get a word out of Jet,' she says. 'And Ruby's a cold fish. She hasn't cried a tear, that girl.'

Rupert sniggers. It's the booze, and the fact that Nicole is so ice-hard. It's rare, in a woman. With the right guidance, she could have gone far in business, could Nicole. Instead, he's watched her make a half-hearted career out of being the Former Mrs Baz Carson. Peddling candles that smell like kids' sweets and occasionally leading 'wellness retreats' where she imparts advice cribbed from greetings cards – *live, love, laugh; dance like nobody's watching.*

'Where's Davey?' she says.

'Davey's probably running a long hot bath and lining up the electrical appliances.'

'Don't.'

'I'm joking, Nic. He was with Jet, last time I saw. Chewing his ear off. Wanted to pen some kind of ballad for Baz.'

Nicole collapses in the chair next to him. 'I don't know how I feel,' she says. 'Is that awful?'

'It's the shock,' he says. 'It's the same for all of us.'

'I don't think Jet's shocked. I don't think Ruby's shocked.'

'They are, Nic. It just hasn't hit them yet. It was always complicated with Baz for them. For all of us. He thought he was so bloody clever.'

'If he wasn't already dead, I could kill him.' She holds her hand out for his glass and he reluctantly passes it over. 'Putting us through this. I made them come here you know. They laughed, said no way. But I could see the invite for what it was. I said if they missed this birthday, they'd regret it.'

'He loves his family,' says Rupert. 'Always did. And he was buzzing on having you all here. It was like the Baz of the old days. He was ready for a party, Nic.'

'I think he saw the big seven-zero bearing down on him and realised he had no one to celebrate it with. No one who isn't on the payroll, anyway.'

'Dear old Davey?'

'Davey'd go to the opening of an envelope.'

'I should think Tallulah would have been company enough for anyone.'

'Don't get me started on her,' hisses Nicole. 'I'm announcing, by the way. Nine o'clock tomorrow morning. All the socials.'

He nods. 'Call me callous, but your boy's right . . . it's not going to hurt the book sales, is it?'

'I don't want to talk about the book. My skin's as thick as it comes, and I know yours is too, but the way he talked about his own kids? He owes them.'

'I hear you, Nic. But if you're talking about the will, don't ask me. He kept his powder dry on that one.'

'But you did everything for him.'

And Rupert had. He'd done everything. Because business didn't float Baz's boat, so as far as Baz was concerned, business could do one. Short-sighted, but whatever, Rupert never complained. Not for a second.

'Not his will though.'

Rupert can see her chewing her lip. Anyone else in her shoes wouldn't expect a penny, but Nicole? He wouldn't put it past her.

'He loves his family,' he repeats. 'Loved. Gordon Bennett, that's going to take some getting used to.'

Nicole mutters something indecipherable.

'What are you going to say when you announce?' he asks. 'We should agree the wording.'

'It's not a bloody press release, Rupes. The plod will be doing that. It's a heartfelt message from the person closest to him.'

'I thought you were the one tweeting?'

'I'm offended.'

'And I'm serious. About the wording, I mean. We don't know what happened, do we?'

The question hangs heavy between them.

'I'm hardly going to go into detail,' snaps Nicole. 'The god-forsaken press will be doing enough of that. Making up stories. Salacious gossip. We're living our darkest hour and they're just selling papers.'

'Until the post-mortem comes through and then they'll all shut up again.'

'Exactly.'

'Unless . . .'

'Don't even go there, Rupes.'

'Don't tell me it hasn't crossed your mind.'

'And who exactly? Who are you pointing the finger at? My granddaughter? That little chef girl?' She gives a shrill laugh that Rupert, in that moment, finds faintly chilling. 'No, that hard heart of Baz Carson's finally gave up on him. End of.'

And maybe it's true. It doesn't matter if you're out to pasture in a coastal pile or still showboating in the London clubs, death will come for you one way or another. Doesn't matter how clever you think you are.

Rupert looks up to the sky again and raises his glass in silent salute. Baz went out on top: friends and family around him; book hot off the press; bank account swashing with enough dollar (well, until he poured it all into this place). You could cry big wet tears, or you could pick yourself up and say hey, that's life. The guy had a hell of a run.

Just then, Rupert sees the silhouette of the pretty chef girl gathering up glasses. She moves across the terrace with a lightness that makes him think of a dancer, as if she might twirl and spin, and arrive at his feet with a flourish.

Hey baby, he imagines saying. But he probably can't get away with that kind of thing anymore. He takes another swig of his drink, his eyes still on her. Who's he kidding? He's Rupert Frost. He can get away with anything.

17

Ally's coffee pot signals the start of the day with a bubble and a hiss, just as the first rays of sun turn the back wall of The Shell House golden. She steps to the window. Outside, the water is a milky blue, the waves pulling in so languidly they're barely there. The island lighthouse stands solid, while the sky riots around it in a blaze of pink, yellow and orange.

It is – as Bill used to say – *some view*.

Ally thinks of Tallulah and feels a pang of compassion so strong it takes the breath from her. She wonders if Tallulah's waking up to this Porthpella day affronted by its beauty, or whether it's some kind of comfort.

As Ally lay in bed last night, numerous thoughts kept her tossing and turning. Not least Jayden's interest in the timing of Baz's memoir. Does it amount to a hunch? Usually, she loves being carried along by Jayden's energies. His questioning mind and his inclusive nature light up her days. But this time she wills there to be nothing in it, and for the police to issue a statement confirming natural causes. Baz's death will be no less sad, but for those who loved him, it's perhaps a simpler sort of grief to reckon with.

However, a small part of Ally – a part that didn't exist before Jayden moved to Porthpella; that didn't exist before Lewis Pascoe was found at the foot of the cliffs – feels a quickening sense of resolve. If there is anything unnatural about Baz's death – *if* – then justice must be brought. Though she can't imagine how she or Jayden might be involved. Thus far, their cases have been the ones the police didn't want or were slightly adjacent; separate investigations that ended up shedding light overall. The death of Baz Carson is headline news. The eyes of the world – the rock-and-roll-loving parts of it, anyway – will be turned on Porthpella. Questions will fly.

Was it a heart attack that killed Baz Carson – or something else?

Ally fills her cup and goes out to stand on the veranda, just as she's done for forty years. It feels like a form of devotion – a small act of worship.

It's dead calm out, no breeze lifting the marram grass, but around The Shell House the dunes buzz with life: the disappearing tails of rabbits, the high whistle of skylarks. The air is soft and already warm, and Ally breathes it in. It's forecast to be scorching again later, but right now, it's perfect.

'Morning Fox.'

Her little dog pushes against her legs, noses her toes. He'll want a walk soon but he's getting old, this boy of hers, and for now he's happy idling with her on the veranda. Even the rabbits don't provoke more than a twitch of his ears. Ally has noted this change, but has she accepted it? That's a question for another day.

The only certainty in life is death. That's what Ally's mum used to say.

Bill was never much for mornings; he was a sunset man. All the better if there was a pint of Doom Bar in his hand, and his shoes kicked off; coals turning white on the barbeque. So many evenings they spent out here together, the riches of the ocean on their plates and all around them. A life of extraordinary blessings.

But now Ally's getting maudlin and that's not on at all. Not when it's a big day: the opening of her exhibition at the Bluebird. Perhaps it's because it feels like a milestone – that's what Gus called it yesterday, *a milestone* – that Ally's mind is turning to change. The inevitable cycles. And the uncertain ones too.

Fox patters to the edge of the veranda. Lifts his nose. He looks back at Ally, mouth open as if he's laughing. Despite herself, she smiles. 'Oh, come on then, let's get out in it. It's no good just watching the day start without us, is it?'

Five minutes later and they're down on the sand, Ally with her mug in hand. She follows a trail of gull prints, as neat as tiny anchors. Fox pokes around in some bladderwrack. The water caught in the tidelines is as warm as a bath. Even at this hour – not yet six o'clock – the heat is on the rise. There's a lone paddleboarder stroking out, and Ally watches them, feeling the glory of the water; a kinship.

'It's Ally, isn't it? The artist.'

Ally turns. She didn't hear the woman's footfall in the sand.

'Tallulah.'

White linen trousers. A loose denim shirt. Her long hair shining white-gold. Ally thought she'd never see her again, but somehow, on this bare beach at daybreak, the woman's presence feels entirely natural.

'I had to get out of that house,' says Tallulah. Then, 'You heard what happened?'

'I'm so very sorry.'

Tallulah tucks a strand of hair behind her ear, says, 'I have no words.'

The two women fall into step. Fox glances back, noting the new arrival, but then trots on ahead. There's something in this shared silence. It's as if threads bind the two of them, no less strong for being invisible.

'God, is there anything more opening than an empty beach? I feel like I want to . . . I don't know. Run right on into the water.' Tallulah heaves a breath, and Ally can feel the tension coming off her in waves. She watches as Tallulah looks out to the sea and her eyes fill. She gently lays a hand on her arm.

'When my husband died, this beach was the only place I wanted to be,' says Ally. 'Everything felt wrong inside the house.'

Those beloved rooms, filled with the objects of a shared life, were suddenly, horribly, emptied. Everything meaningless without him.

'Late night, early morning, that point where one becomes the other, this is where I came,' says Ally.

'And it helped?'

'It helped.'

'It's the shock,' says Tallulah, quietly. 'The shock, and the gap . . . the enormous gap, between the way I thought things would go, and the way—' She breaks off. 'You know?'

Ally nods.

'Five minutes, we had. Five minutes, if that. He met me at the gate, and my God as I saw him coming towards me all the years fell away. I know he felt it too. The connection. Nothing had faded.' She pushes a hand to her forehead. Her giant turquoise rings peal with colour. 'I unpacked. I hung my dresses in the wardrobe. Set out my toiletries in the bathroom. I mean . . . I was doing that, that *fussing*, when Baz . . . when Baz was dying.'

'There was nothing you could have done,' says Ally gently. And she regrets it the moment it's out of her mouth, because she doesn't know, does she? And she can't help feeling Tallulah deserves more than platitudes.

At that moment Ally sees something glinting in the sand. It's a piece of cerulean sea glass. She stoops to pick it up; presses her thumb to its smooth and rounded edges. Then she passes it to Tallulah.

'A heart,' says Tallulah, her voice cut with wonder. She folds her fingers around it; holds it to her chest. 'I shall treasure it.'

Ally feels the pulse of emotion. And, again, it's like a current passing between them.

Tallulah's eyes go to her coffee cup. 'Is there anywhere round here to get a cup of coffee this early?'

'Hang Ten is wonderful but it doesn't open until eight o'clock.'

Tallulah looks at her watch. 'I couldn't be at the house. I had to go. But I'm crashing now . . . adrenalin only carries me so far.'

Ally hesitates. The Shell House isn't far. She turned someone away once before – Lewis Pascoe – and vowed to never do it again.

'I live just back that way,' she says. 'Would you like to come in?'

Tallulah's eyes fill. 'I don't want to trespass.'

'You wouldn't be.'

'Then that would be very kind.'

Together they turn back towards the dunes. Ally checks, to be sure Fox is following. He looks at her enquiringly, no doubt affronted that his walk has been cut short. And he eyes Tallulah with nothing short of suspicion.

~

Settled in wicker chairs on the veranda, Tallulah lets out a low whistle.

'It's some kind of beautiful here, Ally.'

In the early morning light the sea is a soft turquoise, the sand like sugar. There's the slightest streak of white cloud above, like an artist has cleaned their brush on the blue cloth of the sky.

Tallulah turns to Ally. 'You love it here, don't you? This home.'

'I can't imagine being anywhere else.'

'Baz and I used to go to the beach all the time. It was like another world, compared to the Strip. He said he felt peaceful with me in Topanga. Like he could really be himself. No performance.' She takes a sip of coffee. Closes her eyes. 'It wasn't enough though.

Not then. He was young, and he wanted the lights. I could have gone with him, Ally. But I didn't want to. That was the sticking point. I loved the canyon, the wild coast. I didn't want to be in the city. And I didn't want to be in London.'

'Was there talk of moving to England, then?'

'Oh sure. Baz came to LA thinking the American Dream was his for the taking. But it didn't happen. Or he didn't give it the time – maybe that's closer. Baz was impatient. He hated that people didn't see his talent for what it was. For all that he loved me, he wanted to go home. With or without me.' Tallulah gives a sad smile. 'And just like you, I couldn't imagine being anywhere else. I chose the place I loved over the person I loved.'

Ally feels a strength of connection with this woman again. She knows Evie would like her to be in Australia. Her daughter's given up asking, but it doesn't mean that Ally's stopped thinking about it.

'And for nearly forty-five years I didn't regret it. But now . . .'

Tallulah hauls in a breath and closes her eyes. Ally sees a tear slip from her lashes.

'Listen to me, rabbiting on about our past. It's the present that I wanted. I had enough memories. I wanted life. I wanted life with him, before it was too late for both of us. And I just can't . . . believe he's gone.'

Ally lays a hand on Tallulah's arm. What can anyone ever say? The skylarks fill the quiet with their buzzing song; the tide whispers its way in. Around them, the dunes are all gentleness. It's as if the place knows.

Tallulah sets her coffee cup on the wooden balustrade. She shifts in her seat and says, 'Can I tell you something wild?'

'Of course.'

'I'm a spiritual person, Ally, one way or another. I came here because, after all these years, I felt like it was time. I had a very clear sense that it was time. But the thought that kept me up all night, was . . . what if I was sent here for a different reason? Not to be with Baz, like I thought. But . . . to be here *for* him. To be here for him, when others weren't.'

Ally tips her head. Tallulah doesn't need a response; she just wants someone to listen.

'I went to bed last night agonising. All the what-ifs. If I'd driven straight to the house; if I hadn't stopped in for that drink; if I hadn't been so vain, so uncertain, that I needed to charge myself up; if I hadn't been fussing in my bedroom when he was down by the pool . . . things could have been different, Ally. That's what plagued me in the night.'

And Ally understands it, this urge to track back, to try to imagine a different version of the story. By apportioning blame, in however misguided a way, it makes the inexplicable explicable. The universe firing off madly and at random is somehow a more frightening thought.

'But I know self-sabotaging voices when I hear them. Oh, I know them very well. And that's all it is. I went into the Bluebird because I needed to. It was destined. I don't know why yet, but it was. Which means I arrived at Rockpool just when I was supposed to. Ally, a house full of people who pretend to be Baz's nearest and dearest, and one of them had a hand in his death. I know that too. And that's what I told that young policeman.'

Ally feels a prickle at the back of her neck. 'PC Mullins?'

'That's right. Sweet, simple boy, plodding around Rockpool as if he were on holiday. Completely clueless that there was a murderer in his midst.' Tallulah takes another deep breath. 'He'll find out soon enough, when the post-mortem results are in. They all think I'm going to fly on home. No chance of that. I'm staying here until justice is done. That's all I have left. But maybe it's what Baz needed me for all along.'

A murderer in his midst. Tallulah's conviction is startling, but what is it founded on, other than despair? Ally's fingers tighten around her cup. She's aware that Tallulah is looking at her, waiting for a reaction.

'The lady at the gallery yesterday, she said you're a private detective. Ally, if that's really true – and I hope to God it is – then can I take your phone number? Because if we're talking destiny, then I think our paths crossed for a reason. Don't you?'

At that, Fox bumps Ally's legs and gives a low growl; peeved still, probably, about his shortened walk.

'Of course,' she says, and she trips out the digits. Knowing that the very next thing she must do is call Jayden. And, because she'd like to have a bit more to give him, she says, 'Tallulah, who are the other guests at Rockpool?'

18

Mullins is eating a Pop Tart, a chocolate one, but he's cramming the last bite in before really registering he's had the first. He wipes his hands on his trousers, a little irked that he didn't savour it. It was the last one in the pack as well. He takes a slug of tea.

He's taken to having his breakfast down at the station, finding that he quite likes getting in early. Especially on these light summer mornings. The place is quiet – and his mum isn't grumbling on at him. 'You've left the shower dripping again' (*I haven't, it just drips*). 'Your Aunt Jen keeps asking when you're going to stand on your own two feet' (*When I can afford to buy a house, so yeah, tell her never*). 'Careful there, you know we don't do well with sugar in this family, just look at your Uncle Tony' (*I'd rather not*).

Mullins was in the same class as Saffron at school, and look at her now: business owner, landlord, no one getting on at her over her Shreddies. But Saffron's mum had to die before any of that happened.

'I've gone over your notes from yesterday.'

That's what serves for *Good morning* in Skinner speak.

'What on earth's wrong with them all up there?' the sergeant says.

Mullins presumes Skinner is alluding to the fact that in their statements both Tallulah Pearce and Imogen Edwards made a case for foul play – as opposed to the quality of his notes, which he knows he bossed. He used to hate the 'writing it all up' bit, but he's coming around to it.

What's clear is that nobody at Rockpool had any real light to shed on what happened to Baz. Everyone had been upstairs getting themselves ready for 6 p.m. drinks and canapés – very nice canapés too, Mullins can attest to that. Baz's ex-wife, Nicole, and her two grown-up kids, Ruby and Jet, were in their separate rooms. Nicole was using the hairdryer and didn't even hear Imogen's scream. Ruby was waiting for a call from her husband. Jet was reading – which didn't seem like classic pre-party preparation for a rock star's son, but hey, maybe Baz's idea of a party had changed when he cleaned himself up, and Jet knew there was nothing to get too excited about. Davey and Rupert were the only two guests who were together, having a game of pool in the cool of the games room. *Too effing hot out there*, as Rupert put it. *Baz said he'd join us for a game of Cutthroat but he didn't show. We presumed he got distracted. We all knew Tallulah was flying in. That was messing with his head.* When Mullins asked about Tallulah, Davey welled up, said, *The look on her face when Baz wouldn't come round. She was in ruins.*

'So, no one saw anything,' says Skinner, 'including Tallulah. Despite her claims.'

'Tallulah was in love with Baz Carson,' says Mullins. 'And I think she's having trouble accepting he's dead. She flew all the way from Los Angeles just to see him. First time in about thirty years.'

'You sound like you're a little misty-eyed, Mullins.'

'I think maybe it's colouring her judgement. That's what I mean. Plus, Tallulah did have some intel on the other suspects. Witnesses. Whatever.'

'Go on.'

'Bad blood between the old bandmates and manager. Sour ex-wife. Difficult relationships with his kids. Baz didn't have a great opinion of any of the people that were there – and they all knew it. Imogen reckoned he was harsh on them all in his book.

Embarrassing, that'd be, wouldn't it, sir? If my mum aired our dirty laundry in public, I'm not sure I'd take it lying down . . .'

'I don't especially want to think about your dirty laundry, thanks very much.' Skinner rubs his chin. 'Honestly though, crack open any family and you'll find problems. Money, fame, it doesn't protect you from the same old nonsense the rest of us have to deal with, does it? But there's nothing in their statements that gives me reason to doubt that Baz's death was anything other than natural causes. Nothing obvious anyway. And therein the rub.' He smiles thinly. 'What we need is the post-mortem. Because of who Baz is, they won't hang about.'

'What's your gut instinct though, sir?'

Skinner pauses. Strokes his chin again. 'Gut instinct is that this is probably a tragic accident. Stroke or heart attack. He'd had chest pains recently, hadn't he? Rupert Frost said that, though it's not corroborated by any medical records, so he can't have been bothered enough to get it checked out. Unless Rupert Frost is lying, of course. There's always that.'

'What, to make Baz look frailer than he was?'

'It's possible,' says Skinner. 'At his last check-up, about a month ago, the doctor said Baz was in great shape for his age. But . . . say he's by the pool, has a stroke, or a heart attack, then he falls in and drowns. That stacks up. And to be honest, it's our best bet. If there's so much as a whiff of foul play, the media circus will come steaming down here and not a single one of us will care for that kind of attention.'

Mullins nods. Summers in Cornwall are barmy enough as it is. More people who can't reverse their 4x4s in the lanes? Clogging the tables at The Wreckers and asking for mint in their mushy peas and beer in their batter? No, thanks.

But there is something about Tallulah. She seems so certain. And even the kid, Imogen – out of the mouths of babes and all that – seems to think there are real problems in the family. Problems that on a hot summer's day, with tempers and temperatures running high, could easily boil over.

'Your face is a picture, Constable. What, your gut tells you otherwise?'

Mullins blinks. He didn't expect the question to be sent back his way. Honestly? His gut's telling him he needs another Pop Tart. But instead, he says, 'I don't think we should rule anything out at this stage.' And he's quite pleased with that; it's the kind of thing the brass says in press conferences.

Skinner narrows his eyes. 'You're learning.' He walks off and Mullins thinks that's it, but moments later he's back, brandishing a book. Baz's book.

'Get this read,' he says. 'And do me some notes.'

Oh great. Homework. Mullins has never fared well with a set text.

'I thought you were a fan, sir? Don't you want to read it yourself?'

'A fan of The Nick? I'm more of a Chris de Burgh man, myself. "Lady in Red" – now that's a song.'

Well, Skinner pulled the wool over Mullins's eyes when he laid it on up at Rockpool. Anyone would have thought he had The Nick lyrics tattooed down his forearm, the way he was gushing down by the pool. And maybe he wasn't the only one faking it yesterday.

Mullins opens the book at random and a line jumps out at him. *My son Jet is an eternal disappointment to me. Have you any idea how painful it is to write that line?*

Probably not as painful as it would be for Jet to read. And suddenly Mullins is thinking of his own mum – how she'd never say a thing like that out loud.

Mullins settles back in his chair, hoping he doesn't get a call-out. Crime should take a day off, get itself an ice cream and head to the beach. Because this book might be worth reading after all.

19

Saffron steps back from the breakfast buffet and surveys her handiwork. Oven-warm blueberry muffins, homemade granola, a massive bowl of fruit salad. Banana pancakes for anyone who wants them. Bacon set to be grilled, crusty rolls ready to be split and buttered. Jugs of fresh squeezed orange juice so bright it's fluorescent, and cloudy apple juice from a farm just outside Porthpella. The spread looks indecently celebratory, but it's what Baz wanted. And last night, when Saffron sought the advice of Nicole – who seemed to be taking the lead on things – the woman was firm: *keep calm and carry on.* Baz had paid Saffron for her services upfront, and all the food and drink was ordered too. Nicole said she was contractually obliged to be at their service for the whole weekend.

So that means continuing to sleep at Rockpool too, in the hot little attic room where Saffron lay awake for most of the night, listening for things that go bump; it was like the strange energies in the house were running through the crack beneath the door, swirling about in the airless room. Fuelling bizarre dreams (so she must have slept a little).

But Saffron is nothing if not professional. She will do her duty. One of the things she knows about grief is that everyone deals with it differently. All she can do is be kind.

She glances at the clock. She's been ready to go since six o'clock, just in case anyone gets up early, needing that cup of coffee and a good word. Though she's hoping that someone isn't Rupert. Not after his roaming hands last night; his sloppy, drunk voice in her ear. She doesn't want or need a hungover apology. A guy like that, there'd be nothing genuine in it.

This is when Saffron could do with a dunking, but she can't leave the kitchen and go surfing, and the pool is, of course, out of bounds.

Two hours later, the house is as quiet as ever. Eerily so, in fact. If it weren't for the mess of bottles and wine glasses she came down to earlier, she'd be worried. But lie-ins and hangovers? Shock and sadness settling in? That makes sense.

The vibe last night was a mixed bag. Davey, Rupert and Jet clustered together, whisky and cigarettes; Davey trying to initiate a singalong that never really took off. Then the women orbiting the group, while all the time seeming to avoid one another. Nicole and Ruby don't particularly resemble mother and daughter, but last night their differences were sharper than ever: Nicole's energy was full on, as she tossed her mane of hair and swished about in an eye-achingly colourful kaftan, while Ruby sat with her head dipped, her knees pulled up and her arms clamped tight around them, mollusc-like. Tallulah stayed firmly away, the one person who didn't seem to connect to anyone else – or have any interest in doing so. And Imogen was mostly somewhere near Saffron until she realised Saffron had work to do.

Rupert and Davey were the most obviously drunk. Though at least Davey didn't go around trying to grope people. Saffron has chalked Rupert's douche move up to two things: alcohol and grief. She was serious when she told Davey that she'd report Rupert if there was a sniff of any more trouble from him. Though she isn't sure who to. Nicole, her de facto boss? Mullins, so he can offer a warning that Rupert needs to check himself before he wrecks himself on a charge of sexual harassment? Just thinking about the guy makes her skin creep.

Saffron's phone buzzes and it's Broady. She feels a pang for the simplicity of their early mornings together at Hang Ten. Now that Broady's running his surf school out of the next-door annex, they have their routine: bike to the beach, coffee on the deck, drinking in all that early light. He'll be going through his bookings for the day, bent over his laptop wearing the reading glasses that make him look studious, his sun-bleached hair around his shoulders.

The news is out about Baz. It's everywhere. You okay up there?

Saffron replies, then clicks on to Instagram. Her feed is full of the usual. The news about Baz is yet to break among surfers, skaters and coffee roasters, it seems. But the moment Saffron taps *Baz Carson* into Search, the posts flood in. She scrolls through pictures from concerts back in the day. *#RIPBaz*. She wells up, feeling impacted, again, by the bigness of being here. She looks to the wide doors, the empty terrace, the blue of the pool and beyond, the sea. Rockpool House is rimmed by high white stone walls and the electric gates at the top of the drive are firmly closed. But for how long?

Saffron hears a noise and quickly puts down her phone.

'I'm the only one up, am I?'

It's Jet. Jet who barely spoke a word to her yesterday.

His eyes are blurry, dark scoops beneath them. He strokes his shaved head and slides on to a stool at the breakfast bar. Tugs at his necklace, a thin silver chain.

'Coffee?' she offers.

He nods. 'Yeah, coffee.'

It's hard to tell Jet's age. She guesses he's in his thirties, but boyish, beneath the stubble and tattoos.

'How are you doing?'

'Awesome,' he says, without a grin, and she kicks herself. How does she think he's doing?

'But then you know, don't you?' he adds.

She passes him a coffee cup. 'What do you mean?'

'Your mum died.'

Saffron stiffens. How does he know that?

'Though you probably actually loved her, so whole different story.' He bites into a muffin, speaks through his mouthful. 'Dad did his homework. He was nothing if not thorough.'

Jet slides from his stool and moves to the doors. As he tugs them open, Saffron's glad of the air.

'Hear that? Silence. Not for long. Word's out. That's what you were looking at when I came in, isn't it? On your phone?'

And, again, Saffron shifts under his stare. She doesn't like the way Jet second-guesses her. She can't get a handle on his accent either. Not that it matters – people can talk how they want – but he sounds like a posh boy trying to rough up his edges.

'Bloody Rupes. Taking to Twitter with his big broken heart. Stealing Mum's thunder into the bargain. She's going to love that.' Jet's picking at the fruit salad now, going at it like a gull; he tosses back grapes, crescents of apple, cubes of mango. 'She was going to post at nine a.m. Expertly curated, going for that blend of grace and grief.'

He laughs, and the sound makes Saffron want to edge away. *Be kind*, she tells herself. *He's in a bad place.*

'Is Imogen still asleep?' she asks, changing the subject. 'She's lovely, your niece.'

'Yeah, it's surprising, isn't it?' He's moved to the granola now, takes a handful and chucks it back. 'She's in with her mum, poor kid. She probably took one of Granny's sleeping pills just to shut out the moaning and groaning from Ruby.'

Nicole bursts into the kitchen then, her silk dressing gown flaring out behind like a sail. Her face is streaked with some kind of cream, and her eyes are all fury.

'Have you seen it?' she storms.

'Pretty tasteful, I thought. For Rupert.'

'I told him explicitly. We agreed.'

'You agreed. With yourself.'

'*Jet.*'

And for a second Nicole looks like she's about to raise her hand to him. She turns then, seeing Saffron as if for the first time.

'I expect you've been enjoying your moment in the spotlight, haven't you?' She spins back to Jet. 'We should have made her hand in her phone.'

'I wouldn't dream of posting anything,' says Saffron.

'She would have done a better job,' says Jet. 'Rupes made a typo. He's heartbraken, apparently.'

'And you think this is funny?' Nicole slams her hand on the counter. 'Wait 'til I see him.'

'Oh, come on, Mum,' says a bored voice, and it's Ruby looking oddly formal, in a white cotton blouse and a navy A-line skirt. She pours half a glass of orange juice and sips at it, as if each mouthful is somehow costing her. 'It was always going to be Rupert. Old habits die hard.'

'Managers manage,' says Jet, as he tucks into muffin number two. 'Yeah, come on, Mum, Ruby's right, which I rarely admit. If you haven't got the measure of Mr Frost by now, that's no one's fault but your own, is it?' He looks as if he's about to say something else, then changes his mind as another thought lands. 'By the way, anyone seen Davey this morning?'

Ruby makes a dismissive noise. Nicole's thumbs are moving so fast over her phone that sparks are practically flying. Saffron doesn't know if the question is aimed at her too, but as she's got nothing to add, she turns to the stove, stirs the pancake batter. Maybe Imogen would like pancakes.

'Because we should probably check that the old sad-sack hasn't topped himself.'

'Jet, when are you going to grow up?' says his sister.

'Last surviving member of The Nick. And Davey's never liked being left out. What? I'm serious. I'm worried for the guy. I like Davey. He makes me feel better about myself on a daily basis.'

Saffron's trying to tune out their conversation. She wipes the knife she used for the fruit salad and jumps as Jet claps a hand on her shoulder. She turns to face him, recoiling from the touch.

'Some people do that, don't they?' He grins. 'Just by being more messed up than you are. Talk about a public service. You must be feeling pretty amazing, hanging out with us lot. Free ego boost, to go with whatever he's paid you. You're quids in, mate.'

And in that moment Saffron thinks she'd pay good money just to be able to take off her apron and walk out. But she can't. Nicole Carson isn't the kind of person she wants to cross. Plus, in a weird way – beyond the details of the contract, beyond the epic fee – Saffron feels like she owes it to Baz to be here.

20

Gus walks up and over the dunes, perspiration prickling at his brow. It's barely mid-morning and already the sun is beating down, burning the sand beneath his espadrilles. If it goes on like this, he's going to have to resort to shorts. He's already regretting not wearing his straw hat, but the truth is he feels a bit foolish in it when he's out of his deckchair. It feels like too loud a proclamation: *I Am Wearing a Hat!*

Plus, he feels self-conscious enough as it is, because Gus is also carrying a large bouquet of flowers. *I Am Carrying Flowers!* But he doesn't really mind that one. It makes him look like a man with somewhere to go and with someone to see.

The Shell House is the last in the dunes, heading towards the nature reserve. Gus has come to think of the building itself as distinctly Ally-ish. It's painted blue for starters, the same blue as her eyes. Standing out there all on its own, face turned to the sea, you'd be forgiven for thinking that perhaps visitors aren't welcome, but you'd soon realise that's not true at all. As you get closer, Gus thinks, you notice all these incredibly special little details. Like the hundreds of seashells pressed into the wall outside and the edges of the building itself, before the weatherboard takes over. Like the dune-side garden, which bursts with tropical plants – some of them from seeds Ally saved from the shoreline, bursts of exotic life blooming improbably on Cornish soil. Like her studio, a salt-encrusted annex with peeling paint and splattered windows, but once you step inside the colour leaps from her work – her treasure trove of litter-picked plastics and salvaged objects. And it's this last that Gus wants to celebrate. He'll be at her exhibition later, of course. But if he knows Ally, he's sure she's feeling nervous today. And he hopes his offering will send the jitters packing.

Who doesn't like cornflowers? Mona, that's who. *Scraggy things. Weeds, essentially.* He really should stop making comparisons, but he can't help taking pleasure in all the ways that Ally is different to his ex-wife. Gus finds it endlessly fortifying. Of course, there is one key difference that Gus is perhaps less keen on: the fact that Mona loved him. She must have for at least some of those thirty years of marriage anyway (how many, Gus is loath to put a number on; nor to consider his own feelings on the matter). And while Ally has come to value their friendship – to *treasure* it, in fact, that's the word she used at Christmas – he's not certain her feelings run any deeper than that.

Meanwhile, Gus's ability to consider his own feelings inconsequential is a long-held practice. One that occasionally has its uses: not least, self-preservation.

He jogs up the creaking steps and knocks.

'I'm here, Gus,' she says.

Ally emerges from the foliage of her garden, a pair of clippers in hand. She has a basket over her arm and it's full of cut flowers.

'Oh,' he says, 'you beat me to it.' He holds up his own bunch, as if in surrender.

'Beautiful. How kind of you. I wanted to bring some to the gallery, but yours I shall keep at home.'

Gus shifts on his feet. 'The colours,' he says, 'all the blues. I thought they were very you. Not in a *blue* blue way, a depressing way, if you know what I mean.'

Ally laughs. 'I love them. Coffee? Or something cold?'

'Oh please, a water. I'm parched.'

Gus settles on the bench on the veranda, while Ally ducks inside. It's only a matter of time before one of them mentions Baz Carson, he thinks. He doesn't know why he's straying from the subject. Perhaps it's because he spent most of the night thinking about Baz. His death seems to have taken on excessive meaning, hitting Gus in more ways than he cares to dwell on. The fact that the grim reaper could sidle up at any given moment. The fact that time marches on, and by anybody's reckoning Gus is beyond midlife and is now firmly in later life; the version of Gus who belted out 'You Do It For Me', and even sometimes wore a leather jacket, might as well be a figment of his imagination. The fact that Baz's arrival in Porthpella felt like a sign – a sign that this must be the place, that Gus was right to stay and stay and stay. And if the sunset of his life beckons, then spending it in the approximate vicinity of his one-time hero and, yes, this woman who stands in front of him now – in fact, mainly this woman who stands in front of him now – would be a grand way to rage against the dying of the light.

Ally emerges with a tray and a jug of iced lemon water, two glasses.

'Jayden says the news of Baz's death is everywhere,' she says, passing him a glass. 'He thinks we should brace ourselves for a press invasion.'

'Any more known on what happened?' he edges.

Because the truth is Gus avoids the internet. He wants to feel bound up in the Porthpella he knows and loves, not have his thoughts pulled in all sorts of other directions.

'That message I sent you,' he says. 'I fear I was being a bit dramatic. The chance of foul play must be incredibly small. Poor old Baz's number just came up, didn't it?'

Ally hesitates, something crossing her face. 'I'd have said so,' she says. Then, 'I told you I met an old friend of his yesterday?'

'Tallulah Pearce. I was reading about her last night.'

'Ah, so you are carrying on with the book?'

'I couldn't not. I found myself wanting his words,' he says. 'I can't believe you met her. There's a picture – the two of them in LA back in the day. She's astonishingly beautiful.'

'She was his first love, wasn't she?'

'She was. But then he wanted to be in England, and she wanted to be in America, and they just couldn't find a way to make it work.' Gus is on a roll now. 'The whole book is themed around the concept of saying no, and the power you can get from that. That's why it's called *Turn It Down*, really. Baz reckons all the best things in his life have come about as a result of his saying no. With Tallulah, yes, he was in love with her, this angelic woman in Topanga Canyon offering him the American Dream, but when he left her to go back to England, that's when things really took off for him musically. He channelled that heartbreak into his songwriting. And he made the decision count, because there was a lot riding on it.' Gus takes another drink of water. 'That's the drift of it, anyway. Saying no to a life with Tallulah led to The Nick. What's she like? Do you think she bears ill will? She can't do, if she came to his party. And, of course, it was all such a long time ago.'

'I think she's still very much in love with him.'

'She told you that?'

'I saw her again this morning. She was at the beach at first light. I feel so dreadfully sorry for her.'

Gus narrows his eyes. He knows Ally. There's something she's not saying.

'What did you talk about?' he says. 'I should think I'd be speechless if I saw her. Going by her photo in the book, anyway.'

And then he stops himself, because here he is, gabbing away effortlessly, and what does that ease say about his feelings for Ally? The chorus from Baz's big hit rises in his mind.

'She said she's staying until she knows why Baz died,' she says, refilling their drinks. Ice clatters into Gus's glass. 'Though I don't know whether she'll be up at Rockpool itself. She doesn't seem too keen on the company. In fact . . . she's looking for someone to blame. But I can understand that instinct.'

Gus looks at Ally. Her eyes are on the beach, the wide band of golden sand and the azure waters, close enough to touch. It's a stupidly beautiful sight. He knows that Ally takes every possible pleasure from her home; no one could appreciate it more. But he also knows that there's a person missing; perhaps there will always be a person missing.

Gus feels a nudging at his ankles and Fox flops down at his feet. Settles his nose on Gus's toes. He reaches down to stroke his ears.

'Gus, how far off from finishing the book are you?'

'Baz's book? Oh, I finished it in the small hours.'

'I couldn't borrow it, could I?'

'Of course, I'll drop it round. It's a great read, Ally. I mean, it helps if you're a fan. But he has some terrific stories. And you've got to be impressed by his confidence. Puts the rest of us to shame, really. Puts some of his own people to shame too, actually, which is a bit . . . well, a bit much, perhaps. Like we said yesterday. It wouldn't be my way, to say it in a book. But that's classic Baz. Never cared what anyone else thinks. A true rebel.'

'How does Tallulah come across?' asks Ally.

Gus stops to think. 'Well, she's not the one who got away,' he says. 'That was Connie. It was Connie who was Baz's true love. The only person who ever said no to him.'

'And Connie's not staying up at the house?'

'No, no. Connie died five years ago. Most moving part of the book, actually.' He looks at her. 'You wanting to read it . . . that's just curiosity, is it?'

Ally nods.

'And Jayden's going to be reading it too then, is he?'

'I should think he'll want to get his hands on a copy.'

'Right. Gotcha.'

His thoughts rev up again – thoughts he managed to quash last night. The injustice of it cuts like a knife. Death is death and never a picnic, but the possibility that Baz was murdered? Here in Gus's happy place? He tries to rally, but his smile is thin.

'The Shell House Detectives book club,' he says. 'I like it.'

21

Nicole pounds over the lawn. Fury burns in her veins and it's an old, familiar feeling. Everyone else getting it wrong, and she alone a beacon for what's right.

Ruby called her negative once – *you're always so negative, Mum* – and it was like a slap. Not the accusation – of course she was negative, how could she be anything but? – but the fact that she was judged for it. Or that it should be somehow surprising. Because Nicole's negativity is a reasonable response to a set of circumstances called Life.

What no one realises is that Nicole's a good faker. No, she's a *great* faker. The Nicole Carson wellness brand is one of self-love and good vibes and later life lived to the max. And the first part is 100 per cent accurate. She does love herself. She loves herself because no one else will.

She faked it back there in the kitchen. She kept a lid on her anger, in front of the kids and that judgey little hired help. But Rupert tweeting about Baz's death? The biggest news she's ever had to share on her socials, and he gets there first.

They had an agreement. And more fool her, she thought he'd stick to it.

In their marriage, Baz used to accuse her of keeping score – a petty running total of every misdemeanour – as if that was somehow a flaw. Small wonder that Baz didn't like the fact she valued accountability; guilty people always want to let bygones be bygones. It was almost funny that he couldn't see it.

Baz never liked the fact she held a grudge against Rupert either. Well, neither did Nicole. It's much easier to walk on sunshine, isn't it?

Yes, okay, it was years ago now, but Nicole can't forgive Rupert for the fact that when Ruby was a screaming toddler and Jet just born, he pulled Baz out on an impromptu weeks-long tour. Rupert threw the dates together like a kid filling a bag at the pick-and-mix counter. She was broken-bodied, her mind rattling with loose screws, the stench of sour milk and baby sick hanging about the house like a cloud – and he left her on her own. Nicole never told Baz as much, but she phoned Rupert, said *please, no.* It cost her a lot, that phone call, not least her last scrap of pride. But business came first; the band came first. And Rupert saw an opportunity and took it. Who cared if it killed Nicole?

In all the years she's known him since, she's never told Rupert how much it hurt. But she's carried it, like she carries all her grudges; the weight of it only makes her sturdier. And of course Baz put the tour in his damn book, without ever knowing what it meant for her.

You knew what you were getting into with Baz Carson. That's what her own mother said to her once. Had she, though? The first time she saw him he was onstage, and he was electric. She wanted to run off the energy of this guy, that's what she knew; she wanted his power in her life. And okay, she wanted the gold too. When they met backstage, she was surprised to find that in her wedged heels she towered over him, but the crackle of attraction was still there. And when they shook hands, she could feel her whole body lighting up. Then he pulled her in for a kiss.

Now, Nicole stares at the police tape marking the pool – every inch of it. She has never been one to turn away from difficult truths. So, this is how it ends: a dripping-hot clifftop; her dead ex left bobbing like a piece of litter in a canal; his poor man's Hollywood-style mansion behind him, its flash face turned to all, but inside cheap bathrooms and an ancient kitchen and stifling rooms. But if Rockpool House is split between the kids, it'll be a fair whack apiece. Less than they deserve, but still.

Ruby's the executor, but she was tight-lipped last night. *It's not appropriate to talk about it*, she said. Then she gave her mother that same look of disdain that Nicole has known since the cradle. Only, edged with something else, something undecipherable. The trouble is, Nicole doesn't know her daughter quite well enough.

There were dangerous accusations in the air last night. Tallulah's grief had a strange shape to it. Nicole saw the way that American was looking at them all: eyes front, appraising; fearful, even. And little Imogen with her overactive imagination, thinking someone had wanted to kill Grandpa. Surely a heart attack? For the best part of two decades, Baz's heart had beaten only for Connie. Well, that organ of his was on borrowed time these last five years. It was a miracle he made it this long, the pining bastard.

This last thought is the spike Nicole needs as she reaches the so-called cottage. She hesitates before she pounds on the door. It's little more than an outhouse – a one-room granny flat with a bathroom tacked on (what did Rupert do to earn en-suite?), and a prime view of the taped-off pool. On the other side is a games room housing pool and darts; a bird-poo-splattered table-tennis table that must have lived outside at some point – pre-Baz, presumably. The kind of facility for a low-rent holiday house littered with gangly teenagers, not a rock star's *palais*.

She curls her lip at it all. When Baz bought Rockpool, he was buying the view. End of. And Nicole had wanted to see it for herself. She liked that he invited her; that she's one of the ones who mattered, despite everything.

She feels a catching in her chest, and realises it's a sob. For a moment she stands with her face pushed into her hands. She feels grotesque: salty cheeked; heaving shoulders.

Baz is dead.

In that moment Nicole feels so damn sorry for herself that, with a fresh surge of fury, she hammers on Rupert's door. He might have stolen her thunder with his pathetic tweet, but she can strike like lightning when she needs to. *By God, yes I can.*

22

Jayden has the fan going in the campsite office, and its half-hearted whirring is the soundtrack to his thoughts. Usually, he quite likes being here at this time of day. People drop by to pick up maps or ask after a day trip, and he enjoys the chit-chat. Today though, he's preoccupied, and less open to small talk than usual.

Thanks to his conversation with Felix, Jayden now has all the names of Baz's weekend guests, along with a few scribbled notes on each one. *Just in case.* It makes him smile that Ally did the same thing after running into Tallulah Pearce at the beach; Tallulah seems to think someone at Rockpool wanted Baz dead. Ally was guarded in her assessment, saying that her instinct was to trust the woman, but she knew she was also devastated – possibly not thinking straight.

The same can't exactly be said of Felix. *Maybe they were all standing there. Watching him sink.*

Jayden can't work out whether Felix genuinely thinks anyone there wished Baz ill, or whether that was just a journalistic flourish. Felix was clear that he was unpopular among Baz's crowd – with Baz's children, anyway.

I was a teenager, Felix said, *just a bit younger than Jet and Ruby. They hated me. And I'm pretty sure they still do. In fact, I know they do. Jet's already texted me, saying no one wants me there this weekend. Pathetic, really.*

Was that the message Felix received when Jayden was getting his milk? If so, for all that Felix seemed to shake it off in the telling, Jayden could see that, in the moment, it cut him deep.

Felix's mum had met Baz when he showed up at her pottery class one day. She handed him an apron and a ball of clay like everybody else, so the story went. It was the start of a one-sided love affair – but an equal friendship. Baz cleaned himself up, stopped the drugs, stopped the drink, and left his wife and family.

Baz made a big show of the fact that he was leaving Nicole for Mum, but it wasn't like that. They were never together. Not in the way Baz wanted, anyway. But they stayed friends for years. At Mum's funeral, Baz played an acoustic version of 'You Do It For Me'. The one that hit the charts later. It was . . . actually, it was pretty cool.

'Good morning young man.'

Eileen, from plot 7. Here in her caravan for three weeks with her husband Ken. Some rig they've got too, with a doormat, a revolving washing line, and a couple of deckchairs that look more like La-Z-Boy recliners. Eileen and Ken live in a village in the Dales, and she did a double take when Jayden said he was from Yorkshire. *But not originally?* she said. And he forced a grin as he said, *Born in Leeds General.*

'Now, I don't want to complain, but that baby in the little blue tent was making a terrible racket at six o'clock this morning.'

'Not much anyone can do about a baby's crying. If you're being disturbed, we could always move you to the top of the field.'

'What, and walk five miles to the toilet block? No, no, that won't do. Can't you move them? Ken's terrible when he doesn't get his sleep.'

'Ah, I'm afraid not. It's give and take, isn't it? Has to be, on a campsite. Now, anything I can do for you, Eileen? You alright for milk?'

'I bring powdered,' she says, her lips tight. 'Ken can't tell the difference once it's in his brew.'

Jayden pops her a thumbs up, then sighs as she ambles off.

The whole point with a campsite is that you don't put up walls; you embrace the music of other people's existence, while showing a bit of respect yourself. It's the deal, isn't it? Jayden wonders whether they should get guests to sign something when they book: *I hereby agree to live and let live.*

His phone pings. *Saffron.* He messaged her earlier asking how things were going up at Rockpool.

There's a weird vibe but I guess that's to be expected.

Then another drops in: I have to work the full weekend still.

He's about to reply when Felix appears in the doorway.

'Hey, man.'

'Felix, morning! How are you doing?'

'Good. Better. I'm shooting up to Rockpool now. Thought I'd best pay my respects. Listen, thanks for last night. I didn't realise I needed it.'

'Any time.'

'It's all over the media now. This place will be swarming.'

'How big a news story is it?'

Felix shrugs. 'Depends on your angle. The timing with the book's publication amps things up. The fact that everyone who mattered was there. Some of the gutter press will want to make something of that, regardless of the truth.'

He says this calmly, Jayden notes, and with a measure of distance. Felix can't really think anyone else had a hand in Baz's death.

'Have the police been in touch?' he asks.

'With me? Why would they?'

Jayden shrugs. 'Standard procedure, I'd say. You're on the guest list for an intimate gathering and the host dies.'

'You're still thinking like a copper, then.'

'Old habits die hard.'

'Maybe I should beat them to the punch and offer a statement. Look, I'd best get going. If I'm bothering to go up there, I want to at least catch them before they all head off.' He hesitates. 'Hang on, can they even head off?'

'Well, the police will have all their details. But my mate's doing the catering up there and she's been asked to stay on for the weekend as planned, so . . . maybe they're staying put.'

Felix looks lost in thought suddenly. Then he appears to collect himself.

'Alright, I'm off.'

'Good luck.' Jayden claps him on the shoulder.

Felix hesitates in the doorway; turns. 'By the way, I got a message from Davey late last night. After you left.'

In his mind, Jayden runs through what Felix told him about Davey.

Former bandmate. Bit of a drifter after The Nick broke up. Session work, mostly, but he always partied too hard. Made him an unreliable proposition, and his talent wasn't enough to make up for it, you know? I think I probably wrote something like that once, and I'm not sure he's ever forgiven me for it.

Another person who has a grudge against Felix – or maybe he's just a little oversensitive.

'Why he'd reach out to me, I don't know. Like I said, we weren't exactly close. Look, I've got it here.'

He pulls out his phone, thumbs through the messages.

Devastated about Baz. Rupert is too. We loved him.

'Rupert used to manage The Nick, right?' says Jayden.

'That's it. And he still looked after Baz's business affairs – what there were of them anyway.'

'And they all stayed friends?'

That's a question Jayden didn't ask last night because there's a fine line between curious conversation and pumping for information. But maybe he crossed it anyway, because after Felix ran him through the list of guests, he appeared to lose steam; as he yawned and stretched, Jayden took the hint.

'More or less, yeah. Davey was the glue. Loyal as a Labrador, that one. It must have broken his heart when Baz called time on the band, but he never showed it. Rupert had a bit more of a chip on his shoulder. Probably because it was a terrible business move, the band breaking up, and he's never had a big success with another group since. A point that Baz makes with considerable alacrity in his book.'

Or maybe Felix was just tired last night, as he's forthcoming now. Jayden takes it and runs with it.

'He doesn't paint Rupert well then?'

'He doesn't paint anyone well. Except himself, of course. But hey, that's Baz.' Felix turns the phone in his hand. 'It was Rupert who rang and told me Baz was dead yesterday. Probably Nicole made him, thinking I'd stay away once I heard. But I can't do that. No matter what I think of them, I can't do that.'

'My friend Saffron, the chef, she said the atmosphere up there is pretty intense.'

'Intense? I'd say it'll be hell. Anyway, I'm stalling. I'll say hi to your mate while I'm up there.'

'Oh, hey, Felix – Baz's book. Do you have a copy on you?'

'I've got two. I had an advance copy, plus he gave me one the other day. Why, you want to read it? I'll grab it for you, mate. It's in the van.'

He's back in half a minute with the two copies, says, 'Take your pick.' One is a well-thumbed paperback with *Not for Resale* printed across it, the other a glossy hardback. He puts them both on the counter.

Felix tips his head. 'Weird to think he was your neighbour, hey? You want to know more about him?'

'Yeah . . . that's it.'

Felix nods, and Jayden can tell he's on to him.

'Take it with a pinch of salt, okay?' he says. 'Baz is harsh, but everyone around him knows that's his vibe. There's nothing new in here. Just standard Baz, offering his pronouncements on why no one else is as good at life as he is.'

'Still be interesting to read,' says Jayden.

And he's certain that the coroner, if not the police, will agree. But in the meantime, it wouldn't hurt for Jayden to draw his own conclusions from the book, would it? He fancies a little reading on a hot summer's day. The thought of it takes him back to his school holidays, lying on his belly on his bed, tearing through his stack of library books one after the other. He'll have it back to Felix before the day is out.

Just then the light changes in the cabin as a massive vehicle pulls up outside.

'See you later,' says Felix.

As he heads out the door, Jayden sees him do a half-dance with a guy coming in the other direction. The other man steps aside, waves his arm with a grandiose gesture. Then peers inside the cabin with a grin.

'Jayden Weston, as I live and breathe.'

'Sir,' says Jayden, stepping round the desk. 'It's good to see you.'

They clap hands together.

'Surprised?'

'My wife spotted your name on the booking.'

'Ah, foiled.' DI Radford looks at his watch. And, just as Jayden remembers, it's a flash one. 'It's ten thirty. That's what I call a tidy drive.'

'What time did you leave Leeds?'

'Leeds? No, no. That'd be a speed-breaker, especially in the juggernaut. We overnighted in Plymouth. You seen this thing?'

He gestures to Jayden to follow him outside. The motorhome is enormous: brilliant white, with silver trim. A tiny woman waves from the high-up passenger seat. Jayden waves back.

'Keely,' says DI Radford. 'I told her all about you.' He claps Jayden on the back. 'It's good to see you, PC Weston.'

PC Weston.

'It's just Jayden now,' he says. And he's surprised that saying it feels so bittersweet.

DI Radford – ever the detective – gives him a long look. Says, 'Let me get settled in. Then I want to tell you about Plymouth.'

23

Saffron passes Imogen a mug of hot chocolate. It's a scorching morning, but Saffron can always get behind hot chocolate. The girl's gone for the whole shebang too: a mountain of whipped cream and disco sprinkles.

'They're all out on the terrace, I think.'

And it's not that she wants Imogen to go, but she needs to prep for lunch. If anyone's staying, that is. While Nicole might be able to enforce her ex-husband's wishes in keeping Saffron here, she can't exactly make the other guests stick around, can she?

'Everyone's crazy this morning. I'm staying out the way.'

'There's a lot of emotions,' says Saffron.

'Rupert's in big trouble over leaking it on social. Granny's livid.' Imogen dabs the tip of her finger on the sprinkles, eating them delicately. 'And Davey and Rupert got drunk last night so Mum's blaming the smashed vase on them. I thought it was just a standard vase but apparently it's worth thousands, and I guess that's what they're all thinking now . . . who gets this place. Who just lost out on that vase? I think it's gross. Poor Grandad.'

'How's your mum?' asks Saffron.

'Ask her therapist.' Imogen dips her head and licks at the cream, like she's a cat at a bowl. 'Dad's the only sensible one in our family. Maybe that's why he's not here. Actually no, Dad's not here because Grandad hates him. *Hated* him, I mean. God, I still can't believe he's dead.' She looks up. 'Well, he didn't hate him, he just thought he was incredibly boring. It's in the book. Like I told the inspector, it's all in the book. "My daughter married the most boring man in Surrey, just to spite her old man." That's what Grandad wrote. And he is a bit boring, my dad, when you compare him to people like Uncle Jet or whoever, but I think that's what Mum likes about him.'

The inspector. Saffron resists the urge to laugh. She wonders if Mullins is still buzzing about that one. He revelled in Imogen's attention yesterday, especially with her talk of who might be to blame for Baz's death. But Saffron's not going to fan that flame; it's not good for anyone.

'Something's going on out there,' says Imogen, spinning round. 'Listen.'

She darts to the big glass doors and looks out.

'That must be Felix. I wondered when he'd turn up.'

Saffron joins her. From this angle they've a perfect view of the driveway, where a camper van is now parked. They watch as a tall, shaggy-looking guy walks over to the terrace and shakes hands with Jet. Davey, who Saffron hadn't yet seen this morning, pulls him into a long hug. Nicole's face is thunderous. Ruby doesn't even look up.

'Grandad was in love with his mum, Connie. So, my mum hates him. Talk about a long grudge, though. She was a teenager when they split up. I mean, if that happened to me, and there was some other kid suddenly on the scene, I'd get over it. It's not exactly the kid's fault, is it?'

'Felix was the kid?'

'I told you, it's all in the book,' says Imogen, shaking her head. 'Felix is this cool music writer, now. Which makes Mum and Uncle Jet hate him even more, probably, because he ended up doing something that Grandad approved of.'

'Was Baz Felix's stepdad?'

'Oh, nothing like that. Baz lived with them for a bit, when he was drying out. Connie was the love of his life. The book's dedicated to her. Although his old girlfriend's here this weekend, from way back. Tallulah, the American. You've met her, right? Very Californian, Mum says, like that's a bad thing. Tallulah's super-sad about Grandad.'

'I haven't seen Tallulah this morning.'

'I saw her heading out early. There's a secret gate to the cliff path. She's smart, dodging the reporters. She had a bag with her, maybe she was going for a swim.'

Saffron smiles. 'You see everything that goes on around here, huh?'

'No one takes any notice of me, so it's easy.'

'I haven't seen Rupert yet this morning either.'

'Oh, you won't. Mum said he was all over the place last night. He'll be in bed all day, I bet. Rupert and Davey always overdo it. It's their thing.' Imogen turns from the glass doors. 'I expect we'll be leaving soon. Mum's desperate to get back to London.'

'Nicole seems to want everyone to stay on.'

'Well, let's see who wins that one. Anyway, your inspector friend says there'll be a post-mortem. How long does that take?'

'Erm, I've no idea . . .'

Saffron doesn't like the way the conversation is going. She glances at the clock on the wall. It's coming up to eleven o'clock. She tells Imogen that she probably needs to get on with prepping lunch, and the girl wanders out of the kitchen with a slightly dejected look.

In the new quiet, Saffron stands for a moment; breathes. She's suddenly conscious of the clock's ticking, something she hasn't noticed before. *Tick, tick, tick.* She thinks longingly of the outside world. Wonders how Kelly's doing with the Hang Ten morning rush; whether the brownies are outselling the cookies, or if the lemon drizzle will take it. Up here on the clifftop, it's as if Porthpella village and the beach, the dunes, don't exist at all. Just this giant ship of a house, floating up above the sea.

She looks out to the sun-bright terrace. Only Ruby is still sitting there, bent over her phone, beneath a parasol. Saffron thinks she can hear the faint hum of voices moving through the house, but no one comes her way.

Feeling a rush of relief, she turns back to her work. She planned an elaborate salad bar for lunch, and she needs to crack on; these carrots won't julienne themselves.

'Hey. Saffron, is it?'

And it's the new arrival – Felix. He brushes his long hair back from his face and scuffs his feet. Blue Vans, just like hers, only box-fresh.

'I'm Felix. I'm staying at the campsite and Jayden said you were a mate of his.'

'Oh, hi,' says Saffron. 'Nice. It's a great spot.'

'Not quite the gig you anticipated here, huh?'

'I'm really sorry. I only just met Baz but . . . I liked him.'

Felix passes his hand across his mouth. His eyes are sad. 'Yeah. It's a lot. Everyone here . . . they're treating you okay?'

'Sure. Nicole's asked me to stay on for the weekend and . . . I've agreed.'

'You don't have to, you know.'

And Felix sends her a look of understanding, almost as if he was here this morning and heard the way Jet and Nicole spoke to her.

'They're a complicated bunch at the best of times,' he says. 'And right now, it's not exactly that. Don't let them push you around.' He taps his fingers on the counter, a quick-fire rhythm. 'Anyway, I just wanted to look in and say hi before heading off. I told Jayden I would.'

'It was nice to meet you. And . . . thanks.'

He turns to go out of the door, then stops. Says, 'You really liked him? When you met him?'

'Yeah, I did. I thought he was very sincere.'

'Too sincere, for some people. He could be callous.' He rubs at his chin and his stubble crackles. 'I hear you tried to save him.'

'I was too late.'

'But you pulled him from the pool.'

Saffron nods.

'Everyone here reckons a heart attack. Apparently, he said to Rupert he'd had chest pains earlier this year. He didn't put that in his book though. Didn't want to admit the vulnerability, maybe. That all those years of excess might have caught up to him. It doesn't exactly sit with the brand.'

'The brand?'

'Of being perfectly in control of everything.'

And at that, Felix gives a rueful smile, and ducks out of the kitchen.

For the next three-quarters of an hour or so, Saffron loses herself in the satisfying rhythms of slicing and chopping and grating. Her spirits lift as she works. *Maybe people will decide to leave after lunch*, she thinks hopefully. The media are congregating in Porthpella; she's heard the buzzer go at least six times this morning and, on each occasion, Nicole has jumped to it – not that anyone's being let in. Fortress vibes all the way. But it's oppressive, knowing they're gathering, so maybe all the Rockpool guests will prefer to disperse and go to ground back at their homes.

Saffron starts to cut a pomegranate, the sharp knife making short work of it. She turns the fruit and starts to score the sides. She loves this next bit, where she gently prises it open and the ruby-red jewels spill into her hands. It's like finding treasure.

Just then she hears a cacophony out in the garden, a slamming door and what sounds like fast footsteps. *Someone's having a tantrum* – that's what she thinks. And she'll berate herself for it later, this casual disregard of other people's emotions, because then the door flies open and Davey lurches into the kitchen. His face is pure fear. Behind him, a scream sounds – as sudden and sharp as smashing glass.

Saffron jumps. As the fruit skids across the countertop, her knife slips, cutting straight into her finger. Instantly the blood rises.

Davey stumbles towards her, eyes wide with panic. He tugs at her arm, as her finger throbs and blood splashes to the floor. Tears run down his sunken cheeks.

'Help us. You have to help us.'

Mullins has his window down. His elbow rests on the door and he fans his fingers as they lift and drop in the airstream.

'Mullins,' hisses Skinner.

And he feels like a little boy being caught out.

He settles back in his seat, as the view opens in front of them; he tries to ignore the churning in his belly. Up ahead he can see Rockpool House, a white cube perched on the edge of the cliff. The sea is an eye-aching blue. Mullins pulls his shades out of his pocket: police-issue wraparounds.

From here it looks like paradise. But appearances can be deceptive. *Murder.* That was the call that came in.

Out-and-out murder.

'Rupert Frost,' says Skinner. 'Tell me what we know about him.'

'He was pretty shocked yesterday,' says Mullins. 'He was getting started on the drinking early.'

Skinner swings the car into an ascent, and the sea disappears behind high hedgerows. 'And he's a band manager?'

'Retired, mostly. He was with Davey in the poolroom when Baz died. It was Nicole Carson who called 999 this time.'

'Baz's ex-wife.'

'That's it. Sixty-three years of age. Mum to Ruby and Jet. Granny to Imogen.'

Mullins pictures the man from yesterday: Rupert Frost. The sweat shining on his forehead. The glint of his expensive watch. He'd been wearing a Hawaiian shirt with shop-creases running down the front. Rupert was probably around the same age as Baz, just not into all the health stuff; a high paunch sitting above his belt.

'Stabbed in the chest, that's what Nicole said on the call. A lot of blood.'

And it's the Hawaiian shirt that Mullins is imagining, although Rupert probably wasn't still wearing it. Big red splodges mixed with jungle print and dinner-plate flower heads. He feels faintly queasy and turns to facts instead.

'You know, in the witness statements, both Tallulah Pearce and the girl, Imogen, thought there was more to Baz's death,' he says. 'This makes it look more likely, doesn't it? This second one?'

'We'll know soon enough. Good job they're fast-tracking the post-mortem. What the—!'

Skinner slams his brakes on suddenly, as a car bears down on top of them. Mullins's chest slams against his seat belt, and his shades bounce on his nose. He gives a low whistle.

'Close one.'

It's not the other car's fault; the lanes are tight round here. And they were going at some speed. It's up to Skinner to reverse, by rights, but he's showing no sign of shifting. Mullins looks at the other driver – when you're police, people either jump to attention or stick their chests out. You never know which way it'll go.

He instantly recognises the face of the woman at the wheel.

'That's Ruby Edwards, Sarge. Baz's daughter.'

'Now, what's she doing fleeing the scene?'

Skinner shunts them forward and winds down his window. Reluctantly, Ruby does the same. Her face, Mullin notes, is sheet-white. Either from the shock of the near-miss or . . . something else.

'We're on our way to Rockpool,' calls out Skinner, polite as you like. 'It was your mother who called 999.'

'Thank you, Officer.'

Ruby's hands grip the wheel. A big pair of sunglasses hides her eyes.

'Where are you going in such a hurry?'

'My daughter was upset,' says Ruby.

And Mullins clocks a figure in the back, then. Bit old for that, isn't she? Mullins was riding up front about as soon as he was off his booster seat. He has a sudden memory of holding a toy plastic steering wheel while his dad drove beside him. *My co-pilot*, that's what his dad used to call him. Well, Mullins was flying solo soon enough, wasn't he? Not that he had much choice in the matter. He tries to see Imogen's face in the back, but he can't.

'The instructions were to stay at the scene,' says Skinner. 'In the event of any kind of sudden death, we need witness statements. But of course you already know that, I'm afraid to say.'

And the DS doesn't sound particularly apologetic at all. In fact, he's ice-cold.

Ruby pushes a hand through her flat brown hair. 'I panicked,' she says. 'It's . . . a lot to cope with. Imogen was getting . . . hysterical.'

In the back of the car, Imogen gives Mullins a little wave. She doesn't look particularly hysterical.

'There's a driveway just back the way you came,' says Skinner. 'Reverse, then turn around. We'll follow you back to the house.'

There's a moment where Ruby doesn't respond, her gaze fixed straight ahead. Who does that – just makes off, the minute someone's found murdered? Ruby Edwards has either got a whole lot to hide, or she's so innocent that the thought didn't even occur to her.

'You alright reversing?' asks Mullins, leaning across, pushing his shades on top of his head. 'These lanes are murder if you're not used to them. What you want to do is just focus on where you want to go, not what to avoid. Make sure your mirrors . . .'

And it does the trick. With her lips pursed, Ruby changes gear and shoots into a deft, fast reverse. As they drive on, Mullins grins to himself.

'Was that a little bit of tactical mansplaining, Officer Mullins?'

'Might have been.'

'Nice work. Didn't know you had softly-softly in you.'

'I'm a marshmallow, me,' says Mullins. Then pulls his shades down. *Co-pilots.*

~

As they pull up to Rockpool House, there are cars parked on the verge and a cluster of photographers at the gate. Nothing like the kind of scenes Mullins has seen on TV – or even outside the magistrates' court from time to time – but enough to prove that something has happened here. And that there are people that want the telling of it.

Skinner makes an irritated clicking noise with his tongue as one of the blokes turns his camera on them. They must be the first officials here, otherwise this lot would've got wind something more had happened; they're here for Baz, not Rupert Frost.

In the car ahead Ruby barks into the buzzer and the gates open. They follow her in and park next to her on the gravel by the house.

As she climbs out of the car, she looks assertive, as if she's the one to have summoned the police and brought them to the door. She strides towards the house, and only when she's halfway there does she stop and spin, gravel crunching beneath her plimsolls.

'Imogen, hurry up!'

Mullins opens the car door, and the girl peers up at him.

'You alright in there?' he says.

Imogen rolls her eyes. 'We meet again. Don't mind my mum, Inspector, she's wound a little tight this morning.'

'No surprise, really. Do you want to go in with her?'

'I actually think I'm going to stay out here. If that's okay? I won't go anywhere near . . . you know.'

'Okay, good idea. We'll come and talk to you in a bit. Need someone with you? I can get your mum . . .'

Imogen gives a sharp laugh. 'Please, no.'

'Come on!' barks Skinner.

Mullins turns, surprised that he's waited for him.

'Let's get on with this. And be warned, Mullins, it's not going to be pretty.'

Mullins doesn't love blood. But then, does anyone?

He looks around the luscious garden – the perfect lawn, the fancy palms and tropical-looking flowers. The fake-looking blue of the infinity pool – yesterday's crime scene, a tranquil warm-up in comparison – and the big old sea beyond. He doesn't blame Imogen for wanting to stay out here.

He sucks in a big deep breath, determined to take in all these garden scents, all things green and pleasant. But instead, he inhales a passing fly, and he feels it catch at the back of his throat. He coughs, his eyes instantly filling.

'For God's sake, Constable,' says Skinner.

Mullins spits on the gravel, then wipes his mouth with the back of his hand. A creepy nursery rhyme about an old lady swallowing a fly comes into his head. *Didn't the silly boot swallow a spider, then a bird, then a cat, and so on? She definitely dies at the end.* Mullins shakes his head, trying to get rid of the thought, as he follows Skinner. There's already been more than enough death at Rockpool House.

25

No one asked them to gather in the lounge, but it's where they are anyway.

Saffron sits on the edge of a bright white leather sofa, her bandaged finger resting on her knee. It pulses with a pain that, given the circumstances, should really feel insignificant. She bites her lip, trying – and failing – not to think about the nightmare scene in the cottage.

Anyone could see that Rupert was dead, but Saffron checked his pulse anyway, reaching over the spreading red tide. If not her, who else? Davey wasn't going to do it: he was in shock, his voice high and querulous, saying the same thing over and over: *I went to wake him up, the lazy bastard. I went to wake him up.* Then Jet, crowding the doorway, letting out a laugh of disbelief that Ruby, behind him, was mad at him for. But Saffron understood it: when panic hits, no one's in control, and Jet – for all his nonchalance – was as shocked as any of them. Nicole stamped into the room in her metallic cork wedges. Why does Saffron remember the shoes? Perhaps because she was still kneeling, and Nicole was suddenly beside her, with her cherry-painted toes and tanned ankles. Screaming orders over her shoulder: *Ruby, you keep that child of yours away from here!* But then Imogen was suddenly there and the swear word she dropped – a single consonant – spoke for them all.

Two dead bodies in as many days.

And this one, Rupert, was nothing like Baz, who'd looked almost peaceful floating in the pool.

The stab wounds were clear on his chest. And in that moment, the dead body of Rupert Frost was the most terrifying thing Saffron had ever seen. So terrifying, in fact, that her brain seemed to stall.

Until now. Now, with everyone gathered.

Because suddenly her mind is clicking into some kind of action, and a single question pushes to the fore: did one of this lot kill Rupert Frost?

And is everyone else thinking the same thing?

'I'm sorry you got hurt, Saffron,' says Imogen, nudging her.

She tries for a smile. Says quietly, 'Hey, it's nothing.' *Nothing in comparison.* 'I'm not a real chef without a scar or two.'

She squeezes Imogen's arm, then gets up and moves to the window. The blue-and-white police tape still hems the pool, and now there's more being unspooled. Mullins is trudging with his head down, the sun bouncing off his back as he marks off the cottage. White-suited SOCOs bob back and forth.

Saffron turns back to the room. Ruby is slumped in the window seat, the Breton stripes of her top criss-crossing. Jet leans against the far wall, hands stuffed in his pockets; his unbothered vibe shifted. Davey paces by the fireplace, gnawing at his thumb; a small man to begin with, he looks diminished now, especially beside the solidity of Nicole, standing tall in her wrap dress and gold necklaces, arms folded across her chest. Stress radiates from her, as if she might go up in smoke.

'Rupert didn't really care about Baz. He just wanted to make money off him.'

And it strikes Saffron as a strange thing for Nicole to say. What do Rupert's feelings towards Baz have to do with his murder?

'Sounds familiar,' murmurs Jet.

But Nicole doesn't hear, she's too busy tossing words like grenades.

'That's all he was ever interested in. Money. Profile. That's why he leaked the death. He had to grab that moment. And it wasn't his to grab.'

'You were the last one to see him, Mum,' says Ruby in a high, tight voice.

Nicole spins on her heel to face her daughter.

'What?'

'I saw you. Going to his cottage. What did you do? Have it out with him about his tweet?'

'What, you think I killed him? Over a tweet?' Nicole hoots with laughter.

Davey goes over and tries to put an arm around her, but Nicole bats him away like he's a fly.

'No one killed anyone,' says Davey, his voice breaking.

'Erm, untrue,' says Jet.

'But who would?' moans Davey.

'That's why the police are here,' says Ruby. 'It's pointless us speculating. And it's pointless us still being here. The sooner we all just go home and get away from this disastrous weekend, the better.'

'I've a feeling the police will disagree with you there, sis. In fact, I'd hazard a guess that us all still being here is going to be very much, erm . . . mandatory.'

'Oh, shut up, Jet,' snarls Nicole.

'Where's Tallulah?' says Ruby, suddenly.

'Mum, I saw her going out this morning,' says Imogen. 'She's not back yet. She won't know about Rupert.'

There's a beat of silence.

'Well, isn't it strange that she's not here?' says Nicole.

'She was devastated about Baz,' says Davey. 'Totally gutted.'

'So, what, Rupert killed Baz and Tallulah killed Rupert? That's our theory?' Jet laughs. 'While we're at it, I'm just going to point out that everyone's favourite not-quite son came and went pretty damn fast. Shifty, shifty.'

'Felix,' whispers Imogen.

'This is all stupid,' says Ruby, standing up. 'It was clearly an intruder. Wasn't it? And poor Rupert just got in the way.'

'Has to be that,' says Nicole.

'Adrian saw something in the paper about a string of violent break-ins down this way,' says Ruby. 'One in Padstow. Another place beginning with P . . . Perranporth? Targeting luxury houses.'

But that's not exactly near Porthpella, thinks Saffron.

'Well, there you have it,' says Nicole.

'Clever intruder, getting through the locked gates, with a pack of reporters outside,' offers Jet.

'There's the gate to the cliff path.'

'You need a code for it. Baz was very good at locking people out,' says Jet.

Skinner steams into the room then, looking as smooth and solid as a cruise liner. As he docks by the fireplace, Davey skitters away. Mullins lodges in behind Skinner. Saffron tries to catch Mullins's eye, and eventually he obliges with a wink. But the look on his face is deadly serious. She feels a fresh wave of unease in the pit of her stomach.

'Right. Are we all here?' says Skinner.

'Where do you think we'd be?' snaps Nicole. 'For God's sake.'

Skinner ignores her, and calmly announces, 'Given the circumstances of Rupert Frost's death, we need to interview everyone who was at the house this morning. We'll be conducting those interviews at the station and taking each of you into custody.'

But there's a pulsing at Skinner's jaw that gives him away. Not so calm.

Jet grins and says to no one in particular, 'Told you.'

'I don't see why we can't give you our statements here like we did yesterday when Daddy—' says Ruby from the window.

'*Daddy?* Since when has Baz been *Daddy?*' Nicole cuts in. 'And this is a farce. Rupert clearly got in the way of an intruder. Those break-ins Ruby mentioned. Or just some local miscreant who heard there was a full house this weekend and fancied their chances . . .'

Skinner holds his hand up for quiet.

'Where's Tallulah Pearce?' says Mullins suddenly.

'Off being heartbroken,' says Nicole. 'Nobody's seen her today. Put that in your statement.'

'I told you, I saw her,' cries Imogen. 'There's that little gate at the bottom of the garden that leads to the beach path. I saw her go out of it. The sun wasn't even up.'

Saffron sees Mullins making a note.

'I'm obviously not being clear enough here,' says Skinner. 'Nicole Carson, Jet Carson, Ruby Edwards, Imogen Edwards, Davey Hart and Saffron Weeks . . .'

'Yes, yes, Sergeant?' trills Nicole. 'Say what you want to say! Or are you just taking a register?'

Skinner stares back at Nicole. There's the longest of pauses. Saffron realises she's holding her breath.

'No, I'm not taking a register. I'm arresting every one of you on suspicion of murder.'

Saffron immediately looks to Mullins. *Don't worry*, he mouths, *standard procedure*.

26

Ally sits in the shade of a whiskery palm tree, her notebook lying open in her lap. Her attempts at writing a speech for tonight's show are, so far, a series of crossings-out. Mostly because the thought of standing in front of a room of people – and trying to say the right words – makes her want to disappear in a puff of smoke.

Ally turns over the page and instead writes *Baz Carson: is there anything suspicious?*

Beyond the timing of the memoir, and Tallulah's insistence that it wasn't an accident, Ally's got nothing. She wonders how Jayden is feeling deep down, with this drama unfolding just along the lane from the farm. Is part of him wishing his uniform was still hanging in his wardrobe?

Ally turns back a couple of pages and looks at the list of Rockpool party guests that she gleaned from Tallulah: Baz's ex-wife, his two grown-up children, his granddaughter, his former band-mate, his former manager, plus the music journalist who's staying at Cat and Jayden's. And, of course, Tallulah herself. An intimate gathering; in number, if not – according to Tallulah – in devotion.

The ringing of Ally's phone drifts down the garden. Fox lifts his head from his paws and drops it again. It'll take more than a phone call to disturb his sunshine snooze. Ally sets down her notebook and winds her way up the path, sandals crunching on the pebbles.

At this time of year her tough little Atlantic garden is an ocean of bright mallow and drifts of lavender between the terracotta pots: plants that thrive on salty air. Usually, the snapdragons would be swaying in the onshore gusts, but it's dead calm today, just like it was dead calm yesterday. Beyond the dunes the sea is as still as soup.

Inside the house Ally's phone bleats impatiently, and when she gets to it, she sees Tallulah's name flashing on the screen.

When she left this morning, Ally wasn't sure where Tallulah was going. She'd just said she needed to be 'away from the house'. Ally gave her a map of the coast path, because the woman had talked about how much she loved hiking the canyons back in California, and said the heat didn't bother her. Ally pointed out a looping trail from Porthpella that cut back towards Rockpool House over farm-land. She knows that forward motion – the simple act of putting one foot in front of the other – can help when it feels like nothing else might.

Ally drops into a wicker chair to take the call.

'Tallulah, hello.'

'Ally there's been a second death.'

Ally draws a quick breath. Her phone immediately starts beeping with another call, and she holds it away from her to look at the screen. *Jayden.* Coincidence, or has he heard too?

'I got back to Rockpool and it was deserted,' says Tallulah, her words tumbling over one another. 'Deserted of house guests, that is. The press were all outside. And police and CSIs. They've all been arrested, Ally. Everyone who was there.'

'Everyone's been arrested?'

'I thought it was for Baz, but it's not. It's a second death. Rupert Frost, Baz's manager. He was found dead in his bedroom in the middle of the morning. It's horrific. If I'd been there, I'd no doubt be under arrest too, because they sure as hell wanted to ascertain my whereabouts this morning. But I had video evidence.

I recorded sections of my walk on my iPhone. Time stamped. As another murder was being committed at Rockpool I was watching seals at some cove around the coast. Sharing binoculars with a family from Munich – and doing a very good impression of being just like any other rambler, not someone whose world has fallen apart.'

Tallulah's words skip over one another, and her voice is high, unsteady.

'Ally, it goes to show, doesn't it? That what happened to Baz wasn't an accident, or natural causes, or anything like that. Don't you think? It's obvious. My God. It's just *horrific*, what's happening here.'

Ally can feel her heart thumping. The phone buzzes in her hand with an incoming text message.

Another death? It changes everything, surely.

'Ally? Are you still there? I've been reading up on you – you and your partner. Jayden Weston. The things you've done. Please, will you take the case? Money's not a problem.'

'The police will be doing everything they can, Tallulah.'

'And what if it's not enough? I can't have that, Ally. Baz can't have that.'

'I'm so sorry. Really, I am. But a situation like this, we can't get involved.'

'JP Sharpe at Christmas? Lewis Pascoe. You've investigated murders. I've read about it.'

'We don't investigate them directly, as such . . .'

'What did those other people have that I don't? Was it money? Because I told you, that's not a problem. I'll pay you whatever you ask.'

'It's not money.'

'Or is that the point? You don't want to help me because I'm rich? That kid Lewis Pascoe had nothing. I read all about it. You only help the waifs and strays?'

And Ally tells her that it's not that either. Although she knows if she's prejudiced at all, it's inverted. You can't live in Cornwall and not witness the imbalance: the second-homers swanning in and out, while others struggle to keep a roof over their heads or find one at all. But pain is a leveller, and Ally knows that, when it comes to their cases, they go with their hearts. She isn't saying no to Tallulah because she's wealthy.

'I know you understand,' says Tallulah, 'that's why I'm asking. I don't doubt that the police will do what they do, but it's just another case for them – even with the media pressure. There's no . . . compassion. The questions I faced just now . . . they knew what Baz meant to me. They've got that on paper. But they were cold, Ally. Cold and searching.'

'With a murder,' says Ally, 'there's questions they need to ask . . .'

'You and I though, we connect. Don't we? I felt it at the Bluebird, and I felt it this morning. The sea-glass heart, Ally. I walked away feeling like you were somebody who'd be important to me. And through it all, you're a detective? That kind of serendipity must mean something.'

Ally hesitates before she replies. She can see Tallulah's point, she really can.

'Let's wait and see where the police get to,' she says, knowing she's passing the buck. But isn't it the sensible response? Jayden will surely think so. 'And let me talk to my partner.'

∽

Five minutes later, Ally is back on the bench beneath the palm. She stares down at the pages of her notebook. For all Tallulah's entreaties, she was right to stall her. Two deaths in two days and Rockpool

House is the centre of attention. And there's nothing to suggest that the police aren't doing everything right.

She checks her phone again, willing Jayden to call her back. He messaged her before:

There's something going on at Rockpool. FIVE Police cars just went down the lane. I'm heading up there to see what's what.

She tried calling back but there was no response, so she left him a message, filling him in on her conversations with Tallulah Pearce.

What more is there to do?

Ally picks up her pen. Around her, the garden stirs with insects. Beyond, the sound of the sea is as gentle as a lullaby as it laps at the sand. She turns to a clean page and refocuses.

Rupert Frost has been murdered, she writes. *How does it connect to Baz?*

Just then a butterfly, as blue as the sea-glass heart she gave to Tallulah, lands on her notebook. The insect gently fans its wings, resting for three, four seconds, before spiralling skywards. Ally watches as it disappears over the dunes, her heart climbing. Then she picks up her phone and tries calling Jayden again.

27

Jayden's leaning against a gate on the lane up to Rockpool, waiting for a phone signal to drop back in. The field in front of him is sun-blasted, the earth hard and cracked. He feels thirsty just looking at it, and pulls his water bottle from his bag; a short walk, and the contents are already tepid.

The page on Cornwall Live is half loaded, then suddenly the screen fills. Jayden reads it avidly.

> Police attended an address in Porthpella on Saturday at around midday and the body of a man was located inside. A 68-year-old man was confirmed deceased at the scene and the death is currently being treated as unexplained. Six people have been arrested on suspicion of murder.

Six people?

Put like that, it sounds dramatic, but Jayden knows that sometimes arresting everyone present is sensible and cautionary. Especially if it's a closed space, like a luxury pile on a clifftop, full of weekend guests. In the mystery novels that his mum-in-law likes to read, there's always something to stop the police attending – a snowstorm, a bridge out, a tree across the road – but in real life, if the police turn up and gather the suspects in the dining room, they're not going to just say 'Don't leave town' and hope for the best. They're going to slap cuffs on them and hold them for twenty-four hours, while they gather evidence.

He wonders what DI Radford is making of all this action – if he's even tuned into it yet. In Jayden's experience, cops fall into two camps: they either switch on and switch off, lines between work life and home life drawn hard and fast, or they're always on duty, even when they hang up their boots – or swap them for flip-flops.

Jayden hasn't seen DI Radford again since he arrived, but every so often he wonders about what he meant by mentioning Plymouth.

His phone buzzes: Ally.

'You got my message?' he says. 'There's been a second death.'

'I know, I heard from Tallulah. She rang me straight away. I was on the phone with her when you tried to call.'

Ally, close to Tallulah? The first thing Jayden thinks is that it could be useful. The second is that it's unusual for Ally to be on the front foot when it comes to socialising.

'But they arrested everyone. How was she calling you?'

'Tallulah was out of the house all morning. After she saw me, she went for a walk. Jayden, she was devastated about Baz and sure there was more to it. And now this.'

'This piece I'm reading says the victim is a sixty-eight-year-old man. Could be Rupert or Davey.'

'It's Rupert Frost. Baz's manager.'

Jayden gives a low whistle. 'Good intel, Al.'

'But to be honest she was more concerned with how it connects back to Baz.'

'And she thinks it does?' says Jayden.

'For what it's worth, she's certain.'

Jayden can hear a car speeding up the lane, followed by another. The tang of exhaust mixes with the sweet hedgerow scents. This tiny corner of the world is getting busy. It was newsworthy when it was Baz Carson who was found dead, but a second death more than doubles the attention.

'The media aren't saying it's at Rockpool House. Yet. But it's going to break. Any minute, probably.' Jayden counts on his fingers. 'Six arrests. Okay, so . . . the son, Jet. The daughter, Ruby. The ex, Nicole. Davey the bandmate.' Ruby's daughter, Imogen, was there too – Baz's granddaughter. Would she be among the arrests? Possibly. If they're crossing all the Ts and dotting all the Is.

Felix. He was headed to Rockpool this morning.

'What about Saffron?' says Ally.

'Jeez. Yes. Saffron. But they'll release her just as soon as they've established that she has absolutely nothing to do with it. Right now, I'm thinking about our campsite guest. Felix. He was on his way up to the house this morning.'

'Could he have been arrested too?'

'That'd make seven. Unless they're not counting the child. Al, I'm heading up there.'

Ally tells him, then, about Tallulah's request – appeal, by the sound of it – to hire the Shell House Detectives.

'We can't get involved in this, Al.'

'You say that every time. And then we do anyway.'

Jayden gives a low laugh. 'Fair cop.'

'Anyway, you heading up there – what's that if not getting involved?'

'Neighbourly interest vibes. This is my patch, Al. If Cliff lobbed one of his cauliflowers it'd land in that infinity pool. If he put his back into it, anyway. Plus, Felix – our guest – he's a nice guy. I feel for him.'

'He's in the book, isn't he? Connie's son.'

'So you're reading it too, huh?'

'I borrowed Gus's copy. Jayden, I really like Tallulah. I . . . I feel for her too. Losing someone so suddenly . . .'

And she doesn't need to say anything more than that.

'Technically they're both suspects, these new mates of ours,' he says.

'Which makes them even more interesting company.'

Jayden laughs. He loves how Ally surprises him.

'Look, you're right to keep things open with Tallulah. Let's see how today unfolds. I don't think we can let someone hire us if we can't get near the case. We don't know enough, Al. Reading a book, poking about online, that's good background, but if we can't talk to any of the suspects because they're all banged up . . .'

'I know,' says Ally. 'We're on the outside looking in.'

'Big time.' And he knows he sounds rueful as he says it. He switches focus. 'What about tonight? How are things shaping up for the show?'

'I'm dreading it. Which sounds so ungrateful, but . . .'

'You'll love it once you're there. You deserve this, Al. That work's gonna fly.'

'Do you think I need to do a speech? Sunita said I should.'

'Nah. Let the pictures do the talking.'

'Oh, thank goodness for that.'

Ally Bright. She'll go toe to toe in an interview room with a murderer, she'll clamber over rain-lashed cliffs in the pitch-black, but the thought of a bit of public speaking is enough to send her running. *You don't have to be good at everything, Jayden,* his mum used to say when he was a kid. *You just have to find the thing you love.* Then his dad would counter, *But Jayden is good at everything, so how's he supposed to choose?* His parents were both teachers and neither of them imagined him joining up with the police. When he did, he could tell by their faces that they were a little afraid; that they thought there were easier lives there for the taking. But they did what they always did: fully supported him. And when he quit, they supported him in that too.

Even though they're hundreds of miles away up north, his mum and dad are still an anchor point. The way Felix talked about his mum moved Jayden: the intensity of their relationship, single mum and beloved only child. But his detective brain is ticking. How can it not? For all of Felix's laid-back vibe, the guests at Rockpool have beef with him – does that feeling run both ways?

'Al, I'd best go. Jazz is with Sue and I'm supposed to grab her for the afternoon.'

'And you need to get up to Rockpool.'

'Yeah, that too.' He grins. But then the smile fades. Two deaths. Behind the luxurious façade, something very dark has happened in that house.

Jayden knows he probably won't get anywhere; those gates are tall and locked fast. And he doubts Mullins will be there still. The station will be a hive of activity, the media pressure intensifying everything. Back in Yorkshire, Jayden always liked the buzz when something big was going down.

'Tell me, won't you,' Ally says, 'if you learn anything. Because, you know, now that I'm giving up on my speech, I'm rather twiddling my thumbs.'

'Radio contact. Always.' He hesitates, then says, 'And with Tallulah, keep her on ice. All may not be as it seems.'

～

Jayden can hear the thrum of conversation before he rounds the corner and sees the Rockpool gates. In his shorts and t-shirt, without a camera or laptop bag, he doubts he passes for a newshound. Nosy neighbour, probably. Or lost tourist.

The gates are as impenetrable as a prison entranceway. They've always looked imposing, which strikes him as unnecessary because if you carry on down the coast road you get a clear shot of Rockpool House in all its glory. But okay, if it's about access, then the place is well off limits: look, but don't touch.

'What's the latest?' he asks, joining a man on the fringes. The journalist is bent over a tablet, thumbs tapping.

Just then Jayden's phone rings: Cat.

After all the police vehicles buzzing down the lane, Jayden told her he was going up to Rockpool to see what was what. *For the good of the campers*, he said, to which she wrinkled her nose but nodded anyway.

'What's going on, Jay? People here keep asking me as if I've got info.'

'I've just got here. I think it's the manager, Ally said.'

'Ally said?' Then, 'Jay, the guy in plot thirty-seven, do you know if he's left?'

'No. He's just gone out.'

Jayden turns away from the clustered reporters and strolls back down the lane.

'Are you sure? Because the van's gone, and there's nothing left behind. And apparently he told Eileen he was leaving today.'

Did Felix say he was leaving? Not to Jayden. Though it makes sense; there's nothing for him to stay for now. Except the police investigation.

But he'd have said goodbye, wouldn't he?

'Jay, the reason I'm asking is someone just called about a last-minute booking. I said we were full but then I thought, what about plot thirty-seven?' Cat pauses. 'Plus, he's connected to Rockpool, isn't he? Don't you think it's weird that he's just . . . disappeared?'

28

Felix thought it might help, coming to the place his mum loved; a place of calm and stillness and creativity – and, okay, a bunch of cultural tourists milling about in sun hats and chinos. But now he wonders if it's only making it worse. He hums to himself, a nervous habit he thought he'd lost as a teen. He rubs his mouth with his hand as if to forcibly stop himself. Regret swirls in his gut.

Felix left Rockpool in a rush earlier and drove straight to St Ives – like a wasp to sugar water, judging by the traffic. But he had to get away from them all; every single one of them. He didn't even say goodbye – only to Jayden's mate, the chef. But the fumes of all their resentment came with him in the van, and it took having the windows open, his hair blowing all over his face as he drove too fast, to blast it out.

Crazy that now, nearly twenty years since Baz left, Nicole, Ruby and Jet's hatred of Felix burns as strongly as ever. It's so misplaced he should probably feel sorry for them, but that would require a level of maturity and philosophy that he knows he doesn't possess. Not without his mum by his side, smoothing the creases. *You have to see it from their perspective, Felix. They're just hurting.*

Felix draws a breath and exhales, not quite steadily. He picks up a mug, looks at the price, and puts it down again. *Breakages Must Be Paid For*, a sign in the shop says. *Ain't that the truth*, he thinks.

The Leach Pottery. That's why he's here in this choked-up tourist town on a midsummer's day. Running from a scene that, if he's honest, scared him with its intensity. At Rockpool he felt something quicken in his chest that didn't stack up with the story he's been telling himself for the last five years: that he's okay, that he has perspective, that he's moved beyond grief and anger and sadness to a place of acceptance.

So Felix has gone to ground among the smooth lines and muted palette of mid-century pottery.

Like that's going to help.

Bernard Leach was his mum's hero. They came here several times when he was small; a skinny-legged boy hanging on his mum's arm, pretending to admire what basically looked like pretty boring brown pots to him. But he worshipped her, would have gone to the ends of the earth to look at the most tedious examples of claywork if it made Connie happy. And Cornwall did feel a bit like the ends of the earth, that first time. Taking the sleeper train from Paddington, blinking in early morning light in St Erth. Then the little shuttle train that ran on to St Ives, clinging to the cliffside, high above the startling blue ocean. Suddenly, the town itself appearing, all laid out like a painter's dream. *It's not real*, he said the first time he saw it, just as a rainbow was pouring into the sky. *You'd better believe it*, said Connie, her whole body seeming to vibrate with the pleasure of being here.

Now though, it's a bassline of unease that throbs beneath everything. Felix thought this timeless space would calm him and connect him, but it isn't working. Not even close. He looks through the window to a palm tree, its spiked fronds exotic against the blue sky. He wishes he was a long, long way away. Somewhere loud and intoxicating and easy to get lost in. Rio or Bangkok. Anywhere, really.

It was a mistake to have come. Not just here, but to Cornwall. To Rockpool House the first time, and definitely the second. He'd thought he owed it to Baz. He'd thought he owed it to his mum. But the past was lying in wait for him at Rockpool this morning.

It isn't about the book; he reassured Baz on that note the day before yesterday, when they saw each other. Everyone is the hero of their own life, and Baz was no exception – he just shouted louder about it. He isn't going to hold that against him.

No, the hard part is his mum – Baz's death making Felix think of hers all over again, and just the way that things could have turned out differently. The kinds of snap decisions and split-second choices that change the course of life completely. Can Felix track that remorse all the way back to the day his mum brought Baz home with her? *He's going to stay with us a little while.* Connie in Florence Nightingale mode, as if their little redbrick house with the rambling garden studio was the next best thing to the Priory. Whatever Baz loved about Connie – which was pretty much everything – Felix has never really understood what she saw in him in return. Not when she didn't want his love or his money. Friendship, and the pleasure of knowing she was helping Baz: was that really it?

Felix doesn't blame Baz for her death. He doesn't blame anyone. It was an accident. But it is fair to say that if Connie had never met Baz, she wouldn't have been in that place at that time. Or perhaps she would? Crossing town in the dead of night for some other reason? Who knows how the Fates and the Furies work?

What he does know is that grief never really goes anywhere. You just get more used to its presence. Until something happens to make it flare. And rage.

He feels someone staring at him. An arty-looking older lady in a denim dress with green-rimmed glasses. She looks like one of his mum's friends.

'You're bleeding,' the woman says. Whether it's concern or judgement in her voice he can't tell, but as she hands him a tissue he'll go with the former.

He dabs it to his face, and it comes away red.

'Nosebleed,' he says apologetically. 'Had them since I was a kid.'

He looks down at his t-shirt and sees that's stained too.

Felix suddenly feels dizzy. He doesn't want to lose it in here, a flailing arm taking out hundreds of pounds of wares. So, he staggers towards the open door. As he goes, blood splashes on his trainers, and on the slate floor too.

29

Mullins hands Saffron a cup of tea in a polystyrene cup.

'I thought you wouldn't want to risk the coffee,' he says.

'You're right. Bad tea is always better than bad coffee,' says Saffron. 'Thanks.'

It's weird seeing her in regulation grey joggers. But like everyone else, Saffron had to hand in her clothes.

'You know it's all just procedure, right?' he says, glancing towards the door. 'You'll be out of here in no time, Saff.'

'I get it. And hey, I'm all for new experiences.'

But her cheeks are pale, and she looks tired about the eyes. Does she know something? She could know something. Maybe chefs are like bartenders: people spill their problems to them. And as far as Mullins sees it, there are a lot of problems among the Rockpool lot.

'Do you really think one of the guests killed Rupert? I know you can't answer that, by the way. But everyone was there. Everyone was shocked, horrified. You can't fake that, can you?'

'I'm afraid you can, Saffron,' he says, gravely.

'Does this change things with Baz too?'

But then one of the Major Crimes lot comes in – DS Chang, who he knows from previous cases – and that's the end of the chit-chat.

'A word, Officer Mullins.'

Has Chang been listening in? The tips of Mullins's ears go red at the thought. It's not like he's been unprofessional. He's been making the detainee feel relaxed, that's all.

He follows the detective out into the corridor, ready for a ticking-off. It's a long corridor, this custody suite, and it smells different to their nick. As if all the drama and stress and, as Saffron 'Hippy-Dippy' Weeks would say, bad vibes have leached into the walls or something.

'Constable Mullins, I'd like you to sit in on the interviews.'

'What, me?'

'It'll be good experience. And the continuity of your presence might encourage trust. You were there yesterday, after Baz Carson was found.'

Mullins scratches his head. 'What about DS Skinner?'

'We're dividing and conquering. I'd like you to join me. We'll start with Nicole Carson. It appears she was the last known person to see Rupert Frost alive.'

And that's DS Chang's professional way of saying that after Skinner announced the arrests, and an initial beat of shocked silence passed, accusations were fired across the room like arrows, and Nicole took the most hits.

'I'd love that, boss,' says Mullins.

Then his ears go red all over again.

He only wishes that Saffron – behind that heavy door – could hear that he, Mullins, has been requisitioned by Major Crimes.

'Hang on, full disclosure, Saffron is a mate,' he says.

'And that's why Skinner will be interviewing her.'

~

'It's completely over the top,' says Nicole, glowering at them across the table. 'What is it, the local force wanting to flex their muscles and show us who's boss down here?'

'Two men have died,' says DS Chang calmly, 'in suspicious circumstances.'

'One man has died in suspicious circumstances. Which I swear blind will be an intruder, who's probably out of the country by now, while you're wasting time with us. Rupert didn't deserve it. Didn't deserve it one bit. As for Baz . . . we'll never know . . .'

'The results of the post-mortem are due today. We'll absolutely know then, Mrs Carson.'

Mullins is watching Nicole carefully. Her lipstick looks freshly applied, though her make-up is patchy around her eyes; her mascara streaked. Sweat or tears? It's hot in this interview room, just like it's hot everywhere. He notes a bead of perspiration on her forehead and watches it to see if it'll run; it's as if he's a kid again, stuck inside on a wet day, watching raindrops chase each other down the window.

'Let's start at the beginning,' says DS Chang. 'How did you know Rupert Frost?'

There's a pulsing at Nicole's jaw. She's completely ignoring the weaselly presence of the duty solicitor sitting beside her. And that's a sign, isn't it, that she's not taking this seriously? If she was, she'd have called a lawyer of her own – some bigwig from London.

'I've known him forever,' she says, eventually. 'He's always been lurking in the shadows. He managed the band and was there to cash in when they made it big. After they broke up, he went on to other things. Kept his eye in with Baz, still advised him, brokered the Netflix deal a few years ago. But I'd call him small-time.'

'What was your relationship like with him? Were you friends?'

'We went back a long way.'

'Which isn't the same thing.'

'No,' says Nicole. 'I suppose it isn't.'

'You went to see him this morning in his room.' The detective looks down at her notes, but it seems more for show. 'Around ten o'clock.'

'I did.'

And Mullins notes that the drop of perspiration is on the move now, trickling down Nicole's temple.

'Why were you going to speak to him?'

'I had a bone to pick. He leaked Baz's death.'

'Leaked it?'

'He was my husband . . .'

Ex-husband.

'It wasn't his place to say it. It was up to me.'

'Is that what you agreed with the group?' asks DS Chang.

'Yes, Officer,' says Nicole, sarcastically. 'No one drew up minutes, but it was agreed. Not only was I married to Baz for the best part of two decades, but I've a strong social media following. It made sense.'

Mullins has looked at Nicole's social media. Just shy of 10,000 followers. She's a Wellness Entrepreneur, whatever that is. And she put out a tweet this morning that said: The love of my life and the father of my children, Baz Carson, has passed away at the age of seventy. Anguish is not the word. The family asks for privacy at this difficult time.

Mullins found himself wondering that if *anguish* wasn't the word, then . . . what was?

The picture Nicole posted with the tweet was from her and Baz's wedding day: a puffy white princess dress, only it was hacked short and skimmed her thighs. Baz in a leather suit. She was holding up a bouquet of black roses – dyed, surely? – and the blooms obscured at least a third of Baz's face.

'It was disrespectful,' says Nicole. 'Disrespectful to me, at the worst possible time. And that's what I said to Rupert. He knew he'd effed up. But he was sick – hungover, rattling on about the old days. It doesn't surprise me that he couldn't fend off an intruder in that state.'

'So, you kicked him when he was down?'

'Rupert was overreacting, putting himself in the centre of the story. He's just a suit. And he made a mint off Baz's creativity. He's not the star here.'

Mullins glances at DS Chang and she raises her eyebrow in reply. Nicole's head is bent, examining her painted nails. They're the same red as the plonk they serve down The Wreckers. The phrase *blood on her hands* jumps into his head.

'How long were you with Rupert for?'

'Not even five minutes.'

'And what did you do after you left?'

Nicole hesitates. Those nails of hers really are keeping her attention. 'I went for a walk.'

'Where did you walk?'

'I don't know, just in the grounds. I needed to let off steam.'

'You didn't see anyone else in the gardens?'

'No. Everyone was keeping out of my way, probably. They do that, when I'm worked up.'

'So, you were angry?'

'No. I was furious.'

'So after you spent some time in the gardens you went back inside the house.'

'Up to my room, yes.'

'What time would that have been?'

'I really don't know. Ten, fifteen minutes later. Maybe more?'

'And, again, you didn't see anyone?'

'It's a big house, in case you haven't noticed. And like I said, people were keeping out of my way.'

'So, the next time you saw anyone, or anyone saw you, was when you were alerted to Rupert's death?'

'Davey. Wailing like a banshee,' says Nicole, her lip curled with distaste.

'So, what you're saying is that there's nobody who can corroborate your story?' says DS Chang.

And Nicole's head snaps up. As if it's only then that the penny drops.

30

'So, you think it was around 11.45 that Davey came running into the kitchen?'

Skinner's made a temple out of his hands. He smiles but it gets nowhere near his eyes.

Saffron nods. 'About that. I remember looking at the time after Felix left, and thinking I'd best get a move on with lunch.'

They'd be held for up to twenty-four hours, Mullins said, which could mean a night in the cell. She shivers. And despite the heat of the day, the sun burning through the small window high up in this room, beneath the thin polyester sweatshirt her arms prickle with goosebumps.

Saffron has already run through the minutiae of her morning, and who among the Rockpool crew she did or didn't see, the tape whirring all the while. It's a strange experience. She's being completely matter-of-fact, but in this setting, everything she says sounds loaded: her impressions sound like verdicts; her interpretations accusations.

'Tell me more about your conversation with Felix Boyd.'

'It was really short. He just wanted to introduce himself, because he's staying at Cat and Jayden's.'

'Was there a reason for that, do you think? I mean, Cat and Jayden aren't friends of his, he's just parking his van there. Why would he want to meet you?'

'I think he was just being friendly. And Jayden knew I was kind of out on a limb at Rockpool.'

'Where was everybody else, when you were talking with Felix?'

Saffron tries to pull herself back. People had been on the terrace when Felix first got there, but she can't remember anyone else being around when he came to the kitchen to speak to her.

'I think most people were in their rooms,' she says. 'I don't honestly know. I'd been chatting to Imogen, then I was focused on making up for lost time. When Felix came in, I remember it being quiet. I could hear the ticking of the clock. That sticks in my head for some reason.'

'And did you note the time?'

'It was around eleven o'clock. Maybe five past.'

'Around eleven o'clock, maybe five past. And how did Felix seem?'

'Nice,' says Saffron. 'Quite chilled.'

She thinks on this. Was he chilled? There was a slight edginess to him. A fraught energy. But Baz had just died, so wasn't that totally normal?

Skinner nods. He takes a long time writing something down; longer than those three words, for sure.

'So, Davey runs in to the kitchen at around 11.45. What were his exact words?'

'He said, "Help us. You have to help us." I think that was it.'

'He didn't say who was in peril?'

'No. Davey ran down the garden to the cottage and I followed. He was fast; I remember thinking he could move pretty fast for an old guy. But he was panting when we got there. And crying. I think he already knew Rupert was dead.'

'Why do you say that?'

'Just because it looked so obvious. I don't mean . . .' Saffron shakes her head. 'I'm not saying he actually knew. But anyone would think it, seeing Rupert lying there like that.'

And she feels flustered suddenly. She thinks of the recording: *I think he already knew Rupert was dead.* Someone looking at it later in a transcript. Underlining it. But then . . . what if Davey knew that Rupert was dead because he was the one to kill him?

Davey is as likely as any of the others, isn't he? Because the police think someone at Rockpool House killed Rupert Frost.

'But surely it's possible that someone got in from outside?' she says, suddenly.

Skinner eyes her levelly. 'What makes you say that?'

'Just . . . Ruby mentioned there'd been a spate of burglaries. Violent ones, targeting luxury homes.'

'Not on our patch.'

'And . . . well . . .'

But she doesn't say it, because she knows how naive it sounds: *I can't imagine any one of these people being a murderer.*

'We're investigating all avenues,' says Skinner. 'But stabbing someone is a violent, purposeful act.'

Suddenly Saffron feels a wave of nausea. She looks at the un-drunk tea that Mullins brought her. There's a film on its surface from greasy milk, and she holds her hand to her mouth.

'You alright?' says Skinner.

She nods. She's aware of the detective watching her; his appraising stare.

'You're not a trained chef, are you?'

'I run my own beach café.' She tips her chin and meets Skinner's eye. No one disses Hang Ten.

'A strange choice for catering a high-falutin' party,' he says. 'Did you know Baz Carson?'

'No. He asked around locally and I was recommended to him.'

'And you claim never to have met any of the members of the party until this weekend?'

'I don't claim it. It's true.'

'Last night. Rupert Frost was drunk, wasn't he?'

'They all were. Except for Imogen, obviously. And Tallulah.'

'He came into the kitchen to thank you for the dinner, didn't he?'

Saffron creases her forehead. How does Skinner know that?

'Is it correct that you asked him to leave?' he says.

'Yes. I was busy clearing up. Plus . . . he was being a creep.'

'A creep?'

'He was inappropriate. Nothing I couldn't handle though.'

'Nothing you couldn't handle.'

It's one thing to put up with Rupert being lecherous, but another to have it used against her. Saffron sucks in a breath and speaks levelly.

'Rupert came into the kitchen and said, "What's a pretty little thing like you doing hiding away in here?" And he reached out for me, going for my bum, probably. But he was drunk, off his face, and he missed. I told him to leave, or I'd report him for inappropriate behaviour. Davey must have seen because he came into the kitchen and led him away. Davey apologised for him. Said it was the shock and Rupert was a decent guy really. I wasn't really listening, to be honest. I was just glad Davey took him away.'

'You said that you could handle it, yet you were glad of Davey's intervention,' Skinner says. 'So, which was it?'

'Can't it be both?'

Just then there's a knock at the door. A plain-clothes officer says, 'A word?'

As Skinner turns, Saffron's eyes instinctively go to the small window set high in the wall: that slender rectangle of blue. There's a whole day happening out there; people walking about in it, not realising how lucky they are.

Then she thinks of the weight of Baz's body as she pulled him from the water.

The cold feel of Rupert's skin as she pressed her two fingers to his pulse point.

And the ice-cold thought that someone at Rockpool House is a killer.

The sky can wait. Instead of looking up, Saffron looks inward. Maybe she's missed something. Maybe there's a tiny, seemingly insignificant detail that might solve everything. Everything, that is, apart from the fact that two men are dead.

31

Hang Ten is full of sunshine. It streams through the windows, and without an accompanying breeze the wooden beach hut is like a tinderbox. Gus thinks how good it looks, though. Saffron gave the interior a fresh lick of paint for the new season, and the coral-pink walls and powder-blue counter beam with colour. Her wild and wonderful collection of plants is thriving; well suited to jungle temperatures, clearly. Sun bounces off the rainbow-bright skate decks on the walls; the collection that Mona – on her only visit to Hang Ten – enjoyed being so disdainful of. But Mona's mocking was water off a duck's back by then. In fact, Gus rather delighted in her displeasure. Despite never having stepped on a surfboard or a skateboard or any kind of board, he's always felt very much at home in Hang Ten. And that's the Saffron effect.

Gus mops his brow. 'Flat white, please,' he says.

Normally he wouldn't even have to say *the usual*, because Saffron would already know. But Saffron isn't at Hang Ten. She's up at Rockpool House, catering what should have been the dream gig. But it's the nightmare gig, as it turns out. So, it's her pal Jodie that Gus appeals to for coffee, and it's Jodie who says, 'Anything to go with that, Gus?'

Gus's eyes move to the tempting array of brownies, cakes and cookies on the counter. He's got a nice linen suit lined up for this evening. Overdoing it? Probably. But he's going all-out 'arty-farty', as another resident of the dunes once referred to him as – though Gus doesn't like to think about Roland Hunter too much; with some sort of ingrained muscle memory his cheek starts to tingle where he got socked. Back to the suit. It's a little tighter on the waistband than he'd like it to be, and that's all wrong. Linen is supposed to look relaxed and effortless, not straining.

'Maybe one of those smaller cookies,' he says. 'The ones with the nuts.'

'Those are toffee,' says Jodie. 'Is that cool?'

'The lemon drizzle, then?'

Jodie cuts a wedge two inches thick.

'Have you heard from Saffron?' he asks.

'*Nada.* They only let her have one call though. And obviously that was to Broady.'

'They're running a tight ship up there, aren't they?' And he wonders who's in charge, in the absence of Baz. His money is on Nicole. The way she's painted in the book, Gus can't help seeing a little of Mona in Baz's ex-wife. Or maybe he's just looking for connections. The pints they could have had at The Wreckers, lamenting the years spent with the wrong people. Would Tallulah have got her happy ending this weekend with Baz? He wrote about her with fondness, but not a great deal more than that. It was as if he'd consigned Tallulah to her place in his history: the Californian interlude, the end of which set him on his true path. It was clear to Gus that Connie was the only woman for Baz. He wonders if Tallulah realised that, reading it too.

'Well, they have to, right? Though arresting everyone is crazy. It's well heavy-handed. Still, Saff'll have a good story.'

Gus blinks as she passes him his coffee. He takes a sip. 'Arresting everyone? Who's been arrested?'

'Erm, everyone. Including Saffron.'

The coffee goes the wrong way and Gus finds himself in a coughing fit. Jodie eyes him with alarm, as if he's about to expire. He waves his hand to communicate that he's fine, but realises it makes him look more like a man drowning than a man collecting himself.

'Alright there, mate?'

And it's Broady. The picture of youth and health, with his sun-bleached locks and tanned face and muscled shoulders. Baz has never felt more decrepit.

'Coffee . . . wrong way . . .' he croaks.

Broady claps him hard on the back. Unnecessarily, thinks Gus. It's not like it's a coffee bean that's lodged in his windpipe; so much for surf-school first aid. But whether it's the shock or what, Gus is surprised to find he's righted.

'It's not true, is it? That Saffron's been arrested for Baz's death?'

'For the second guy,' says Broady. 'Who – by the way, Jodes – is someone called Rupert Frost. They've just released it. Small-time music mogul. Another old guy.' He glances at Gus. 'No offence.'

Gus's eyes widen. A second death is news to him. But since seeing Ally this morning he's been working at his novel, the outside world all closed out. He'd felt a burst of something akin to inspiration as he walked back over the dunes. *Why not bang out a few words while the going's good?*

Tonight, he's going to buy a picture. A small one. Not the smallest, but perhaps the second smallest. Although, of course, the Bluebird isn't a large space, and Gus isn't sure how many pieces are in the show – what if the second smallest turns out to be, in fact, quite large? Gus has always been careful with his money. The extended lease on All Swell is the only financially reckless thing he's ever done, and even then it was the result of some careful spread-sheeting. And now there is a new column on that spreadsheet. *Art.*

But as gestures go, it's a pretty good one, he thinks.

Gus brings himself back to the present moment. *A second death?* Broady fills him in. Jodie serves the next customer. And the next. On this baking summer afternoon, the beach is busy, and a steady stream is making its way inside Hang Ten. Bare toes and bikini tops. Seawater dripping on the wooden boards. Gus tries to concentrate on what Broady is saying.

'The party's got to be over up there,' says Broady. 'She'll be back working here tomorrow. Crazy times.'

'Rupert Frost,' says Gus again, slowly shaking his head. He can hardly believe it. 'And it's really murder?'

'Oh yeah.' Broady holds up his phone. 'Read all about it.'

'But what does that mean for Baz?'

Just then Gus is aware of a presence at his shoulder. He steps to the side, thinking the queue needs more room. But the man doesn't budge.

'Did you say Rupert Frost is dead?'

Maybe there are more fans of The Nick around than Gus realises. This guy looks to be in his thirties. A muso type, if ever there was one. Long hair. The sort of complexion that looks like it's more suited to cavern bars than outside spaces.

'Apparently so,' says Gus, with a small shake of the head. 'It's terrible, I don't—'

The man's feeling in the pockets of his jeans. 'Crap. My phone's in the van. When? When did this happen?'

'This morning,' says Broady. 'Felix, isn't it? I took you out yesterday.'

'What? Oh yeah. Yeah.' And the man looks hunted; haunted. 'Yeah. You did. In fact . . . that's why I was coming by. Grabbing a coffee then . . . booking a lesson. Another lesson. It clears the head, y'know? But . . .'

This man, Felix, looks from Gus to Broady. He runs his hand through his hair.

'He died this morning?'

'Stabbed in his bedroom,' says Broady. 'Brutal.'

'Americano, no milk?' says Jodie.

'I think your coffee . . .' begins Gus.

But the man's gone, bumping through the queue; a little kiddie's bucket and spade clatters in his wake. A dad, with a sharp Home Counties accent, protests.

Gus raises his eyebrows at Broady.

'Guess he doesn't want that second lesson after all,' says Broady with a shrug.

Suddenly Gus feels weak in the legs. 'Baz. Now Rupert Frost. They're dropping like flies,' he says. And maybe he even totters a little, because next thing he knows, Broady's guiding him to a chair. As if Gus is the old man he suddenly feels like.

32

Ally sits at the big table in The Shell House. She has the shutters partially closed to keep out the heat of the afternoon, and sunlight falls in stripes across the caramel surface of the table and over the pages of Baz's book.

Ally is focused on a photograph of Rupert Frost signing the first contract with The Nick. It would be a strange picture for Baz to include in his memoir – a moment of administration; meaningful at the time, but surely more so for the manager – except for the fact that the caption says: *Always the clown*. So, really, it's about Davey Hart, not Rupert Frost. Davey, dressed in a black vest and pirate-like bandana, his arms as skinny and knotted as rope, has his fingers held up behind Rupert's head. It's the bunny-ears sign that Evie and her friends used to do to one another when they were little. And it's the only photo of Rupert in the whole book. Not the most flattering inclusion, a moment of mild ridicule. But then, from what Ally has gleaned so far, flattery is not Baz's style.

Ally jumps to Google, interested in what the gesture means. Apparently, it can be interpreted as a signifier of infidelity: the cuckold's horns. Was Davey cheating with Rupert's partner at the time? Or was it just a childish prank?

And is she reading far too much into it? Probably.

She's gone through all the main news bulletins about both Baz's death and what is now confirmed as Rupert's murder. Away from the more speculative write-ups, that's how the two incidents are being formally described – *Baz's death* and *Rupert's murder* – and Ally wonders how Tallulah feels about that. Ally hasn't heard any more from her since the phone call earlier, but she has a feeling she will.

She turns back to the book, and flicks to chapter three. The first to mention Rupert.

> *Rupert Frost heard we were doing something differ-*
> *ent, so he came to see us at The Elevens. Greasy little*
> *guy, as wide as he was tall, but he knew music and*
> *he knew the business of music.*

The only description of Rupert in the book and that's it. No surprise that this memoir of Baz's has ruffled feathers. Ally tries to imagine what it must be like to be someone who says and does exactly what they want, without a care for others. Is there ever a reckoning? The memoir is full of casual cruelty to the people closest to Baz – so casual, you'd almost miss it. Like a magician, he deflects with occasional compliments, while putting the knife in time and time again.

Unfortunate phrase.

Ally goes back to her notebook, where she's written pages on Rupert, all stories gleaned from Baz's memoir. There are three, perhaps four, revelations, and if they weren't widely known among Baz's crowd, then there's a chance that Rupert might have had to face the music this weekend. She calls Jayden again. As it rings, she holds the phone away from her ear; she can hear it outside.

Then he's here, jumping up the steps, swinging through the door with 'Hey, Al!'

But there's something a little strained in his smile.

Five minutes later he's joined her on the mint tea – *actually kind of refreshing, Al* – and then he comes out with it. His concern about Felix. How Felix was going up to Rockpool to pay his respects and would have been there, or close enough, at the time of the murder.

'And you haven't seen him since?' says Ally.

'I mean, that's not unusual. People go off on day trips all the time. It's not like we keep tabs. But I got the impression he was just sticking his head in up there. That he didn't want to stay. You know?'

'Could he have been one of the arrests?'

'It's possible,' says Jayden, 'but . . . I don't think so. I called Mullins . . .'

'Oh, you did?'

'. . . and obviously he wasn't going to give out any names, but he did say everyone they arrested was staying up at the house. Which Felix wasn't.'

'Including poor Saffron.'

'Exactly. I spoke to one of the journalists at the gate. They definitely saw someone with pink hair in the back of a police car.' Jayden picks up the book. 'I've speed-read this. Felix lent me a copy. Have you finished it?'

'I combed through it looking for mentions of Rupert. I haven't read every word.'

'Did you get to the epilogue?'

'I did.'

While the memoir is themed around all the positive ways in which Baz said no through his life – positive for Baz, anyway – the epilogue focuses on a moment when he said yes. And how he'd regretted that yes every day of his life since, because of the tragedy that followed: the death of Connie.

'Connie is Felix's mum,' says Jayden.

'Yes. Presumably Felix already knew the circumstances of her death though?'

'I'm sure he would have.'

'But the part that Rupert played in it?' says Ally.

Jayden's brow wrinkles. 'I'm sure he would.'

Baz writes of how he went for dinner with Connie, the woman he describes variously as his pottery teacher, his best friend, his saviour, guardian angel, and 'the only woman who ever turned me down romantically'. He writes how painful the occasion was, because Connie was telling him she had a new partner and that things were serious – they had plans to live together. 'It was like she was breaking up with me, only we weren't in a relationship. What she was doing was worse. She was shattering the dream I still had, even after so many years, that we might one day be together.' After the dinner Baz called Rupert, 'because I knew he'd give me what I needed'. And, sure enough, Rupert was hosting a boozy gathering at his house, and he folded Baz into it. *Come and drown your sorrows, mate*, and it was the worst thing he could have said. It was meant as a kindness, a bloke's way of saying *I feel your pain*. Rupert never took me getting clean seriously. None of them did. I was the ultimate party pooper as they saw it.' Baz had one drink and it went straight to his head, 'and my heart. I felt like I'd lost everything Connie had given me. She'd made me a better man and I was about to drink it away again.' Rupert phoned Connie in the middle of the night, asking her to come and get him. And, according to Baz, Connie did what she always did – she came to save him. To get him away from that party before it went any further.

'Baz is big on consequences,' says Jayden, 'linking actions together to make a good story. Sometimes it makes sense, sometimes it doesn't. The epilogue is a weird one. He's blaming himself for Connie's death, even though she ran a red light and a truck hit her car.'

'And he's also blaming Rupert.'

'For calling Connie and asking her to come and get him when he could have just stuck him in a taxi. Exactly. But that was Rupert trying to do the right thing, because he knew the one person who could help was Connie. But it was also Rupert who gave Baz the drink that meant Connie was out on the road in the first place. Late at night, bad weather, she's in a rush to get to him before things get worse. But . . . it was an accident, pure and simple.'

'It reads like a confessional to me,' says Ally. 'Most readers' responses would be to sympathise, I'm sure. To say of course no one was to blame.'

'But at the same time, they'd understand why Baz felt guilty. Or, though it's not explicit, why Rupert might.'

'Or why Rupert should? I doubt Baz gave a second thought to how he was painting Rupert in the story. His focus is on the fact that his weakness, as he calls it, led to her accident. But if you were tracking everything back, you could say it was Rupert's action – giving a sober man a drink – that set events in motion. And then his phone call to her later.'

'But Baz says he called Rupert, the subtext being he knew Rupert'd be partying. So, it's back to Baz. And at the inquest it was all clear. Connie ran a red light. It was dark and raining hard. The roads were slippery. She didn't see the truck. Everything about her death was to do with what happened at that intersection.'

'But she'd never have been at the intersection if it hadn't been for Rupert's phone call to her,' says Ally. 'Rupert's party, Rupert's alcohol, Rupert calling Connie to pick up the pieces.'

Jayden's on his feet, pacing the boards of The Shell House.

'When I spoke to Felix, he didn't act like the memoir was revealing anything he didn't know. In fact, he worked on the first draft himself, so he knew all the stories. He kind of saw the funny side, the fact that Baz was celebrating his birthday with all the people he'd so freshly dissed in the book.'

Ally puts on her reading glasses and flicks through her notebook.

'There are other people who have reason to be unhappy with Rupert,' says Ally. 'According to the book, anyway. Nicole. Jet. Davey. Baz tells stories in here, involving Rupert, that would be quite painful for each of them to read. And even more painful to have shared publicly.'

'But this is all conjecture, right? We're looking at the memoir because it's the only thing we've got access to.'

And the frustration in his voice shows Ally that Jayden is thinking about this case just as much as she is. Even without Tallulah's entreaties.

'Have you heard any more from Tallulah?' he asks, as if he's a mind reader.

'No, nothing. But Jayden, I think you're right when you say that the timing of the publication feels relevant. It's Rupert's death that complicates things, in a way. Or perhaps makes it simpler. Who would have motive to kill both Baz and Rupert? It narrows the field.'

Jayden nods. He passes his hand over his close-shorn hair. Says with a sigh, 'Yeah, I agree.'

'What are you thinking?'

'I'm thinking about Felix. I should probably let the police know that he was headed to Rockpool this morning. But that feels . . .' He shrugs; goes for a smile. 'That feels like the campsite might be heading for a really bad review on Tripadvisor.'

33

Davey Hart is like a cartoon old rocker. Even without his accessories – Mullins remembers a bandana, a series of leather bracelets – and kitted out in regulation custody gear, he just has that look. Plus, the drawling voice to go with it. He says 'man' a lot – even to DS Chang.

'Last night, you and Rupert were the last ones awake?'

'I wouldn't call Rupert awake, man. He was . . . slumped on the sofa.' Davey scrunches down in his chair to demonstrate. 'Like this. Can't take his drink like he used to.'

'The incident with the chef. Have you seen Rupert behave in that way before?'

'When he's drunk, sure.'

DS Chang filled Mullins in on Skinner's interview with Saffron earlier. Mullins felt a heat in his chest – was this what they meant by 'blood boiling'? *Is she alright?* he asked DS Chang, and the detective assured him that she was.

'How did you know he'd gone into the kitchen?'

'I saw him. And I know what he's like. Baz dying like that, it hit us hard. We were all messed up. That's why this morning, when I saw him lying there' – Davey rubs at his stubble, his eyes moist – 'my first thought was . . . that he did it. That he killed himself. Because of Baz dying. That's what I thought.'

'Why would you think that?'

'Because I was gutted,' says Davey. 'And . . . I woke up low. Real low. And then, seeing Rupert like that . . . I just went to the obvious place. What I thought was the obvious place. Not . . . murder.'

'What was the atmosphere like in the house last night?'

'Heavy. Nicole was on one. She's a time bomb, that woman. You never know when she's going to go off. Dive for cover, man.'

'Did Rupert and Nicole have a particular problem with one another?'

'Nicole has a problem with everyone.'

Davey's fingers are still working his stubble. *He looks nervous*, thinks Mullins. *Proper nervous, for all his slow rolling talk.*

'Rupert got up people's noses, man, but we all do. Suicide? Yeah. Tragic stuff . . .' His voice breaks, but he goes on. 'But that would have made sense to me. More sense than murder. I even said to Felix he should get up here, because Rupert always liked Felix, even if Felix was a . . . even if Felix didn't respect him.'

Is it Mullins's imagination, or does DS Chang lean a little closer at the mention of Felix's name? They're trying to trace him: officially a person of interest.

'When did you have this conversation with Felix?'

'I sent him a message last night. He was down for the weekend like we were, but no one had seen him yet. That's Felix though – he's always kept his distance. Acted like he didn't need Baz. Like he's above the rest of us. That's critics. Who watches the watchman, huh? Anyway, he came.'

Mullins saw Felix's name in Baz's book when he skimmed through it, but can't remember much about him. Apart from that he'd been raised by his mum, Connie, whose death Baz felt guilty about. But that end section struck Mullins as a bit of a getting-the-violins-out moment. Like Baz was trying to show a soft side, after being The Big I Am through the whole book. Anyone could see that it had been a simple road accident.

Davey narrows his eyes. 'You've spoken to him, huh? Felix Boyd.'

'Not yet,' says DS Chang.

She doesn't add that he appears to have disappeared off the face of the earth.

'I'm feeling a little uneasy here, Officers,' he says, his hand going to his chin again. 'First Baz, now Rupert. I'm the last man standing. The only one left who was there at the start. Are you saying I should be looking over my shoulder?' His voice notches up. 'What if I'm next?'

'Tallulah Pearce was there at the start,' says Mullins. 'She was there before the start.'

'Tallulah?' Davey's worried face brightens a tad. 'Talk about a blast from the past.'

'Did she read Baz's book in advance of its publication?'

'How would I know? They were pen pals though. That was Baz's new thing. Writing to Tallulah. He always had to have a thing.'

'Had you met her before this weekend?' asks DS Chang.

'Erm, yeah. You don't forget Tallulah. We played a one-off gig in the Nevada desert about thirty years back, and she came. A reunion gig. Baz always said no to stuff like that, and people asked a lot, man. But Rupert made it happen. I was busy touring with someone, can't even remember who, but I got a free pass for it. Too good to miss. And yeah, Tallulah was there. She wore a yellow dress; came backstage. Or something.'

Two spots of colour have risen in Davey's cheeks. *Well, it is hot in here*, thinks Mullins. He's pretty sure his own face is lit up red. But DS Chang is writing something in her notebook, like Davey just said something important.

'I'm serious,' says Davey, pushing up the sleeves of his sweatshirt, revealing a mosaic of ropey tattoos. 'You need to find who did this. Okay? Reckon you can do that?' And as he looks at them both, Mullins thinks of a cornered animal: fear in their eyes, claws out.

～

As they wind their way through the corridors of the custody unit, Mullins struggles to keep up with DS Chang's stride. She's much shorter than him, but she's a powerhouse.

'What do you think, boss?'

'I think Davey Hart has a crush on Tallulah Pearce,' she says, looking down at her phone.

'I mean about the case.'

'It is about the case,' she says. 'Tallulah's got an alibi for this morning though. She left Rockpool early doors and went walking the coast path. Plenty of people who can attest to that; she's a memorable individual, which is the only reason she's not in here with the rest of them. The woman's devastated. The only one who really is, if you ask me. Well, Davey too, under all the layers.' She glances back over her shoulder. 'PC Mullins, you know part of an officer's duty is to keep up their physical fitness?'

'Yes, ma'am,' says Mullins, with confidence. Because he lifts weights every Friday night down The Wreckers. Pint-sized, but plenty of them. 'Why are we running anyway?'

'Message from the DI. We're needed in the briefing room. Post-mortem's in on Baz Carson.'

They pass the cell where Saffron is, and Mullins slows. He thinks about just ducking in and seeing if she's okay.

'Come on, Tim,' says DS Chang – *Miranda*, though he'll never call her that – 'you can't miss this.'

Just then, two of the Newquay lot charge down the hall towards them, looking like hounds who've caught a scent.

'Felix Boyd's been sighted,' one says. 'We're going to pick him up.'

'He can join the queue of suspects,' says DS Chang.

'Dunno about that. VIP line; he'll be right at the front.'

And they're gone before either Chang or Mullins can ask any more.

'They must have something on him,' the sergeant says with resolve. 'Something tasty, too.'

Mullins licks his lips.

34

Jayden's phone rings as they're rumbling down the track through the dunes, Ally at the wheel. It's Cat. As he answers, he sees a delicate blue butterfly, as bright as one of Jazzy's stickers, land on the windscreen.

'Be there in five,' he says. 'Less than five. Ally's running me back up.'

'Jay, the police are here. They're looking for Felix Boyd.'

When Jayden hesitates, Cat says, 'You know, the guy in number thirty-seven. He's still not back by the way. I reckon he's checked out. That's what I said to them, but they want to talk to you.'

The blue butterfly is, implausibly, still on the windscreen, surfing the track with them.

'Alright. Couple of minutes and I'm there. Who is it, DS Skinner?'

'No one I know.'

And it's no surprise. A case like this, there'll be a team from Major Crimes. Jayden says he'll see her in a second and hangs up. Turns his phone in his hand.

'Did you hear that?'

Ally nods. 'They're searching for Felix. Look, that butterfly! I saw one just like it in my garden when I was thinking about Tallulah . . .'

As they swing on to the coast road and pick up speed, warm air flows in through the open window. The butterfly finally leaves them, twirling off on its blue wings. Jayden settles back in his seat. The sea is deep blue all the way to the horizon, the sky as clear as he's ever seen it. It's crazy beautiful. And as they crest the hill, the bulbous white shape of Rockpool House comes into view on the headland. *Crazy* is definitely the word there.

Where's Felix gone? And can he really be a killer? It seems to Jayden unlikely. Call it gut instinct. That's something his partner Kieran – the best of men – always believed in: *You don't belong to uniform, Jay. You've got a detective's head on you, and better still, you've got the gut.*

Jayden glances at Ally, his new partner. Whatever qualities Kieran claimed to see in him, Jayden knows they're in Ally too. He wonders if Bill ever saw it. He remembers when Ally told him that now and again, she and Bill would discuss cases. Never in a way that broke professionalism, but small pieces swapped here and there, and she'd loved being included in that way.

The sign for Top Field Camping appears, and they turn into the entrance. Tyres crunching on gravel, past the 5 mph sign that Jayden hammered in with his own bare hands – and Cliff promptly came and redid five minutes later. *Crosswinds off the headland. Don't underestimate them, Jayden.*

The patrol car is parked outside their cabin office. Two officers are standing around, one in uniform, one in a creased suit. Cat's in her denim cut-offs, shades pushed high on her head. Easy-breezy from a distance, but he can tell from the way she's holding herself that she's tense.

'Ah, here he is,' Cat says, as soon as he steps out of the car. As if Jayden's the one who'll make everything fall into place.

Jayden turns to thank Ally for the lift, but she looks like she's got no plans to drive off. She climbs out and leans her arms on the roof. Waves hello to Cat.

'How's it going?' says Jayden; he holds out his hand, and in turn the officers shake it.

'Your reputation precedes you,' says the detective. 'The JP Sharpe case.'

'And that's my partner, Ally Bright,' says Jayden, nodding. But Ally doesn't come over.

'You two aren't getting tangled up in this business, are you?'

'Not at all,' says Jayden, shaking his head. 'So, what's—'

'Felix Boyd. Any idea where he is?'

There's a mild disruption as a Labrador rushes past with a ball, followed by a pre-schooler on a scooter. A harried-looking mum follows.

'What time's the pizza van coming by tonight?' she asks. 'Hugo, wait!'

And she could be calling to the boy or the dog.

'Here from four o'clock,' says Jayden, with a grin.

'Will they do gluten-free?'

Cat comes over. 'Sure,' she says, trying to manoeuvre the woman away.

'What's all this?' says a strong Yorkshire voice, and it's Ken – Ken of Eileen-and-Ken fame – a newspaper tucked under his arm. 'Something afoot?'

'Nothing's afoot,' says Cat, turning on the mega-watts.

'Apart from the massacre next door, that is,' says Ken with a chuckle. 'Bleeding drama. My lot have been on the phone all morning. Tell us what's going on, Kenny! We came here to get away from it all, and now look. But I'll give my tuppence if any reporter asks.'

'Mazda Bongo, white,' says the constable. 'Incoming.'

'Boyd,' says the detective.

And as the vehicle rumbles slowly towards them – obeying the speed limit – it's as if time slows down too. Jayden feels relief climb in his chest. No one's done a runner.

The detective steps out on to the path and holds up his hand. Felix comes to a stop.

'Felix Boyd. Step out of the vehicle please, sir.'

There's a beat of hesitation. Jayden wonders why they're talking to him like that – and why Felix isn't immediately getting out of the van. He shifts on his feet, an instinctive readiness flowing through him. But then Felix slides out of the driver's seat, holding up his hands.

His t-shirt has what look like bloodstains on it. *Seriously?*

'Hey, listen,' says Felix, 'I only just heard—'

Then the constable is by his side, and there's the glare of sunlight on metal as he pulls out the cuffs.

'I'm arresting you on suspicion of murder,' says the detective. 'You do not have to say anything, but it may harm your defence if you do not mention when questioned something which you later rely on in court . . .'

And there's a force, and speed, to the arrest, that makes Jayden certain there's more to this. They wouldn't be slapping on the cuffs like that otherwise. They wouldn't be shutting down any kind of dialogue.

The dog and the scooting child careen by, oblivious. The mum in the wetsuit hisses, 'Hugo! Get here!'

'Bloody hell, this is better than TV,' says Ken.

As Felix is walked towards the car, he meets Jayden's eye. 'Mate,' he calls out, 'I don't know what this is.' And the confusion in his face looks as genuine as Jayden's ever seen.

Jayden feels the urge to get in the car with them, like it would be the most natural thing in the world. But instead, the detective slaps his hand on the bonnet, nods to them, then drives away, dust flying. Definitely doing more than 5 mph.

35

Mullins can feel the electricity humming around the briefing room. His knee's jiggling in response, his dumpy black shoe scuffing the table leg.

'Stop fidgeting,' hisses DS Chang.

'We've brought in Felix Boyd,' says DCI Robinson, eyes gleaming with satisfaction. 'He was arrested at Top Field Camping. He's declined the duty solicitor and has a lawyer coming from London. The only one of the Rockpool guests to do so, which is telling. Witnesses put the suspect at Rockpool House for a period of about thirty-five minutes. He arrived at ten fifty, and spent around ten minutes talking to Davey Hart, Jet Carson, Ruby Edwards and Nicole Carson outside on the terrace. He had, apparently, come to pay his respects. He then went inside the house to the kitchen, ostensibly to speak to Saffron Weeks, the chef, but likely to secure an alibi. What he didn't reckon on was the accuracy of her timekeeping. He left the kitchen at around five past eleven and there is then a period of twenty minutes where his movements are unaccounted for. A witness, Jet Carson, saw Boyd walking at speed towards his van, carrying an object. Carson Junior can't recall the time, nor offer any more accuracy as to what Boyd was carrying. But he said that the image stuck with him. Boyd was seen leaving the property at around eleven twenty-five, his vehicle – a white Mazda Bongo – recognised by journalists at the gate. We believe in this twenty-minute window it's possible that he killed Rupert Frost.'

There's a glow about DCI Robinson, and good on him, too. A tidy wrap-up, especially when so many eyes are on them. But is Boyd really any more of a prime suspect than anyone else they have under lock and key (excluding Saffron, of course)?

'Motive?' says DS Chang.

'Felix Boyd is an outsider,' says Skinner. 'Invited to the party, but instead of staying in a luxury guest room he's in a tatty van at a campsite down the road. His relationship with Baz was a source of discontent among the others. Jet Carson views him as a chancer. Nicole feels he should never have been invited at all. Ruby Carson, who seems to all intents and purposes a reasonable woman, reserves a special distaste for him.'

'Not exactly a motive,' Chang says, her bob shifting.

'What about this thing he was supposedly carrying to the van?' says Mullins.

'The vehicle's been seized. And Forensics are conducting a thorough search as we speak.'

'Mullins,' says Skinner, a flicker at his jaw. 'You made your report on the contents of Baz Carson's book. Can you offer us a precis on Felix Boyd?'

And he's on the spot now. *Felix Boyd, Felix Boyd.* A bit part in the story; a walk-on, at best. It was Connie who was star of the show. But maybe that's the point.

'Well, it's all about his mum, really,' says Mullins. He coughs, adjust his seat. 'She died five years ago. And there's a bit at the end where Baz talks about how he blames himself for it.'

'So, Felix Boyd has a motive to kill Baz Carson. Why not Rupert Frost while he's at it?'

It's an officer Mullins half recognises. Sneery-looking bloke, who he's pretty sure nicked a stapler from them once when he was down at theirs for the Helena Hunter case.

'And that's my cue,' says DCI Robinson, fanning his hands. 'Thanks to some fast-tracking, we've had the results of the post-mortem on Baz Carson. Pathologists confirm he suffered a cardiac arrest. It's a hung jury on whether the cardiac arrest killed him before he drowned, or the other way around. Either way, it's our supposition that he fell in the water as a result of the cardiac arrest and drowned shortly afterwards.'

Mullins's eyes widen. 'So, it was just a heart attack.'

'A cardiac arrest,' says DS Chang.

'Natural causes, either way,' says Mullins. 'Tallulah Pearce was so sure there was more to it.'

'Or death by misadventure,' says Robinson. 'Because here's the interesting bit. Or perhaps, given the circumstances, the predictable bit. Toxicology shows that Baz Carson had recently taken cocaine. Cocaine that very likely provoked the cardiac arrest.'

'But he didn't do drugs,' says Mullins. 'It's all in the book. He gave everything like that up when he met Connie Boyd.'

'I reckon,' says Skinner, 'that Baz Carson talked a good talk.'

And Mullins can't argue with that. The bloke banged on for three hundred pages: the world according to Baz.

'Tallulah Pearce won't like it,' Mullins says.

'I checked the Amazon rankings for *Turn It Down* before news of Carson's death broke,' says DS Chang. 'It wasn't troubling any bestseller lists. It's a different story now though. It's number seven in Memoir and Biography.'

So, thinks Mullins, *on Friday night Baz takes cocaine. First time in a long time – or maybe not. And it kills him. Bad luck for the birthday boy, but how does that connect to Rupert being killed by Felix Boyd the next morning?*

Mullins pulls those last pages of Baz's book up in his memory. He's pretty sure Rupert's mentioned in them.

'It's right at the end,' he says. 'Something about Felix's mum and Rupert. I haven't got the book with me now. Erm . . . Baz had a drink, I think. He wasn't drinking, then he was, and . . .'

'It's here,' says DS Chang, fingers tapping at her screen. 'The epilogue. Baz says, "I phoned Rupert because he was a fixer and, misguidedly, I thought I needed fixing. Rupert's response was instant. *Come and drown your sorrows, mate,* and it was the worst thing he could have said. It was meant as a kindness, a bloke's way of saying *I feel your pain.* Rupert never took me getting clean seriously. None of them did. I was the ultimate party pooper as they saw it. But that night I went to Rupert's place like a moth to a flame."'

Mullins blinks.

'Kindle download,' says DS Chang, without looking up. Her eyes scan left and right. 'Mullins is right. Baz broke his sobriety when Rupert gave him a drink. And even more interestingly, it was Rupert who saw the state Baz was in and called Connie to come and get him. It was on the way over to Rupert's house that Connie was killed in a traffic accident.' She taps her finger on the screen. 'He writes, "It doesn't matter what anyone says, I'll always feel guilty for her being on the road that night." What if Felix didn't know the full circumstances of his mother's death? What if he only learnt about the Rupert factor when the book was published yesterday?'

'But it's Baz who's claiming the guilt,' says Mullins. 'He's not pointing the finger at Rupert. If Baz doesn't blame Rupert, then why should Felix?'

'It's possible that Felix blames them both,' says Robinson. 'Carson dies, effectively by his own hand, so then Felix kills Rupert to draw a line.'

'So, the deaths are connected, then,' says Mullins. 'Kind of. It'd be weird if they weren't. Wouldn't it?'

'Alright,' says DCI Robinson. 'PC Mullins, look for reports of Connie Boyd's death at the time. See if the name Rupert Frost features in any press coverage. If it doesn't, this is a decent line of questioning. The fact that Boyd didn't know the details of the part he played – until yesterday.' He checks his watch. 'We can't talk to Boyd until his brief gets here, so let's use the time wisely. Look for more connections between Felix Boyd and Rupert Frost. Felix is a journalist, go through what he's published. Meanwhile, let's talk to the others again. Jet Carson's clearly got a grudge against Felix. Let's see what he knows about him and Rupert. See if there's any history there.'

'Davey Hart was scared,' says Mullins. 'He said he was worried he'd be next. Like someone was picking off everyone who was in the band or connected to it.'

'Well, unless Felix Boyd magically caused Baz's heart to stop, I think Davey can relax there. We'll be issuing a statement to bring the press up to date on the toxicology. It'll take some of the heat off. Put a stop to any "Double Murder at Rockpool" headlines.'

Skinner, his hands wedged deep in his pockets, rocks back and forth on his heels. He says, 'If Boyd murdered Rupert Frost, it's no surprise he didn't stick around afterwards. So, what was he thinking, going back to the campsite? He could have been halfway back to London by then. It doesn't add up.'

Just then the DCI's phone buzzes in his pocket. He holds up a hand as he answers it. As he hangs up, he turns a look of triumph to the room.

'Well, team, we have ourselves a murder weapon. Almost certainly.'

In the background, someone, Mullins isn't sure who, sings out *nailed it!*

'A bloodied knife, wrapped in a towel, was found stashed in the back of Boyd's van,' says Robinson.

Mullins gasps involuntarily. No wonder Robinson was grinning through that phone call. Solving a high-profile murder within twelve hours? That ought to be beers all round at The Wreckers. But Robinson is probably more of a country club man.

'Fingerprints?' says Skinner. And he manages to sound pernickety, even though it's the natural question.

'Forensics are on it as we speak,' says Robinson. He clenches a quick fist in victory, then collects himself. 'Alright. The Rockpool suspects will remain in custody overnight. No one's going anywhere until Boyd's confessed, or we hit twenty-four hours. In the case of Boyd, we'll apply to extend that, if we need to.' He turns to DS Chang. 'Miranda, I'd like you to lead the interview with Boyd.'

Mullins sees Skinner's moustache turn down.

'Here's what we have,' Robinson goes on. 'The murder weapon – the *likely* murder weapon – was found in Felix Boyd's van. There's a twenty- to twenty-five-minute window where his movements at the house are unaccounted for. And a newly published memoir publicly states that Rupert Frost was directly involved in a sequence of unfortunate events that led to the accidental death of Felix Boyd's mother. These are incontrovertible facts.'

'Well, sir,' says DS Chang, 'the last is according to Baz Carson. So not quite incontrovertible.'

'And it makes no sense whatsoever that Boyd would go back to the campsite,' says Skinner again.

'Call me old-fashioned, but I like him for it,' says Robinson. 'Now, let's get that release out about Baz Carson and his marching powder. Today's shocking news is debauchery among the rich and famous: hold the front page.'

36

At a little after five o'clock Ally walks over the dunes, bound for the Bluebird. The sun is still as fierce as it was at high noon, the air thick with heat, so she moves slowly; half so she doesn't arrive sticky and dishevelled, half just to take it all in. Every so often Fox stops to look back at her, brush tail waving madly.

After the kerfuffle at the campsite, Ally was reluctant to leave. She wanted to talk it over with Jayden, and she knew he did too. But she planned to start out on her walk at five o'clock, and even a dramatic arrest couldn't stop that. Careful planning is her way of managing her nerves around the private view, and a slow amble into the village is just what Ally needs.

She focuses – step by step.

There isn't a cloud in the sky. The sea is pure blue, a stretch of immaculate fabric, only the occasional ripple close to shore. The sand beneath Ally's sandals is hot with the sun as she follows the rabbit path. She breathes deeply. This has been her home for more than forty years, and she can honestly say that there hasn't been a single day when she's taken it for granted. The beauty of this place is that it changes; all the time, it changes. With every shift in weather, the sea shows a different face. And even though the sky has been an unreal blue for days now, sunrise and sunset are a riot: a spectrum from pink to orange to purple; mind-blowing technicolour. Every day, Ally falls in love with Porthpella again.

It's different with people. With Bill, certainly. He was solid, her rock-steady friend and companion. He didn't change. He was, she thinks, the same Bill at sixty-five as he was at twenty-five. The day he died, he made their morning coffee, and they drank it together on the veranda. He kissed her on the cheek before he walked out the door. *See you, Al.* For all the unpredictability of his job, he was like the tide: he left, but he always came back in.

Oh Bill, if you could see me now. Because she has changed; she knows she has. And it breaks her heart a little bit that it might even be for the better.

Evie messaged earlier, to wish her luck for tonight.

I'm so proud of you Mum. Life is what you make it, isn't it? And sometimes amazing things come out of the hard stuff. We could all take a leaf out of your book.

Deep inside Ally's shoulder bag she can hear her phone buzzing. She reaches for it reluctantly, unwilling to break the moment. *Jayden.* She presses her fingers to her eyes before she answers.

'Ally, he called me from the custody unit. I was his phone call.'

'Felix?'

'Felix. He doesn't understand why they've arrested him, but he's afraid of how certain they seem.'

'So, they haven't interviewed him yet?'

'He's requested a lawyer from London. An old university friend. They can't start until she gets here.'

'Why did he call you?' she asks. But she can guess the answer. If Ally was in trouble, she'd call Jayden too. And it took her no time at all to feel like that. The morning Lewis Pascoe was found at the bottom of the cliffs is etched in her mind; as is the concern and kindness that Jayden showed her.

'I guess he knows my background. We talked last night about the police. And he knows what I do now with you, too. Maybe he thinks I'm someone down here who can vouch for him . . .'

Ally can hear the strain in Jayden's voice.

'Why do you think he's waiting on this London lawyer?' asks Ally. 'Doesn't it make him look . . . as if he has something to defend?'

'Maybe he thinks someone's pointing the finger. And what about the way they handled the arrest? That was showboating. They seized his camper van too. Took it off on a truck in front of some of our more excitable guests. We won't hear the last of that.'

Ally pauses at the path that turns inland. She takes a last look back at the sea, then plunges on to the footpath, briars catching at her linen trousers.

'So, what happens now?' she says.

'They've got twenty-four hours. They can only extend that if the circumstances are viable.'

Ally stands to one side to let a couple pass, their dainty whippet dancing on the end of his lead. She swaps smiles with them. 'Lovely day,' the man murmurs.

'Do you think he did it, Jayden?'

'There's no way I can say. But . . . if you're asking for a gut feel?'

'Always.'

'Then, no. I don't think he did it. Anyway, look. I'll leave you to it. I'll see you in an hour, okay? Can't wait to raise a glass, Al. And, hey, you know I'd buy a piece if I could afford one, don't you?'

'Jayden, I'd pay you to take one.' She laughs. 'I'll see you soon.'

'You're not nervous, are you?'

'Oh, very.'

'It'll be a walk in the park, Al. A walk in the dunes. Tell me Fox is coming? Because that's Jazzy's condition of attendance.'

'Coming? He's leading the way.'

183

They swap a few more words, then Ally hangs up. Her reflective mood is broken now, which is probably good. Instead, she thinks of Tallulah. Has she stayed on in Porthpella, as she said she would? She said she gave her statement and, unlike the other Rockpool guests – unlike Felix Boyd – is free to come and go.

Ally opens the internet browser and taps in the name Rupert Frost, to see if there have been any news updates. Her eyes rove her phone screen as she walks. This is not the way that Ally likes to travel, but she has an impulse to know the very latest.

She stops dead.

Baz Carson in drugs death.

Ally reads on.

Following a post-mortem, the cause of death is a cardiac arrest likely caused by cocaine usage.

She tries to picture the scene. The swimming pool; Baz Carson falling into its waters. Would it have been as sudden as the flicking of a switch? Or would it have been a terrible moment of awareness? Ally realises her breathing is ratcheting up, and she stops; tries to steady herself.

She thinks of Tallulah, and how she must be taking this news. She was so sure of foul play.

It was his time. That's what someone said to Ally, after Bill died. She can't remember whose words they were, but eventually they became a kind of comfort because some people don't get nearly as many good years. Kieran, for one; a young man with his whole life ahead of him, and Jayden's best partner. No matter how many cases she and Jayden work together, no matter how many they crack, she knows the important people are irreplaceable.

Tallulah didn't say if there had been anyone important in her life after Baz. Ally presumed there must have, but perhaps not. For all the years they were apart, maybe he was irreplaceable to her too.

These thoughts take Ally across the patchwork of fields, over the sun-scorched stubble and past waist-high mallow. They take her into the narrow lanes and past the sturdy little church and across the bunting-festooned square, until there – with a window full of colour and light – is the Bluebird Gallery and tea room.

And that colour and light? It's all her.

The sugary sweep of Porthpella beach, the island lighthouse, a sky blazing with pink.

So many tiny fragments of plastic, each piece of litter picked over many years, not just from here, but from beaches up and down the coast. Sorted by colour, stowed, repurposed. Never in her wildest dreams did she expect her work to fill a gallery window.

'No one can walk past without stopping to look,' says Sunita, standing in the doorway. Her grin is broad as she says, 'You look lovely, Ally. As do you, Foxy. Come on in. I should say something first though, so you're not shocked.'

Ally feels a thrum of unease. 'Oh, what?'

'It's never happened before,' says Sunita, 'not before the private view. I hope your guests won't be too disappointed.'

But she's smiling as she says it.

37

'Come on, Jay, we can't be late for Ally.'

Jayden scowls, because of course he's got no intention of making them late for Ally. He scans the most recent piece about Rupert and Baz, then slaps his laptop shut. *This afternoon officers made a significant arrest.* No mention of Top Field Camping, which is a good thing. They don't need journalists crowding the site, disrupting the pizza van queue or getting soundbites from the likes of Ken.

'I'm set,' he says. 'Has Jazz got her shoes on?'

'She's got her brand-new sandals on, no less. She's ready to rock. And Jay, let's try not to get collared by any guests. Eyes front. Hey, by the way, you checked in Martin Radford? I saw his girlfriend earlier. She's very friendly.'

'Yeah, I did. It was weird. Blast from the past.'

'Nice they booked to come here, hey?'

'Yeah, nice,' says Jayden vaguely. If they weren't flying out the door, he might have said how strange it felt when the DI called him PC Weston. But that feels like a bigger conversation. And not one he really wants to have: mostly because he hasn't got a sharper adjective than *strange.*

Outside in the yard the heat hits them like a wall. Jazz toddles ahead, quick as a fish in her lime-green playsuit and sunshine-yellow sandals. Jayden catches up to her, places a hand on her mass of dark curls and steers her towards the Land Rover. On an evening as sweet as this they'd usually stroll it, but Jazzy's staying up past her bedtime, and a long walk uphill with a tired toddler is no one's idea of fun. He hoists her up into the car seat.

'Any news?' says a voice at Jayden's shoulder.

'Ken.' Then, because he feels like it, 'News of what?'

'That bloke that got arrested. The killer.'

'He was arrested. That's all.'

'My money's on him though,' says Ken. 'That was some slick operation by the Old Bill. Lying in wait like that. Were you in on it?'

'They weren't lying in wait,' says Jayden.

'Okay, Jay,' says Cat, tapping the bonnet, flashing a smile, 'we'd best make tracks. Ken, have a lovely evening.'

And Ken – rendered a little speechless by Cat's beauty; especially tonight in the blue dress she's wearing – simply nods and holds up a hand. Whether in farewell or surrender, Jayden's not sure.

As they turn out of the campsite gateway and on to the lane, Cat squeezes his knee.

'You were a little defensive there, Weston. You've only known this Felix guy five minutes.'

'I didn't like Ken's tone. Guilty until proven innocent, that's his vibe.' Jayden slips his shades from his shirt pocket and puts them on. 'Plus, what's "this Felix guy" all about? Before he was just "Felix".'

'Okay, Just Felix.' She laughs. 'Come on, Jay. It's horrific, but it looks like the police have jumped right on it. Which is great because it's not exactly a selling point, having a house of horror up the road from the campsite.'

'House of horror?'

'Two deaths in as many days?' she says in a low voice, glancing back at their daughter.

'Baz took drugs and had a cardiac arrest,' says Jayden. 'I told you, the news just broke.'

'But Rupert Frost was murdered, wasn't he?' Cat whispers the m-word. 'I can't believe Saffron's been taken in too. Though now they've got this Felix guy – sorry, Felix – they'll be releasing the others, won't they?'

'Depends,' says Jayden. 'It might not be that simple. In fact, I'm willing to bet that it won't be.'

They swing out into the square and there's a bubble of excitement from Jazzy in the back. It looks like the stage is set for a midsummer party: strings of bunting and colourful parasols outside The Wreckers; bright paper lanterns in the trees beside the Bluebird. Jayden smiles, thinking of Ally inside. They find a parking spot in a side lane and he turns off the engine. He sits for a moment, hands still on the wheel.

'You okay?'

'Yeah. Just . . . thinking.'

'Not your case, Jay.'

'No.'

'And Felix, you don't really know him at all.'

'Okay.'

'The good news is you look great in that shirt, babe.' She pats his arm. 'And this is a big night for Ally. She's going to love that you're here.'

'As if I'd miss it.'

'I think we should buy one of her pieces.'

'Cat, we can't.'

'Dad said he'd lend us the money. As an investment.'

'An investment?'

'Could be really worth something one day,' she says lightly. 'You know Dad, always needs the business angle. But seriously, wouldn't you love one? We could hang it in the cabin, set the tone when people check in.'

'Course I would. But . . . not like that. Not paid for by your dad.'

Cat gives a huff of dissatisfaction. 'It's an amazing offer. Good for Ally too. Dad's being really generous.'

'I know he is. But . . .'

'So, what's the "but"?'

And there are so many answers that Jayden could respond with, but none that would really make sense to Cat. Because she's right: it is a generous offer. And of course he'd love one of Ally's pictures; they can't afford to buy one, and he'd never accept a mate's rate from her. But he's saved by the bell – or, more accurately, a tap at the window: a smiling Gus. He gives a thumbs up, and Jazzy laughs in response.

'You look cool,' says Jayden, clapping him on the shoulder.

'Cool's definitely not the word,' says Gus, plucking at his denim shirt. 'I'd have been better off in a singlet, but I didn't think Ally would thank me for lowering the tone. I hope it's not too hot inside.'

Jazzy breaks into an impromptu tap dance as they walk along, eyes darting in Gus's direction.

'New shoes,' whispers Jayden.

'Jasmine Weston, what fantastic sandals,' proclaims Gus. 'Now, where could I get a pair like that?'

'Can't!' Jazz shouts, as if it's the most outrageous thing she's heard.

'Jay,' says Cat, from the doorway of the Bluebird, craning inside, 'I'm seeing a lot of red dots. We need to get a move on if we want one.'

'What, really?' says Jayden, holding the door open for the others. 'That's awesome.'

Sure enough, the first picture is sold. It shows the coast path in springtime, clumps of sea thrift in the foreground; he knows the

189

name now and points them out to his daughter. They were just pink flowers when he first arrived. Jayden leans closer to see what the petals are made of. He identifies a Smarties cap, a twist of cable, part of the thong of a flip-flop.

'Incredible, isn't it?'

Jayden straightens up and smiles back at the American who looks like she's stepped from the pages of a magazine. Her hair is a sleek platinum-grey and falls well past her shoulders. She's wearing a white dress with a broad leather belt. She looks, he thinks, like a Greek goddess.

'Already sold too,' says Jayden.

'It appears so,' she says. Then, 'You're Jayden, aren't you?'

'I am.' And she's got to be Tallulah Pearce.

'Ally said you were bringing your little daughter.' She gestures to Jasmine, her silver bangles sliding down her wrist. 'I figured there aren't too many fun-sized fine-art lovers in this town.' She touches his arm then, and her eyes turn to his. They shimmer with sadness. 'I'm looking forward to getting to know you better. I'm Tallulah. Did Ally mention me?'

'She did. I'm sorry for your loss, Tallulah.'

'You've heard what the police are saying?' she says, leaning closer. 'It doesn't make sense. I called them myself. I spoke to that Skinner guy, the one who came the first day. I've never felt more disregarded.'

Well, Jayden knows that one. The first time he tried to offer some information to DS Skinner – vital information, as it turned out – he was given the brush-off too. *Playing detective*, was the exact phrase. He listens, nodding, conscious of Cat and Jasmine drifting away into the crowd.

'Skinner said that no one could argue with the facts. That Baz took cocaine, had a cardiac arrest, fell in the pool and died.' Her voice is calm, quiet, but her eyes are searching. 'But Baz would categorically not have taken coke. Right now, Ally's my only ally, Jayden. But I hope you will be too.'

Jayden's aware of Gus at his shoulder. The guy looks entirely star-struck.

'Hey Gus,' says Jayden, 'this is Tallulah Pearce. Tallulah, Gus is another good friend of Ally's.'

Tallulah glances briefly at Gus, then dismisses him just as quickly. Says, 'Ally's going to talk to you, Jayden. I know you make your decisions together. But she wants this case. And I want her to take it more than anything on earth. In fact, I bought up the whole exhibition just to show her how serious I am.'

'You bought all the pictures?' gapes Gus.

'Consider it a deposit,' says Tallulah to Jayden. 'A down payment to secure your services. I'll go by the rate card from here on in.'

'But the police are all over this. We can't get involved.'

'They're focused on the murder of Rupert Frost,' she says. 'Which of course is terrible. But they're not focused on Baz. Not anymore. Not since the drugs. And Baz is my focus.' Her voice cracks. 'Baz is my only focus. I love him, Jayden. That's why I came here to England, to tell him that I love him. I wanted us to have a life together. Share the sunset years. Go out in style.' She takes a deep breath, collecting herself. 'So, you see, it's not just Baz I've lost. But the life we could have had together.'

At that, Tallulah sends Jayden a last appealing look, then melts away into the crowd.

'Blimey,' says Gus.

'Exactly,' says Jayden. And he breathes out, not realising how much he was holding on to it. Tallulah's story has moved him, and he gets why it moved Ally so much too. Knowing what a fan Gus is of The Nick, he readies himself: *Take the case, Jayden!*

'I can't believe she's bought the whole lot,' says Gus. And, at that, he wanders away with his head down.

38

Mullins has been face to face with murderers before. Down The Wreckers, pint in hand, he might claim he gets a feeling – a shiver in his timbers – as soon as he looks into a killer's eyes. *I just know.* But the truth is, he doesn't. And he probably never will. And that's the scary bit, isn't it? That you can be shoulder to shoulder with someone, toe to toe, and still not see the blood on their hands.

In the time it's taken for Felix Boyd's London lawyer to get down here, two things have been confirmed. Confirmed *incontrovertibly*, as the DCI would say (Mullins is going to start saying that too, as it sounds good).

One: the knife found in Felix's van is the murder weapon. Rupert Frost's blood was on the blade, as well as on the towel it was wrapped in.

And two? Felix's prints are all over the knife and the towel.

So that's basically a slam dunk. What with Boyd having a perfect alibi-less window to carry out his plan in. And motive and then some.

But for all this, Felix Boyd just looks like an ordinary guy. Okay, a guy who thinks he's a bit cooler than your average – 'hipster poser' is how Mullins would categorise him, if anyone's asking – but still basically ordinary. Grey stonewashed jeans and a daft short-sleeved shirt the colour of those foam shrimp sweets that Wenna's always chomping on. Scruffy hair that Mullins is willing to bet is the result of careful styling and pricey products; that stubble of his probably measured by the millimetre.

Right now, Felix is running his hand through said hair and staring up at them. Eyes of a killer? Not exactly. *He looks sad*, thinks Mullins. *Sad, and a little bit scared.*

Or maybe he's just a good actor.

'You left the kitchen at around five past eleven, saying you were going home,' says DS Chang, 'but according to witnesses you didn't leave the property until half past eleven. What were you doing for those twenty-five minutes?'

Felix shakes his head. 'Twenty-five minutes? I don't know.'

He knows better than to question the timings. With the journalists gathered at the gate and his distinctive white camper van, Felix's departure time isn't up for debate. But he could have argued the toss over when he left Saffron: his word against hers, close that window for murder until it's barely a crack.

'I didn't know it was that long,' he says.

'What were your exact movements after your conversation with Saffron Weeks?'

'I sat quietly in the garden for a bit, then I went back to the van.'

'Sat quietly?' echoes DS Chang.

Felix knots his fingers. His hands are pale; they don't look like they see a lot of sun. A music journalist, apparently. Mullins doesn't really see the point of reading about music when you're supposed to be listening to it, but fair play if he can make a living from it. Though his camper isn't the newest. And he's wearing a watch that looks like it belongs to someone's grandpa, with a chewed-up old leather strap. Maybe it's not much of a living.

'I wanted to be by myself for a bit. It was a lot to take in, being there. Seeing everyone. I wouldn't say I was especially welcome. Not beyond Baz.'

'So, you were on your own. Did you go down to the cottage?'

'No.'

'But surely that's the natural place to walk? The focal point. The path leads to the pool, the viewing platform, the lower terrace.'

'I went to the other side of the house because I wanted to be on my own. I knew Baz had some of my mum's work in the garden, these giant urns with intricate glazing. I wanted to see them.'

'If you were so keen for solitude, why did you seek out the chef in the kitchen?'

'I just stuck my head in to say hello.'

'So, you didn't go to the kitchen to secure an alibi?'

Felix almost looks amused by the suggestion. 'No, I didn't go to the kitchen to secure an alibi.'

Beside him, Mullins can feel DS Chang sit a little straighter.

'I put it to you that you went to the kitchen and deliberately struck up a conversation with the chef. You then went to the cottage where Rupert Frost was staying—'

'I didn't,' says Felix. 'I told you. I was on my own, just killing time.'

'Killing time?'

'I didn't drive straight off, because I never thought, in a million years, that anyone would be watching or wondering what I was doing. I was just on my own. I was thinking about my mum. I was thinking about Baz. There's this corner terrace on the other side of the house, with a bench and palms. Like I said, some of my mum's pots are there. That's where I sat. If no one saw me, I can't help that. I wasn't anywhere near the cottage. Or Rupert Frost.'

Mullins watches him keenly as he says the man's name. Rupert Frost. Is there an extra flicker of emotion in his face? A crackle of tension at his jaw?

'Let's talk about your mother and Rupert Frost,' says DS Chang, changing tack. 'They knew each other, didn't they?'

'Only through Baz.'

DS Chang holds the silence that follows. Beside her, DCI Robinson is as still as a statue, and just as stony-faced.

'And your relationship with Rupert. Can you describe it?'

'We didn't really have one. He was in the industry, so our paths crossed from time to time over the years. But he was off the scene, Rupert. Basically retired. He still managed Baz's affairs I think, but that was pretty much it.'

'You once wrote a piece where you asserted the opinion that, after The Nick broke up, Rupert failed to push his career forward. That he was a one-hit wonder, much like the band.'

Davey Hart confirmed this in his interview, and it cropped up in the searches Mullins did earlier too. In the article that he read, he thought Felix Boyd came across as a jumped-up little so and so.

'It was a passing comment. But the fact is he's probably made a reasonable living from The Nick's success over the years. Especially after the Netflix show deal. But it will have stung him, that he hadn't had any hits with other bands. Professionally, it makes it look like The Nick was just luck.'

'So, he bore a mild grudge towards you, let's say. What were your feelings towards him?'

Mullins looks from DS Chang to Felix Boyd and back again, feeling like he's at a tennis match. Personally, Mullins would rather watch paint dry than tune into Wimbledon, but his mum is glued to the box for the whole two weeks, keeping her eyes peeled for royals in the box. She'll be watching it now. *Pock, pock, pock.*

'Indifference,' says Felix with a shrug.

'Indifference?' DS Chang taps her pen on the desk. She tips her head sideways. 'Did it come as a shock to read in Baz's memoir that Rupert was with Baz on the night your mother died?'

Felix sits back in his chair, drops his hands in his lap. The tempo of the rally has changed.

Chang goes on: 'That it was, in fact, not only Rupert who gave Baz the drink, but who then phoned your mother asking her to come and get him?'

Felix gives a vague shake of his head.

'It was Rupert Frost's proffering of alcohol, his disregard for Baz's vulnerability, and his certainty that your mother would come running after him, that meant she was driving late at night, and in the rain, leading to the accident in which she died.'

'No,' says Felix quietly.

'Baz's memoir was published yesterday. Prior to that, Rupert Frost's name was never publicly mentioned in connection to the accident that night. Nor was Baz Carson's, other than articles simply citing their friendship. I put it to you that you read the epilogue in the book and, for the first time, learnt something new about the events leading up to your mother's death. That finally you had someone to blame, for what was otherwise presented as a tragic accident.'

'She ran a red light,' says Felix.

'She was rushing to reach a man she was afraid was going to make a terrible mistake.'

'She helped people. That's what she did.'

'And she was only in that position, Baz was only in that position, because of Rupert Frost.'

Felix heaves a sigh. 'You're wrong,' he says. 'Baz was in that position because of himself. His choice. Just like it was Mum's choice to take the phone call from Rupert, and then drive out to go and get Baz. I'm not playing a blame game. I never have. And what's more, you're not telling me anything I didn't already know. Mum died five years ago. Baz told me everything. Way before his book.'

'Including about Rupert Frost?'

Felix scratches the stubble at his jaw. 'Including about Rupert,' he says. 'Plus, I worked with Baz on the book. You won't find my name in the acknowledgements because that's not his style, but I started a first draft for him. He didn't like it, so he struck out on his own.'

'And expanded the section about your mother's death?'

'Look, I even read the finished thing months ago. Advanced copies were sent to press. If you're so certain it gives me motive, why didn't I act back in the spring, when it first landed on my desk?'

'Okay,' says DCI Robinson, speaking for the first time. A new player stepping into the game. 'But what does add up is the science bit. The science bit makes perfect sense. Felix, your fingerprints are on the knife that killed Rupert Frost. And the knife that killed Rupert Frost was hidden in your van, wrapped in a towel, also covered in your fingerprints.'

Robinson's served a zinger. Mullins swivels his head to Felix.

'Now, how do you explain that?'

39

The rambling beer garden of The Wreckers Arms has an especially festive mood this hot July night. The tables are packed, kiddies up past their bedtime tumble and roll on the grassy slopes, beady-eyed gulls stalk the perimeter, every so often dive-bombing for chips and causing a right old ruckus that everyone can get behind.

Despite being in the middle of the throng, Gus feels a little downhearted. Not even the prospect of penning a letter to Clive and Rich – *There I was, drinking with Baz Carson's first love, the wildly glamorous Tallulah Pearce* – can lift his spirits. In fact, Tallulah is the main reason for Gus's change in mood. Though he can't quite put his finger on why.

Okay, the fact she stole his thunder and bought up every damn picture in the show might have something to do with it: Gus's big gesture rendered moot by a land-grabber. That this looms so large in his mind tells Gus two things. One, that he's pettier than he ever thought; being married to Mona all those years must have given him a misleading sense of his own rationality. And two, while he's a fan of The Nick, he's clearly a bigger fan of Ally Bright. Because sitting across a pub table from a woman who is one step removed from the late, great Baz Carson means less to Gus than having the opportunity to impress Ally.

No, that's not quite it.

Show Ally. Show Ally how much she means to him.

Gus takes a slug of Doom Bar. Beer on top of the gallery wine is probably a bad idea, but there's something comforting about wrapping his hand around a pint. Though Tallulah clearly has other ideas about what they should be drinking. He watches as she fills four champagne glasses: for Ally, Jayden, Sunita and herself.

'Sure you can't be tempted?' she says to him.

'Thanks, but beer's more my speed.'

Which means he truly is pettier than he thought.

'To the artist,' says Tallulah, raising her glass in Ally's direction. 'And my new Ally Bright collection.'

Gus stares down into his pint, then at the last minute raises it to join in the chinking. He catches Ally's eye, and she smiles at him, more benevolently than he probably deserves.

'Jayden?' says Ally. 'Do you want to say it?'

Jayden nods. 'Tallulah, Ally and I have talked about it, and . . . we'd like to help you.'

'You'll take the case?' she says, and Gus watches as she looks from one to the other. 'Really? You will?'

'We know how much this means to you,' says Ally.

'But we also want to be honest with you,' says Jayden, 'because the trouble is, us wanting to help you and us being *able* to help you are two different things. I said to Ally that I'm not sure how we can prove anything, in this situation. Or what answers we can give you.'

'But we can try,' says Ally.

'Yes. Yes!' cries Tallulah. 'That's all I'm asking. To have you in my corner. To try.'

'We're definitely in your corner,' says Jayden. 'But . . .'

And then Tallulah's pulling Ally into a hug and raising her glass all over again.

'To getting justice,' she says. 'Or trying to, anyway.'

Jayden hesitates, then says, 'I'll always drink to that.'

'Ally and Jayden, I can't thank you enough. And Ally, I'm so grateful to you for letting me stay at The Shell House tonight, too. I was so distracted I failed to book in anywhere, and of course I can't go back to Rockpool.'

Gus's eyes widen. Beyond her own family, has Ally ever had a house guest at The Shell House?

'I'm beyond grateful,' says Tallulah, and nudges Ally's shoulder like they're a couple of schoolgirls.

'You were stuck,' Ally says, 'and it's no trouble.'

'As to answers,' says Tallulah, setting down her glass with a clink, 'I think you can prove that someone forced those drugs on Baz. Well, can't you?'

Jayden rubs the back of his head. 'Erm, maybe. But only if someone admits it – and that's a massive if. We don't exactly have access to the suspects. They're all in custody.'

'Where they're being asked all the wrong questions,' says Tallulah.

'And even if someone admits it,' Jayden goes on, 'they couldn't have known it'd cause a cardiac arrest. There's just no way. In that respect, it's still a tragic accident.'

'There's nothing accidental about it.'

Tallulah's focus is all wrong, thinks Gus. *It's Rupert who was brutally murdered. Baz took drugs and died.*

'Tallulah,' says Ally, gently, 'you said you think Baz's death is connected to Rupert's. When that case is solved, you may well have your answers about Baz too.'

'I don't care about Rupert!' cries Tallulah.

And Gus's head snaps up, stunned at the admission.

'They've got someone for it, haven't they?' says Sunita, in a keep-the-peace voice. 'A new arrest. But they haven't said who it is.'

'It's a guy who's staying up at our campsite,' says Jayden. 'And for what it's worth, I think he's innocent.'

'So, you're ready to proclaim one person's innocence where Rupert is concerned but you don't want to accept that someone is guilty of Baz's death?' says Tallulah.

Jayden's brow furrows. He opens his mouth to speak – to set her straight, Gus hopes – but Tallulah isn't finished yet.

'It's Felix Boyd, isn't it? Connie's son. He had reason to hate Rupert Frost.'

'Could he have killed both of them?' says Sunita.

'Listen,' says Tallulah, 'Baz always spoke the truth to me, but there's a lie in that book of his. I don't know why, but there is.'

'What's the lie?' says Ally.

Tallulah looks at each of them, and with her giant sunglasses it's impossible to read her expression.

'Baz didn't drink whisky at Rupert's house the night Connie died. He took cocaine.' She picks up her glass again and drains it in one. 'I know that for a fact, because he told me. He was devastated, after. Which is why I'm one hundred per cent convinced that he would never go near that drug again. For Baz, it was symbolic of so much destruction.'

'So why would he lie about it in the book?' says Jayden.

'Because he was human. Fallible. He probably didn't want to admit that he'd fallen so far. Especially considering what happened after, to Connie.'

'Tallulah, did you tell the police this?' asks Ally.

For the first time, Tallulah looks evasive. 'In all honesty, I didn't, Ally. I didn't feel like it was my story to tell.'

'But it does provide a link, doesn't it, between what happened the night Felix's mother died, and what happened to Baz? A tentative link, but . . .'

'And Rupert,' says Tallulah. 'Because they were Rupert's drugs then, just like they could have been Rupert's drugs now. Though anyone in that house could have brought the coke in, frankly.'

'I think you should tell the police everything you know,' says Jayden.

'But I'm telling you. My detectives.'

And it strikes Gus then that perhaps Tallulah isn't paying for detective services at all. She's paying for people to listen to her.

He has another slug of Doom Bar, then says, 'Just to play devil's advocate, if Baz took drugs and lied about it back then, isn't there a possibility that he might do the same again?'

Gus feels like everyone is looking at him. Everyone *is* looking at him.

'I mean, he was rock and roll. It's why we loved him. And we did. I did. I was a big fan of The Nick. Still am.'

Ally offers him an encouraging smile, and Gus musters a smile back.

Tallulah slowly pushes her shades up on top of her head. Her eyes – a piercing blue; an unreal blue – fix on his.

'Gus, isn't it?' she says coldly.

He nods.

'Then, if you're such a fan, you should know better than to question his integrity, Gus.'

And the way she says his name, it's like a sledgehammer's come down clean on top of his head.

40

'I've worked it out,' says Felix.

And Mullins sees relief on the suspect's face: straight-up relief.

'Because it's crazy, right, that my prints are on the knife. It makes no sense at all. And I've been going mad, thinking . . . how? When have I even *held* a knife in Cornwall? I mean, seriously, let alone one that could kill someone. I'm camping. I've been eating beach food. Burgers and things. I haven't been anywhere near any puny little cutlery knives, let alone . . . whatever kind of blade killed Rupert Frost. Except for two days ago. Two days ago, I was at Rockpool House. And I did use a knife in the kitchen.'

DS Chang looks sideways at DCI Robinson. DCI Robinson raises an eyebrow. No one looks to Mullins for his reaction, but if they did, his feelings would be clear.

The dog ate my homework, sir. No really. Gobbled it down with his Pedigree Chum.

'That's got to be it,' says Felix. 'That's the only way that it's physically, humanly possible for my fingerprints to be on a knife found anywhere at Rockpool. I was up there two days ago. Baz invited me, you'll see that from my phone records. And I told Jayden Weston too.'

DS Chang gives the briefest nod.

'Anyway, while I was there, I made lunch. Grilled cheese sand-wiches for me and Baz. And I used a knife to cut the cheese. It's got to be that. It's got to be the same one. There's no other possible explanation.'

Well, there is another explanation, thinks Mullins.

'You used a knife from the Rockpool kitchen to make a sandwich on Thursday?' says DCI Robinson.

'Baz's request,' says Felix. He shakes his head. 'He was getting nostalgic. Years back, when he was staying with us, I used to make them sometimes. I was a teenager, and it was the only thing I could cook. Not much has changed there, to be honest.' He gives a nervous laugh. 'But . . . that explains the fingerprints. Doesn't it? It has to. It was a kitchen knife. Sharp, I guess. I used it then just stuck it back in the block where I found it. I probably didn't wash it properly. I just rinsed the blade, dried it off.'

'You seem to have a very accurate memory around the knife,' says DS Chang. 'Especially considering you didn't know how vital it might be at the time. What about the plates? The pan used to make the sandwiches? Can you be similarly accurate about your washing up, or lack of, with those items?'

And it's a fair question.

Felix gnaws at his lip. 'Look, I know how it sounds. But it's the truth.'

'Anyone who can prove that you were in the Rockpool kitchen on Thursday, Felix?' says DS Chang. 'Using this knife?'

'Well, no. Only Baz.'

'Nobody else enjoyed one of these sandwiches that you made?'

'It was just me and Baz.' He darts a look at Mullins. 'You have to believe me. It was what happened.'

'Let's rewind,' says DCI Robinson. 'Why were you meeting with Baz in the first place?'

'He said he wanted to clear the air before the party.'

'So, there was a problem between the two of you?'

'We'd drifted since Mum died. We weren't close anymore.' Felix rubs his face with both hands. 'Then he hired me to ghost his memoir but changed his mind and sacked me. But that was fine, I didn't care, and he paid me well anyway. No, the issue was, he'd sent me an advance copy of the book, thinking I'd review it. That was the thing with Baz, he always expected people to do what he asked. But I didn't want to review it.'

'Why not?' says DS Chang.

'Because it's no good,' says Felix. 'It's badly written. It's self-absorbed. He comes out of it looking smug, like a know-it-all. I wasn't going to deliver that verdict in the press. I wouldn't do that to him. But I wasn't going to falsely flatter him either.'

'Did you tell him that?' says DS Chang.

'No. At the time I told him there were lots of competing titles, that page space was limited, that I'd done what I could but blah blah blah. I don't think he bought it for a second. He credits me with more influence, maybe.'

'But then you cleared the air over a grilled cheese sandwich?' says Robinson.

'I was more honest with him. I said it didn't portray him as the man I knew he was. I thought it did him a disservice. I played it as a kind of back-handed compliment.'

'How did he take it?'

'Oh, he had his own interpretation. He put it down to sour grapes. He said the only reason I thought the book didn't do him justice was because he'd taken me off the project.'

'So, let me get this right,' says DS Chang. 'You'd drifted from one another, but when you thought there was an opportunity to work together you went for it with both hands?'

'Welcome to freelancing. I could have done with the gig sticking. But hey, even though I thought he was making the wrong decision – objectively speaking, it would have been a better book if he'd let me write it – I could respect it.'

'It seems to me,' says DS Chang, 'that it's surprising you agreed to come to the party at all. Given your history.'

'Our history? That's the only reason I came. Mum would have wanted me to.'

'Your recent history. The issues surrounding the writing and reviewing of the book.'

'None of that was a big deal. Not to me, and not really to Baz. It was an ego thing for him, the review. That's all. And his ego's so big, he's capable of tweaking the narrative to suit him. So, for him, it was about my sour grapes. And it meant he could deliver a speech about how I must be mismanaging my finances if I was so desperately in need of a ghostwriter's fee.'

'And are you? Mismanaging your finances?'

'My overdraft sees some action. Again, welcome to freelancing. But how's that relevant?'

'Yet you're considered successful, aren't you? Felix Boyd the music writer.'

'Doesn't mean people pay promptly though. I live month to month like the next man.' Felix looks to his lawyer. 'Look, I can't add any more. I've told you why my fingerprints are on the knife. I've told you where I was in the twenty minutes before I left Rockpool House. I can't do more than that.'

Out of nowhere, Felix looks as if he might cry.

'I didn't kill Rupert Frost.'

'But we've only your word for it,' says DS Chang. 'And the way I see it, you have every reason to lie.' Then she adds, almost as an afterthought, 'Felix, just because you made Baz Carson a grilled cheese sandwich on one day, there's nothing to say you didn't use the same knife to kill Rupert Frost on another, is there?'

41

Ally joins Jayden at the bar. He proffers a stool, and she takes it. Propping up the bar in The Wreckers? That's new. Her eyes go to the model of the lugger on the shelf behind, its red sails and blue hull. Evie always loved that boat when she was little. If they ever came here for a family tea Bill would let her take the froth off his pint; get her a bag of Scampi Fries. Her *aperitif*, he called it.

'Al, you're sure you're alright with Tallulah staying at yours?' He says it quietly, one eye on the door to the garden.

'Of course.' Then, 'She asked me, Jayden. I couldn't turn her down.'

'We could loan her a tent but . . . something tells me she's not going to be into camping.'

'It's okay. I know she's a little . . . forceful. But she's going through such a lot.'

The truth is, when Tallulah asked, Ally was taken right back to the moment when Lewis Pascoe came to her door looking for help last spring. How could she turn her down after that? And she really does like Tallulah Pearce.

'What Tallulah said about Baz lying in the book and taking cocaine. Do you think that's relevant?' says Jayden.

'Well, as much as I believe Tallulah's said that in earnest, I think Gus is right. There's every chance Baz took drugs of his own volition.'

'Yeah, a line of coke isn't exactly a reliable murder weapon. There's no way anyone could predict he would have a cardiac arrest. Unless it was known that his heart was in bad condition, so the risk was greater? I wonder if the cops are talking to his doctor.' Jayden purses his lips. 'Even then, it's a big stretch. The thing is, Al, it's like I said, I don't know what answers we can give her that wouldn't come up in the enquiry anyway. Rockpool will have been thoroughly searched. If there are any drugs, they'll be found. And maybe then someone will admit to having seen Baz take coke. Maybe they already have. We can't know what's going on at the cops' end.'

'It's Rupert,' says Ally. 'That's what I keep coming back to. Why was he killed, the day after Baz died? I know Tallulah doesn't want to think about it, but there must be a connection.'

Jayden glances to the garden door again. 'Yeah, about that. The first answer that springs to mind is . . . revenge. You get that, right?'

'Jayden, Tallulah was nowhere near Rockpool House at the time of the murder. She was walking the coast path. When she got back to the house it was a crime scene and the police took her statement there and then. Her alibi must have been watertight, or she would have been arrested along with everyone else, wouldn't she?'

Jayden has to admit that she would. 'You're sure you're okay with her staying though?'

'Absolutely. Jayden, don't look so worried. If Tallulah is a danger to anyone – and I truly don't think that she is – it's surely the Rockpool guests, not me.'

'Vengeance though. Someone blaming Rupert for Baz's death. The police will be following that line of enquiry, I'm sure of it.'

'So, who cared enough about Baz to kill someone in his name?'

'I just don't think that's Felix.'

'Tallulah was heartbroken,' says Ally. 'But it was her view that no one else there really cared about Baz.'

'What about the other musician, Davey Hart? He's the most obvious connection between Baz and Rupert, right?'

'According to Baz's book, Davey was a lost soul. Problems with drink and drugs over the years. Never found a home with another band.'

'That fits with what Felix said about him too,' says Jayden. 'I wonder how resentful he was of Baz, deep down. Because it was Baz's decision to break up the band. Then Baz enjoys the lion's share of the royalties, because he's credited with writing their big hit single-handedly, isn't he? Meanwhile Davey drifts from session gig to session gig. The version of the song that was used in that TV show a few years back was an acoustic version that only Baz recorded. So, no pay-out for Davey there either.'

'But we're not looking for someone who's resentful of Baz, are we?' says Ally. 'We're looking for someone who cared enough about him to commit murder in response to his death.'

Jayden drums his fingers on the bar. 'Okay. Here's a scenario. Early Friday evening, there's drugs going around. Baz gets involved. Maybe he's encouraged into it, maybe it's all on him. But someone there – maybe someone who knew Baz was too old for that sort of thing or was worried about what it might do, health wise – knew it was a bad idea. So, when Baz suddenly dies, they're lashing out, looking for someone to blame. And, for whatever reason, it's Rupert.'

'Keep going.'

'Well, the question then is why would someone *not* want Baz to die?' says Jayden. 'Beyond the obvious response of a normal human being, I mean. Or, to put it another way, why would they need him to be alive?'

'So *here* you two are.'

And it's Tallulah, placing a hand on each of their shoulders. Her earlier exuberance has dimmed, and her cool blue eyes look bleary; misted.

'Ally,' she says, 'I'm beat. I wonder, could I take your keys and go on ahead, if you wanted to stay on out? Would that be an imposition?'

'Goodness no,' says Ally, 'I'm more than ready to go home.' She looks at her watch. 'I haven't been out this late in years.'

'Al,' says Jayden, tapping her on the arm, 'to be continued.'

~

'I'm so grateful to you for letting me stay here,' says Tallulah, settling against the cushions on the wicker sofa, drawing her silver-threaded pashmina around her.

As they took Porthpella's one and only taxicab down to the dunes, Tallulah was quiet, her face turned to the window, and Ally felt sure she'd want to go straight to bed. But as soon as they walked up the steps and into The Shell House, she found a second wind. As Ally tentatively offered her a mint tea, Tallulah said, *Or something stronger?* And so here they both are, nightcaps in hand.

Ally can feel Fox looking at her quizzically. He's up past his bedtime too.

'Baz really loved Rockpool,' says Tallulah, pressing the tips of her fingers to her eyes. 'I remember his letter when he first bought it, a few months back. He said it nearly took up all his funds, but it was worth it – though I expect the former was an exaggeration. I can't bear to go back there though. Not now.' Tallulah gestures, and her drink tips in her glass. 'This place, Ally. Are there ghosts here for you?'

And Ally's startled by her directness. But isn't it a valid question? When Evie once said she didn't think there was anything left for Ally in Porthpella, maybe that was tantamount to saying, *How can you bear to be here, without Dad?*

But The Shell House is full of a love that can't be lost.

'No,' says Ally. 'I see Bill everywhere. Every day, I see him. But not in a bad way.'

'*See him* see him?' says Tallulah. 'A haunting.'

'No, no. I just picture him here. Doing everyday things around the house. It's a comfort. Well, now it is, anyway.'

'Warren Zevon,' says Tallulah with a sad smile. 'He wrote a hell of a song about something like that.'

She sighs, and Ally feels her heart clench. She can only imagine the swell of memories, of regrets, that Tallulah must be feeling. She never got to have the everyday with Baz.

'As to Rockpool . . . I expect Baz's children will sell it as soon as they can.'

'Do you know anything about Baz's will?' asks Ally.

And the question feels a touch callous, but Ally's in detective mode; she's with a client, even if it doesn't feel like it.

'No idea. He despaired of his family, but he'll have felt duty-bound, I expect. I'm sure Jet and Ruby will be anticipating most of his estate will go to them.' Tallulah pushes her hand to her forehead. 'Ally, it's too surreal that we're having this conversation. I feel like I'm in a waking nightmare. Speaking of . . . I really do need to get to bed. I didn't sleep at all last night.'

Tallulah stands up. She sways a little, but whether it's from fatigue or the effects of the nightcap on top of champagne, Ally can't be sure.

'You're so kind having me here tonight. And I promise it is just one night. Tomorrow I'll find a hotel.'

'You really don't need to, Tallulah.'

'And you and Jayden,' she goes on, 'I know you're a little at sea with this right now. But I trust you. I trust you to work it all out.'

As Tallulah walks towards the back bedroom, putting a hand to the wall to steady herself, Ally feels pressure sitting in the middle of her chest.

She really doesn't want to fail her. Not when Tallulah's already lost so much.

42

Jayden feels like a burglar as his torch beam sweeps the wooden walls of the cabin office. He doesn't want to turn the lights on and make the place shine out like a beacon; he can just imagine Ken getting his neighbourhood-watch vibe on at that.

Jayden was almost asleep when the thought came to him: *The other copy of Baz's book.* The advance proof, made for industry people. When Felix first gave it to him, Jayden had a quick flick, but then he chose to read the hardback instead. He thought he'd handed the other version back to Felix, but can Jayden see the book in his mind's eye, pushed to one side of the counter? If it's still there, then he needs to check something.

Something that could make a difference.

'Aha!'

The book cover jumps out of the darkness and Jayden cuts behind the desk to grab it. He quickly flicks to the end. Then he turns back several pages, making sure there's no way it's been misformatted.

'I knew it.'

But he feels no triumph. Sure, it means Jayden's recall is solid, but it doesn't look good for Felix.

Jayden tucks the book under his arm and locks the cabin.

As he walks back across the yard, the air is warm and silky around him. He looks up to see an almost full moon, just a smudge missing from its right-side outer edge. He doesn't want to go back to bed yet, his head is too full. Up the field is DI Radford and his massive great motorhome. Jayden tries to picture what he might be doing. Fast asleep, resetting after months of shift patterns? Up late with a crime novel? Or, despite his holiday, going over case notes, mind thrumming, just like Jayden's?

Jayden lets himself back inside the cottage. In the kitchen, the bright light is startling. His laptop and the hardback copy of Baz's memoir are on the table: evidence of a hasty departure. He gets the coffee on. *Because that'll wind you down nicely, Weston.* But the fact is, he doesn't want to wind down. He wants to get stuff done.

He checks his phone. He said to Ally to message him if anything occurred to her. *Or if you need me.* Ally sent him a weird look as he said that. It's not that he doesn't like Tallulah but she's basically a stranger, and now she's staying with Ally at The Shell House.

Jayden pours his coffee, adding a half-spoonful of sugar to take the edge off. He uses the 'I Love You Daddy' mug that Jazzy gave him for Father's Day. Every time though, he translates it – *Uv Ooo Dadatz* – and it never fails to make him smile. Then he settles down at the table, the hardback and the paperback proof copy side by side. He flicks through them, checking the chapter openings against one another. Not forensic, but good enough. Because it's all about the epilogue.

And here's the thing: the epilogue in the hardback, the one that was published just yesterday, is about the night that Connie died: Baz's regret; Rupert's role too – implicit, but no less stated. And in the paperback proof copy? There is no epilogue. It doesn't exist. Jayden scans through the rest of the book, looking to see if the text has been inserted elsewhere. But there's no mention of the circumstances leading up to Connie's death at all.

Jayden sits back in his chair.

The proof copy that Felix read months ago, after losing the writing gig, makes no mention of how Connie died, beyond a reference to the crash in an early chapter. There's no description of Baz's heartbreak at the news of her new relationship and how he turned to drink (or drugs, if Tallulah is to be believed). And there's no implication of Rupert's involvement.

So, there's every chance that Felix read this account for the first time on Friday, when it was published. Learning, at the same time as the rest of the world, what really happened the night his mum died.

Which sharpens his motive.

Except . . . Jayden doesn't really think Felix Boyd killed Rupert Frost, does he?

He hears a creak above his head as Cat shifts in bed. Jayden waits to see if she wakes, feeling his absence beside her. When all falls silent again, he opens his laptop.

Beyond Felix, revenge for Baz's death – however it occurred – is the most obvious motive for someone killing Rupert. So, Jayden looks elsewhere.

He taps *Nicole Carson* into Google. She has her own website, though it's not immediately clear what she's selling. There are photos of her in strappy dresses arranged against various backdrops: a terrace at sunset; a yoga pavilion. Jayden clicks on the 'Discovery' tab, and sees dates offered for 'self-discovery retreats', led by 'wellness practitioner Nicole Carson'. There's a range of scented candles, too – at joke prices.

Next, he clicks on 'About'.

> Married to musician Baz Carson for nearly two
> decades, life was a roller coaster of parties,
> touring, late nights, and then, when the babies
> came along, early mornings too. I wanted to

be everything to everyone. But Muse and Homemaker don't exactly fit together. Baz was happy. The kids were happy. But me, the juggler, the plate spinner, mashing carrot one minute then pulling on a latex dress the next? I wasn't happy. And it takes courage to admit that. It's that courage, and dedication to self-betterment, that led me to the Nicole Carson I am today. To paraphrase the immortal words of The Nick . . . I Did It For Myself. Sounds better, doesn't it?

Jayden clicks on another page: a pomegranate-scented candle could be his for £63.

Okay, he thinks, *let's be cynical*. Nicole is trading on Baz's name, but her story wouldn't lose anything if her ex was dead – in fact, it might even enhance the narrative. How could it be a catalyst for killing another man in cold blood, though?

He clicks on her social media, and sees the same message posted to Twitter and Instagram:

The love of my life and the father of my children, Baz Carson, has passed away at the age of seventy. Anguish is not the word. The family asks for privacy at this difficult time.

There are loads of replies, but none she's engaged with. And there's no mention of Rupert's death, although that's no surprise given how quickly the arrests happened afterwards.

Jayden thinks of Saffron, and how he'd love to get her take on the Rockpool guests. But right now, she's still in custody; he's sure she'd have messaged him if she was back home. So as confident as Felix's arrest seemed, the police are clearly being cautious when it comes to the other suspects. By Jayden's reckoning, the twenty-four-hour time limit will be up by midday tomorrow.

Saffron is, once released, their best point of access. Jayden wants to ask her how people responded to Baz's death, and what the dynamic was like with Rupert afterwards. He's especially interested in Jet and Ruby, because wouldn't they have had the most visceral response to their father's death? According to Felix, they both still harboured grudges towards him, despite Baz and Nicole breaking up years ago. An idea lands. Could a grudge be enough to frame Felix for Rupert's death? But it's not easy to frame someone, not beyond initial appearances anyway.

Jayden wishes he knew what evidence led to Felix's arrest. He looks to his phone: Mullins is just a call away. But one, it's the middle of the night, and two, Mullins wouldn't spill the details of a murder case. Three? There's no way Jayden would ask him to.

He can't get near anything or anyone solid.

It was only after they moved to Cornwall, and everything with the Lewis Pascoe case, that Jayden told Cat he'd been thinking of going for detective back in Leeds. How on the day Kieran died, Jayden had shared his plans and his buddy had said, *You'll smash it, bro.* Jayden had been quietly building up a portfolio, showing skills that'd confirm him as detective material: research, interviewing, the gathering and presentation of evidence. He'd been eying an attachment with CDI, maybe even in DI Radford's division. But all that fell away when Kieran died, and he and Cat left Yorkshire. Jayden thought any kind of police work was behind him. But the day they found Lewis on the beach, and he saw that look on Ally Bright's face, something was reawakened.

Maybe DI Radford will rib him about the Shell House Detectives, think it's all stolen camper vans and surf-comp cheaters, even if he's heard about Helena Hunter and JP Sharpe. Though what does Jayden care? He knows better. But with this murder investigation unfolding just steps away from his house, he feels every bit the outsider. While he enjoys that a lot of the time – it means he's free of so many of the things that frustrated him about the police – the fact is that when it comes to cracking a case, their resources are limited. He hasn't got a network of buddies – head-scratching detectives and world-weary pathologists – that he can tap for information. And even if he did, if he convinced himself that he was putting the Greater Good before due process, would these experts break confidentiality? Not likely.

No, Jayden has Ally. Together, they have their wits. And tomorrow, if they're lucky, they'll have Saffron. But that's about it.

And, this time, it doesn't feel like nearly enough.

On that thought, Jayden claps his laptop shut and reluctantly makes for bed. He doubts he'll sleep, because the question that'll be whirring through his mind is this: should he tell the police what he's discovered about the epilogue? Maybe it's having DI Radford here, but he feels more compelled than ever to play by the rules – even if he's not in the game anymore. PC Weston would 100 per cent be phoning through that evidence. And noting the discovery of it in his wannabe detective portfolio too.

43

Saffron stands outside the police station, vowing never to take the outside world for granted again. The early morning sky is already a true blue, and the sun feels golden on her face. She can't hear the sea from here, but she can in her mind. As soon as she's back in Porthpella she's going to hit the water.

But before that? Coffee. *Good* coffee.

When an officer came to her cell telling her she was going to be released, Saffron imagined they all were; like closing time in a pub, everyone tipped out on to the street at the same time. But as far as she can see, it's just her. Well, cool. With a bit of luck, she'll have time to get back to Rockpool House, grab her things without seeing anyone, and leave the place behind her for good.

The guy on the front desk said there was a bus stop at the end of the road, and although she has her wallet and phone back, he gave her a free ticket. Newquay to Porthpella by bus though? That's going to be at least an hour. Probably two, if it stops everywhere along the way. She wants to get back to Hang Ten, to Broady, to days where the only stress is whether she either over- or under-bakes the brownies (who's she kidding? They're always perfect). And she wants it all as soon as possible.

So, train it is.

Saffron's just stepping off the pavement when a patrol car appears out of nowhere and comes to a showy stop in front of her. The window flies down.

'Alright, Saff?'

'Jeez, Mullins. What is this?'

'Your limo awaits. Jump in.'

'You're giving me a lift?'

'I heard you were getting out.' He winks. 'What did they give you, bus ticket? You obviously didn't pass the attitude test.'

'Attitude test?'

'If they like you, you get a lift. If they don't, they palm you off with a ticket.'

Saffron rolls her eyes. 'Or maybe they've got better things to do than play taxi service?'

'What, the custody lot? Not exactly the coalface, Saff. Nah, they probably heard you complaining about the coffee. Snob.'

Even hearing the word *coffee* makes her salivate. She goes round to the passenger side, but Mullins hollers out. 'Jump in the back.'

'Seriously? You're going to make me go in the back?'

'Rules are rules. And I'll do several laps of Porthpella just so everyone can see.'

Maybe the train would be a better bet.

Inside the car she looks around at the scuffed interior, her memory flashing back to the arrests, the deaths. A queasy feeling hits her, and she closes her eyes. But then she catches the scent of something. She opens her eyes.

Mullins is twisted in his seat, holding a coffee cup out.

'Newquay's finest, apparently. I googled it.'

'Oh, Mullins. I think I love you.'

'Yeah, yeah. I'll be billing you after. There's a croissant-type thing in the bag as well.'

'No, I really do. I love you.'

He turns back to the wheel. The tips of his ears are burning red. Saffron smiles as she takes the first sip, followed by a bite of butter-soft pastry. She closes her eyes.

'Home?' says Mullins.

'Home,' agrees Saffron.

~

Not quite home, but to Rockpool. With the house emptied, only a couple of die-hard journalists are still at the gates. They turn cameras on the car as they approach, and Saffron dips her head; slides down her shades. Mullins taps in a code, and as the gates part, the car glides through.

'I like doing that,' he says, eyes on the rear-view mirror.

'Power trip?'

'They're like Mum's rabbits though. Leave the hutch open for a second and one of them'll shoot out. Cheeky blighters.'

'With you around? They wouldn't dare.'

They pull up in front of the house.

'I'll be quick,' she says. But doesn't move.

'There's no rush, mate. The main house has been cleared. It's just the cottage and pool that are still cordoned off.' He swivels in his seat. 'Want me to go in too?'

'Yeah, I do actually.' She chews her lip. 'I keep playing it over in my head, Mullins.'

'Which bit? The bit where you pulled Baz from the pool and gave him CPR? Or the bit where Davey ran in screaming for help and then you found Rupert covered in blood?' Mullins rubs his chin. 'Or before. Rupert being a creep. That bit.'

'You know about that?' She puffs out air. 'It's a lot, right?'

'It's a lot. Don't blame you for feeling freaked, mate.'

'But the bit I can't get out of my head . . . it's the knife. Skinner was asking me whether I noticed if one was missing from the kitchen. I mean . . . I brought my own knives, but I do remember there was a knife block. A tatty-looking one, but then nothing in that kitchen was very swanky. And it wasn't full. In fact, it was practically empty. If anything, it wasn't that one knife was missing, it was all of them.'

'This is a lot of thinking about knives, Saff. You're not responsible for hiding sharp objects. And anyway, it's not about where it came from, it's about what it was used for. And where it ended up after. Alright?'

Saffron looks through the window, down towards the cool blue of the pool and the white stone cottage with its potted palms by the door. Police tape criss-crosses it all.

'I've just got this horrible feeling I could have stopped it.'

'Like how? If you mean Baz, he was probably dead by the time he hit the water. Not many people survive a cardiac arrest, Saff. As for Rupert . . . Felix Boyd was on the property for less than an hour. Slinking about with his long hair, acting like the grieving friend of the family. And you spoke to him for all of five minutes. There's no way you could have guessed what he was up to.'

She nods. She knows Mullins is trying to help.

'Is Felix being charged?'

'Any minute now,' says Mullins. 'Robinson reckons they've got enough evidence. I probably shouldn't be telling you that, by the way.'

'I just can't believe it. He was so . . . normal.'

'Master of disguise. Nutter pretending to be a nice guy.' Mullins scratches his nose. 'Anyway look, we'd best bust a groove. I'll be needed back at the station.'

'Sure, sorry. Let's get this over with.'

And they're out, slamming doors, walking towards the bright-white house. Saffron feels nerves prickle in her stomach. But why? There's no one here but them. Nevertheless, she's glad of Mullins beside her, scuffing through the gravel.

She puts the key in the door – the key Baz gave her when she arrived on Friday – but it won't turn. She tries the door handle, and it swings open.

'Not locked,' she says, turning to Mullins, her eyes wide.

'Tallulah Pearce, maybe?'

'Oh yeah, of course.' Saffron had forgotten all about Tallulah, assuming she'd been arrested along with all of them. 'And you said Imogen's dad came to pick her up, right?'

'Yeah. He turned up fuming, apparently. Uptight guy in a Ralph Lauren polo shirt. Didn't love his daughter and wife being questioned over a murder. Whisked her straight back to Surrey, probably.'

Inside the cavernous hallway, the house is still. The crystal chandelier glitters in the sunlight from the wide windows. Their feet squeak on the polished granite floors.

'Hello?' Mullins calls out.

No answer.

'My stuff's in the attic,' she whispers.

'Go on then. I'll wait here.'

Saffron runs up the stairs, taking them two at a time. *In and out.* Grab her few things from the room, then straight to the kitchen to get her apron and knife set. *If it's still there*, the voice in her head chips in. Or should she do a proper clear-up? She wonders if everything is as she left it: half-chopped, wilted veggies. Plus, the fridge is full of food that'll probably never be cooked now. What a waste. Maybe she should leave a note, in case any of the others are staying tonight, and they want to throw something quick together. She feels a thud of indecision. But Mullins needs to get back, and Saffron really doesn't want to stay here without him. Maybe, for once in her life, she can leave a job half done – and try not to care.

Saffron's mind is full of this as she's rounding the top of the landing. Head down, she barrels straight into someone coming from the other direction. She throws up her arms and screams.

'Who the hell are you?' a man screams back.

44

Ally sits quietly on the veranda, coffee cup in hand. Fox is nosing about among the snapdragons. There's not a whisper of wind nor the slightest swell. A lone paddleboarder, perhaps the same one as yesterday, strokes silently across the bay. Tallulah is yet to emerge from her room, and the last thing Ally wants to do is disturb her sleep. Besides, Ally is quite grateful for this pocket of still morning.

Fox, too, is finding another presence in the house a little hard to fathom. He keeps going to the door of the guest bedroom, sending an enquiring look in Ally's direction. Tallulah and Fox haven't exactly hit it off. Ally's little dog is sensitive to indifference, and Tallulah has too much on her plate to pay him much attention.

Can they help Tallulah at all? That's the question that Ally went to bed with, and it's the question that's risen with her this morning too. She thinks Jayden was probably right when he said he didn't know what answers they can give her. That it's the solving of Rupert's murder that's likely to shed light on Baz's death; or at least somebody's reaction to that death, if not the incident itself. And they've got nothing.

Perhaps Gus is right: Baz was a wild child, even at seventy. Even with his talk of clean living. But Tallulah – Tallulah, who knew Baz far better than anyone else – had such a virulent reaction to that suggestion. Ally felt quite sorry for Gus at the time. *He didn't seem himself all evening*, she thinks. Perhaps he was a little awed by the presence of Tallulah; after all, anyone connected with The Nick is sprinkled with a little stardust, as far as Gus is concerned. She must send him a message and thank him for coming to the show. And thank him again for the flowers, too. The flowers that are in a vase on her bedside table: she saw them as she woke up, her first smile of the day down to Gus.

Ally's phone buzzes with a message. It's Jayden.

Morning Al. You okay? So I've just told the police something that doesn't help Felix's case. Alright if I drop by?

She replies instantly: I'll get the coffee on!

The dots appear as he replies, and then they disappear again. If he's driving, he'll be here in no time at all. Ally puts her phone down. Should she tap on Tallulah's door and offer her breakfast, or let the natural sounds of Jayden's arrival drift through? She decides the latter. But Ally's ready for Tallulah when she does emerge. She's picked a small bouquet of wildflowers and set them in a jam pot; she'll prepare her a breakfast tray and then give her whatever space she needs. With Bill, it was only when the initial shock of his death ebbed that true grief flowed in.

Moments later, Jayden's swinging through the gate. Fox darts to meet him, planting his paws on Jayden's knees as he crouches to fuss him. When he looks up at Ally, his face wears a heavy expression.

'Middle-of-the-night brainwave,' he says. 'Wish I hadn't. Is Tallulah up?'

'Not yet.'

As they settle on the veranda, Jayden tells Ally what he's discovered about the proof copy and the missing epilogue; how the version of the story Felix read months ago contained nothing about the night of Connie's death.

It sounds an awful lot like motive to Ally.

'I know,' agrees Jayden. 'It wouldn't be enough, not on its own, but if there was something physical to connect Felix to the scene, or a witness, then that'd explain the showy arrest.'

'So, the police know about the difference between the books?'

'No way of telling. But the bit that's bugging me is that Felix didn't mention it. I mean, we talked about the memoir together, and he was kind of casual about it. I'm alright at reading people . . .'

'You're brilliant at reading people, Jayden.'

'Well, it makes me think that Felix had only seen the version without the epilogue at that point. What if he flicked through the final published version and spotted the epilogue later that night? Or a friend messaged him about it? It'd only been out one day, right? It was hot off the press.'

'Tell me again how you ended up with the two copies.'

And Jayden does. Ally listens, brow wrinkled.

'Well, the only thing that strikes me is that if Felix was aware of the difference between the two editions, and it was a problem for him – enough of a problem to make him want to blame Rupert – then it seems unlikely that he'd bring them both to you.'

Jayden slowly nods. 'Yeah, okay. Agreed.'

'Especially knowing you're a detective. So perhaps he had no idea about it.'

'Or he did, but he'd already made his peace with it. I hope the police are doing the same thinking.' Jayden rubs his face with both hands. 'I was the one that he contacted from custody, Al. He wanted to tell me he was innocent. Phoning the police with this, I feel . . . I don't know.'

'You did the right thing telling them. And if it's nothing, then Felix will explain.'

'I wish we knew what else they've got. We're just clutching at straws, otherwise. They must have some other evidence, right?'

He sounds so disconsolate. 'You did the right thing,' she says again.

They both turn at the sound of footfall, and Tallulah's there, in a pair of white silk pyjamas. Her cheekbones shimmer, and as she comes closer Ally catches a fresh and floral scent. For all her brave face, she looks hollowed-out. Her eyes distant.

'Good morning,' Ally says, encouragingly.

'Good morning,' echoes Tallulah softly. 'Ally, I slept like a baby. Against all odds. It's this place. Your kindness.' She sweeps her hand. 'And I woke up this morning with the most extraordinary sense of conviction.'

Ally sees Tallulah look to Jayden and then back to her.

'All I want,' she says, 'is for Baz's name to be cleared. For the right story to be told. Which means someone taking responsibility for what happened to him.' She leans against the wooden balustrade, crosses her ankles. 'I don't want the police involved. No one needs to go to prison. That's not what this is about. Ally, I want to settle this privately. I just want to know what happened. Nothing more. That's why it's you pair that I came to.'

Jayden looks hesitant. 'But if there *is* anything untoward – which is pretty much unprovable unless someone admits it, or witnessed it – it could be deemed manslaughter, Tallulah. That's a prison sentence.'

'What matters,' she says, 'is the truth. You more or less said it – that Baz's death couldn't have been planned. I can see that now. I was . . . overreacting. There is, what, a million-to-one chance that taking cocaine might result in a cardiac arrest?'

'Regular usage is known to increase risks of heart problems,' says Jayden.

'What I'm saying is that I'm not seeking to blame anyone.' Her eyes fill. 'I just want to know what really happened to Baz. That's all. Blame won't bring him back. I just want to know the truth. For myself.'

'We understand,' says Ally. And she looks to Jayden. For all his natural compassion, she can't help feeling he's pushing Tallulah a little.

'So, it isn't about his legacy?' says Jayden. 'That's what you said before, and—'

Tallulah presses a hand to her forehead, cuts in: 'I sure can tell your friend used to be a cop, Ally. I feel like I'm the one under investigation here.'

'It's about how we approach it,' says Ally, in what she hopes is a reassuring voice. 'And what's possible. That's what you're working out, isn't it, Jayden?'

Jayden nods. 'That's it. Right now, we've got no access to any of the suspects. But that's going to change. By midday, it'll be twenty-four hours since those arrests were made. They'll only be able to extend that under certain circumstances.'

'So you're saying they'll all be back at Rockpool?' says Tallulah.

'They'll be free to go,' says Jayden. 'Maybe under certain restrictions though. It depends. Whether they'll return to Rockpool or not will be down to what those are. If it was me, I wouldn't stick around. I'd get the hell away.'

'But their belongings are still in the house, aren't they?' says Ally. 'They'll need to go back to collect them?'

'They sure will,' says Tallulah. 'And that's our moment. Isn't it?'

'Tallulah, even if we succeeded in getting the full story, essentially a confession, it wouldn't be admissible.'

'In court? I told you, I don't need that.' Tallulah looks at her watch. 'It's just past nine. That gives us less than three hours to make a plan. I just need to know for my own sanity, that's all. No police. No recrimination. Just . . . truth for truth's sake.'

With that, she lifts herself from the balustrade and goes back inside the house.

Jayden turns to Ally, eyebrows raised. 'Truth for truth's sake,' he repeats. Then, 'Do you believe her, Al?'

45

'Sorry he scared you, Saffron.' Imogen peers up at them through her fringe. 'But to be fair, I think you scared him too. I've never heard Daddy scream like that.'

'I didn't scream, darling,' says Adrian Edwards. 'I shouted. Distinct difference.'

'Alright,' says Mullins, 'let's calm it down.'

Although everyone's fairly calm. They are now, anyway. As soon as Saffron and this man collided, Imogen came bursting out of one of the bedrooms. *Dad, it's only Saffron! Saffron, it's only my dad!* And Mullins, who was puffing like a dragon by the time he got to the top of the stairs, manhandled the bloke that little bit more carefully as he said, *Get off her.* Still breathing fire, mind.

Mullins looks at Adrian Edwards now. The guy's patting down his hair, still righting himself after that silly scream.

'My daughter has had enough shocks already without the two of you barging in here unannounced.'

'Saffron works here,' says Mullins. 'And she's staying here too.'

'It was you who was shocked, Dad,' chips in Imogen.

'It's all good,' says Saffron. 'I'm just here to get my things.' She looks to Imogen. 'Are you doing okay?'

'She'll be a damn sight better when she has her mother back,' says Adrian. 'Absolute debacle. It's one thing taking a statement, quite another taking her into custody. But keeping her overnight? That's overstepping the mark.'

Mullins can't put his finger on whether this is a man who enrages easily, no matter what lights his wick, or only under certain circumstances.

'This is a murder investigation,' says Mullins. 'So it's no stone left unturned.'

'Your mum will be home soon,' says Saffron to Imogen. 'She's just helping out the police, like we all did.'

'Did you stay here last night?' Mullins asks Adrian.

'They said it was fine,' he says quickly. 'The house isn't out of bounds.'

'Didn't say it was,' says Mullins. 'You weren't invited to the party then, sir?'

'Not my scene.'

'Grandad Baz wasn't the biggest fan of Daddy,' says Imogen.

'The feeling's mutual there, darling. And this latest incident with Baz – well, this final one – is indicative of why a leopard can't change its spots. Though by God they'll want to tell you all the ways they have, a hundred times over.'

'I know people who've turned their life around,' says Saffron. 'Anyone can change.'

'I agree with Saffron,' says Imogen.

Adrian shrugs. 'Pleasant as this is, I suspect we all need to get on. Don't you have a murderer to catch, Constable?'

Mullins doesn't like his tone. 'We're close there, as it happens.'

Very close.

Late last night DS Chang uncovered a motive that, with the cast-iron means and opportunity, makes Felix Boyd look like a slam dunk. That's why Mullins didn't feel too bad telling Saffron, as it'd be announced in no time. Chang had been combing through reviews of Baz's book online, and came across one that drew attention to 'a

230

late addition – or, more likely, a last-gasp assertion of conscience'. The epilogue, the one all about what happened the night Connie Boyd died, wasn't included in the early version of the book that went out to journalists. It was added later, only showing up in the published version, and this reviewer had spotted the difference.

Despite Felix saying he'd always known what had happened with his mum, there was no one to prove that. So, DS Chang put it to him that just two days ago he learnt the full truth about her death – and, by Saturday morning, Rupert was the only person left alive to blame.

It was enough to get DCI Robinson licking his chops, saying, *Get the CPS on speed dial.* Skinner was the only person in the team who didn't look convinced that they were ready to charge him. But the way Mullins sees it, that's force politics. Skinner has never liked someone else getting the limelight. It was DS Chang who dug up the good stuff (even if Jayden phoned through the exact same observation hours later – what is this, bookworm central?). Either way, zero points for his grumpy boss.

Now, Mullins narrows his eyes. 'You don't seem very cut up about Rupert's death, Mr Edwards.'

'Perceptive of you,' says Adrian.

'What was your relationship with the deceased like?'

'I was teeing off just as Rupert was breathing his last. Richmond Golf Club. Threesome with Michael Pendleton and Jeff Sutton.'

Mullins smirks and shoots a glance at Saffron. *Threesome.* Then he straightens his face. 'I wasn't asking for an alibi.'

'Dotting Is and crossing Ts,' says Adrian, with a smirk of his own. 'Anyway, I've heard the latest. The new arrest. A showy affair, by all accounts, so presumably you've got your man. Now if you'll excuse me, my daughter and I—'

Imogen cuts in suddenly, looking to Saffron and Mullins. 'Can I tell you about something I found in Grandad's room?'

'Oh, for goodness' sake, Imogen. I told you to go nowhere near—'

'Wait, I'll get it. It's not *drugs* or anything.'

And it won't be. A thorough search has taken place. There's nothing of interest left in this house; there wasn't anything of interest in it before, either. No drugs stash or bundles of bloodied clothing; nothing that would give the investigation team the smallest thing to go on.

'I'll be two seconds,' Imogen calls over her shoulder.

Moments later she's back, carrying a box. She plonks it at their feet and draws out a string of bunting. Adrian huffs and puffs in the background as Mullins picks out the letters A, P, P, Y, B.

'It's party stuff,' says Imogen. 'That's a birthday banner. And there's balloons too. A bag of party poppers. It was under his bed.'

'Okay,' says Mullins, a tad confused. 'Well, you were here for a party.'

Saffron crouches down by the box. She pulls out a silver packet of helium balloons, a number seven and a big glittery zero.

'Don't you think it's sad?' says Imogen.

'I think it's really sad,' says Saffron quietly.

And Mullins feels it too, then. When you get to seventy, someone else is supposed to throw you a party. You don't buy your own balloons. You don't hang your own banner. When Grandad Jack turned seventy – it was his last big birthday, though they didn't know it at the time – Mullins got his felt-tips out and made a whopping great poster for the hall. It was decent, too, better than anything he scratched out in Art at school. His mum made a mountain of sandwiches, cut in posh triangles. There were gold and silver balloons (though Grandad Jack would probably have preferred black and white, for Kernow). The important thing was that the birthday boy didn't lift a finger; just pint after pint of Doom Bar.

'I think we should put these up,' says Imogen. 'For Grandad Baz.'

'Oh, for goodness' sake,' her dad says again.

And maybe the guy's got a point. Grandad Jack's wake was down The Wreckers, and it was a right knees-up, but there would have been a few raised eyebrows if they'd got the jukebox going before the funeral.

Imogen holds up a packet of jumbo sparklers. 'Grandad Baz got us all here for a party. And, okay, it's all gone very wrong, but I think he'd still want us to have that party. And Rupert would want it too. I think once everyone's back here, we should make it happen.'

'Everyone apart from the stone-cold killer, you mean?' says her dad. 'No invite for him? Imogen, I've heard some ideas in my time. As soon as your mother is free of this ridiculous charade it's home to Teddington, no horses spared.'

Imogen hangs her head. And she looks so sad that Mullins finds himself saying, 'I reckon it's a great idea, Imogen. And I bet you anything your Granny Nicole will agree.'

46

'Okay let's head to Hang Ten,' says Jayden, jumping into gear. 'As soon as Saffron is out, she's going to be messaging Broady.'

Ally hesitates. 'What about Tallulah? I'm not sure about leaving her.'

'Can't Fox keep her company?'

'Fox is being a little stand-offish, truth be told. Give me two minutes.'

And at that she zips back inside.

Jayden bounces on his heels and the boards of the veranda creak. He's eager to be off. Eager to get this plan rolling, whatever this plan might be. The only thing that's clear is that Saffron is their best hope. Just then Jayden's phone bleats with a message. He pulls it out of his pocket, hoping there's no problem at the campsite, that this free day of his isn't going to disappear before it's started.

But it's Saffron.

I'm out!

Ally comes back out at that exact moment, and he holds up the phone jubilantly.

'Thank goodness,' she says.

The phone buzzes again and he grins as he reads her message.

'Don't you love serendipity, Al?' he says.

'She's at Hang Ten?'

'She's at Hang Ten.'

At that, they head up and over the dunes, Fox hurtling ahead, sand flying.

~

Saffron's on the bench outside the coffee shop, Broady beside her. She holds up her glass, a bright yellow smoothie.

'Mango, coconut and chia seeds. Want one?'

Jayden would love one.

'I'll make it, mate. They're my new speciality,' says Broady, jumping up. 'Ally, for you too?'

Ally says no thanks and goes to Saffron; gives her a hug.

'Broady's been amazing,' she says. 'When he's not coaching, he's been here, getting under Jodie's feet. But the customers love him.' She blows out air between her lips. 'Crazy few days, huh?'

'How are you doing?' says Jayden.

'Me? I'm great.' Saffron squats to stroke Fox; runs his ears through her fingers. 'I mean, how can I complain?'

'Don't you want to go home, catch up on some sleep?' says Jayden.

'I had to come here; check it's still standing. Talking of, did you hear a storm's coming?'

'Cliff said that too. Doesn't feel like it though, does it? Maybe it'll blow by.'

'I don't know,' says Ally, 'it's starting to feel muggy.'

Saffron wrinkles her nose. 'I guess you're not here to talk about the weather . . . I've got to ask, is this a Shell House thing?'

Jayden looks to Ally. 'Where shall we start?'

'Saffron, the other guests from Rockpool, have they been let out too?'

Saffron shakes her head. 'I don't think so. But they will be soon, right?'

'Twenty-four hours,' says Jayden. 'So, we've got less than three. Saffron, have you been back to Rockpool yet?'

'Just to get my stuff. And I can safely say I'm never going back.'

Jayden chews his lip. 'Yeah, about that,' he says.

Just then, a couple of customers spill out on to the deck and lean on the balustrade with their coffees. One has a laptop bag swinging from his shoulder, another a camera case. They're talking about the hot weather, but it's obvious they're not in Porthpella for the beach.

'Walk and talk?' says Jayden.

On cue, Broady appears with the smoothie and tops up Saffron's while he's at it. She kisses his cheek and says, 'We're just heading out for a quick walk.'

'Take it easy though, okay babe?'

Jayden's glad to see his concern, because there was a time when Broady was a lot more casual in his affection. Since the JP Sharpe case at Christmas, Jayden's felt a little bit protective of Saffron. He can't help wondering if they're trespassing on her good nature, asking her to get involved in something she's trying to put behind her.

But Ally's straight in, telling Saffron how they've taken the case for Tallulah.

'She bought up Ally's whole show,' says Jayden. 'Called it a down payment.'

'Say what?' sings Saffron. 'That's nuts. Brilliant, but nuts.'

Ally looks a little embarrassed. 'It's got nothing to do with us taking the case though.'

'No, I get it. It's a sad story. Super-sad. Of course you want to help her, but . . . they're saying no suspicious circumstances with Baz's death. Hey, can we sit? I suddenly feel like I'm going to drop.'

They settle in the sugar-white sand. All around them, the heat's already pumping, no clouds in the sky yet. Days like this, Cornwall feels tropical. With the full sun and turquoise sea, Jayden thinks of Maracas Bay, where he used to holiday as a kid. Maybe Saffron, who spent the start of last winter in Sri Lanka, looks out and thinks of Ahangama. Maybe that's where she wishes she is now. She sits with her legs crossed, her elbows on her knees, and her eyes are tired, faraway. Ally's watching her, her face concerned.

'Tallulah says she just wants to understand what happened. And she thinks someone knows more than they're saying,' says Ally.

'What, so she thinks it's dodgy?'

'She's certain that Baz wouldn't have taken drugs. She's not looking to blame anyone, she just wants the truth.'

Saffron hesitates. 'Yeah, okay. I guess if one of the Rockpool lot was doing drugs with Baz then they wouldn't necessarily admit that to the police, would they? Not if they didn't have to.'

'After he was discovered in the pool,' says Jayden, 'that same person could have put two and two together. Disposed of the drugs. There'd be nothing to link them, evidence wise.'

'And what about Rupert Frost?'

'Yeah, well, Tallulah's quite single-minded, isn't she, Al? It's all about Baz for her. And that's what she's hired us for. Which is, erm, lucky I guess, as we can't get anywhere near the Rupert Frost case.' And he can taste his own frustration as he says it.

'But Jayden thinks Rupert's death is connected to Baz's,' says Ally. 'That whoever killed Rupert might have been avenging Baz.'

'Which would probably make that same person less likely to admit they knew anything more about Baz's death,' says Jayden. 'So, my theory doesn't help Tallulah in the short term.'

'Mullins let slip about Felix Boyd,' says Saffron. 'He's about to be charged.'

Jayden's jaw drops. 'Charged for Rupert's murder?'

It's not that he's Team Felix. But . . . yeah, okay, he's Team Felix. Because nothing about the guy suggested he was capable of cold-blooded murder.

'They must have something really concrete,' he says. 'The motive around the night his mother died isn't enough for a charge, let alone a conviction. No way.'

'I think they've got the murder weapon,' says Saffron. 'No one said, but . . . I kind of read between the lines.'

Jayden sinks back in the sand with a depth of emotion that surprises himself.

Is that it? They've got the murder weapon?

Could Felix Boyd really have stabbed someone to death? An argument getting out of hand; a push, a shove, an accidental death. That's one thing. But deliberately setting out to stab someone on a Saturday morning? A whole other level.

Jayden hates not having all the facts. He wants the board in the incident room. He wants the briefings, everyone gathered round, sharing what they know. He wants, suddenly, to be part of the machinery of getting things done. Not sitting on a beach with Ally and Saffron, trying to hold someone accountable for a man's cardiac arrest.

'Jayden,' says Ally carefully, 'if they do have their man in Felix, it makes it seem more likely that one of the others might speak freely about what happened to Baz. Once they're released.'

And she's right. Jayden should focus on what they have, not what they haven't. Shouldn't he?

He sucks in a deep breath. 'Saffron, the thing is, we've only got this window to try and get Tallulah some kind of truth. When the others are released – which will be round about now, probably, if Felix has been charged – then they'll be going back to Rockpool just like you did, right? Even if they're getting out of Dodge straight after.'

'Well, if Imogen has her way, they might not be heading off quite so quickly,' says Saffron, draining the last of her smoothie. 'She wants them to have a party. And flipping Mullins told her he thought it was a good idea.'

Jayden and Ally look to each other. A ripple of possibility runs between them.

47

Saffron sits with her chin cupped in her hands, eyes on the tide. With the predicted turn in the weather, there's finally a decent swell forecast for tomorrow, but she'll take what she can today; just paddle out and bob in the blue. If Hang Ten is her Happy Place, then the water is her Everything Place. She can't pretend to only feel the good vibes out there: adrenalin rocketing through her as she pops up on the sheer face of a wave; deep-water hold-downs that make fear scrabble in her chest; total out-of-body elation. It's where she goes to lose herself. To find nothing but the moment and her own place in it.

And it's what she needs now: the cool kiss of the sea.

'Guys . . . I'm sorry. I just don't think I can do it.'

And because Ally and Jayden are Ally and Jayden, they understand. Which only makes it worse.

It was bad enough going back to grab her stuff – and she could have done without the fright from Imogen's dad on top. The girl asked the same thing of her: *Please say you'll stay and cook for the party, Saffron?* But her dad shut it down, saying there would be no party. So, Saffron gave Imogen a hug, wished her well – she felt weirdly teary doing this – and then booted off with Mullins in the patrol car.

'I'm going to send Nicole a message saying I've left, and that I'll give back the fee Baz paid me if she tells me where to send it. Or donate it to charity. Whatever they want.'

She feels strange being paid for any of it, given the circumstances. And all the food was pre-paid for by Baz, so she won't be massively out of pocket.

'Have you sent the email yet?' asks Ally.

'Erm, not yet. But I told Imogen I was going to.'

And the girl was gutted.

'Look, no pressure,' says Jayden. 'No pressure at all. But if you decided you were up for it, we'd be right there with you, Saffron. It wouldn't be like before.'

'What, you're promising no more deaths? Well, that's good. Because that's a clincher.'

'I'd be your sous-chef,' says Jayden. 'I wouldn't leave your side.'

'So how would you do any detective work if you were stuck in the kitchen as my minion, huh?'

And she knows this lightness makes her sound as if she's willing.

'Ally,' says Jayden. 'Ally would be circulating. She'd look like she's topping up glasses and dishing out canapés, but she'd be all eyes and ears.'

'I think you'd be far more effective at mingling than me, Jayden,' says Ally.

'Toss you for it,' he says.

Saffron scoops a handful of sand; lets it run through her fingers. 'You guys really have it all worked out, don't you?'

Jayden laughs. 'Yeah, no. Not at all. But if there's a party then that's a way in. Well, it could be.'

'I think it's believable that you might want to bring in reinforcements, if this is to be the party that Baz originally wanted,' says Ally. 'I'm amazed you were ever doing it all on your own.'

And Saffron agrees with her there. 'And what will Tallulah be doing?' she asks.

'Yeah, we haven't figured out that bit. Or if she'll even want to come,' says Jayden.

'If she talks to people, if she's honest about what it means to her, they're more likely to open up, aren't they?' says Saffron. 'Respond to a genuine emotional appeal, rather than you two basically being . . . nosy staff.'

Ally nods. 'You're right. She'd agree, I'm sure. Look Saffron, anyone would be feeling reluctant in your shoes. They really would. Why don't you explain to the Carsons that you're not able to cater the party yourself, but you have some friends who can step in?'

Jayden laughs. 'Nice, Al. But much as I love a bit of cheffing – and Jazzy's a big fan of my omelettes – I don't have Saffron-level skills. No way. We'd be rumbled.'

'What if Saffron prepared the food at home and we simply heated it up and served it?'

Heated it up? Saffron thinks of the menu she'd planned. She was looking forward to this fire-pit feast. A huge paella with shellfish and monkfish. Garden salads dancing with colour. Roasted pineapple and coconut ice cream.

Saffron takes a deep breath. 'You two really want to help Tallulah find the truth, don't you?'

Ally nods. 'Yes. Very much.'

'And you do too?' she asks Jayden.

'She flew all the way here to see her long-lost lover,' says Jayden. 'And he dies before they get more than five minutes together. If we can help her in any way then, yeah, I want to. And I agree with you, Saffron. If this plan is going to work, then Tallulah needs to be in on it too.'

Saffron shakes her head. 'We don't even know for sure if the others are being released.'

'Twenty-four hours is almost up. And they've got Felix's fingerprints on a murder weapon. They'll be released.' Jayden's face looks pained as he says it.

'And Imogen's mum might think a party is the worst idea ever,' says Saffron. 'They all might.'

'Yeah, there's a lot of moving parts to this plan,' says Jayden. Then he corrects himself: 'This *possible* plan.'

And it's the lack of assumption that seals it. Saffron stands up. She looks to that true blue horizon. It'll be there waiting for her; it always is.

'Alright,' she says, trying to ignore the prickle of foreboding in her chest, 'count me in.'

48

Ally finds Tallulah on the veranda, an envelope of photographs in her lap. She sits down beside her, and Tallulah passes her a picture. It's a young Baz lounging bare-chested in a hammock, a guitar held lazily in his arms. Dense canopies behind him, as if he's in a treehouse.

'My place in Topanga.' Tallulah touches the tip of her finger to Baz's smile. 'But he wanted the lights. That was who Baz was then, or who he was becoming.' She dips her head. 'Now though? He'd come full circle – back to where I was. We fitted together again.'

She looks to Ally, her eyes shining with tears.

'I have so many letters from him from these last few years. Tender, intimate, honest letters. He was so wrapped up in Connie for so long, but after she died . . . we found one another again.'

'Tallulah,' says Ally gently, 'we have a plan forming. But we'll need your help.'

Ally explains – while also mentioning the uncertainties. Tallulah looks faintly taken aback.

'But I thought hiring you meant that you got the answers.'

'This isn't like our other investigations. We think, in these circumstances, it'll come down to trust, whether we get to the truth or not. Questions coming from you will seem natural. From us, it'll look like prying. Prying when, to all intents and purposes, a case is closed.'

'But I don't know if I can hold it together, being up there. With all of them.'

'It might involve a little bit of . . . faking it.'

Fake it till you make it. Jayden's line, for whenever Ally finds herself hesitating, or thinking she hasn't got the confidence to pull something off.

'Tallulah, if you stay away from Rockpool but the other guests know you're still in the area, then they'll suspect you want something still. Maybe even that you distrust the police's verdict.'

'Damn right I distrust the verdict.'

'But that won't help us get to the truth. Isn't it better to come across as someone who wants to remember Baz with the people that mattered to him? Who's with them, not against them?'

'He's not in the ground, Ally. This isn't a wake. This is a bunch of people who want to throw a party at a dead man's expense. In his house.'

'It's a little girl wanting to give her grandad what he wanted. And . . . a prime opportunity to slow down the inevitable departure of everyone else, so we can find out what really happened. As far as anyone is concerned, Baz's death was a tragic accident, and Rupert's murderer has been near-enough caught. It's perfectly plausible that you'd come back, under those circumstances. Come back and want . . . connection. Conversation. To express your condolences. Because whatever you think of them, and whatever you think Baz thought of them, they are his family.'

Tallulah slowly slides her pictures back inside the envelope.

'But I don't feel like that, Ally. I feel entirely separate from them. I feel all alone.'

Ally reaches for her hand. 'You're not alone.'

For a moment, they sit in quietness. A bumblebee bumps its way along the veranda. A single gull goes screeching overhead.

'Fake it, huh? Well, I guess I have lived in LA my whole life. Maybe I can pull it off.' Then, 'I packed the most fabulous dress. For the birthday night. You think I should wear it?'

'I think you should wear it,' says Ally.

'I'm going to be so damn radiant,' says Tallulah, 'they won't be able to keep away from me. Bees to honey.'

'And I'm going to be a caterer. Invisible, until someone's looking for a refill.'

All they need now is for this party to go ahead. Ally checks her watch. Saffron will be on her way back up to Rockpool now, telling Imogen she's onboard with the plan after all and trying to persuade Imogen's dad. When the others return, she's been briefed to persuade them too. Saffron thinks Nicole will want the sparkle – especially after a night in a police cell. And Davey and Jet are likely to go where the free alcohol is. Ruby may be a sticking point, but Imogen's emotional appeal could win the day.

Jayden seemed confident as he left. *Stay in radio contact, Al?* They agreed that as soon as they had word from Saffron, they'd head straight to Rockpool together. The waiter and the sous-chef, all set to cater a luxury party. Well, they've been in stranger places together, haven't they?

Ally looks to the sky. It's still clear. No suggestion of the reported break in the weather, apart from the muggy air. Usually, she can feel a storm coming, see the slightest shift out on the water, but there's nothing. She takes it as a sign: make hay while the sun shines.

49

Jayden's hauling one of the overflowing bins out from behind the barn. While Cat's given him a free pass for today there are still a few jobs on his list. *Blue jobs,* she said with a wink, at which point Jayden was tempted to offer some banter on the topic of equality.

He stops to wipe his arm across his forehead, trying to ignore the ripe smell of rubbish that the heat's drawing from the bin. His phone is in his pocket and he's waiting on news from Saffron. At her word, he and Ally – and hopefully Tallulah – will jump into action.

And honestly? Jayden's keen to ask some questions up at Rockpool – and not just about Baz's death. Tallulah's the paying client, but he can't stop thinking about Felix.

At the sound of scuttling, he turns his head. He thought he saw a rat in the back of the barn yesterday, as big as a cat with a whip-like tail. He can face a lot of things, but rats? Rats freak him out. Which is something Cliff seems to enjoy far too much. *Farm life, Jayden. You give me emmets, I'll give you rats.*

Jayden turns back to the task at hand – hefting the bin – and sees a holidaymaker on the approach. One who raises his hand in a friendly wave. DI Radford, ice-white legs in beach shorts. Flip-flops slip-slapping across the yard. The campers rarely drift to this part of the farm – *good job too,* thinks Jayden, *considering the wildlife.*

'I've been waiting for a chance to bend your ear,' he says. 'Now a good time?'

Is it? Not really. But Martin Radford carries an authority with him, even in his holiday garms. So Jayden says, 'Sure. Of course. Let me just shift this.' At least this time he drops the *sir*.

DI Radford looks at his watch. 'It's past the yard arm isn't it, Jayden? Anywhere we can get a fizzy pop around here?'

He could suggest The Wreckers, but it'll take time to get there. Time he might not have.

'Only thing is, I'm waiting on a call. I might have to run. Do you want to come to the house?'

'Let's do that then,' says Radford.

Five minutes later, they're at the wooden picnic bench in the strip of garden behind the cottage. A gnarly old apple tree throws dappled light. The swing he made for Jazzy hangs from the upper-most branch – well, the swing he initially made, then Cliff came along and modified it. Obviously.

Radford raises his can of Korev. Jayden has an apple juice. They chink.

'Weather always like this here?'

'Oh yeah, 365.' He grins. 'Apparently, it's set to break though. You'll be glad you're not under canvas then.'

'It's a helluva spot you've got here.'

'We're lucky.'

'Bit of an adjustment?'

'What, at first? You could say that.'

'What you went through, Jayden, it's about the worst thing that can happen to a cop.'

He nods. He thought Radford might go there.

'No one blamed you for wanting out,' says Radford. He lifts his can for a swig. 'Time passes, though. What's it been, two years?'

'That's right, yeah.'

And the way Radford says it, it sounds like it's a long time. But it isn't. It isn't a long time at all. The night Kieran died is as sharp in his memory as if it were yesterday.

'So, here's the thing,' says Radford, setting the can down with a clunk; steepling his hands.

Gear-change alert. Even when Radford was a DS, he had the cut of someone who was climbing higher. The kind of cop who fared well in boardrooms, as well as on the street. And he was good on the street; Jayden always liked that about him.

'I'm not going to beat about the bush. I've got a proposition for you.'

Something quickens inside of Jayden, and it's like the sun is shafting harder through the leaves above. He wipes a bead of sweat from his forehead.

'I'm relocating to Plymouth next month. Leading a County Lines task force. There's a lot of drugs coming in, and they're making their way down here too: the party towns on the coast. You ever see anything like that?'

'Not in Porthpella,' says Jayden, forcing a grin. But even as he says it, he's thinking of Rockpool House. The white line that stopped Baz Carson's heart.

'You know the score. We're talking organised crime. Vulnerable kids falling prey to gangs from up-country. Plymouth has always had its problems, but something's shifted lately.'

'Big change for you from Leeds,' says Jayden, conversationally. 'How did you like it, on your stopover?'

'Keely was at university in Plymouth back in the day, so she took me on a tour of the best bits. It was quick.' He laughs. 'Joke. I'm all in for the move, Jayden. And I'm all in for the job, as well. But I want the right people around me. And I straight away thought of you.'

'But County Lines is CID.' *And I run a campsite now.*

'You'd come back in as a PC, but with an attachment to CID. Take your exams when you're good and ready. A little bird told me that was on the cards, anyway.'

Jayden wants to ask who, because the only person he told was Kieran. Apart from Cat. He has a sudden vision of DI Radford talking to her in the cabin office. Or was it Keely? Cat said she'd spoken to Keely. But that's not the point. Jayden left. He quit. He's not going back.

'You were a hell of a response officer, Jayden. But people had already noted you had skills that could be used elsewhere. And what you've been doing since, down here, the private work, it's impressive. I talked to DCI Robinson. Decent lad.'

'You talked to DCI Robinson?'

'It was your thinking that cracked a cold case from Surrey, and your fast action that prevented a murder in Porthpella.'

'It was me and Ally.'

'Then Sharpe, the chef murdered in Mousehole? Without any resources at all – except for you and a neighbourhood watch lady, curtain twitcher in the dunes – you nailed that one too.'

Radford grins at him, but Jayden doesn't return it. 'Ally's a bit more than neighbourhood watch,' he says gruffly. 'I wouldn't be doing any of it without her.'

'I think you're ready for more. And I'll bet that wife of yours does too. Take what's happening now, events up at Rockpool House. You don't want to be on the outside looking in, do you? One of your own guests gets hauled in on murder charges and all you can do is stand and watch? Tell me you're not itching to get involved.'

Jayden rubs at his temple.

'I know you've got a life here, a family, but none of that needs to change. Plymouth's commutable. We steamed down here in an hour and a half this morning. In full summer. In a juggernaut.'

'It's not the school holidays yet. You should see the roads then.'

As if that's the point.

'Or you could rent a place. Pied-à-terre. We could make the shift patterns work for you. Divide your time between the great western city of Plymouth and the Cornish wilds. Sounds very suave, doesn't it?'

Jayden laughs. It's crazy talk.

'Or maybe it's time for a change for the whole family. Cat liked being in the city too, didn't she? There must be bits she misses about urban life.' He waves his arm. 'A place like this'll look after itself, now it's up and running.'

'She loves it here,' says Jayden. Then, 'I love it here.'

And, as he says it, he realises it's true. But loving Porthpella doesn't exclude other feelings.

'I'm flattered,' he says. 'Massively. And I really appreciate you coming here, sir, but—'

'Look,' says Radford, cutting in. 'I don't want an answer straight away, I just want you to think about it. Jayden, don't you ever feel like you're wasting your days down here? You're young. You've got a lot to offer. You've got things to offer you haven't even begun to tap into yet. You can run a campsite and play surfboard detective when you're retired and sitting on a nice pension. You might need to find yourself a new partner by that point, but . . .' Radford laughs. But, seeing the look on Jayden's face, he corrects himself. 'Gallows humour. Sorry. But Jayden, the mark we leave. It matters. If Kieran was here now, what would he say to you? I'm willing to bet he'd say "Go for it, Weston."'

It's a cute angle, playing the Kieran card. Inside or outside of the interview room, Radford always knew the questions to ask.

Jayden's phone goes then, and he makes an 'excuse me' face to Radford and pulls it from his pocket.

'Saffron,' he says. 'Are we on?'

50

Gus can't settle to his writing today. He blames the heat, because it's simplest. And it's true that All Swell – little more than a wooden hut, in truth – is as hot as a furnace inside. These last few days the sun has burnt into the walls, and even when he opens all the windows, it can't escape. He'd try to write outside, but squinting at his laptop screen *en plein air* doesn't work either, even if Gus paints a slightly different picture in his letters to Clive and Rich. *Life as a beachside writer.* Maybe he should convert to longhand. Buy a new notebook and start again from word zero, working out on the deck. There's something both tempting – and devastating – about the thought of starting the book all over again. He's heard of writers who do such things, but they've always seemed like sadists to him.

No, Gus prefers this way. The slow chip, chip, chip, so that he hardly knows where one draft ends and the next begins: it's all the same lump of rock. It changes shape, but neither grows smaller nor larger (unlike actual rock, of course). Gus applies this gentle inertia to deadlines too, liberating himself from all targets and expectations. On good days he feels like a rebel, sticking up two fingers to task-orientated conformists. Why can't he just *live* this novel of his, rather than simply inhabit it for a spell then leave it in his rear-view mirror? On the less good days, he wonders if it's all a ploy: avoid sticking his head above the parapet because he's bumbling about in the castle. *Sandcastle.* He looks to the window. It's golden out there, a sunlit stretch punctuated by colourful windbreaks and those little tents that appear to have become all the rage. But what's a seaside holiday if the sand isn't blowing in your sandwiches, and you don't go home with a sunburnt neck?

His email pings, and he jumps on it.

Even though he and Ally have never emailed one another, it's Ally he thinks of as he clicks across to his inbox. He hasn't heard from her today, and he's been wondering how it's going with Tallulah as her house guest.

But it's from Jacqueline Clifton. The owner of All Swell.

> Hi Gus, hope the start of the summer is treating you well. I wanted to let you know that we've decided to put the beach house on the market. With property booming as it is, we'd be fools not to. I wanted to give you a heads-up, in case you were interested yourself. Also, to pre-warn you that there will be viewings, organised via the agent, and you might find it easier to vacate the property ahead of this happening, to minimise inconvenience. We don't anticipate it being on the market for long. I'm sorry if this comes as a shock . . .

Gus stops reading.

The beach house. Until he got to the part about vacating the property, he honestly thought this email was about a different place altogether. Not All Swell. Not his home. Not . . . here.

He pushes back on his chair, the legs squeaking on the lino. He looks round at the pine-clad walls. The nautical striped curtains. The chalkboard with *Happy Hollibobs* painted on it.

It has been a happy hollibobs. It's been the happiest hollibobs he's ever had in his whole life. And he thought he could make it last forever.

Gus feels a burning in his throat, and suddenly the room is blurring.

Oh, but he's an old fool. Who was he to think things could stay the same? When Mona pulled the rug from under him, he found his feet again here. And he sunk them deep in the sand. But he's been duped. These ever-shifting dunes, the sea that literally never stops, all this time he's been surrounded by change, yet he thought he was immune to it. Or that it could be on his own terms.

He starts to type a reply, his fingers heavy.

> Hi Jacqueline. Thanks for your email.

Then he deletes it; starts again.

> Hi Jacqueline. No thanks for your email. You do realise you've ruined everything, don't you? Who do you think you are, wanting to sell your own house?

Then:

> Hi Jacqueline. Fantastic. Obviously, I'll jump at the opportunity to buy. I've half a mill burning a hole in a suitcase under the bed.

No, he'll reply another day. With a wipe of his eyes, he decides to go to The Wreckers.

～

By the time Gus has tramped along the dusty footpath and across the baking fields, he feels sun-addled and faintly mad. The village square shimmers, mirage-like; maybe this whole place has been a mirage. Outside The Wreckers he ignores the picnic tables with their stupidly jaunty parasols, and steps into the dark interior.

After the brightness it's as good as pitch-black and he feels his way to the bar, blinking. He orders a pint of Doom Bar. *Doom – that's about right.* Plus a bag of Scampi Fries, because Mona thought they were a disgusting invention and right now he feels like socking it to anyone and anything. He makes for a corner. He doesn't want the sun-filled garden, with all its holidaymakers who are just fine with staying a paltry week and filing back up the A30 to their regular lives.

Then he sees himself, already sitting there on his own, bent over a pint like the sad sack he is. He does a double take. He really must have sunstroke. He realises exactly who he's looking at.

'Oh,' he says. 'I thought for a second I was going mad. It's you.'

The man looks up and his eyes are as sad as a bloodhound's. 'The one and only.'

Whenever Gus imagined bumping into Baz Cason in Porthpella, he always pictured himself handling the situation as if their lives were made to intersect. *Hey, man. Good to see you.* But Gus also knows, deep down, that this is fanciful. More likely he would have lost his words, shuffled his feet, when what he wanted to say was . . . wow. But now Baz is dead, and here's Davey Hart: the only surviving member of the band.

You can either define the moment or let the moment define you.

'Davey Hart,' says Gus. 'You're a hell of a drummer. That solo on "Leapfrog". Everyone goes on about "You Do It For Me", but the drums on "Leapfrog" are sizzling.'

Davey looks confused for a second. Then he breaks into a slow grin.

'Now, that's what I've always said. Who are you? Other than a bloke who knows his music.'

'Gus Munro.'

'You want to join me, Gus Munro?'

And Davey nods to the empty chair. Gus plants himself in it before the guy can change his mind.

'Local?' asks Davey.

'Local,' nods Gus. 'Sort of. I came down here nearly a year and a half ago and . . . stayed.'

He feels a swell of emotion, so decides he might as well go the whole hog.

'When I heard the news about Baz, I was devastated. And then Rupert Frost too. Condolences, my friend. I can't imagine the pain.'

Davey Hart drains his glass. His hand goes to his head. The bald head that Gus – sun-soaked, sad, a little mad, frankly – mistook for his own.

'It hurts,' says Davey, his voice low, eyelids drooping. 'Baz, he went out blazing though. Didn't he? Maybe he was fed up of living by all those rules he set himself, huh? But Rupert . . . that's cold blood, that is. That's different. That's terrifying, man.'

'Terrifying,' agrees Gus.

'I'm just out the slammer,' says Davey, peering into the bottom of his empty glass. He licks his lips, then darts a look at Gus. 'And I don't mind telling you, I was alright with being there. Because after Rupert, and before we knew what Baz was up to, I was looking over my shoulder big time. I mean, what if they were picking us off? That's what I said to them. I was safe in there.' He picks up his glass then puts it down again. 'But they've got someone now. Felix Boyd. Jumped-up-streak-of-piss music journalist. Never would have thought he'd have it in him, man.' Davey shakes his head. 'I need another one of these.'

Gus immediately gets to his feet. 'What are you on?'

'Some local drop.'

'Doom Bar?'

'That'll do. Thank you, my man. Much obliged. Here, bag of crisps too while you're at it.'

Gus walks to the bar, his heart pounding. *I'm drinking with The Nick. I'm drinking with The Nick.* Somehow this day has taken an upward turn – even if the company might be considered downbeat. Is it a sign, that things might turn out all right for Gus, after all? That right now his inbox might be pinging with an email from Jacqueline Clifton, subject header 'Change of heart'. *What was I thinking, selling your home from under you? In fact, Gus, I hereby bequeath . . .*

'That who I think it is, over there?' asks the barman.

It's someone Gus doesn't recognise: a summer season worker.

'No, mate. Just looks like him,' says Gus, and he returns to the table, pint and crisps in hand.

'Much obliged,' says Davey again.

'Can I play superfan for just a moment?'

'That's my favourite tune,' says Davey, taking the top off his pint. And he does seem to have brightened a bit.

'Is it true that when you were a kid you used to use your granny's knitting needles as sticks? That that was how you got started?'

'She wanted to tan my hide, when she saw her half-made scarf in a heap on the floor. But she had these big wooden needles, and I tell you what, they weren't bad sticks.'

Gus laughs. 'And is it true that you never go anywhere without your lucky gloves? Even when you're not playing?'

'That one's an exaggeration.'

'What about the story that you bought your first proper kit when your car blew up? Citroën 2CV, wasn't it?'

'Famous for going up in smoke that model, apparently. And yep, insurance just about covered a Ludwig. Lovely kit, that was. Worth the singed ears.'

'That how you lost your hair?' says Gus, and to his delight Davey cackles.

'Takes one to know one, brother.'

But then Davey drops his head suddenly, as if he's remembered laughter's out of bounds.

'My turn,' he says quietly, splitting open the bag of crisps. 'You knew Baz did you, living down here?'

'Never had the pleasure. I always hoped I'd run into him. Your music has meant such a lot to me, and I'd have liked to have been able to tell him that.'

'Well, you're telling me.' Davey taps his fingers on the table – with impeccable rhythm, of course. 'You ever catch the record I put out with The Levels? Late nineties.'

'I don't think I did,' admits Gus.

'Never mind,' says Davey sadly, and crams a handful of crisps in his mouth. 'For what it's worth, there's some decent drumming on that too. Not "Leapfrog" but . . . decent.'

'I'll check it out.'

Davey looks at him sideways, licks the salt from his fingers. 'You've cheered me right up, you have.'

But he sounds anything but cheery.

'If you're a fan, you'll know about Baz and Tallulah Pearce. She came all the way over here just to see him. First time in donkey's years. Sad story, that. Beautiful lady and a sad, sad story.'

'Terrible,' says Gus. 'I actually met her last night.'

'What, Tallulah? She's still in town?'

Gus nods.

Davey sits a little straighter. 'How was she?'

'As you'd expect.' And it's a careful answer, because the way the conversation is flowing so nicely, Gus doesn't trust himself to just come out and say that, actually, he thought she was a little full of herself.

'Still beautiful though, huh? More beautiful than ever.' Davey shakes his head. 'It's a joke, isn't it? Life. Only I don't know who's laughing.'

'Maybe we have to,' says Gus. 'Maybe that's the only way to make it through.'

Davey slaps the table. 'I like that. Maybe that's why we're having a party up at Rockpool tonight. To laugh through it. I wish I had a way of contacting Tally. She should be with us. I never got to tell her . . . that we're here for her. We were all so wrapped up in ourselves that first night. And then the next morning she was gone . . .'

'You're having a party?'

Davey looks faraway suddenly. And then he stares at Gus as if he's a total stranger. Which of course he is.

'A party at Rockpool House?' nudges Gus.

'Yeah. The kid wanted one. Imogen. Baz's grandkid. She found a box of decorations Baz had been keeping and thought it was a pity they weren't being hung. She gave it the waterworks and, well, how could anyone argue with that?' Davey shakes himself; slaps his shoulder. 'It's what Baz would have wanted. Isn't it?'

'I'd say so.'

Then, as casually as if he's offering him a crisp, Davey says, 'You want to come, Gus Munro?'

51

'Well done, Tim,' says DCI Robinson, shaking his hand. 'You played your part. And well done, Miranda.'

The ink's still wet, but Felix Boyd has been charged with the murder of Rupert Frost.

DS Chang smiles, and her neat bob swings. 'It's a result, guv.'

It's Forensics who can really claim it. They found one of Felix Boyd's hairs – a long, dangly, music-person hair – at the scene. Felix didn't need another nail in the coffin, what with the knife in his van, his fingerprints, the clear-cut motive, the lack of alibi, but . . . might as well make sure it's hammered tight.

'Right, press conference,' says Robinson, with relish. 'DS Chang, join me?'

And the two power out.

Mullins catches Skinner's eye at the back of the room. He wanders over.

'That it then?' says Mullins.

'That's it. On to the next one. Another day in paradise.'

'Boyd wasn't exactly remorseful,' says Mullins.

'It's because he's not guilty.'

Mullins blinks. 'You can't think that, Sarge?'

'That's Boyd's line and he's sticking with it. Remorse won't help that plea. Anyway, what are you still doing here? You're off shift.'

Mullins shuffles his feet. 'I thought there might have been beers or something.'

'You want a party, do you, Mullins?' Skinner rolls his eyes. 'Paperwork awaits. You'd better get out of here before I send some your way.'

Mullins heads for the door. Then he stops and turns. Skinner is hunched at his desk, shoulders rounded as he glowers at his screen.

'That stuff you said, Sarge. About why Felix Boyd drove back to the campsite instead of just legging it . . . it is a bit odd, isn't it?'

Skinner doesn't turn around. 'Murderer not thinking straight? That's a well-ploughed furrow, that is.'

'So, it does make sense to you now?'

Skinner spins on his chair. Growls, 'No. No, it doesn't.'

'But criminals do make mistakes. Most are stupid, Sarge. We're always saying that.'

'But Felix Boyd isn't "most criminals". The only reason his prints are in the system is because he got a caution for criminal damage back when he was nineteen. Graffiti. By someone else's estimation – not mine, incidentally – it'd probably be considered art. So no, Mullins, since you're bringing it up, I don't buy that Boyd would go back to the campsite in his van after committing a murder. Especially as we've since learnt he was carting around the murder weapon too. There was absolutely no reason for him to do that.'

'He went up to St Ives first though, didn't he? Some pottery place that his mum used to like, or so he says. The woman there confirmed it. He bought a ticket. Deliberate sort of alibi, I'd say.'

'What, alibi for *after* the murder? Then down to Hang Ten for a coffee and a chinwag with Broady Holt? Pull the other one, Mullins.'

'Same thing, isn't it? Trying to present as a regular guy doing regular things. Quite clever, when you think about—'

'Or, in fact, a regular guy doing regular things,' says Skinner. 'Anyone consider that? No. Because no one wants to hear good old-fashioned reasoning when there's forensic evidence, do they? Boyd had an explanation for those prints on the knife. No one to prove it, but he had an explanation. Maybe he'll have an explanation for how that hair of his ended up at the crime scene too. But now that he's charged, we won't know until it goes to trial. And if the whole thing falls apart, that's egg on a lot of faces. And if it doesn't? An innocent man behind bars.' He holds his hands up. 'But I'm out-numbered. And the DCI was feeling the pressure and reckoned he had enough for a charge. So, there we have it.'

Mullins chews his lip. He feels an odd tug of loyalty to Skinner.

'Go on, clear off. Have your celebration.'

'Did you say all this to the DCI, Sarge?'

'No, Mullins. I thought, seeing as you're the brains behind the operation, I'd best bring it to your door. What do you think? Course I told him. Near enough put my job on the line, the way I set to. But he wasn't buying it. Because he wants the quick result, doesn't he? Everybody always does. Now go on. Your pint's getting warm.'

~

Mullins strolls across the square towards The Wreckers. It's silly now, this heat; it needs to stop. His mouth waters at the thought of an ice-cold lager, the frosted glass. He could use it for his brain, too. A Thinking Pint, as Grandad Jack used to call it. Because he can't shake Skinner's words. The DS is never a fan of the Major Crimes team stomping about on their patch, but he'd be the first to say that a win is a win is a win.

Is there any way that Felix Boyd didn't do it?

And is it possible that someone else wanted to make it look like he did?

With these questions humming in his head, there's no kick in Mullins's step. He's just trudging up the pub steps when Gus and another bloke barrel out together. Tweedledum and Tweedledee, sun glinting off their matching bald heads. *Davey Hart!* Since when have these two been pals?

'Tim, hallo!' cries Gus heartily.

'Officer Mullins,' says Davey, holding out his hand. 'We just heard. You've got him.'

Mullins shakes it. 'We've got him.'

'Thank you, brother,' says Davey, solemn suddenly.

'A job well done,' agrees Gus. And there's colour in his cheeks. *These two have had a pint or two*, Mullins reckons. *Or three or four.*

'We're off back to Rockpool House,' says Gus, shining as he says it. 'Bit of a celebration.'

Davey waves his hand. 'It was for Baz's birthday. But now it's about justice for Rupert too. You want in, Officer?'

Mullins looks from one to the other.

'Baz might have been teetotal, but he got in enough booze to sink a ship,' says Davey. 'And you've got a thirsty look about you, fella. We do owe you boys in blue.'

Mullins weighs it up. A solitary pint in a corner of The Wreckers or socialising with a group of not particularly likeable people who were – until just hours ago – suspects. Who, if Skinner is to be believed, still *are*.

'Saffron's cheffing up an enormous paella, by all accounts,' says Gus.

'I'm in,' says Mullins.

52

'Baz always had a thing for paella,' says Nicole.

Saffron watches as she hovers near the stove, leering at the fish stock. When Nicole turns back to face Saffron, her forehead is beaded with sweat. She clomps across the kitchen in her wedged sandals, her vivid pink dress taut across her back; a cloud of hairspray and perfume – and fish stock – following her.

Saffron is surprised Nicole's lurking with her in the kitchen, but since she's been back, her mood has changed. Saffron expected to see anger that she'd spent the night in custody, and a desire to get away from Rockpool at all costs, but Mullins was right: Nicole jumped at a party. Maybe knowing that Rupert's death was nothing to do with the fallout from Baz's was freeing. Saffron overheard her telling Imogen's dad earlier, *I did give him both barrels about his tweet*, to which Adrian replied, *Have you ever given just the one, Nic?*

'People always made a lot of my and Baz's differences,' says Nicole, leaning against the counter, arms folded tight against her chest, 'because they like to stir. With holier-than-thou Connie around, Baz reckoned he was leaving all his party days behind him, but I always knew that wasn't him. He was trying to be someone he wasn't. No good ever comes of that. So, Baz wanted a little bit of Charlie on his birthday? That's the Baz I knew.' Nicole narrows her eyes at Saffron. 'Charlie. Cocaine. I expect you kids call it something different.'

And it strikes Saffron that Nicole is weirdly validated that Baz's death was drugs-related.

'I think Jet calls it breakfast,' Nicole says with a high laugh, and maybe there's something in Saffron's face because her tone changes abruptly. 'Are you judging me? Us?'

Saffron attends to her stock, shoulders tense. 'Of course I'm not. I'm just sorry for your loss.'

When she looks back, Nicole's still glaring at her. The feeling of unease returns. They're a volatile bunch, this Rockpool crew, and Nicole switches with the wind. But Saffron is doing this for Ally and Jayden. Ally and Jayden who, right now, are setting up drinks and canapés in the pagoda. With the sky still clear – for now – the outside plans are still on. With Jayden in a crisp, white shirt and Ally in an apron, they pretty much look the part. Maybe she'll put them to work down at Hang Ten as payback when all this is over; they can take the summer rush, while Saffron paddles out.

'I'm going to check on the fire,' she says, and exits the kitchen with a little gust of relief.

As Saffron passes through the central hall, Jet slides up behind her. 'Hey, chef.'

He's another one who's taken the night in a cell in his stride.

'I know you're only doing this for my niece,' he says.

And for a second, she thinks, *Who?* because she doesn't think of Jet as an uncle. He seems too untethered to be anybody's anything.

'Which is very heroic of you. A different form of imprisonment, huh?'

'We're happy to do it,' she says, and she sounds as stiff as Jayden's white shirt.

Jet rubs at his stubble, eyes narrowed. 'Felix Boyd. You talked to him, didn't you?'

And Saffron wonders how he knows this. She didn't notice anyone else around when Felix came in the kitchen. But then Jet is someone you don't really notice; he slinks about, occasionally making mild quips when he can be bothered.

'I always thought you could see evil. Like it's this toxic kind of . . .' – he waves his hands, looking for the word – '. . . cloud. But it's just ordinary. It creeps in, says and does all the right things, then, when the moment comes . . . executes.' His eyes are a flat grey, his face dispassionate. 'He was a creep as a kid, though. I could have called it then. Should have called it then. Poor old Rupes. Ultimate insult, to be taken out by a sad little music critic.' Jet suddenly crows with laughter. 'Hatchet job. Get it?'

He strolls out, laughing to himself still.

Saffron follows, eyes seeking out Ally and Jayden.

'Saffron!'

Ruby. Ruby who, unlike her mum Nicole, isn't dressed for the party at all. She's in a crumpled cotton blouse and cropped trousers; hair pulled into a joyless ponytail.

'My husband will want to get involved with the fire. Don't let him. He's basically a pyromaniac. All men are.'

'Erm, okay.'

'He doesn't want to be here. Well, newsflash, none of us do. But this party is the one thing Imogen's shown any enthusiasm for in weeks, so . . . there we have it.' She chews at her thumb as she talks, eyes darting nervously. 'My mother is highly stressed. She'll drink too much, shout, fall over, then fall asleep. Just go with it, okay? The last thing we need is sniffy staff. But if you get the chance, add Perrier to her champagne. Might as well soften the blow.'

And Saffron's trying to work out how that would even be possible; perhaps Jayden has some stealth moves.

'Ignore my brother Jet. Most of the time he's too lazy to antagonise anyone, but once he decides to, he's a vile little menace. Don't rise to it. His trump card is that he doesn't care. Not about anyone or anything. Which makes him unoffendable.'

'He must care about your dad dying,' says Saffron.

Ruby gives a strange laugh. 'I think he probably feels ridiculously liberated. I know none of it makes sense to someone like you. You've probably got the perfect set of parents at home, but our family wasn't like that. We're crooked. Broken. We were before Baz met Connie Boyd and we were after too. And with him and Jet it was always . . . difficult.'

Saffron can't be bothered to set Ruby right. 'Why did you all come here?' she asks instead. 'If I didn't get on with my family, I'd give them a wide berth.'

'We're sadistic,' says Ruby, doing that odd little laugh again. 'We do love a twisted family gathering. No, it's for Mum, of course. It was important to her. She said seventy was a milestone and however much life has veered off course, we're all still here to mark it. Ironic, huh?' Ruby dabs her eye with a finger, but Saffron can't see tears. 'And there's the book. Mum wanted to soak up some of the reflected light from the publication. She didn't anticipate that she'd be painted as a gold-digging good-time girl. But that's one thing my mum and dad do – did – have in common: they see what they want to see. So, she's utterly unbothered.' Ruby drops her head. 'Drugs at his age. What was he thinking?'

Saffron reaches out a hand and squeezes her shoulder. Ruby looks at her, and suddenly the years fall away. She looks like a small child, not a thirty-something mum. She offers Saffron a thin smile.

'Rupes might have been ruthless in business, practically Machiavellian, but he wouldn't have hurt anyone directly. Connie Boyd was hit by a truck. Felix must be pretty messed-up if he thought he could blame him for that. But then he is, isn't he? Messed-up.'

'I guess,' says Saffron.

'I tell you what else is messed-up . . . the will.' She checks her watch. 'Mum's called a family meeting. I'd give my right arm to get out of this. Where's Adrian? I need him by my side.'

Imogen appears in the doorway then. She has a plastic Hawaiian-style garland of flowers around her neck, and a grin on her face. Whatever she's been through, this is the party she wanted.

'So, Davey's just turned up. He's been boozing in the village and he's brought some straggler with him. Plus, that lovely inspector.'

Saffron and Ruby follow her out. There's Mullins standing on the driveway in his off-duty gear. A drink has already found its way into his hand. And is that *Gus*?

'Classic Davey,' murmurs Ruby. 'He'd party with just about anyone.'

But it's not just anyone, thinks Saffron. She looks to Ally and Jayden, wondering if this is all their doing, but by the expression on their faces they appear to be just as surprised by the new arrivals.

She does a quick tally. *Six of them and five of us.*

Just then the big gates open, and Tallulah Pearce sweeps through. She's a vision in a floor-length maxi dress, long silver hair alight in the sunshine. A pair of aviators make her look pure seventies chic. Davey and Gus swivel. Davey's jaw pretty much falls to the floor, then he moves towards her, arms wide open in welcome.

Saffron is happy to see her too. Tallulah's Team Porthpella. Or are they all Team Tallulah? Either way, her arrival makes it six-all.

53

Ally is impressed by Tallulah's entrance. She's a pro. And she's found a composure that Ally doubts she could muster in the same circumstances.

They've already discussed the plan, and how important it is for Tallulah to pay no particular attention to Ally and Jayden. Nobody at Rockpool today would have seen them at The Wreckers the night before. Except for Gus. And what's Gus doing here anyway? At the first opportunity Ally must intercept him, and make sure he gives no sign of knowing that Tallulah has hired them. If their plan is to work – and it's tenuous, at best – then they're relying on people relaxing, talking freely, perhaps getting emotional. And Tallulah hearing what she needs to hear: the truth.

Truth for truth's sake.

Mullins is an unexpected element. His presence could hinder things too. Although, by the look on his face, it's as if he's the guest of honour.

'You thinking what I'm thinking?' says Jayden in a low voice.

Ally turns. Jayden in his crisp, white shirt and black apron, holding a magnum of champagne.

'Why are they here?' says Ally.

'They better not blow our cover,' says Jayden.

'Oh gosh, I didn't think of that.'

'I'm on it. And so's Tallulah, by the looks.'

And he's right. Tallulah has moved off with Davey, as though deliberately to split the group. Ally watches as Jayden slides smoothly up to Gus and Mullins, tray in hand. She can't see Jayden's face, but she watches Gus open his mouth to say something then close it just as fast. Mullins shoots a look in Ally's direction, then takes a glass of champagne from the proffered tray. His hammy 'Thank you, waiter!' booms across the lawn.

Then Tallulah's at her elbow. With Davey Hart.

'This man needs some food in him,' says Tallulah, with a graceful smile. 'What have we got here?'

'We have,' says Ally, 'some rosemary and sea-salt crackers, homemade of course. Black olive tapenade. And a selection of Cornish charcuterie, from a farm just along the coast.'

'Sounds delicious. Davey, graze here a while. You need to soak up some of that booze.'

'You know what, Tally—'

'Don't call me that. Only Baz called me that.'

'That geezer over there, the baldie, I said to him, "I wish I had a way of getting Tallulah to come tonight." I thought you were lost to us.'

'I wouldn't miss it,' says Tallulah.

Ally busies herself, rearranging crackers. But neither Tallulah nor Davey are taking the least bit of notice of her. She's staff. She's invisible. Across the lawn Jayden is circulating, topping up glasses. He's swapping a joke with a young man in ripped jeans who Ally guesses is Jet, Baz's son.

'Oh Davey, if only I could have stopped him taking those drugs.'

'Stop Baz? You're joking right? No one could stop Baz doing anything. You know that better than anyone, Tally. Tallulah. And some of those decisions he made? Plain stupid.'

'Like taking cocaine.'

'Like leaving you in LA.'

'Ancient history,' she says.

'I never understood it. Not then, not now. You know I didn't.'

And Ally notes the way Davey's voice breaks; the depth of his emotion.

'Come on, you don't mean that,' says Tallulah, her voice soft. 'There wouldn't have been The Nick without Baz going back to England. You've read the book, haven't you? We all know how the story goes. And where would you be without The Nick?'

'Yeah, yeah,' he mumbles. 'And I've just lost two of my best friends in as many days. I figure that means telling the truth. I still remember Baz showing us the photographs of you. The girl he left behind in America. I thought he was mad then, and I thought he was mad years later when you and I met. You know I did. You do remember, right?'

Ally catches a strange look cross Tallulah's face, fleeting as a cloud.

'Were you with him, Davey, when he took the drugs?'

'You think Baz would have showed us the real him? He was Mr Clean and Sober. You've read the book, haven't you?' And as he parrots back her line, he nudges her.

'Touché. What about Rupert? Was he with him?'

'With Baz? No, we were playing pool. Waiting on Baz to join us. We never thought he was off getting loaded.'

'When was the last time you . . . indulged?'

'Too old for all that.'

'Not what I heard.'

'What, the book again? Veiled references to my . . . what did he call it . . . hedonism? Nah, Baz was way out of date. Rupert though . . . Rupert was different.'

Beside her, Ally can almost feel Tallulah stiffen.

271

'There was nothing in the news about Rupert's post-mortem and drugs.'

Davey takes another cracker and a heavy scoop of tapenade. For a second, Tallulah and Ally's eyes meet – although it's difficult to tell through Tallulah's shades.

Tallulah flicks her hair over her shoulder. 'It would mean the world to me to know what really happened to Baz. The worst thing is, I don't think there's anyone left alive who can give me that. I wish there was . . .'

'If wishes were horses,' says Davey, running his hand over his head.

Tallulah touches Davey's forearm. 'You're right. Beggars would ride.'

'Huh?'

'That's the expression. If wishes were horses, beggars would ride.' She smiles enigmatically. 'It means there's no point just standing around wishing. You've got to act. You've got to make what you want happen.'

Davey crunches the cracker. 'Exactly,' he says. 'That's it.'

Tallulah glances again to Ally, then says, 'I'm going to speak to little Imogen. I hear we owe it to her that this party's happening at all.'

'I'll come,' says Davey.

But Tallulah has already peeled away; gone without a backwards glance.

'Top-up?' says Jayden, appearing suddenly.

Davey holds out his glass. 'If wishes were horses,' he says.

54

Ruby wipes her sticky palms on her trousers and glances across at Adrian. She's glad, as she almost always is, of his sobriety, his formality. With his starched polo shirt and creased chinos, his open, sturdy features, he's the definition of law and order.

They're gathered in the same room as where that shiny-suited detective said *I'm arresting every one of you on suspicion of murder.* Wide windows overlook the terrace, the two waiters circulating with drinks for those left outside: Davey and his stragglers, Tallulah, her daughter (strictly on Fanta). Meanwhile, inside, it's just the inner circle: her brother, her mother. And Adrian. Thank God for Adrian.

Ruby was eighteen when Baz left. It was somehow still a shock, even though she knew they weren't the happiest family in the world; her mum and dad so rarely saw eye to eye that she often wondered what had brought them together in the first place. Partying, probably. And that's where the real hurt came in. As a teen, Ruby had known her dad overdid it, but he was a musician, all his friends were musicians, it seemed like it came with the territory – or that was the song they played, anyway. But the day that Baz decided he didn't want to live like that anymore was the same day he decided to leave them. As if it was his family who were responsible for his hangovers, his shaky hands, the sharp tang of vomit in the bathroom after another one of his parties. Baz's famous conversion to clean living – he wouldn't shut up about it – was as much to do with flushing his family away as it was to do with falling for Connie. That archangel in a potter's apron, who somehow got her clay-sticky hands on him and wouldn't let him go again. Ruby never believed that they weren't romantically involved. Jet always reckoned it was all tantric. But it was too complicated to hate their dad, so instead the pair of them took those feelings and pinned them on Connie and, their closest adversary, Felix. *Felix.* The replacement child. The lank-haired fanboy who sucked up to Baz just to get what he wanted: bylines; pretentiously bleating on about music in the press. Plus, getting the drip-down from whatever handouts Connie was enjoying, because how could you make a living doing a stupid job like pottery anyway?

Felix would have been laughing all the way to the bank if he hadn't been so stupid as to kill Rupert. Jet always said Felix couldn't be trusted. Well, now that's astonishingly official, isn't it? He stabbed Rupert and shot himself in the foot at the same time.

Which means Felix can't have known about the will.

'So, come on,' says Nicole. 'Out with it, Ruby. We all know you're Baz's executor. Which means we all know that you know what's in the will. You might have thought it tacky to talk about it any sooner, but it's downright strange to leave it any longer when we're all here together.'

Ruby looks to Adrian, and he rolls his eyes at her. She loves him, in this moment.

'I have no personal expectations whatsoever,' says Nicole. 'All I want to know is that you two are getting what you deserve.'

'Yes, are we?' drawls Jet. 'Are we getting what we deserve, Ruby?'

And Ruby glares at him, because Jet already knows the answer. He was far from a perfect son, and maybe she wasn't a perfect daughter, but that wasn't their fault, was it? They were shaped by these parents of theirs. Pummelled and stretched and moulded like Connie's damn clay. And if that's passing the buck, then so be it.

'There's not much to get,' she says.

Nicole turns a look on her that's so confused it's almost comedic. Jet starts humming a little tune.

'Baz was always very private about his finances . . .' Adrian begins to say.

'Which is a polite way of saying that Baz was too pig-headed and prejudiced to ever seek Adrian's advice, which of course was about as short-sighted as we'd expect from him. Because if Adrian had ever seen his financial records, he'd have told him he was spending far too much. He'd have advised him on investments,' says Ruby. 'And we wouldn't be where we are now.'

'What are you talking about, "where we are now"?' demands Nicole.

'This place is his principal asset,' says Adrian. 'Rockpool House.'

'In terms of cash money, Adrian and I have got more in the bank than him,' says Ruby.

'Show-off,' says Jet, airily.

'He's squandered it. I mean, we'll need to see bank statements to really understand it, but he's pissed it all away. Adrian and I wanted to talk to him about it this weekend, but we never got the chance. You were going to make some recommendations, weren't you, Ade? Try to help him out. Because whatever advice he was getting from Rupert, it was lousy.'

'To be fair, I don't imagine even Rupert could impact Baz's thinking,' says Adrian. 'He was very single-minded—'

'And, you know, herbal teas can be very expensive,' chips in Jet. 'Plus, he was probably paying his yoga instructor top dollar. I expect he was bankrolling Felix's pathetic little career as well. But come on, Ruby. Dad's spending habits aren't exactly the headline here. Tell them the real news.'

Nicole is collecting herself; Ruby can practically hear the machinery clunking.

Ruby sucks in a breath. Her chest aches with anticipatory pain for the fallout she knows is coming.

'Baz left this place to Felix,' she says.

'Boom-tish,' says Jet.

Nicole is on her feet. 'He wouldn't have done that.'

'He did,' says Ruby.

'Oh, he did,' says Jet. 'And now the idiot's going away for life, so he can't even accept the keys.'

'That can't be true,' says Nicole. Her voice low; a warning growl of thunder.

'Jet and I are provided for elsewhere. We're each to receive a cash sum. Thirty thousand each.'

'Thirty thousand?' says Nicole.

'Adrian and I don't need the money. We weren't counting on it.'

'And contrary to popular belief, nor was I,' says Jet. 'Thirty's a nice little handout as far as I'm concerned.'

Nicole looks from one to the other. 'But it's . . . outrageous. It must be contested. Especially given the circumstances. Felix can't be arrested for murder and inherit a fortune. It's fishy. Fishy as anything.'

'He killed Rupert, Mum,' says Jet. 'He didn't kill Baz.'

'Didn't he?' trills Nicole. 'I think this casts a very different light on things.'

'There's nothing to say Felix even knew about the will,' says Ruby.

'And there's nothing to say that he didn't!' she cries.

'It's a fair point,' says Adrian.

'How long have you known about this, Ruby?' Nicole is breathing fire.

'Only a week or so. Baz said he'd been doing some thinking and had set right a few things. Then he sent me the will.'

'A week? A week, and you've never mentioned it?'

'I was letting the dust settle. And, frankly, Adrian and I were getting our heads around it. I told you, we intended to talk to Baz this weekend. Not about the Felix part, but about how little he had in the bank. Like I said, Adrian had some ideas . . .'

'Felix said he was here at the house,' says Nicole. 'On Thursday. He said he came to see Baz. Didn't he? Jet? Didn't he? What if he found out then? What if he found out, then killed your father?' Nicole's voice is rising and rising.

'But it was a cardiac arrest,' says Jet. 'We all saw how Felix butchered poor Rupert. Kill a man like that, you're not going to be clever enough – or sorcerer enough – to induce a heart attack, are you?'

'But he had *reason* to kill Baz,' says Nicole, flopping back on the sofa, her head in her hands. 'To get his hands on the house. He did. He had reason.'

Ruby doesn't know what to say. What she really wants to do is get in the car and drive straight home. Back to sanity and normality. Their tree-lined street. Her immaculately tiled bathroom. To drink a cool glass of wine standing in her kitchen looking out over her green-striped lawn and borders full of peonies. That's what she wants. Adrian in the background somewhere watching golf videos. Imogen shut up in her room being a teenager. Ruby possessed of only a standard anxiety: fretting about school-gate politics or whether they owe the Hemsworths a dinner; holding her mother at bay over everyday irritations, not this out-and-out warfare that makes every nerve in her body tingle with stress.

'Did you know about all this too, Jet?' Nicole's tone is accusatory.

Jet shrugs. 'Ruby filled me in, yeah.' Then he stands up and stretches, like he's been asleep, before wandering over to their mum. He settles on the sofa beside Nicole and wraps his arm around her shoulders.

Ruby has a sudden flashback: twenty years ago, and the rubble of Baz's exit. Ruby with this same gesture for their catatonic mother and how she was batted away. Jet didn't have it in him as a teenager to offer anyone any comfort. He just raised his drawbridge and stopped talking to any of them.

'Mum, look,' he says. 'When Ruby told me I couldn't believe it either. But hey, it was Dad's choice. We didn't really understand him in life, so let's not try to in death. This whole weekend is messed-up on so many levels. You know what I think the main thing is? We're still here. We're still standing. Dad's not. Rupert's not. Neither's Felix; not really. I call that a victory, don't you? Who cares about money, compared to the fact that we get to walk away and carry on living. So let's get back out there and do this party tonight. For our Imogen, as much as anyone. And then let's just get on with life.'

Ruby can feel a sting in her eyes. Her little brother is full of surprises. She's not crying, is she? She pushes her hot palms to her eyes. Then she goes and sits on the other side of her mum and tentatively leans in.

'Now we're talking,' says Jet. 'The fabulous three.'

'The only ones I could ever count on,' says Nicole, her voice choked.

And Ruby wills her not to go and ruin the moment.

'Come on, Adrian, get yourself in here,' says Jet. 'It's a love-in.'

Adrian hesitates, then grins. 'Thanks for the invite,' he says. 'Better late than never.'

55

'Alright,' says Jayden, once Davey has trailed off across the garden in Tallulah's wake. 'The Gus and Mullins situation is contained. They bumped into Davey Hart in The Wreckers and the rest is history. Gus reckons Davey's got a crush on Tallulah.'

'I think Gus might be right,' says Ally.

They're standing in the shade of the pagoda, palms fringing the sides. The terrace has all but emptied; perhaps people are finding the house cooler, because the heat is sticky now, the air heavy. But Jayden's light on his feet. And that's got a lot to do with his last conversation.

'Gus also wanted to tell me all the rock history gems he'd gleaned from him,' he says. 'From first kits and lucky gloves to . . . what was it . . . nicking his granny's knitting needles as his first sticks. It's safe to say Gus is a little star-struck.'

'And Mullins?'

Jayden feels a pulse of excitement. 'Okay, Mullins. At first it bothered me that he's here, in case his presence throws people off. Our whole play relies on people letting their guard down.'

'Oh God, you're right.'

'No, it's all good, Al. Because Mullins let his own guard down. He's in a weird mood. And, wait for it, he just let slip that Skinner's got doubts about Felix Boyd.'

He looks at her triumphantly.

'But they've charged him,' says Ally. 'Haven't they?'

'Yeah, they have. And it was obviously a rash move. I think, for the first time ever, DS Skinner and I might see eye to eye.'

Whatever Skinner said about Felix has stuck with Mullins. Jayden's first reaction to Felix's arrest was biased: basically, he likes the guy. Plus, it was a little self-protecting, because Jayden think he's good at reading people; that's why it was a shock when Felix Boyd was charged. He knows these things about himself. But for DS Skinner, it would be a whole lot easier for him to be onboard with his colleagues: everyone celebrating closing the case together. Jayden remembers those days, and it was a buzz. Even when he was on the peripheries as a PC, he felt the energy coming down the hall from CID.

'But Jayden, we don't have any of the information.'

'We've got some of it,' says Jayden, with a grin. 'Mullins wouldn't spill. Not at first, and good on him. But I think he's between a rock and a hard place. On the one hand the case is wrapped, on the other, his boss is uneasy. I told him that if there's a possibility they've got it wrong, then tonight is our best chance to set it right. All the suspects in one place? Us here too? When's that going to happen again, right?'

'He really told you what evidence they have? But Jayden, he could get in terrible trouble for that.'

'I know. I shouldn't have pushed his buttons. But Mullins's instincts are telling him to trust Skinner, and I'm the only other person voicing doubts about Boyd. Look, Al, the murder weapon was found in Boyd's van. Plus, his prints are on it.'

'Then it must be him,' says Ally.

'Exactly. Which is why I'm even more certain that it isn't! Because even knowing all the details, Skinner has doubts. What if someone really wanted to make it look like Felix is the killer?'

'You mean someone framed him?'

'It's possible. Isn't it? It crossed my mind before, but it wouldn't stick. But now . . . it'd explain why there's evidence on some levels, but also why it doesn't stack up on others. Anyone can plant a murder weapon. The prints . . . okay, that's trickier. But we do know that, beyond Baz, Felix isn't exactly popular with the Rockpool crew. He told me that loud and clear.'

'But unpopular enough to be framed for murder?'

Jayden rubs his chin. 'Well, yeah. The question there then, is whether Rupert's death was above all about framing Felix, and Rupert was just the fall guy, *or* if it was about killing Rupert first and foremost and pinning it on a convenient person. Two birds, one stone.'

'I think you need to talk to DS Skinner,' says Ally.

'You're kidding, right? DS Skinner never wants to hear from me. And anyway, if Felix is charged, he's charged. Even if Skinner's harbouring private suspicions, he's not going to discuss them with me. Or you.'

'But you've proven yourself, Jayden. Time and time again.'

'I'm not police, Al.' And he can hear the wistfulness in his own voice, so he snaps out of it; reframes it. 'And tonight, that's the best thing we've got going for us.'

'So is Mullins here because' – Ally's face is worried, her eyes wide – 'he thinks Rupert's killer is still out there?'

'No. Mullins is here because he fancied a pint. But if you're asking whether I think Rupert's killer is still out there . . . ?'

Jayden's eyes rove the garden. There's a scattering of guests on the terrace now. Tallulah and Imogen wandering by the pool, still cordoned off with its blue tape. Saffron bent over the fire, with Ruby's husband, Adrian, beside her.

'Yeah. I do, Al. And the fact that Skinner does too is everything I need.'

'We're here for Tallulah. We must remember that.'

'We are. And we will be. But . . . we can't actually do that much for Tallulah. We agreed that her best shot at hearing what happened is by learning it for herself, right? And she's doing a great job of pretending to like these people.'

'She is. Fake it till you make it.'

Jayden grins at that. 'We're her eyes and ears. And I don't know about you, Al, but I've got 360-degree vision right now. Test me.'

'Where's Davey Hart?'

'About to crash and burn with Tallulah, probably.'

'Alright, what about Jet?'

'Jet. I was just with Jet. He's floating about. Quietly getting obliterated. Right now, I think he's probably sunk in one those beanbags on the terrace. Vaping aimlessly.'

Ally peers over his shoulder. 'You saw him go there.'

'No, but I told him they looked comfy and he looked like he needed a sit-down. So, what have we learnt about Jet Carson? He's suggestible.'

'Nicole?'

'Nicole. She's the butterfly. Okay, I don't know where Nicole is.'

'She's heading this way, Jayden,' says Ally.

'Alright, well, look. What I'm saying is . . . we've got smarts to spare.'

He sees Ally's brow furrow. 'Do you think DS Skinner suspects Felix has been framed too?'

'He must do. But he obviously couldn't make a compelling enough case internally to delay the charge. The police get it wrong sometimes, Al. And sometimes juries do too. Felix came here to do the right thing by his mum. And now he's been charged with murder.'

'And Tallulah came here to tell Baz she loved him and never got the chance.'

'These are our people, right? The ones getting the hard end of the bargain. That's who we're in this to help. That's Shell House.

And we've got until the end of this party to figure out who Rupert Frost's real killer is.'

'Can I offer you some Cornish charcuterie?' says Ally loudly, suddenly.

'I want some of this lovely boy's champagne,' says Nicole. 'He's neglecting his circling duties and I've run dry.'

'Fixing that now,' says Jayden, and fills her glass.

He's taken aback by her changed appearance. Her eyes are red, and her cheeks pale. She looks burdened in a way she didn't before.

'And I'm not paying you two to stand around and gossip,' Nicole says tartly.

Pretty sure Baz is footing the bill for this one, thinks Jayden. But, instead, he says, 'How about I stay by your side? That way you'll never run dry. It's Nicole, isn't it? I go where you go, Nicole.'

'At last, a sensible suggestion.'

Nicole slips her arm through his. And her grip is more forceful than Jayden might ever have imagined.

56

It's hot everywhere, but by the fire it's insane. Saffron drains another bottle of cool water as she watches over the paella.

The pan is stuffed with monkfish and giant prawns, mussels and cockles and clams, strands of salty samphire and strips of fennel and fine shavings of garlic. Everything simmering away in silky, saffron-yellow juices. It's not the biggest she's made – she's done cook-outs down on the sand for forty people or more – but it's the one she's maybe been most attentive to. Cooking as a distraction? Yes, please.

She glances up at the sky and sees a bank of tall clouds; the first in days. And the first sign of weather on the way.

Saffron has no idea if things are going as they should, but the last time she looked at Ally and Jayden they were deep in conversation with people. Tallulah seems to be turning heads wherever she goes – whether she's also getting the response she wants is a different thing.

'God, this smells amazing,' says Imogen. 'If you like fish. I don't actually like fish.'

'Oh Imogen, you're kidding.'

'Joke. I saw the man dropping it off before. It looked like he was giving you aggro.'

'He wasn't giving me aggro.'

But he was concerned that Saffron was back here after all that's happened. It was a pretty fatherly vibe, to be honest.

Imogen catches Saffron's arm. 'Thank you. For doing this. I think it's going brilliantly. Considering, I mean. We're celebrating Grandad Baz, but we're also celebrating that the man who killed Rupert is caught. Thanks to Tim.'

'Tim?'

'Well, he's not an inspector or a detective so I thought I might as well get it right. It's a nice name, Tim.'

And Saffron can't quite believe it, but Imogen looks a little dreamy.

'By the way, there's tension bubbling. Granny Nicole's just found out from my mum that Grandad Baz left this house to Felix in his will. She's furious. Especially as he didn't have nearly as much money as anyone thought.'

'Oh dear,' says Saffron. 'Are you okay?'

'I don't care about money,' says Imogen. 'Mum and Dad have loads anyway.'

Saffron nods. Easy not to care about something when you don't have to.

'Okay,' she says, 'I think this paella is about ready. Imogen, do you want to rally the troops?'

At that, Imogen darts off, and Saffron watches as she goes up to people in turn. Imogen's parents are together, leaning against the balustrade, deep in conversation. Jet is swamped in a beanbag, vape in one hand, phone in the other. Mullins has taken the adjacent beanbag and is pitched at a weird angle; he's on his phone too. Nicole and Tallulah are sitting at opposite ends of the wicker sofa. Davey and Gus have pulled up chairs nearby. Jayden is still circulating with champagne. Music drifts from the speakers, and Saffron doesn't know whose choice it is, but it's classic stuff: Zeppelin and Dire Straits. She's pretty sure she heard 'Hotel California' earlier too.

The first breeze in days catches the bunting that Imogen hung earlier. Saffron watches it jump and flap as, in the distance, cloud builds over the headland.

'Can I help serve?' asks Ally.

Saffron thanks her and starts loading plates. The aroma is perfection. The long terrace table is perfectly laid, though the guests seem slow to move towards it. Imogen's rallying hasn't achieved much.

Just then there's the chink, a call to order, and Tallulah's on her feet, tapping her glass with a knife. All heads turn towards her.

'Before we sit down to eat,' says Tallulah, 'I wanted to say a few words: a different form of grace, I guess. Though Baz wasn't religious and nor am I. But I do want to express gratitude for this gathering.'

Saffron and Ally swap looks; Tallulah's playing it well. Her voice is clear and true.

'It was Imogen who reminded us all why we were here in Baz's beautiful home in the first place – to celebrate his birthday. It's testament to Imogen's big-heartedness that we're still here now. Because amidst the loss, there are still things to be glad of. Not least the fact that the police have moved so swiftly in catching Rupert's killer.'

There's a murmur of agreement from the terrace. Saffron's pretty sure she hears Mullins say, *You're welcome*. But then she catches the uncomfortable look he sends Jayden. Mullins is about as easy to read as a kids' comic.

'Listen,' says Tallulah, and for the first time all evening she pushes her sunglasses on top of her head. Her wide eyes glisten as she looks around the terrace. 'Over the last five years, and over many letters, Baz and I re-found the intimacy we once shared. This reunion . . . so many years after we last saw one another, it was supposed to be . . . special.'

Next to her, Nicole is fidgeting, crossing her legs and slurping her drink. Tallulah pauses, sending her a piercing look. Then she appears to reset.

'Baz's book. That's what I really want to talk about. We all know Baz was tough on the people around him. But I hope you all also know that he loved everybody here a great deal. I think that's probably what this weekend was all about. Telling you all that he loved you. Perhaps he realised that the book . . .'

'Was lacking in that department?' offers Jet.

'You don't need to tell us how he felt, Tallulah,' says Nicole. 'He was part of our lives. Not in letters, but in real life. Whatever you thought you had with him . . .'

'Mum,' says Ruby, with a note of caution.

'I want to appeal to your better natures,' says Tallulah.

'Good luck,' says Jet.

'I'm flying home tomorrow. And I want peace.' Tallulah places her hand on her heart. 'I can't fight the fact that Baz is dead. No more than Rupert's beloveds can fight his death.'

'I'm not sure Rupes had any beloveds,' says Davey. 'Except for us. Poor sod.'

'Rupert's funeral will fall to us then,' says Ruby. 'But who knows how long it'll be before they release the body. All these post-mortems and such.'

'It's all Greek to me,' says Davey with a shrug.

'*Post-mortem* is Latin,' drawls Jet, 'but Rupes is with his beloved Hermes now.'

'Baz bought me a Hermès bag when we were married. A Birkin,' says Nicole.

'Oh, Mother,' groans Jet. 'Trust you.'

Ally looks to Tallulah as this small talk ripples back and forth. She feels for her, trying to hold the attention of such a reluctant crowd.

'Listen!' cries Tallulah. '*Please.*'

Quiet, surprisingly, falls. Nothing but the rustle of bunting in the breeze.

'What I want to say is that I think a kind of peace can be found in understanding what happened. I would give anything to know, personally. So, if there's anyone here who could tell me more about Baz and those drugs, you'd have my eternal gratitude. In fact, name your price. Because it means more to me than I can say.'

Her voice breaks. Beside her, Saffron feels Ally shift. Was this speech part of the plan?

'Tallulah,' says Nicole, 'you're talking to his wife of twenty years. His children. His grandchild. His son-in-law. His bandmate. Whatever you think your loss is, it's nothing to ours.'

Tallulah pushes her shades back down. 'Death's a wonderful opportunity for revisionism, isn't it? You hated him, Nicole. And you turned his own children against him too.'

'Oh, give us some credit,' says Jet lightly. 'I think we did that all on our own, didn't we, Ruby?'

'Your precious Baz wasn't the man you thought he was,' says Nicole, getting to her feet. 'He turned his back on his own family, twice: in life, and in death. Jet and Ruby never did anything to deserve being overlooked in such a cruel and insulting—'

'Mum,' says Jet, his voice pacifying. 'It's cool.'

'It's this woman,' says Nicole. 'She's pushing me.'

'Tallulah, let me translate. The contents of my father's will came as a shock,' says Jet. 'That's what this is about. I know, I know, we're a total cliché.'

Adrian, who's standing next to Saffron and Ally, leans towards them. He says in a low voice, 'Buying this place practically cleaned him out. He might have played the rich man, but he didn't have nearly as much as anyone thought. If he'd had the sense to ever ask my advice then I'd have taken care of his affairs, but he was too pig-headed. And now we're paying the price.'

'Why, are there a lot of debts?' says Ally.

'Not debts,' says Adrian, his brow wrinkling. 'But the will's hardly going to change anyone's life.'

Saffron looks away. This whole scene's making her queasy. And then she looks to the paella, congealing on the plates. She wonders about scooping it back into the pan, but she can't do that, not when she's scattered the herbs so perfectly: the fine sprinkling of chives and chervil and tarragon. Maybe they should take the plates to the table before the guests sit down: *Major hint, guys. Grub's up.*

Nicole moves towards Tallulah.

'Adrian!' Ruby cries.

Adrian tries to intercept. 'Easy, Nic. Emotions are running high.'

'And what's so bad about that?' snaps Nicole, batting him away. 'Why's everyone always so afraid of emotion? Tallulah's not. Are you? She's here, telling us all how we feel. Telling us how Baz felt too. What about Rupert, huh? Do you want to tell us how he felt too? And Felix?'

'I should think Rupert felt pretty peachy,' says Jet, who's now practically horizontal on his beanbag. 'Up until he didn't, anyway.'

Saffron can see Mullins struggling to get to his feet, but the beanbag keeps sucking him back in.

'Don't even bother, dude,' says Jet, puffing his vape in his direction. 'It'll soon blow over.'

'I'm sorry,' says Jayden, stepping between the two women, an easy smile on his face, 'but I'm under strict instructions to let you all know that dinner is served.'

And somehow Jayden smoothly steers Nicole towards the table; her face pinched with anger, chest heaving.

Beside Saffron, Ally picks up a bowl of green salad – but her eyes are casting about the terrace. If she's looking for Tallulah, she's nowhere to be seen.

Way out west, the sky darkens.

57

'Okay, Al. Team meeting.'

After the heated scenes on the terrace, the kitchen is like a sanctuary. Saffron's quietly working on dessert: fire-roasted pineapple and coconut ice cream. It's a safe space, but all the same, Ally pulls the door closed.

'That speech was Tallulah's play,' says Jayden. 'She handled it well – mostly. Observations?'

'I admire her. But I'm not sure how well judged it was, given the crowd. It felt a little . . . preachy. Didn't it?'

'Did you see the way Davey Hart was looking at her?'

'Gosh, yes. Hanging on her every word. I think if he knows anything at all about Baz, then he'll tell her.'

'I can see it. The band back together – what's left of them anyway – partying like the old days. But Davey will have been swabbed when he was arrested. Drugs would have shown up then. And the same for Rupert with the post-mortem.'

'But they could still have been together?'

'Yeah. But everything I read about Davey in the book is that he's a party animal. Still going hard at sixty-eight. Is he likely to have turned down coke, if Baz was offering?'

Ally shakes her head. It's another world to her. Another world entirely. 'Like you said, I think Davey will want to help. To give her that peace she talked about. Even if he fabricates it.'

'You think he'd do that?'

'I think when someone wants to comfort someone, they do the kind thing. And overhearing Davey with Tallulah before, I think he'd say anything to be in her good books.'

'Plus, he's drunk and getting drunker. Loose lips sink ships, right?'

'Jayden, what do you think all that was about the will? What Jet was saying about them being shocked?'

He shrugs. 'Honestly, I'd have put money on this lot arguing about Baz's will.'

'But could it be relevant? Adrian, the son-in-law, said Baz had a lot less money than anyone thought.'

Jayden scratches his head. 'Relevant to how Baz died? I don't know. As for Rupert . . . I don't see how it could connect. Why would anyone want to kill Rupert over Baz's will? Unless he was set to inherit the lot. Which feels . . . unlikely.'

'Guys,' says Saffron, wiping her hands on her apron as she comes over, 'Imogen told me that the stress over the will is because Felix is inheriting this place.'

'Felix is inheriting Rockpool House?' says Jayden.

'Apparently.' Saffron shrugs. 'I know, it sounds wild, but when Baz was telling me about all the guests, he said that he was genuinely proud of Felix. He was rough on his own children, but he only had good things to say about Felix.'

Ally looks to Jayden. 'Felix can't have known he was inheriting. Unless Rupert was going to contest it in some way . . . and that was his motive.'

'Why would Rupert contest it? He's not family. But you know what, Felix's inheritance could help his defence. Thanks, Saffron, that's helpful.'

'I was watching everyone as Tallulah spoke,' says Ally. 'When she mentioned Rupert's name, no one blinked an eye. Then Davey volunteered that Rupert had no beloveds.'

'Yeah, "poor sod" was the term. Not much of an epitaph, is it?'

'If there is a murderer at this party, they're about as cold-blooded as they come.'

'Davey looked really gutted.'

'He did.'

'But whether that was for Baz or Rupert or for both, I don't know.'

'However he's feeling, Gus seems delighted to have met him.'

Jayden nods. 'Yeah, all those stories.'

Ally watches him, her head tipped. 'You're mulling something, aren't you?'

'The questions that Gus was asking Davey in the pub.' Jayden has a fixed look of concentration. 'It's made me think. If Felix's fingerprints were on the knife . . . *why* were they?'

'You mean, if Felix wasn't the one holding it?'

'I mean if he *was* the one holding it. Which is the basis on which the police are pressing charges.'

Most of the time Ally thinks she keeps pace with Jayden fairly well. But not now.

'What I mean is, Felix is a smart guy. If he really wanted to kill Rupert, why didn't he wear gloves? It's the one thing someone can do to cover their tracks – or, in this case, prints. It's a no-brainer, Al.'

'Perhaps he panicked. Heat of the moment.'

'And, what, Felix just happened to be carrying a kitchen knife when he called on Rupert in his room? It doesn't stack up. If the murder was premeditated, the killer would be wearing gloves.'

'But how on earth could Felix's prints be on the knife otherwise?'

'I'm thinking he could have been set up. He could have been handed the knife at some point or forced to pick it up. Just enough interaction to get his prints on there. It could have been orchestrated, if someone was cunning enough.'

'But how does that link to Gus's conversation with Davey?'

'Ah,' says Jayden with a grin. 'This is where you'll have to bear with me.'

'I'm bearing.'

'Okay, so do you remember the bit in the book where Baz is talking about people not taking responsibility for their own destiny? He goes off on one, this whole soapbox moment about people's crazy superstitions and misplaced belief in fate – all that kind of thing.'

'I remember it,' says Ally. 'Their bassist, I forget his name, always used to have a full fry-up for breakfast on gig days. Three eggs. Four sausages.'

'And four rashers of bacon. And he died of a stroke at fifty-five. And he calls out Davey too. Baz mocks him for always carrying his lucky gloves. Apparently, wherever he goes, they're always with him. Like other people carry a wallet, Davey carries his drumming gloves.'

Ally sees where this is going. *Maybe.* 'Go on.'

'Chatting to Gus earlier, he was passing on all the rock trivia he'd gleaned. Knitting needles as drumsticks, Davey's car blowing up and buying his first kit. Gus said he asked Davey about the gloves, but he said that it was an exaggeration.'

'So, either Baz was making something out of nothing in the book, or Davey didn't want to look silly? Or . . . he had something to hide?'

'Or he had something to hide.' Jayden's holding up his phone. 'Look. Put into Google "Davey Hart lucky gloves", and there's a bunch of entries. It's a thing. So why would he deny it? Why not just laugh it off? I think we need to ask Gus how Davey responded in that exact moment. Because you know what, Al . . . Davey could have done it. He could have made Felix hold the knife at some point – set up some innocent situation – then killed Rupert

294

wearing those lucky gloves of his and tossed them before the police got here. That way, only Felix's prints would be on the murder weapon.'

'But surely the police would have found the gloves when they searched?'

'All Davey had to do was chuck them in the sea. Time wasn't on his side, but he could have dropped them from the cliff. I was checking it out earlier, the gate at the bottom of the property. It leads straight on to the cliff path, and there's a bunch of sheer drops. If I wanted to dispose of something, that's what I'd do. Sure, they could have snagged on a rock, and the search team might have found them, but . . . they're his lucky gloves, right? He took the risk. Or he could have. What do you think?'

Ally loves Jayden when he's in this mode (she loves him all the time, really). What does she think? She thinks it's all perfectly possible.

'But why Davey?' she says. 'So, he's got the means and the opportunity, but what about the motive?'

'Yeah, I'm still working on the motive. Any thoughts?'

'And why would he want to frame Felix?'

'I don't know. Maybe he didn't care who got the blame, Al.'

'If it was Baz who was murdered, you could almost imagine it was out of jealousy. Davey wanting to be with Tallulah, maybe.'

'Exactly . . . So why would Davey want to kill Rupert? Perhaps there's some ancient history that we don't know about.'

'Something that only came to a head after Baz died,' says Ally.

'Royalties,' says Jayden. 'Could be, couldn't it? Who gets Baz's share now? But I don't think anyone would act this quickly.'

'And even if they did, is it enough to kill over?'

'What, money? Definitely. Especially if Davey was in financial difficulty. Ordinarily the police would have been checking all that, but with the Felix factor, maybe not . . . I think sometimes you see what you're looking for. And with prints on the knife, they're not thinking about someone else coming along afterwards and wearing gloves.'

Ally steps back; smooths her hands on her apron. On the other side of the kitchen Saffron's working away, as if she's used to this kind of background talk in the kitchen.

'We need to talk to Gus next, don't we? Find out more about how Davey responded to that question of his.'

'Exactly. Good old Gus, wandering in all innocent and potentially unlocking this whole thing.' Jayden checks his watch. 'The clock's ticking on this party, Al, but I reckon we just got a little bit closer to finding our killer.'

58

The sun is dropping fast towards the horizon, partly obscured by a bank of cumulonimbus that seems to Gus to have come out of nowhere. The pyrotechnics are even more dramatic for the purple clouds and electric outlines. Is he the only one watching? Everyone else seems pretty wrapped up in each other, their phones, or the bottoms of their glasses.

Gus knows his clouds. Should he tell people there's a storm coming?

Earlier, Ally passed carrying a stack of plates and she gave him a half-smile. He nodded and waved, then remembered that he's supposed to be pretending not to know her. Or is he? It's perfectly plausible that, in a place like Porthpella, he would know Saffron's helpers. He neglected to voice this to Jayden, when he first intercepted them at the gate. Mullins all but laughed: *What, undercover?* To which Jayden coolly replied, *Don't knock it till you've tried it.*

How peculiar for them all to be here. This place. This time. The two-fold loss hanging over this fancy house. No wonder emotions are running high. Nicole Carson has a touch of Mona about her, though brasher – and more flammable. Gus is giving her a wide berth tonight. In fact, he's giving everyone a fairly wide berth.

Whatever bonded Gus and Davey in the pub seems to have loosened here. Davey's hardly spoken to him since Tallulah Pearce turned up. *Classic.* He was looking forward to more rock-and-roll tales. Maybe swapping notes on the eighties – were you even there if you could remember them, et cetera. Well, yes, Gus was there. Marking geography essays, mostly; striding the odd fell, whistling 'You Do It For Me'. But still.

Meanwhile, Jayden and Ally are flitting about, doing their thing. Mullins has been all but commandeered by Baz's granddaughter, Imogen. She's showing a lot of interest in his pet rabbits, which, if you don't know Mullins, might make him sound creepy.

The bad bit about being on his own means Gus is alone with his thoughts too – as much as he's tried to give them the slip.

He hauls himself to his feet. If Ally's in the kitchen washing dishes, then perhaps he can lend a hand. It's not how he thought he'd spend his first rock-and-roll party, but he'd like a chance to speak with her and he's handy with a tea towel. He'll have to tell her at some point about the email from Jacqueline Clifton, and perhaps tonight is as good as any.

He'd rather have a plan to go with the news, because, as it is, Gus looks a lot like a man who's not in control of his own destiny. He felt so wild and free, deciding to stay in Porthpella on the spur of the moment, but with one email, the plug's been pulled on that. And he's been left with nothing but a sense of his own precariousness.

Because the fact is, it's not just about losing All Swell, is it?

He's just padding across the terrace, the buffet of wind at his back – *that's new, wind* – when he sees Ally coming towards him with a focused look on her face. It's as if he's conjured her. As she reaches him, she lays her hand on his arm, says in a low voice, 'Can we talk?'

And his heart jumps.

Gus nods, following her into the cool of the house. Inside it feels vast and empty; he can hear his shoes squeaking on the polished granite floor, his heart banging in his chest.

It's a long time since he last went to a party. But parties are where things happen, aren't they? Where lines are blurred, and people take the risks that seem, by daylight, to be off the cards. He's done his fair share of huddling in corners, music swirling as two people fall. A lifetime ago, but nevertheless.

Ally leads him into the kitchen and closes the door. The lights are bright in here and there's Jayden, leaning against the fridge, a serious look on his face. All hopes of romance instantly fizzle. He was a fool to think it at all.

'Sorry to pull you away,' says Ally.

'Gus,' says Jayden, 'we want to ask you about Davey Hart.'

'What, my new best friend? Nice bloke. Not that I've seen much of him since we got—'

'Gus, you know you told me the story about Davey's lucky gloves?'

'What? Oh yes. Well, the non-story. But he was forthcoming on everything else. I got a quite forensic description of that first Ludwig kit. Skins and all. I think he was glad of the distraction to be honest, poor bloke. He's devastated about Baz and Rupert. I'm sure he's got people looking out for him, but—'

'Did you bring up the gloves or did he?' asks Ally.

'Oh, it was me. I knew, of course, but I read it in the book, and—'

'Did you notice anything about his reaction, when you asked about them?' says Jayden.

'Not especially. Why all this interest in Davey's gloves, folks?'

Ally sends Jayden a look of enquiry, and he responds with a just-perceptible shake of his head.

Suddenly, Gus feels very tired. Whatever Ally and Jayden are up to, he's not part of it. Just like he's not really a part of this party either. Is he even a part of Porthpella? An emmet who's scuttled in, hiding beneath a rock, kidding himself that it's home.

He feels peevishness sweep in like a wave, so has a crack at bucking up.

'You can't think Davey was involved in the deaths somehow, can you?'

'We're considering all the possibilities,' says Ally.

'I should say it's unlikely,' says Gus.

'Based on what, Gus?' says Jayden.

'Based on . . .' And he's got nothing. Nothing at all. 'Do you want me to pump him for a bit more info? We were getting on handsomely before, and—'

'Cheers, Gus, but I think it best you keep your distance,' says Jayden. And to his side, Ally nods.

And that's Gus's cue.

He holds up his hand in a wave. 'I think I'll shove off then. Get my beauty sleep.'

'Cheers, Gus,' says Jayden again, distractedly.

Ally catches him at the door.

'I'm sorry it's been such a strange night,' she says. 'If I knew you were coming. Well, it'd have been no less strange, but . . . I would have explained.'

'Ah, no problem there,' says Gus. 'I'm as surprised as you that I'm here. Right. Okay. Good luck and so on.'

'See you tomorrow,' she says, with a squeeze of his arm.

'Right you are.'

Then he's back out into the hall. He's making for the door when he has a sudden thought: he should say goodbye to Davey. It's the done thing, isn't it? And he's sure Ally and Jayden are barking up the wrong tree – otherwise he wouldn't be going within a country mile of the bloke, obviously.

Gus wanders deeper into the house. He ducks his head into the vast lounge. Dusk has rolled in, hustled on by those storm clouds, but inside it's as if the white walls are holding the last of the light.

The whole place seems to shimmer, an iridescent almost-pink. But it's empty of people. He wonders if Baz has a music room, and imagines a whole set-up, an immaculate Telecaster, a Ludwig kit, in case Davey ever dropped by. Framed records and photos. Oh, how he'd like to nose around in there.

He stops then, hears voices. Is that Davey's gravelly laugh? And a woman's voice, coming from a room at the rear.

Gus isn't sure why, but he edges his way carefully, instead of just striding in with a hearty *Cheerio then!* Perhaps he wants to get the measure of the conversation, before he briefly intrudes. Or perhaps the Ally-and-Jayden effect is lingering after all.

'You said you wanted the truth.'

Gus freezes at the words.

'You know I do. It's all I want.'

Tallulah. And her voice is seductive, blatantly so. Gus's eyes widen. He presses himself against the wall. *Are you considered a voyeur if you can't actually see anything?* He's been here before – Helena Hunter; peeping Tom accusations – and it was deeply unpleasant. Not to mention inaccurate.

Should he dash and get Ally and Jayden? But there's no time. The conversation could be over by then.

Gus holds his breath and listens hard. Outside, he hears a far-off rumble of thunder. He has a sudden feeling – one of absolute conviction – that whatever happens next will matter.

59

Finally, Davey has Tallulah all on her own. And all to himself.

They're in a small room off the main hall, a kind of sitting room with doors leading to a garden at the side of the house. It's sparsely furnished, the light poor. Not a party room. And no danger of anyone disturbing them.

Davey's perched on the edge of a chaise longue. He's not sure what he's going for with this posture, but he's too drunk to have much of a say in it. Tallulah, meanwhile, is resplendent in a wing-back armchair by the fireplace: silver hair spilling over her shoulders and her long, tanned arms; the folds of her dress hanging just so. She looks like a goddess, but then she always has. He stares at her, feeling faintly stunned. She glitters back.

Davey will tell her what she wants to know; lay the gift of truth in her hands – or some of it, anyway. Then, perhaps, they can mourn together. Find comfort in one another.

Like they found comfort in one another in Nevada thirty years ago.

Davey knows what that night was about – but this doesn't take anything from it. Tallulah hadn't seen Baz in years, and by the time their paths crossed again in that dusty spot, Baz was with Nicole. Tallulah was gutted, anyone could see that. She turned up to the gig and danced and sang and was radiant; she wore a dress as yellow as the sun. Davey could feel the desire coming off Baz in waves; he was lit up. But he was a decent bloke, Baz, and he wouldn't do that to Nicole. So, the way he handled it was to play a killer show, then take himself off. No afterparty that night. Baz couldn't stand to be around Tallulah in case he was tempted.

Enter Davcy.

He had a good way about him back then. Time was yet to chew him up and spit him out; disappointment wasn't scratched all over his face. *I've seen a photograph of you,* he told her, *but 2D's got nothing on the real deal. Baz was loony to ever walk away.* But even at the apex of their night together, Davey knew he was a consolation prize.

You and Tallulah, huh? Baz said the next day.

Me and Tallulah, shrugged Davey, like it was no big thing; like it wasn't the best moment of his off-stage life.

Davey would never say it's why The Nick broke up, and nor would Baz; there's no word of it in that book of his. But Davey always felt like a little something was altered after that: a key change.

'Davey, please,' says Tallulah now. 'The truth. You know how much it means to me.'

And there's a confiding note in her voice. Seductive, even. Is he reading that right?

You know how much it means to me because you know the real me. You've lain with me as the sun burst over the mountains and the desert dust danced. Tequila and smokes out on the balcony, the pool below as still as a teardrop. 'Do Not Disturb' sign on the door. The maids passing, thinking, what sweet music is that?

Davey was never a songwriter.

'I don't want to tarnish Rupert's memory. What's the point in that?' says Davey, his voice slurred from Baz's champagne.

'What about Baz's memory?' says Tallulah.

Baz's memory. Davey's memory of Baz. They were just Northampton boys, art college boys, boys who stepped clear of the shoe factories their old men made a wage in, and threw about paint on canvas, fierce marks of lead pencil, built things out of trash and said it was sculpture. The lads played their guitars at each other like they were in a bullfight: courting and killing, all majestic swoops and furious bellowing. And Davey's drums the heartbeat beneath it all. They called themselves The Nick because they used to rehearse in an old garage behind the remand centre. They made music because they felt banged up and wanted to escape. And it was all Baz. He went away to America, but when he came back, he said, *Boys, I've got it. We're The Nick.*

We're The Nick.

Davey's sucked under by the past, now. It's a fight to stay clear of it. His throat burns; his eyes too.

'Davey, come on, darling. You've been a good friend to Rupert, but it's not helping anyone now. And it's not helping me. Is it? Or you. Because I know it's eating you up too.'

She leans forward and sets her hand on Davey's knee. He looks down at her slender fingers, her silver and turquoise rings. Her touch travels all the way through him.

He feels a flutter of hope.

'You really want to know?' he says, his voice low; broken, really.

'I really want to know.'

Her eyes so blue, fixed on his.

'Alright. Alright. It was Rupert. It was Rupert who gave him the drugs.'

'Gave him the drugs?'

'Spiked his drink. Some herbal thing.'

'*Spiked his drink?*'

Tallulah takes her hand back, but Davey can still feel the touch of it there – like a phantom limb, a ghost of affection.

'Why didn't you tell the police?'

'Hmm, what's that?'

'I said, why didn't you tell the police, Davey?'

Her voice is suddenly cut glass. He blinks.

'But what difference would it have made? Baz's heart packed up. No one could have seen that. Total tragedy but that was the gods, that. That wasn't Rupert. We lost our Baz, because . . . it was written.'

And he sounds nonchalant as he says it, trying to smooth things over. He thought he'd meet her in grief, but she's turning to anger. Meanwhile Davey's own grief is rising as fast as an incoming tide. *We lost our Baz.* He feels like he's getting sucked beneath it; choking for breath.

'Rupert would have been arrested there and then. That's the difference it would have made.' Then, after a moment's pause, she adds, 'Which means Rupert would have lived, wouldn't he?'

'But aren't you glad he's dead? Considering?'

'Glad?' Another pause. The silence thrums. Davey wonders about reaching out to her knee this time. Reaching out and holding on for dear life, because he feels like the current's changed.

'Whatever happened to Rupert has happened, but this man they've arrested – Felix Boyd – I've heard what that was all about,' says Tallulah. 'His mother Connie dying. The role Rupert played that night. Felix was heartbroken, Davey, and he was looking to blame someone. And honestly? I don't blame him at all. Don't you see, darling, if Rupert had been arrested on Friday night, then Felix would have been spared his fate.'

Davey shakes his head. Tallulah sounds more concerned for Felix than for Rupert; more sorrow for the man who was pushed to murder than for the victim.

'That need for revenge,' she says, quietly, 'I understand it. Hate born out of love is the strongest kind.'

She pushes her hair from her face and looks steadily at Davey. She's beautiful, so beautiful. His head spins, and he wishes he went slower, or stopped drinking sooner, or just . . . wasn't him. He wishes he wasn't him.

If he can just stay with her, he'll be okay. He holds out his hand and she takes hold of it. He feels the press of her rings – pleasure meets pain.

'But how did you know? Did Rupert tell you?' says Tallulah softly.

'He confessed it. He was in pieces.'

'Why did he tell you, Davey?'

'Because I'm his friend.'

'You weren't in on it together?'

And Tallulah's voice has changed again. If it was glass before, it's a diamond now. Sharp as you like.

'What? No! Never. I wouldn't pull a trick like that.'

'So why would Rupert?'

And suddenly he wants to say it. He wants to be free of it. He wants to be so free that he'll float away. Because with Baz dead and Rupert too, doesn't he have it coming?

'Because Rupert was fed up with Baz lording it over everyone, thinking he was better. Because he wanted to take him down a peg or two. Because we missed the old days . . .'

Davey hears her quick intake of breath.

'We?' says Tallulah. 'You said *we*.'

But he's on a roll now. He won't stop. He can see the great wide open, the freedom of the truth, even though his vision's blurring. Perhaps *because* his vision's blurring.

'. . . we used to have fun, man. He was one of us. Then he wasn't. And the way he saw it, the rest of us were failures. Good for nothing. He was the only one who ever got it all right. And he loved telling that story to the whole world, didn't he? So Rupes wanted to just . . . we just . . . we never thought it'd kill him. What? Why are you looking at me like that? Tallulah, you know how he was. He picked you up and then he dropped you. Didn't he? He did the same with me . . .'

He sees her change. Transform, before his eyes, like in a Disney movie where the beauty becomes the beast.

'You killed him,' she says. 'You killed Baz.'

And she's on her feet. She spins to the fireplace, reaches for something. She's crying, her hair falling in front of her eyes. And this is so far from what Davey thought – hoped – would happen. But when has he ever got it right?

That's what Baz would say.

Loser. When did Davey Hart ever get it right?

'Tallulah . . .' he starts to say.

But then he stops short, because she's got a poker in her hands.

There's no fire in the grate, but she's holding a poker.

She's lifting it above her head, and her face looks like he's never seen it before.

He starts to back away; words falling from his mouth, but he doesn't know what. She cries out as she raises her arm. He turns and pelts through the doorway, feet skidding. Behind him he can hear her sobbing, and it wrenches at whatever's left in him to wrench.

When Davey gets to the end of the hallway, he turns. He sees someone else step into the light. It's the bloke from the pub. He watches him go into the room. Then Davey hears another sob, and a crash.

A moment of stillness descends.

In this quiet, Davey can feel his heart pounding in his chest, and he presses his hand to it. Maybe his ticker's got a timer on it too. Well, that's poetic justice.

Then there's the slam of a door. The sound of thumping footsteps on the stairs. It's the other bloke from the pub, the copper, taking them two at a time. Davey locks eyes with him, for no more than a second, then he's off and running.

Whatever's happened back there, it's all over.

It's all over for Davey.

60

Mullins hears the shout when he's halfway down the stairs. At first, he thinks he's being ticked off for wandering about in the house – he just wanted a snoop – but you don't make a sound like this for a thing like that.

He moves fast down the stairs, the night's excesses swirling in his belly.

As Mullins skids in the corridor, he just catches a glimpse of Davey's startled face – then his rear end disappearing out into the garden. Jayden hurtles in from the other direction.

'Through there,' cries Mullins.

And they move into the room together; steady now, two cops, assessing a situation. Mullins sees the body straight away, lying by the open garden doors. His heart drops.

'It's Gus.'

There are footsteps fast behind them, and he hears Jayden turn. Says, 'Saffron, can you call an ambulance? Al, stay back. It's okay.'

Mullins kneels by the body. *Gus.* In his summer shirt and khaki trousers. That tanned bald head of his running with blood. Blood that Mullins can't look at. His hands are juddering as he checks for a pulse. He finds one – just. He leans close to Gus, listens for his breathing. Gently tips his head, listens again. His chest isn't rising, his chest isn't falling. He checks the pulse again.

'We need to do CPR,' he says. His voice comes out high, trembling.

Jayden's instantly there. He does the same checks and he's rock steady as he says, 'Okay, let's do this. Alternate?'

'I haven't . . . I've never . . .' Mullins has all the training, but he's never actually had to do it. There's always been someone else; someone better qualified, or faster off the blocks. 'You do it, Jayden,' he says.

And Jayden already is.

Chest compressions. Breathing. Counting. Like the pro he is.

Mullins feels a burn at the back of his eyes, and he grits his teeth hard.

'Ambulance and police are on the way,' says Saffron.

And Mullins is aware of her hand resting on his shoulder. Then Ally's there too, and it's looking up at Ally's face that makes the tears come for Mullins.

'He'll be okay, Mrs Bright. Jayden's got this,' he says.

Ally kneels beside Jayden. Mullins hears her say, 'Stay with us, Gus. Stay with us.'

He can't look. An image suddenly lands – and Mullins snaps his head back up.

'Davey Hart. He was running away. It must have been him.'

Beside him, Saffron's response is instant. 'Stop him.'

'Run, Mullins,' says Jayden, without looking up, still working on Gus. 'Run.'

And suddenly Mullins is on his feet, and it's like he's super-charged, like he's ready to bust his way out of the cloud of panic and move towards the light.

He grips Saffron's hand, and because she's Hippy-Dippy, because she's got the powers, he says – quietly, so Ally can't hear – 'Don't let him die, Saff.'

Out in the garden it's properly dark, but the terrace is lit by spot-lights. Nicole, Jet, Ruby, Imogen, Ruby's husband Adrian – they're all there, in this sinister kind of light. The wind's up, and it pushes at Mullins's back.

'What's going on?' says Adrian, getting to his feet. 'We heard a bit of drama.'

And the way he says it – *drama* – it's like it's insignificant; something even a little bit silly.

'Anyone see Davey Hart?' A rumble of distant thunder half smothers his words; it better not be coming this way. Mullins shouts it again.

The way they look at him blankly, he's on his own here. Can he hear sirens? He wants to hear sirens. He wants the cavalry to come charging up the lanes.

'I saw someone,' says Imogen, jumping up. 'I saw someone heading down the garden. Is Davey okay?'

'There's been an incident,' he says. 'Police and ambulance are on their way. You all stay here. alright? Nobody go anywhere.'

Mullins pulls his phone from his pocket and switches on the torch. As he moves down the garden, he casts it left and right. He can hear their raised voices behind him, but he can't think about how that pack might scatter.

If I was Davey, where would I go?

The guy has no vehicle – Mullins remembers him moaning about the train journey on the way here – so he's on foot. He's on the run.

Why would anyone want to hurt a guy like Gus? And if Davey did this, did he kill Rupert Frost too?

He dials Skinner, who answers instantly.

'What is it?'

'Davey Hart is what. Are you on your way to Rockpool? Because I'm here, and I think you're right about Felix. I think it was Davey because now he's tried to kill Gus too.'

'Mullins, listen carefully. Go after the suspect. Restrain him.'

And now that it's an official order, Mullins baulks. He wants to say that he's off duty, that he doesn't have any of his gear. But then he thinks of Jayden – who right now is saving Gus's life – and how he's always off duty, he never has any gear, but he gets stuff done all the same.

Jayden would stop Davey Hart.

And it's that thought that reboots him. It sets his thinking straight too: if Davey Hart wants to get away, then he'll use the gate at the bottom of the garden that leads on to the cliff path. It's the only other exit point apart from the main gates. And once you're through the main gates then you're stuck on a lane, hedges as high as prison walls and just as thick. Davey won't run the risk of being picked out by police headlights there. He'll slip out on to the cliffs. Weasel-like. Thinking he can just disappear.

Mullins sprints past the glinting waters of the pool. The police tape gives him jetpacks. *We're on this, we've got this, let's do this.*

Through the gate, the garden walls high behind him, the cliff path feels like it's cutting between sea and sky: a narrow trail of semi-darkness. The water stretches endlessly, gleaming silver. The moon is bright, even if fast-blowing clouds keep blotting it out.

The temperature's dropped and Mullins shivers. Something swoops close to him and it's as if he feels its wingbeat. Bat or gull?

You've got this.

'Davey? Are you there, Davey?'

Here's what he knows about Davey Hart. He's pushing seventy, he's as drunk as a skunk, and he just tried to kill Gus. The first two facts make Mullins sure that he can catch him. The third? He doesn't know what he'll do when he does.

Because Gus is about the nicest man Mullins knows. It's not like they've spent a lot of time together, but whenever they do, it's just . . . decent. Gus is one of the few people around here who doesn't treat him like he's a little bit stupid.

'Davey!' Mullins shouts again.

Two choices: left or right.

What would Hippy-Dippy say? *Oh, left.*

So he goes left. Because it's away from the village, and maybe that's in Davey's head.

It's narrow, the path here. It's not the official coast path, but a walkable section of clifftop that will, Mullins figures, eventually join up with it. He's got a dim memory of capering about up here as a little boy, a box kite flying from his fingers. The memory sharpens suddenly, as Mullins's foot skids. He remembers the gust that took that kite once, making Mullins yell out in delight, as the sails of his coat were filled and he was pulled along. Pulled closer and closer to the edge – not that he knew much about it. Then his mum, screaming like a gull, flying towards him like he'd never seen her fly before; the way she threw her arms around him and held on to him tight. Saved him, really.

His mum, who's grown old now. Who barely leaves the sofa and has custard creams for breakfast.

They hung on to each other, then; the kite slipping from his fingers and sailing away without him.

Now, Mullins feels the strangest thing: love, pure love, flowing through him.

He won't let Davey Hart get away. And Gus won't die.

And this absolute certainty leads him on like a light in darkness. Somewhere far below, the faint sound of sirens lifts on the night air. Then thunder growls, closer this time, as if the sirens and the weather are racing each other. Mullins feels the light patter of rain on his shoulders.

61

He didn't think it would end like this. But then who does?

If Gus had ever imagined it, he'd go gently in his sleep, blissfully unaware of his own departure. Mostly because it was the only option – *option?* – that felt tolerable. Without a church to lean on, he's never seen the silver lining of the big full stop. Life eternal? *Well, sure. But can we make it earth-side, please.*

This, though.

The pain went as suddenly as it came, a split second of agony as immense as an explosion. And the aftershock? This drift. Bodyless, more or less. Floating on slow currents.

Gus has never been much of a swimmer. He's never cared for the stench of chlorine, so it isn't for him, the swimming caps and boring lengths in marked lanes. He's made the odd cautious foray into lakes and rivers over the years, though such occasions were often cut short by feeling the eerie slip of a fish at his middle or a twist of weed around his ankle. But since being in Porthpella, he's taken dips. In then out, slap of wave, face full of salt. That sort of thing. Not in midwinter – he's not a lunatic – but under a full sun you might find him wading out. Earlier this week he floated like a starfish. Bobbed on still waters, stared up at an endless sky. And it was a moment of total happiness.

Perhaps that was an indicator. Some joker on high, declaring, *Let's give him one last hurrah*, before he checks out.

Afterwards, he walked along the beach with Ally and Fox. They stopped in for a coffee at Hang Ten. The sunshine made Ally's hair glow bright white.

Total happiness: squared.

Now here he is. Floating again. Weightless. Swathes of blue. Neither here nor there.

Not so very different – apart from the happiness factor. Instead, there's a whacking great regret factor. And it's a regret so powerful that if he had any breath of his own, the mere thought of it would punch it out of him.

Such a cliché, to die with an unspoken wish at your lips.

Because here's the thing. Gus really does want to tell Ally that he thinks she's smashing. That he thinks she's smashing in all the ways that a person can be. He wants to tell her that with no expectation of return.

Just for it to be said.

He really does wish he at least managed that.

62

Jayden watches the ambulance disappear through the Rockpool gates. Now that the initial shock has ebbed, other emotions flow in. Jayden rubs his face with both hands: rain and salt water.

'Right, okay then,' says Skinner, clapping him on the back, 'where's PC Mullins?'

He takes a beat to answer. Part of Jayden is in that ambulance with Gus and Ally. Part of him is still bent over Gus, hand to heart and mouth to mouth.

'What's that?'

'Mullins. Where is he?'

Jayden turns. Police are on the terrace. The crackle of radios. Uniforms doing what uniforms do. Meanwhile the rain starts falling harder. DS Skinner looks at him, not unkindly.

'You did what you could for Gus. Muscle memory. The training kicked in. You okay, son?'

Jayden nods. Tries to keep the tremor from his voice as he says, 'Mullins went after Davey Hart. He was seen running from the scene.'

'He called me. Told me the same thing.'

'I think Davey killed Rupert Frost,' says Jayden.

'Felix Boyd has been charged.'

'But you don't think he did it.'

'Mullins blabbing? That's a breach right there.'

'If Mullins has caught up with Davey,' says Jayden, 'he'll need assistance.'

'What are you waiting for, then?' says Skinner. 'Come on.'

Jayden hesitates. He looks to the uniforms again. Part of him wants to be in the mix, giving chase, backing up, doing all the things he's been trained to do. Instead, he says, 'You don't need me here.'

'Any other exits?'

'There's a gate at the bottom of the grounds.' Jayden scans the lawn, sees torch beams moving over the wet grass. 'Your officers are already on it.'

'Alright, son.'

Jayden hauls in a breath. He should be behind the wheel, following the ambulance. When Gus is taken in, he should be standing there right beside Ally.

'I've got to go,' he says.

'You do that,' says Skinner. 'But tell me why Davey Hart.'

'Lucky gloves. He never goes anywhere without his lucky gloves.'

~

Jayden finds Ally at the end of a long, quiet corridor. She sits statue-still, her hands folded in her lap. She's still wearing the apron Saffron gave her. When he says her name, she looks up at him, and he sees the smear of blood on her cheek.

Jayden sits down beside her, shifting the plastic chair closer. He covers her hands with one of his.

'He can't die,' she says, in a very small voice.

'No,' he says.

But they both know that people do.

Jayden drops his head. There's a pain blazing in him that he doesn't know what to do with.

316

'You brought him back, Jayden. He was gone, and you brought him back.'

He nods. He can't quite look at her.

'You were . . . amazing.'

But none of it matters, if it doesn't work. The compressions, the breaths, the pitch-perfect technique: if it doesn't work, he might as well have not tried at all.

'What have they said to you?'

'He's in surgery. Jayden, I can't get the image of him out of my head. Gus lying there. Not moving.'

Ally turns to him. She looks old. And he never thinks of her that way. The lines on her face are deeply grooved, and there's a frailty about her that's pure stress.

'Your jacket's wet,' she says.

'It's tipping down out.'

'Jayden, I think I saw something. Something that didn't fit. I saw a tiny blue object. It was on the floor . . . near Gus.'

Her voice is cautious, but focused. It trips a switch in him.

'What was it, Al?'

'I shouldn't have noticed it. I don't know why I did, with everything happening, but . . . it was a piece of sea glass.'

'Okay. What are you thinking?'

Ally's fingers toy with the edge of the apron.

'Well, it could be nothing. I mean, Baz could very well have some as an ornament. I didn't look closely at it, this piece of sea glass, but I did register it. And, the way I remember it, it looked awfully like a heart shape.'

Jayden gives her a sad smile. Because maybe she wants a sign. Maybe in the same way that some people believe in white feathers, or a fisherman like Wilson Rowe tucks a little black china cat in the wheelhouse of his boat.

'Could have been, Al.'

'Jayden, it looked almost exactly like a piece of sea glass I gave Tallulah yesterday.'

'Tallulah?'

'I didn't see Tallulah, not afterwards. She would have come to me, I know she would have. But . . . she didn't. Did you see her?'

He shakes his head. He didn't see her at all. His mind whirrs as he says, 'The police will be taking everyone's statements. If there's anyone missing, they'll find them.'

Ally shifts in her chair. 'Jayden, listen. Tallulah said she wasn't looking for retribution. She just wanted to find a personal kind of peace. That was she told us. And it's what she said in her speech to everyone. But . . . what if she didn't mean it? If you're right about Davey killing Rupert, she might have figured that out too.'

'But for Tallulah it wasn't about Rupert's death. She was only focused on Baz.'

'We've always said the two deaths could be linked. We just don't know how.'

Jayden sits back in his chair. His thoughts churn. He tries to order them: one by one. Just like Ally sifts through her shoreline treasures. Just like she notices a glinting piece of blue sea glass in a moment of such shock and fear that most people wouldn't take anything in at all.

'Mullins saw Davey running from the scene,' he says.

'If it was Tallulah's sea glass, it means she was in that room.'

'You think she was involved?'

'I don't know what I think,' says Ally.

And it's like all the wind goes from her then. He feels her sag beside him, and he reaches out to her.

'But please tell the police that, Jayden. Tell them about the sea glass.'

318

63

When Mullins sees Davey on the rock, it's as if he's been waiting for him. He's crouched like a goblin, staring out over the dark sea. A spike of lightning illuminates the sky, then on its coattails comes a roll of thunder that Mullins feels deep inside of him.

He shivers. Looks behind him hopefully; no one else is coming. Not yet.

Mullins thinks of the tales his Grandad Jack used to tell: the mermaids that bask on rocks, luring sailors to their deaths. Davey Hart is no fish-tailed beauty, but here he is, not shifting an inch – and there's something scary about it.

Without cuffs, without backup, his best bet is to get him talking. And keep him at it.

His only bet, really.

The phone in his hand, with its torchlight playing over the wet rocks, is Mullins's lifeline; but he can't spook Davey by calling it in. Instead, he taps out a quick message: Out small gate, go left, half a mile. Rocks. If they're bringing in the big boys, they'll be able to see his location by his phone anyway. And Mullins hopes they're bringing in the big boys.

'Davey,' he says. 'It's Tim.'

When Davey doesn't move, Mullins goes a little closer.

Is he dead?

And is that even possible, to die sitting upright and stay put? Not sunk in a sofa like the old-timer he saw on the Carrick estate months back, TV blaring, but here on a rock. A sentry. A piskie. A new-ager doing yoga under a stormy sky.

Mullins shivers. He can feel goosebumps prickling his rain-streaked cheeks. What did he expect? A rugby tackle, a tussle; pinning him down, urging the sirens on. Maybe even taking a hit himself, because Davey is a tough little bloke, wiry and quick. Whatever Mullins expected, it wasn't this stillness.

'You okay there, Davey?'

As Mullins moves closer, he sees that this outcrop of rock that Davey's perched on is a marker. Edge of the land, start of the sea, and between the two? Nothing but air. A sheer drop. Mullins's throat is dry as he swallows. He can hear the sea far below, hissing at the foot of the cliff. The lazy summer swell has been replaced by something with more bite, and it sounds even bigger when it's hitting rocks in darkness.

How close is this bloke to the edge?

Or maybe that's the point.

Any kind of scuffle here would end badly. Mullins thinks of action movies, two tough guys rolling around on the wing of an aeroplane, miles high. Only, no stunt doubles here. He has to keep him talking.

'You're a bit close to the edge there, Davey. With this rain, it's slippy too. Can you move back a tad? That's it, just a few steps. You're okay.'

But Davey's not budging. Not one inch.

'Could you do that for me, Davey?'

To Mullins's horror, Davey draws himself upright and takes a step forward.

'You seen the lightning?' says Davey.

As if on cue, a corker splits the sky. Thunder booms in its wake.

So, what, we're storm-watching? He attacks Gus and then he wants a nature walk? But anything to keep him talking.

'Quite a show, isn't it?' tries Mullins. *Brainwave.* 'I've got a better angle on it from here, actually. Why don't you just—'

'I love a good storm.'

'Me too. Nothing like it.'

And this is barmy talk. But it's talk – and talk is good. Mullins has sent his message, and help will be coming. He just needs to keep going on about thunder and lightning for a bit, doesn't he? That's his job. *Stay in your lane, Mullins. Don't think about Gus.*

'I'm not afraid,' says Davey. 'There's stars up there and I'm alright with joining them.'

Joining the stars? Davey's got it all wrong. If he steps off that rock, he's not going to sail upward, starlight, supersonic. He's crashing down. That's it. End of. Mincemeat, not stardust.

'We're getting soaked out here,' says Mullins.

'Don't care.' Davey's words turn into a wild whoop as another spike of lightning hits.

And Mullins is no good at this. He's had the de-escalation training. But Davey isn't angry or ballistically sad. He's caught up in the storm.

And he's standing inches from a massive drop.

Mullins thinks of Lewis Pascoe, and his dad before him. It doesn't take much to go over. And on a night like this, probably even less. But Lewis Pascoe is a good thought, because Mullins did okay there – in the end.

'I grew up here,' says Mullins. 'I used to play on these cliffs as a kid. Fly my kite.'

Davey doesn't say anything. But he doesn't take any more steps either.

'Where did you grow up, Davey? London, was it?'

'Northamptonshire. Other end of the country.'

'I've never been to Northamptonshire. Nice . . . is it?'

Bolt of lightning. Clap of thunder. Northamptonshire doesn't stand a chance.

Instead, Davey says, 'That bloke, he was a mate of yours, was he? Russ?'

So we are going there. Mullins feels a punch of emotion. But he knows he can't lose it. Not here, not now.

'Gus. Gus Munro. And yes, he's a mate. A very good mate . . .'

Mullins clenches his phone in his hand so hard it could crack. There's a reply to his message: Received.

'Rupert was a good mate. Baz was too. They had their ways. Wound people up. Wound me up. But we had history. Lot of shared history. Especially me and Baz.'

Davey's voice is jagging, and he sways on his feet. One hasty move and he'll startle like a rabbit. But if Mullins isn't quick . . .

'We did amazing things together. Then Baz wanted to quit. When he stopped the music, we all had to get off. But he gave me the best days of my life. And I . . . I thought the world of him. I did . . .'

Davey lurches suddenly. Mullins shoots forward – already knowing he can't get there – but instead of going over, Davey sinks to the ground. He plants his palms on the wet rock and dangles his legs; leans his head down towards his knees.

Mullins draws himself up. He holds his breath; no sudden movements.

He thinks again of his mum. The kite. The way she held him. Good thoughts, that's what he needs. Not Gus lying there. Not Gus not breathing.

'I'm going to sit with you,' Mullins says. 'That okay? Just here.'

He takes Davey's shrug as permission. He edges into place. He doesn't look down.

Good job it's dark, he tells himself. But that's not even true. Because while he can't see how high they are, and that's a positive, there's nothing to ground him either. It feels like they're drifting in space, held by just a tiny bit of arse on rock. The sky above, split by electricity, heavy with thunder, feels like it's coming down on top of them.

Mullins has never had a head for heights.

He looks sideways at Davey.

'I said it was a bad idea. But that's the way it's always been,' slurs Davey. 'Nobody listens to Davey. Davey's nobody.'

'Nobody's nobody.'

'Yeah, yeah. Nobody, I am. No point to being a nobody, is there?'

Mullins has his hands on the cold, wet rock, palms flat. No grip. But so long as he just sits here, stays still, feels that centuries-old rock strength pulsing up through him, he's alright. Unbudgeable. Isn't he?

Or is the greater evil not a slip, but a strike, burnt to cinders by a lightning spike?

'I feel like that sometimes,' he says.

'You a copper? Big man? Yeah right.'

'I don't know what I'm doing half the time.'

And he's astonished at how his voice cracks. Is this contagious, or what? *Confiding in a killer? Nice one, Mullins.*

'I just make it up. I make it up, and hope no one notices.'

'It's tiring, innit,' says Davey, quietly.

'You're not a nobody though, Davey. You might have made a few mistakes, but nothing that can't be figured out.'

And Mullins hears himself say it: *a few mistakes.* Then, *don't think of Gus. And don't think of Rupert Frost either.* His job is to keep this man safe. And he'll do it.

Mullins can hear movement back on the cliff path. They're coming. He prays for a torch beam to pick them out.

'She tried to kill me. And okay, I deserved it. I did. I broke that beautiful woman's heart. But that poor Russ bloke didn't.'

Poor Russ bloke?

'Who tried to kill you, Davey?'

'I didn't just hurt Baz. I hurt Tallulah too. And Rupert . . . I don't know . . . All I know is that when I looked for my gloves, they weren't there. And that's a sign. It's got to be. End of an era. Everything up in flames.'

Mullins realises then that Davey is crying. The footsteps are close now and something in Mullins unclenches. Help is here. He puts an arm around the man's shaking shoulders.

'It's alright,' he says quietly. 'We've got you.'

And there it is, the torch beam.

'Police!'

The officer's voice behind them is too sudden. But then it's immediately eclipsed by a clap of thunder so loud that it shakes the entire cliff.

Davey starts forward, like a startled animal going to ground. Only the ground is endless feet away and swirling with seawater.

Time slows.

Mullins lunges for him. He lunges without thinking of his own tethering. All he knows is that if he doesn't stop him, this man will fall.

His fingers close around the fabric of Davey's shirt. Something rips, but he holds on. He can feel his arse-end slipping on the granite. Still, he holds on. A strange sound is belting out against the night, louder than any thunder: his own roar. Still, he holds on. He kicks out a leg and his foot meets a jut of rock. He doesn't know how, but it does, and Mullins pushes all his weight against it.

That one foot counteracting a dangling man.

But then hands are fastening around his shoulders. Suddenly Mullins is not the only one hanging on to Davey. The weight of him lifts, and they're pulled clear.

Mullins rolls on to his back, puffing like a steam engine. Delayed fear shudders through him. He looks up at the sky just as the clouds part and the moon shows its face.

The rain stops. Everything stops.

Beside him, Mullins hears Davey mumble something. It might be 'Thanks, man'. But if it is, he doesn't want it.

64

After that last epic clap of thunder, the storm passed. The rain is barely drizzling now, and the breeze has gone back to wherever it came from. After everything at Rockpool, it's eerily quiet down in the dunes. Saffron walks up to The Shell House, Ally's key in her hand.

She gave her statement to the police, and they let her go. It was all she could do not to run.

Ally went with Gus in the ambulance, Jayden following behind. And Mullins. Who knows where Mullins is? Saffron feels a tug as she thinks of him. *Don't let him die, Saff.*

As if she's ever been able to stop anyone dying.

As she draws near the house, she sees that Ally left the lights on. It looks as welcoming as it always does: the last place in the dunes; nestled in the sand, a sea of marram grass, blue weatherboard. Out to her left the ocean glimmers silver. A giant moon hangs in the sky. Saffron's eyes fill.

She's been here before: stopping in for Fox, with Ally at the hospital. Last time it was Jayden, and now it's Gus. She's going to give that little dog the hug to end all hugs. She hears Fox bark then and it's as if he's heard her thoughts. Broady's coming with pizza, and they're staying the night here. Ally said she didn't know when she'd be back.

Saffron's phone pings with a message: Jayden.

You still at Rockpool?

No, she messages back. The Shell House. I've gone for Fox.

Did you see Tallulah?

No sign.

She's about to ask after Gus when suddenly, Fox is at the gate. 'Hey little guy, what are you doing out here?'

His paws are up and he barks again. Saffron bends to fuss over him. Did he get out somehow? Ally would never leave him to run loose.

Saffron stuffs her phone in the back pocket of her jeans and heads through the gate. Fox twines around her legs as she crunches over the path and up the wooden steps. She tries the door.

It opens.

She's about to call out *Hello?* when something stops her. Everything looks as it always does. The big wooden table. The pictures. The white-painted boards and sea-blue cushions.

But there's something different: the smell.

A thick and musky perfume. It's not an Ally sort of perfume. In fact, Saffron doesn't think Ally even wears perfume.

Saffron's phone buzzes in her pocket just as Fox, who's sticking to her like glue, gives a low whine, followed by a sharp bark.

'How did you get back in? I shut you out—'

And it's Tallulah, her voice harsh as she flies into the room. She pulls up short when she sees Saffron.

'Oh,' says Saffron. 'Oh, hi.'

Tallulah stares at her. Her hair falls in front of her face, and she rakes it back with her fingers. For someone who's usually so immaculate she looks ragged; undone. Saffron notes the bag over her shoulder. The car keys in her hand.

'The police are looking for you. They were worried, when . . .'

Tallulah's craning past Saffron. 'Who's with you?'

327

'It's just me. You heard what happened to Gus? Ally's at the hospital, and—'

Saffron stops. Tallulah's hunting through her bag, not listening. 'My letters, where are my letters?'

Is she drunk? Or in shock? And why is she here? The whole point of the party was for Tallulah to find her truth.

'Did you leave early? Someone attacked Gus, and . . . what letters?'

'From Baz. I had them with me. I . . .'

Tallulah spins on her heel, swearing under her breath, and flies back towards the bedrooms.

Fox growls.

'Foxy, it's okay. It's just Tallulah . . .'

Saffron remembers the message and pulls her phone from her pocket. Jayden again.

The police want to speak to Tallulah in connection with Gus. If she turns up at The Shell House call them. And don't approach.

Saffron reads it twice. *Don't approach?*

Her phone in her hand rings then, and the sound makes her leap from her skin. She answers, eyes darting towards the bedrooms.

'Mullins.'

'Skinner said you went back to Ally's.'

His voice is high; croaky. He doesn't sound a lot like Mullins.

'I'm here now. Mullins, are you okay?'

'Saff, this is important. If Tallulah Pearce shows up, lock the door. Don't let her in.'

Saffron turns, cupping her hand as she whispers.

'Erm, little late for that. She's already here. She's about to leave.'

'Leave? Alright. Hold tight. We're on our way.'

'What's she done, Mullins? Jayden said something about Gus—'

'It was her, Saff. We've arrested Davey but he had nothing to do with Gus. That was Tallulah.'

'Tallulah attacked Gus?' Saffron whispers. Then claps a hand to her mouth.

'Just keep her talking, do your friendly thing. We'll be there in seconds, okay?'

Saffron hangs up, her heart thudding.

She can hear movement in one of the bedrooms, the sliding of drawers and banging of doors. She already knows that when Tallulah finds whatever she's looking for, Saffron won't get to do her 'friendly thing'. She'll steam past her, out to her car, and be gone.

And yeah, okay, maybe the police will intercept. Tallulah's a tourist, she won't know the lanes, they'll catch up to her. But . . . isn't it better not to give her the chance? Because there's no way Tallulah Pearce is getting away with this. Not on Saffron's watch.

She runs into the kitchen. Yanking open a drawer, she finds what she's looking for.

'What are you doing with that?'

Tallulah's in the doorway, her eyes on the knife in Saffron's hand.

'This?' Saffron looks at the blade as if she's surprised to see it. 'Oh this. Nothing, I'm just . . . I need it.'

'You don't need a knife, Saffron,' says Tallulah, her voice level. 'Give it to me.'

'I don't want to.'

'Then put it down on the ground.'

'I don't want to put it down,' says Saffron. And there's a quiver in her voice that she hates. Tallulah takes a step closer, and Saffron's hand tightens around the knife. 'Why did you attack Gus? Why would you do that?'

'It was . . . a mistake. I thought he was someone else.'

'And that makes it better?'

Tallulah steps closer, and Saffron holds the knife higher.

'I don't want to hurt you,' says Tallulah.

And Saffron wonders why Tallulah's talking about hurting anyone. Isn't she the one holding the knife? But then Tallulah moves suddenly, grabbing a huge conch shell from the mantelpiece. Saffron looks at the spiked shape of it; imagines the skull-splitting weight of it.

My God, am I actually going to have to use this knife?

'I just want to walk away,' says Tallulah, holding the shell aloft, 'and get on with what's left of my life. So, step aside.'

'There's no point. The police are on their way.'

'You're lying.'

'I'm not.'

'I never meant to hurt Ally's friend,' cries Tallulah. 'She was my friend. She was good to me. But . . . I won't let it be the end of my life. I won't let those people destroy me like they destroyed Baz. *Move!*'

In a flash, Tallulah jerks forward. Saffron sees the spiked conch looming at her. She dodges to the side, and with no target to meet, Tallulah's sent sprawling. The conch smashes on to the floorboards. Fox cowers and barks.

As Tallulah screams in frustration, or pain, or both, Saffron spins on her heel and pelts for the door. She crosses the veranda and leaps down the steps, Fox close behind her. She sprints through the garden and out on to the track.

Tallulah's hire car. A silver BMW.

Saffron does what she planned all along. Crouching, she rams the knife as hard as she can into the rear tyre's sidewall. She pushes the blade deeper, pulling it to the side. The rubber's tough, but the knife is sharp. She yanks it out, tumbling back on to her heels. Then she jumps up and does the next one, then the next.

And something stirs in her.

Saffron has pretty much never, ever done anything wrong.

She's never parked in a blue-badge bay or snuck away from a table without paying. She's never sprayed a brick wall or slipped a lipstick into the pocket of a coat. She's definitely never hit anyone; she can't remember the last time she raised her voice in anger. When Rupert Frost drunkenly lunged for her in the kitchen, she quickly sidestepped – and then let it go.

But as she plunges the knife into the last tyre, a fury she didn't know she had pours out of her. She gives a cry of total ferocity. As she rocks back, tears streaming, she sees Tallulah framed in the doorway. The woman is limping down the steps, something in her hand. Saffron thinks of the broken conch shell and how sharp a shard would be. She staggers to her feet, her chest heaving.

Her fingers tighten around the knife.

But then blue lights fill the dunes. And she's never *ever* been so glad to see Mullins.

65

Jayden's eyes are on the clock in the corridor, trying not to second-guess what all this time means. As they wait for news, he feels a deep ache for his wife and daughter. Cat offered to come but he told her no need; once he knew Gus was okay, once he knew Ally was okay, he'd be home.

He doesn't know when either of those things will happen.

If they will happen.

Jayden's phone rings. 'Skinner,' he says, turning to Ally. 'Answer it.'

'Sarge.' And he's on autopilot, not realising his mistake until after.

'Two quick headlines. One: we've arrested Tallulah Pearce for the attempted murder of Gus Munro. Ally was right: sea glass at the scene. Tallulah thought he was Davey Hart, a case of mistaken identity. We intercepted her trying to attack Saffron Weeks with a whopping great conch shell. Right up your street, you Shell House Detectives.'

His attempt at levity falls flat.

'And two: Davey Hart's admitted that he and Rupert Frost spiked Baz's herbal tea with cocaine. He's probably looking at a charge of involuntary manslaughter. How's Gus?'

'No news yet.'

'Alright. So, I'm not disturbing?'

'No. What about the gloves?'

'Lucky gloves. You're right, there's something in it. Davey confirmed that they're missing. But he said he's got no idea who took them, and he denied having anything to do with Rupert's death. I believe him. If Felix Boyd did this, then it's possible Boyd took the gloves.'

'But why would his prints be on the knife then?'

Skinner makes a noise that could be frustration, or concession, or both. 'A grilled cheese sandwich,' he says.

'Say what?'

Skinner groans. 'Boyd maintains that's the only way his prints might be found on any knife at Rockpool. On Thursday they had a one-on-one meet, and he made Baz a grilled cheese sandwich.'

'But that's it. Surely? That explains it.'

'But nobody can prove it. Felix's word is his only defence.'

Jayden's mind ticks over. So, Felix used a knife in the Rockpool kitchen, hence the prints. But how did the killer know to use that exact same knife to kill Rupert? Someone else must have seen.

'I've got a couple of people lined up to search the area again at first light,' Skinner says, 'seeing if we missed the gloves the first time. But with the charge made, my resources are limited. As far as anyone else is concerned, this case is closed.'

'Where was the murder weapon found?'

Jayden can feel Ally's eyes on him. Ordinarily, neither of them would ever expect Skinner to answer a question like that.

Skinner hesitates. 'Back of Boyd's van.'

Jayden snorts. 'Convenient.'

'After murdering Frost, Boyd takes himself off to the bloody Leach Pottery in St Ives. Wanders round looking at crockery and whatnot. Then meanders back to Porthpella via Hang Ten. All that time, the murder weapon's sitting pretty, wrapped in a towel in his van.'

'Okay, how did this charge fly?'

'Means, motive and opportunity. Plus, prints on the knife. And a hair at the scene.'

'A hair at the scene?'

'Well, in the cottage.'

'So, if he'd been in the cottage at any point, say if Baz was giving him a tour, that'd explain that.'

Skinner grunts. But Jayden knows they're on the same side here. Otherwise, why would he be telling him so much? It's unprecedented.

'There is an argument that Boyd wasn't thinking straight. That in the aftermath of the murder he was directionless, looking to retrace old footsteps. His mother was a Bernard Leach fan. He was happy up at your campsite. Maybe he was lost, confused. Spinning in circles.'

'I was there when he was arrested,' says Jayden. 'He looked confused alright. Like he couldn't understand why the cuffs were being slapped on him.'

After that, Skinner hangs up. *He sounded defeated*, thinks Jayden. But his own mind is thrumming. A version of events is building.

Someone must have framed Felix.

'I heard most of that,' says Ally. 'Skinner doesn't sound himself at all.'

'It was Tallulah who hurt Gus. I'm so sorry, Al.'

She shakes her head. 'Because she thought he was Davey? I . . . can't think about it.'

Jayden squeezes her arm. 'I know. It's too much. But you were right about the sea glass.'

Beside him, Ally buries her face in her hands. Then she looks up. 'So, who on earth would have framed Felix?'

Jayden looks at her. 'I thought you didn't want . . .'

And he can see the need in her eyes; they burn with it. She wants the distraction.

'Keep talking, Al,' he says.

'It's the same question we asked before, isn't it? Was Rupert's murder primarily about killing Rupert, or framing Felix, or both?'

'Exactly. You want to do this now?'

'I want to do this now,' says Ally.

'Okay.' He rubs his hands together. 'Let's narrow our field. Who would have motive to kill Rupert while also hating Felix so much they'd want to frame him for it?'

Ally nods. 'Really, it's who's left. Not Tallulah, not Davey. All we have are the Carson family, past and present. Nicole, Jet, Ruby, Ruby's husband Adrian, and the child, Imogen. Those are our five suspects.'

'Okay,' says Jayden. 'Let's discount Imogen. And then let's talk about why anybody would hate Rupert.'

Ally folds her hands in her lap. Jayden sees her turn her wedding ring, something she does when she's thinking.

'His connection is business,' she says. 'And whether he's a true friend or more of an associate, Rupert's an important part of the picture. From the book, it sounds like he looked after everything. Brokered the deals, organised the tours. Anything financial or administrative was him.'

Jayden's on his feet, his trainers squeaking on the linoleum. It feels good to be doing something constructive, because there's nothing worse than waiting for news in a hospital.

Except for getting the wrong news.

He refocuses. He needs to stay positive for Ally.

'Baz had no interest in anything beyond the music,' says Jayden. 'He writes about that in his book, doesn't he?'

'Baz said one of the keys to success is surrounding yourself with people who like doing the things that you don't. That way you get to concentrate on what you love. He said he turned away from the business side completely.'

'That's a lot of control to give someone, isn't it? A lot of trust.'

Ally looks up suddenly, her eyes bright. 'Could Rupert's murder be to do with money?'

'Go on.'

'We know there was discord about the will. Adrian, Baz's son-in-law, said that Baz wasn't nearly as wealthy as anyone thought. That most of his money was in Rockpool House. And we know from Saffron that the house was left to Felix.'

'Yep.'

'So . . . what if someone blamed Rupert for Baz's financial situation?'

Jayden considers it. Rupert's link was business, so was it business that got him killed?

'I like where you're going with this, Al, but unless Rupert specifically failed Baz in some way, lost him a lot of money, brokered a series of rubbish deals, it's hard to see how he could be held accountable for the guy's bank balance.'

'Unless he was taking more than his fair share. Or they suspected that he was.'

Jayden stops. 'Rupert stealing from Baz?'

Ally nods. 'It's possible, isn't it? If Baz turned away from anything financial and Rupert held the purse strings. Baz could have had no idea.'

'And then the family find out, and instead of having it investigated they kill Rupert instead.'

'Hmm. That doesn't quite feel plausible, does it? If there was any suspicion of wrongdoing they'd report him, surely? There would be nothing to gain from killing him.'

Jayden's running through all the Rockpool guests in his mind. Who is the most emotional, reactionary, chaotic?

'Nicole said that Ruby and Jet lost out in the will,' says Ally. 'She was furious about it, wasn't she?'

'She was. But I can't see her being devious. She seems so upfront with her emotions. And framing Felix is such a specific thing.'

'You said Ruby and Jet held the grudge against Felix?'

'That's what Felix said,' says Jayden. 'And it was Jet who messaged him before the party telling him he wasn't welcome.'

'I can't see Ruby stabbing Rupert to death. Still waters might run deep but . . . that kind of capacity for violence?'

'Then we're left with Jet,' says Jayden. 'Process of elimination. But he seems too . . . lazy to kill anyone.'

Ally almost smiles. 'Well, yes. I agree with you there.'

Jayden drops down next to Ally, just as if they're side by side on the bench on The Shell House veranda. Then they both turn at the sound of footsteps. A nurse is hurrying along the corridor, and they look to her expectantly – Jayden hears Ally's quick breath – but the nurse goes by without looking at them, her eyes fixed on her clipboard.

Beside him, Ally sags.

Jayden nudges her. 'Okay, Al, let's try this. The family see the will and learn there's nowhere near as much money as they thought. Maybe Jet was counting on it. Baz goes on about how directionless he is in the book, doesn't he? But maybe Jet smells a rat. Thinks Rupert took advantage of his dad's disinterest in the business side to cheat him. So, he goes to challenge him about it and . . . ends up killing him.'

'But it was premeditated,' says Ally. 'It would have to be, to frame Felix. Perhaps Jet already challenged him about it, the night before? Rupert denies it. Which of course might be perfectly genuine. All it would need is for Jet to *think* he'd been stealing. And Jet, consumed by grief for his father, devastated to be receiving so little in the will, loses all sense of proportion and . . . plans to kill him.'

'While taking down Felix, the guy he hates, at the same time.'

They face one another.

'Jet,' says Ally.

'Jet,' says Jayden. Then, 'Well, it's a theory.'

'I think it works though. Doesn't it?'

'Kind of. There are a lot of ifs. But as a line of enquiry? Definitely. Whether it's enough for Skinner, considering Felix is already charged, who knows . . . I'm just trying to picture Jet having this theory about Rupert, and why killing him felt like a better idea than talking to anyone else about it.'

'Unless he did talk to someone else.'

'What, and other people were in on it too?'

Jayden thinks back to Tallulah's speech, everyone gathered on the terrace. All the Carsons rubbing up against each other, the snide back and forth. It didn't speak of any kind of unity – however twisted. When Davey said *It's all Greek to me*, he might as well have been talking about the whole gathering: why they would even want to be in each other's company. If Jayden's family was that messed up, he'd keep his distance.

A thought hits.

Jayden holds it for a moment; light flows in.

'Hermes,' he says.

'Hermès? That's a fancy brand, isn't it? Nicole said Baz gave her a Hermès bag.'

'She did. And Jet rolled his eyes. Because Jet wasn't talking about that Hermès. Jet was talking about the Greek god.'

'He was?'

'It's possible. I mean, it makes sense. He was riffing on what Davey said about it all being Greek to him. That's why he mentioned Hermes. You know why, right? Hermes was the god of thieves.'

Ally shakes her head. 'How do you know these things?'

'I had a book as a kid. My dad was mad on Greek myths. Hermes ferried souls to the afterlife and he was god of a bunch of different things, including thieves.'

'What was it that Jet said about Rupert and Hermes?'

'"His beloved Hermes". A quip that didn't land with anyone, but maybe that's the point with Jet. He's wrapped up in himself, he doesn't care.'

Ally looks thoughtful. 'It's obscure,' she says.

'That's why I love it,' says Jayden with a grin. 'And Al, if you hadn't suggested that Rupert could be stealing money, I'd never have made the connection.'

'That was utter speculation on my part.'

'True, but we've built a theory out of it. A solid one, I reckon.'

'Phone him,' says Ally. 'Phone Skinner.'

'Jet Carson,' says Jayden quietly, turning it over. 'He's the last person I could imagine killing someone. Except for . . .'

'. . . Tallulah,' finishes Ally.

Just then a doctor comes down the hall. Her stride is purposeful; her white coat flaps behind her. This time? This time they know.

Ally gets to her feet, and Jayden goes to stand beside her.

The doctor nods to them both – and for a moment Jayden thinks she looks too serious.

'Gus is awake. You can see him.'

Jayden breathes deeply. 'How's he doing?'

She gives a half-smile. 'He's doing well. Don't be alarmed by the machines. They're there to monitor him. And the ventilator is to take the strain of having to breathe for himself. There's no sign of a blood clot or swelling, but we'll continue to monitor this.'

Ally's hand is at her mouth. Jayden squeezes her shoulder.

'Talk to him as normally as you can,' the doctor says. 'Chat about TV, or the weather or what the family are up to. Touch is good, too. So do hold his hand. Don't worry that he isn't responding.

After an injury like this, consciousness varies. But interaction can help. Do you both want to come in?'

Ally looks to Jayden. Nods. 'Please.'

'Definitely,' he says. 'Thank you, Doctor.'

~

Inside the room, Ally sits beside Gus's bed. The light is low. The machines click and whirr and occasionally beep. The ventilator whooshes. Gus's head is bandaged, and his eyes are closed. Ally gently takes his hand.

'Can you talk to him, Jayden,' she says in a low voice. 'I don't know what to say.'

'So, Gus, mate,' says Jayden. 'It's been a big night here, but we're on the case. Ally and I reckon we've cracked it. But the only thing to worry about now is you getting on your feet again. And that's going to happen in no time at all. Isn't it, Al?'

She dips her head. Her fingers are woven with Gus's.

And Jayden gets why she can't speak, but he really wishes she would. Because he knows that if there's anyone's voice that Gus would want to hear right now, it's Ally's.

'Man, you should have heard the storm earlier,' says Jayden. 'It's cleared now though. The moon's back – and it's huge. That means a spring tide, doesn't it, Al?'

She nods.

'That's when, what, the high tide's really high and the low tide's really low? But then you know all this, Gus. Proper ocean-dweller now.'

Jayden hears Ally say something. He jumps on it.

'What's that, Al?'

'Spring tides are good for beachcombing.'

'Hear that, Gus? Ally's going to be getting her beachcombing vibe on. Sorry, *wrecking*. You Cornish lot call it wrecking.'

340

Jayden sees a tear slip down Ally's cheek as she holds Gus's hand tighter.

It's now or never.

'Al,' he says gently, 'I'm going to call Skinner. You're okay here, aren't you? I'll be right back.'

Ally nods. Then says, 'I don't know what to say to him, Jayden.'

'Yeah, you do, Al.'

66

'I didn't go looking for you, but you came anyway. I can still remember the first time I saw you, down on the sand. You told me a woman had gone missing. I think you thought you'd got it wrong, that wisecrack about me being a glamorous divorcee, but really, you got it all right. And you had no idea. No idea at all. That's one of the lovely things about you, Gus.

'The thought I keep returning to is this: Bill would have liked you. He would have liked you a great deal.

'The trouble is, I thought I would go on loving Bill forever, that I would be no less married to him after his death than I was when he was alive. And the first part is true. But the second . . . He's not here anymore, Gus. And there are so many things I miss.

'I miss the companionship. Having someone to just . . . do it all with. I didn't know how much that mattered to me until I lost it. I used to think that for all I loved Bill, and loved Evie, what I really treasured was being on my own.

'God, I was wrong about that.

'I was spoilt to have someone beside me for forty years. Someone who made everything so easy that I could take their existence for granted.

'Perhaps you thought you had that once in Mona. We've never talked about her much, have we? But I know that the way she treated you at the end made you doubt yourself. Lose your confidence. And I can't bear that she did that to a man like you.

'But in another way, I'm oddly grateful to her. I wonder if you'd ever have come to Porthpella, if life had just rolled on. Perhaps I do you a disservice, and writing your novel by the sea was always going to be your future. All Swell just waiting for you.

'Gus, whatever first brought you here, I'm immeasurably glad that you stayed.

'And I think you've really come to love it. That's the other thing I dwell on. That Bill would have liked you, and that you love Porthpella just like I do. You love our place in the dunes. And that's the strangest part of it, really. That I've come to think of it like that. Ours.

'Perhaps I should have said some of these things to you before. But I think life is rather like that, isn't it? We think we have all the time in the world. Even when things happen to show us that we don't, we really don't, we still fall back into our own ways. We presume tomorrows.

'Gus, it was Jayden who brought you back. And of all the many things that Jayden has given me, that is perhaps the greatest gift of all.

'So, I shan't waste it. I promise. If you're alright, if you can just be alright, I won't waste another minute.'

Ally turns as she hears the door quietly open behind her, and Jayden steps back into the room. She wipes her face with her palms.

'Gus,' says Jayden, his voice cut with wonder, 'you're awake. Al, he's awake.'

Gus smiles a slow smile. 'Hello,' he says.

67

Mullins shifts on his pillows. His curtains are thin and the light from that big old moon is filtering through. Normally he crashes out, he's never been one for tossing and turning, but tonight – well, technically this morning – it's not happening. In this silvery half-light, the bedroom he's slept in his whole life looks different. It feels different. He clamps his eyelids shut and tries to keep them that way.

But his head's buzzing like a hive. And his body feels as frazzled as if that lightning had hit.

It was a result. Wasn't it? DCI Robinson said as much. A bit of embarrassment around the Felix Boyd charge, but a result none the less.

Davey Hart, a man held together by not much in the end, confessed to spiking Baz's drink with cocaine. He and Rupert were in it together apparently, and they'd never intended for it to go so wrong. *Take the wind from his sails, that's all we wanted. Knock him off his perch. Bring him back to the good old days.* That stupid, dangerous prank had cost Baz his life, and nearly Davey's own too, if Mullins hadn't hauled him back from the edge. And Gus? Gus's life had hung in the balance for a while back there. And maybe that wasn't down to Davey – *Tallulah, blimey, I'd never have seen that coming* – but it was still connected.

Mullins rolls on to his other side. Beneath him the bedsprings protest.

When he sat beside him on that rock, Mullins saw Davey's pain. It glowed from him, as bright as any full moon. He even felt a little bit shining into himself.

Mullins hadn't expected that.

He can feel his throat burning and he yanks the sheet up around his ears; tries to get a hold of his emotions.

It was a busy night, that's all. A big, busy night. All he wants to do is go to sleep but this head of his won't switch off. He tries to stop thinking about Davey, and Hippy-Dippy darts into his mind instead. Even after everything with Davey on the cliff, there was no way he was staying on the sidelines when Saffron was involved.

She really let rip on those tyres of Tallulah's. As they turned up in the car, blue lights blazing, Mullins never expected to see a look like that on Saffron's face. She was sunshine, that girl. She didn't need to wear a 'Good Vibes Only' t-shirt, because it was so obvious just looking at her. But she'd been through it up at Rockpool the last few days. Sure, she'd wanted to stop the suspect from getting away, but maybe shredding rubber was her way of letting off a little steam too. And if Tallulah had come at her again with that whopping great seashell? That's not a question Mullins wants to think about.

Tallulah gave them more trouble than Davey, in the end. She was upset about Gus Munro – mostly because she'd got the wrong man. As soon as Davey had let slip to Tallulah his own part in the drink-spiking, it didn't matter that Baz's heart did the rest – Tallulah lost control, and the poker from the fireplace was her weapon of choice. It was just bad luck that Gus ran into the room so soon after Davey ran out. In the half-light, Tallulah thought he was Davey. And she really had wanted to kill Davey.

He's had word from Jayden that Gus is stable. Talking, even. He's going to be okay, which is the best news ever. Trouble is, Mullins knows that, in the moment, he bottled it. He bottled it, and Jayden didn't. Jayden, who actually had a friend, a fellow officer, die beside him in the line of duty. While Mullins is really glad that Jayden saved Gus's life, he's also all too aware that he didn't.

It's not a nice feeling, that.

You saved a man tonight, Tim, Skinner said to him back at the station. *Saved him and nicked him. That's some effort.* And then the sergeant shook his hand.

But saying any old thing to a guilty bloke to stop him jumping is a different thing to literally breathing the life back into someone who is about as innocent as they come.

Or do all lives weigh the same, in the end?

Mullins feels tears pushing into his eyes now. He can't stop them. It was a big night, that's all. A big, busy night. And he can't shake it.

There's a tap at the door, then. No one ever taps at his door.

'Tim, love, you alright?'

He's about to do his default grunt, but then the door nudges open and his old mum's face appears in the gap. She's in her nightie, the same one she's had forever.

He hesitates, then says, 'Not really, Mum.'

68

Jet's no stranger to a sunrise – they're usually his sign to call it a night – but he's never seen one quite like this. It's an explosion of fire across the sky, and this morning it's a show that's all for him. A reward. A celebration. The universe saying, *I've got your back*. But he knows better than to expect a rush of emotion in response.

He stretches out on the cool grass. Pulls on his vape and watches the molten-metal ocean do its thing. After days of dead calm, the swell's up. Is that to do with last night's storm? He never paid attention in geography.

Behind him, the house, white as a sugar cube, sits quietly. The curtains drawn; everyone asleep. Three nights in Cornwall. Two here, death knocking, and one in custody. Not the weekend people planned, but a memorable one, nevertheless.

Jet doesn't understand everything that's happened. Davey and Rupert spiking Baz's drink with coke? He hasn't processed that one yet. He might decide he won't at all; just push it to the back of the cupboard and slam the door on it. Davey's gone to pieces anyway. He was one of the few people who really loved Baz. The idiot.

Tallulah. She was another. Feisty customer, as it turns out. The word is that she's been arrested for attempted murder. That bald-headed bloke who, yeah okay, looks a bit like Davey in the right light. Or the wrong light, as it happens.

Rupert?

I always said Felix was bad news. That was Jet's line. As if it was only a matter of time before Felix acted: stole their father then killed their friend. *Called it.*

Jet lies there on the sun-scorched grass in a pose of rest and relaxation as the sun climbs higher and higher in the sky. Occasionally he looks at his watch, but the passing of time seems a pointless thing. Time only matters to people who have something to do. Normally his bones are stilled by a different sort of vibe: basic apathy. Nothing gets him worked up because it takes energy, it takes emotional commitment, to care – and most of the time Jet has neither.

Those two years at drama school, back when he was trying still, they weren't totally wasted: he can, on occasion, do a good impression of giving a damn. Like yesterday. It fooled his mum and sister, it even fooled that loser Adrian, as he brought them in for a group hug.

There was a time when life had been different, probably. No taller than a Fender, Daddy's boy Jet, with a scrapbook of Baz's boarding passes and his plectrums stowed in a piggybank. Singing The Nick on the way to school, splashing through puddles in his grey knee socks; his mum humming behind. But it's so far back that it's pointless. Just another page in a rubbish history book.

Jet should have felt something when Baz died. As he stared down at his father's body by the side of the pool – soaked; lifeless – it was as if he was looking at a dummy that they'd use in a lifesaving class; it'd be shoved back in a cupboard later, limbs askew, until the next time.

Jet should have felt something when Ruby said the house was left to Felix and not them. That this place where they'd all gathered, this symbol, supposedly, of all that Baz was – and worth a bit too – was being handed to an interloper in a two-fingered salute.

Jet should have felt something when Ruby told him Baz had peanuts in the bank. Peanuts for someone like Baz, anyway. And that all he and his sister would walk away with was a handful of said peanuts apiece. But instead, Jet thought, *Bloody Rupert.* Because Ruby and Adrian might be scratching their heads, wondering what exactly Baz had been spending all his cash on, but Jet knew. Jet has always known, probably. Rupert was a subtle conman: not smash and grab, but a skimmer. Quietly robbing Baz for years? It fit. Did he overhear Rupert on the phone once? Did he look at his latest car, watch, house, holiday, and think, *Yeah, really?* Jet can't remember – can't be bothered to remember – and certainly has nothing approaching evidence, or any intention to make the accusation to anyone who matters. Instead, as his sister rambled on, fretted on, was so completely suburban about the predicament, he simply thought, *Bloody Rupert.* The clarity he experienced was as instant as a needle in a vein.

But even then – no father, no house, no money (to speak of) – did he snap?

No, Jet didn't snap.

But what was interesting was that he felt that he probably *should* snap. That a normal person would snap, under the circumstances. And suddenly he wanted it. He wanted that grief, that anger, that repulsion. For once, he wanted to feel *something.*

Jet shifts on the grass, hearing a car on the road outside. How long exactly has he been here? Time creeps. The sun is fully up; the sky's lost its drama and is relentlessly blue again.

And someone's headed for Rockpool.

He half gets to his feet, but the gates are already being buzzed open and it's a police car crunching up the driveway. The piercing sunlight shines directly off the windscreen, and he squints. The ache behind his eyes goes all the way to the back of his skull. He pats his head for his shades but they're not there. He must have lost them at some point.

Perhaps there are things to tidy up; questions to be asked. But Tallulah and Davey are behind bars. So is Felix.

Jet saunters to meet them, just as Imogen skips down the steps.

'Uncle Jet! The police are back.'

And Jet has a weird feeling then. She's so innocent, Imogen. She just wanted a nice party for her grandad.

'Go back inside, Imo.'

'Back inside?'

'What kind of teenager are you? You should be sleeping till twelve. Go on.'

And as he sees rejection cross her face, something tweaks inside him. It's not feeling, as such; you couldn't put a name on it. But suddenly he remembers being her age.

'Jet Carson?'

It's an officer Jet half recognises.

'Would you come with us?'

Jet shrugs. 'Why?'

But it's for show, that *why*?

'We found Davey's gloves. Your prints are all over them.'

Ah.

'So?'

'On the inside, Jet.'

He scratches at his stubble. Wants to grin and say *alright, the game's up.*

He only took Davey's gloves for fun. It amused him, that the silly old sap's lucky gloves should be put to such a use. But he didn't want to stitch Davey up – or himself – so, afterwards, he lobbed them from the cliff to be taken by time and tide. Obviously, that didn't work. It's a wonder the cops missed them the first time.

'But you've charged Felix Boyd. Felix killed Rupert.'

Said with no conviction; with mockery, if anything.

There's a glint of metal and again the sun catches it. A spear of light. Jet rubs his eyes. Handcuffs. *Really?*

'Jet Carson, I'm arresting you on suspicion of murder . . .'

And Jet stops listening. He walks calmly towards the police car. As he goes, he pays attention to his body, but there's no whirring in his head, no fluttering in his chest. No nothing. He's just a guy walking towards a car.

He knows there will be questions, and he's interested – in an abstract kind of way – as to whether he'll feel compelled to answer them. Or whether he'll save them the bother and just come out with it. Easier all round, that way.

I decided to confront Rupert as I thought he'd been stealing money from my father, robbing me of my inheritance, you see, Officer. Mr Frost had a good laugh about it. Denied it, of course. But I'd come prepared. It didn't really matter what he said. Gloves and knife, it was easy, in the end. Afterwards I stashed the knife in Felix's van. Yes, I was setting him up. I didn't overthink it though. A half-hearted attempt, probably. I'm sure you've seen better. So, a nice surprise when it turned out his prints were on the knife already. Lovely little nod from the universe there, that he deserved everything coming to him. Who am I to argue with that kind of fate?

He holds out his wrists. 'Slap them on, Officers,' he says. 'But I won't give you any trouble.'

I killed a man in Cornwall, just to watch him die.

As the song doesn't go.

As Jet slides into the back seat, he sees a small congregation of people at the top of the steps to the house. His sister. His niece. His mum. And Adrian, the most boring man in Surrey.

His mum starts forward. Her nightdress flaps against her legs and her hair's flattened from sleep. Her arms are thrown wide, as if she wants to rescue him, or as if she wants to be saved herself.

'Can we go?' he says to the driver. And then he shuts his eyes. He waits to feel something; anything.

69

'Now! Now, now, now. Dadatz,' says Jazzy, clambering into Jayden's lap, dragging a massive picture book behind her.

'Alright, Dadatz is here. Let's do this. What have we got? Oh man, not the Hungry Caterpillar again.'

Jazzy collapses in a peal of laughter and leans her whole body into him. Jayden wraps his arms around her, her weight in his lap so reassuring.

One of the things about being a dad is that tiny children don't let you live anywhere except the moment. *Now, now, now.* For instance, it's six o'clock on a Monday morning, and Jayden's had exactly no sleep. He drove Ally back to The Shell House in the small hours. He invited himself to sleep on her sofa too, but she wasn't having it. She said that she was really and truly okay; that Gus couldn't be better looked after, and Jayden needed to get home to his family.

So, he's here. Home with his family. Early morning sunshine streams through the window as if last night's storm never happened. Cat is making bacon rolls and getting the coffee on. He can hear her singing in the kitchen. She told him to go on up to bed, but that's not what he wants. Jayden wants the beautiful chaos of his everyday. He wants Jazzy and her picture books. His wife's insanely out-of-tune voice. He'll even take this crashing feeling of exhaustion. Because it's all gold.

'Dadatz.'

'Yes, babe.'

'Weed.'

'Weed? You've done a wee?' he says, tickling her.

'Weed, weed, weed!' she screams with laughter. 'Weed!'

'Oh, *read*! You want me to read this book, do you?'

He catches Cat leaning in the doorway, smiling at them.

'You're going to crash so hard later, Weston,' she says. 'One book, one bacon roll, then bed, okay?'

'Yes, Sarge,' he says.

⁓

Later, Jayden's down in the cabin office and the light dims. It's DI Radford's juggernaut, parked hard to the window. He springs to his feet. The DI is checking out earlier than planned. Jayden probably doesn't need to say goodbye because they talked earlier, at the bench under the apple tree again. Jayden got his three-hour power nap in, and it felt like enough. He fell asleep instantly, no tossing and turning, no thinking about everything. There are things he *needs* to think about – but for now, he'll take the break. Because Gus is awake and talking. Davey, Tallulah and Jet are locked up. And Felix? Felix will be on his way home: all charges dropped.

Even though there was no one around to prove that Felix made Baz a grilled cheese sandwich and used the same knife that went on to kill Rupert, when you have a tatty old drumming glove – covered in bloodstains and DNA – not to mention a confession from the killer himself, the grilled cheese bit is kind of irrelevant. Ally cracked it, when she said that Rupert's murder could be linked to money. Jayden put the Jet Carson theory to Skinner, and as soon as it was light enough a search team found the gloves: snagged on a gorse bush, just outside of the area the clifftop teams had originally been looking in. A couple of hours later and they had the prints they needed to haul Jet in. The guy apparently confessed everything without even being asked. *I've seen psychopaths display more emotion*, Skinner said. So, when Radford came knocking at the cottage door – eager for a first-hand account of 'what the hell's gone on at Rockpool' – Jayden was happy to oblige.

Plus, they had other things to talk about.

Radford holds out his hand to Jayden.

'Safe travels,' says Jayden, shaking it.

Cat appears at his side, Jazzy sitting high on her hip. 'Sure, you're not tempted to stay on? You booked three more nights.'

'Tempted,' grins Radford. 'But much as I pretended this was a holiday, I had one job in mind. And that's done. So . . . see you guys soon, okay?'

Keely calls down from the passenger seat, 'He got me here under false pretences. But at least we're stopping at the Eden Project on the way back. See you in Plymouth!'

As the motorhome rumbles out into the lane, Jayden slips his arm around Cat's waist.

She turns to him. 'There's still a lot we need to talk about,' she says.

'Yeah, I know.'

'How's now? Beach walk?'

'Beach walk.'

'Wot Pimmouth?' says Jazzy, with astonishing precocious-ness. But she's already struggling to get down. She heard the words *beach walk* too. And she's tearing off before they need to answer her question.

70

'Nice big coffee and a couple of brownies please, Saff.'

Saffron folds her arms and raises an eyebrow at Mullins.

'A couple?'

'They're getting smaller. What's that about, credit crunch?'

'They are not.'

'Well, maybe I'm in need of extra fuel. Big night for me, wasn't it?'

'Yeah,' she says. 'It was.'

He saved Davey Hart's life, so the story goes, out on those stormy cliffs. And he almost lost his own (though not the way he tells it). It was a big night for Mullins, alright, and he looks pretty done in by it.

He's reaching for his wallet when Saffron says, 'On the house.'

'No, mate, I pay. I always pay.'

You didn't use to, thinks Saffron. But instead, she grins and says, 'Not today you don't.'

'Well, in that case, chuck in another brownie, will you? They really are getting smaller.'

And she rolls her eyes.

For all the drama of the weekend, it's just another day in Porthpella. Monday lunchtime and here she is, back behind the counter at Hang Ten. The view through the wide-open door and wide-open windows is of a wide-open sea and a wide-open sky. All that blue is back again – with bells on. The swell's picked up and

Broady's out on the water with a group of beginners. Wipe-outs a-go-go. They'll all stream in here afterwards, for the après-surf slot; bashed to pieces, aching from head to foot but buzzing. She'll bring out iced coffees and pots of ice cream and wedges of cake. She'll spread word of the cook-out at the weekend. And she'll be thankful for every damn second of this glorious life that, somehow, she's landed.

'You okay, Saff? After, you know, everything.'

'I'm okay. Are you okay?'

She won't forget the way Mullins looked at her before he ran off to catch Davey. *Don't let him die, Saff.* And she won't forget the hug he gave her after Tallulah was bundled into the patrol car. *Suppose you would be handy with a knife, what with all the cheffing.*

The bit that Saffron can't think about is what she would have done if Tallulah had come at her again. Turned and run? Probably. Maybe.

'I'm great, mate. And much as I'd like to stay and chat,' says Mullins, 'I've got a hot date.'

'Oh, yeah?' Sceptical as she sounds, her 'good news' antennae are up. 'Who's the lucky girl? Or guy? Not gonna presume.'

Mullins takes a bite of brownie – which basically means putting most of one in his mouth. Maybe they *are* getting smaller.

'The lucky person,' he says, chewing, 'is my mum.'

'Aw, what – really?'

'I don't normally go on about work. She doesn't get it. Thinks I just plod about giving people parking tickets or something. But . . .' – he hesitates, rubs the back of his head – '. . . she got wind of the stuff on the cliff. Porthpella grapevine, right? Anyway, she said that deserved a fish and chip supper.'

His cheeks are red as he says it. And Saffron realises this: Mullins is quite loveable. Once you get past all the ways in which he's annoying, anyway.

'Don't you get fish and chips every week though?' she says.

'Not here, some fancy place up the coast she's heard about. Not too fancy, I hope. I don't want mint putting in my mushy peas. And the cod best be hanging off my plate.'

'Maybe you'd be better off down the chippie. Known quantity.'

'Maybe. But it's Mum's shout. Here, have you spoken to Jayden and Cat today? I saw them on the beach earlier and they looked like they were having a proper serious conversation. I didn't interrupt.'

And Saffron thinks Mullins really is changing. 'That was tactful of you.'

'And I wanted to get in here and have my brownies before it clogged up with emmets.'

There it is.

'Yeah, we messaged earlier. Ally's back at the hospital seeing Gus. I'm going to see him tomorrow hopefully, when he'll be out of the ICU. Want to come?'

'Course. I like Gus.'

'Everybody likes Gus.'

'I told one of those reporters that Ally and Jayden helped crack the case,' says Mullins.

'Did you? Not claiming it for yourself then?'

'Ho-ho. Well, it was Jayden who made the link between Davey's gloves and the real killer, wasn't it? And Ally put it together with the strife over the will, and Rupert being held accountable by whoever did the deed . . . Which, somehow, they made out to be Jet. Funny guy, that. Didn't seem like he could be bothered to do anything, let alone pull out his finger and kill someone. Plus, Ally saw Tallulah's piece of sea glass at the scene. Though, to be honest, I'm being generous to Ally there, because that woman's prints were all over the poker. Anyway, I wouldn't be surprised if they get a few more high-profile cases coming their way now. Which is obviously going to cause us professionals a problem or two. Bloody amateurs,' he finishes with a grin.

A new customer comes in then, and Mullins steps aside. Then stops. He looks uncertain, suddenly.

'Alright there?' he says.

'Hey,' says Saffron. 'How's it going?'

Felix gives a double thumbs up. 'Freedom's good.'

'There were some of us who never thought you did it, you know,' says Mullins.

'Well, that gives me faith in the system,' says Felix, 'but thanks anyway.'

He looks at the chalkboard and Saffron wonders if she should say something. After all, Felix must know she was interviewed. Is he wondering what she told them? *Yeah, creepy guy. Looked like he was up to something.*

'There's a smoothie on here called Blue Juice,' he says. 'Is that as good as the film?'

'Even better than the film,' says Saffron, 'and that's saying something.'

'One of those then.'

'Coming right up.' Then, 'Are you sticking around for a bit? Or can't wait to make tracks?'

He runs his hand through his hair. 'Dunno yet. Ruby Carson just tipped me off that I'm in the will. She's the executor. I don't think she was supposed to tell me, but she did anyway.'

'Have you landed his fortune?' says Mullins, on to his second brownie.

'Something like that. If it's true, you might be getting a new neighbour.'

Saffron gets the blitzer going. When she passes Felix his smoothie he toasts them with it, then wanders out the door.

'Some people get all the luck,' grumbles Mullins, under his breath.

And she can't tell if Mullins is joking.

Saffron watches as, outside, Felix leans against the balustrade, his eyes on Broady's surf lesson. If Rockpool House really is to be his, maybe he will stick around. Stranger things have happened. But it's probably more likely that he'll sell up, and some rich person will roll in – and then roll out again just as fast when the sun goes down, or the novelty fades, or something else, somewhere else, feels more important. Porthpella nothing more than a page in a portfolio of investments. A line on a spreadsheet. An occasional weekend, *commitments permitting.*

A soulless way to live a life.

And then there are the people like Gus. And the people like Jayden. The ones who just get it. Who come and slot in like they were meant to be here all along; like Porthpella was just waiting for them to find it. Would Baz have been one of those people too?

'Seriously,' says Mullins, 'Rockpool House is worth a fortune.'

'Mullins, you don't need cash, because apparently wherever you go these days you get free stuff, right?'

'Speaking of . . . that Blue Juice looked decent. I could do with an energy boost. Did I tell you it was a big night?'

'Yeah, yeah,' she says. But she's already reaching for the blueberries, double scoops, because she could use one too. It was a big night – Mullins was right about that. It was a big weekend, too. But it's behind them now. And what lies ahead? Summer in Porthpella, that's what. Sunrise surfs and fires at dusk. Skating the coast road. Trays of fresh baked brownies and a new coffee roast that people should write songs about. And every morning Saffron will throw open the doors of Hang Ten, feeling like she's the luckiest person alive.

'Might as well chuck in a cookie, while you're at it, Saff. A nice big one.'

71

On the way home from the hospital, Ally stops in at the Bluebird. Sunita comes out to meet her and hugs her hard. Ally hugs her back. She hugged the doctor earlier too. This is, apparently, becoming a habit. She was never really a hugger before.

'Do you know,' says Sunita, 'I thought that woman had this weird intensity when she came in wanting that iced tea. We had the "Closed" sign up and everything.'

Ally bites down a smile, although there's nothing funny about it. She's probably light-headed, still. She hardly slept last night. Though she did doze off beside Gus this afternoon; their hands entwined.

I was talking to you, he said. *Then I realised you'd fallen asleep.*

She stopped a smile at that too.

'I feel sorry for her,' she says now. 'Despite everything.'

'I suppose it's not like she wanted to hurt Gus,' says Sunita. 'Wrong place, wrong time.'

And it did make it better, in a way. Because the truth is, Ally really did like Tallulah. She's never made friends easily – not in the past, anyway – but there was something about the woman from Topanga: they just clicked. And the way Tallulah talked about her love for Baz was moving. Ally would never have imagined that love could evolve into something so violent; that Tallulah would have that capacity. But perhaps anyone can lose control, and that's what Ally is trying to think – that it was a moment of madness; that Tallulah didn't go to Rockpool with murderous intentions that night. Because if she did, then the uncomfortable truth is that they played a part in enabling her.

Gus isn't up to dispensing wisdoms yet, but Ally remembers his words of comfort when she felt culpable before, in their very first case. And she keeps those words in her mind now too.

She tried to be a friend to Tallulah in her moment of need. She couldn't have known how it would turn out.

The sea-glass heart has been taken into evidence. Not that it will be vital, because Davey gave a full statement, and Tallulah a full confession. But strange to think of it there, nevertheless. Washed on tides, found on a strandline, pressed into the hand of someone who needed it. Then bagged and filed. The end of its journey.

If Gus was unlucky, he was also lucky.

Just as Jet Carson was lucky that the knife he grabbed from the kitchen at Rockpool happened to be the very same one that Felix had used two days before. Jet's clumsy framing looked a lot more convincing with that detail.

If Jayden hadn't kept pushing, if, together, they hadn't come up with an alternative scenario for Skinner, then Felix would still be in custody.

Luck, lack of luck, the way the world turns both discriminately, and indiscriminately, makes Ally's head spin sometimes.

'So, Ally, what do you want to do about the pictures? They're bought and paid for but . . .'

'I've honestly got no idea,' says Ally, with a sigh. 'Can we refund the money? I don't . . . want it.'

'Of course. And you've got the space until the end of the week. I can reach out to the guests from the night. I know some were disappointed there were none left.'

Ally tells her that anything goes. That they can donate them all to public spaces, if she wants, and Ally will pay Sunita her cut anyway. Perhaps the hospital would take one? It was so terribly drab in those corridors. Not that she isn't grateful for every inch of the place. Every single millimetre.

'Ally Bright, you're the least commercial artist I know,' says Sunita.

They hug again, and then Ally's driving out of the village, on to the dune road. Sand spins beneath her wheels, and towering mallow brushes the metalwork. The bay opens wide as she drives towards home, and she thinks how the sky and the water, newly blue after last night's storm, are the brightest shades she's ever seen. It's as if all the colours of the world have been turned up. That's how she's felt since she opened her eyes back at The Shell House this morning, Fox curled at her feet, and she remembered that Gus was in hospital, that he was terribly hurt, but he would be okay. A full recovery would be his. If he took it slow. Gentle. No upheaval.

'Ah,' he'd said, earlier this afternoon, 'about that.'

That was when Gus told Ally about the email from Jacqueline Clifton and her plan to sell All Swell.

'But that's wonderful,' Ally said. 'I mean, that you can remember it. That's a good sign.'

'Ally,' said Gus, 'I hear you. But . . . it's All Swell. My home.'

'I know,' she said, squeezing his hand. 'But we'll think of something. I promise.'

Ally doesn't know how much Gus heard of what she said to him as he lay sleeping last night; that period of time when he was neither at shore nor at sea. She doesn't know if he heard any of it at all. Perhaps it'll come up one day. Or perhaps it won't. She spoke from the heart, that much is true; a heart blown wide open, after being under lock and key.

If you're alright, if you can just be alright, I won't waste another minute.

She can't imagine Gus not living in the dunes. But compared to him not living at all, it feels like a surmountable problem.

As Ally's car rolls down the track, The Shell House comes into view. And just as he said he would be, Jayden's waiting for her. He holds up his hand and waves, and she presses the horn in reply. But then she sees that he's not on his own. At first, she thinks it's Cat – later she'll blame the sun in her eyes, but more likely it's because her own daughter was the last person she expected to see. Ally sees then that the boys are here too. She can't believe the size of them: her little big grandsons. Her heart jumps in her chest. Evie must have heard – heard and come. But then Ally does the calculation – it's not even twenty-four hours since the party. Evie would have been in the sky as Gus's life hung in the balance.

'Mum.' Her daughter is at the car and in her arms before Ally's even out.

'But what are you doing here?' She laughs delightedly.

'Taking a leaf out of your book,' says Evie. 'Doing something different.'

～

Ally treads out on to the veranda, closing the door behind her. Evie is unpacking, back in the bedroom that was hers as a child. She was a little disconcerted to find the bed had recently been slept in. *Long story*, Ally said. *Give me a second to find you fresh sheets.* The boys and Fox are re-establishing their acquaintance and finding they're just as fast friends as when they last saw each other six months ago.

'Jayden,' she says. 'I'm sorry. I wasn't ignoring you, but Evie . . . I was so surprised.'

'It's very cool, Al. A spontaneous holiday. I love it.'

The voice of caution sounds in Ally's head again. 'She said Scott was too busy with work to make the trip at such short notice. I hope there's not more to it.'

'You think there might be?'

'There was something in the way she said it. And I know Evie,' says Ally, 'she's not especially impulsive.'

'People can change though, right?'

They share a smile. 'Oh yes,' she says. 'There is that.'

Jayden's dark eyes are suddenly full of something she can't quite read.

'You're exhausted,' she says. She briefly touches his cheek with the edge of her thumb. 'You should go on home.'

'I wanted to see you,' he says. He shifts on his feet. 'To tell you something. But you've got your hands full here, so . . . another time. I'll drop by. Tomorrow, maybe. Or the day after. Whatever works. There's no rush.'

'Are you sure?'

'Yeah, sure.' And he's almost too eager, walking back down the steps; lifting his hand in a wave. 'You're busy here, so . . .'

Ally follows him into the garden. Once, she would have taken more or less any exit from a conversation. But not now. Not with Jayden.

'Jayden, talk to me.' She lays a hand on his arm. 'What is it? You look upset.'

'I'm not, Al.' He passes his hand across his mouth. 'I'm really not. It's a good thing. It's just . . . change. It's a lot of change. I'm still getting my head round it. But it is a good thing. A great thing.'

'Jayden, I think I know what you're going to say.'

Because Wenna knows everything that happens around here, and it turns out a great juggernaut of a motorhome going through Porthpella turned a few heads. She got on the phone to Ally straight away.

'I think it's a wonderful opportunity,' says Ally, 'if it's what you want.'

Jayden wrinkles his brow.

'"Head-hunted" was the phrase Wenna used. By an old colleague of yours. And I'm not surprised. Not at all. The only surprising part is that it took them so long.'

Ally doesn't add that she'll miss what they do together; that she'll miss it dreadfully. Jayden doesn't need that laid at his door. Besides, after everything that's happened these last few days, she knows more than ever to be grateful. Because haven't they had the most wonderful time, as the Shell House Detectives? Before Jayden, Ally never could have imagined such adventures. Just looking at him, she feels a wave of emotion so strong that it threatens to knock her from her feet. Does this young man have any idea how much he means to her? Well, this time she won't leave it until it's too late – almost too late – to tell him.

But before she can say anything, Jayden suddenly laughs. He laughs wide and true.

'Al, I'm not leaving Porthpella for Plymouth. And I'm sure as hell not quitting us.'

'But why not?' she says, incredulous.

And maybe that's a question for another day. Or, maybe it's one, deep down, she already knows the answer to. For now, her friend, her partner, just shakes his head.

'Al,' he says. 'Cat's pregnant. We're having another baby.'

~

In the early evening, Ally finds herself alone again. There's a gentle breeze stirring, and while the air is warm, the stifling heat of the last few days has gone. Behind her, in the house, her daughter is asleep, her grandsons too; their jet lag finally getting the better of them. Fox is also dozing, his nose between his paws.

How Bill would have loved seeing Evie arrive out of the blue like this. He'd have whooped and swung her round as if she were waist-high again. Their laughter would have been heard all along the dunes.

The picture is so vivid it's as if it really happened. Past and present blurring; Porthpella the only constant. It's because there are so many memories stitched into this landscape. So many versions of the three of them, over the patchwork of years. But new memories are being made now too. Where the land meets the sea, there is movement.

A subtle reshaping.

From her spot on the veranda, Ally can see the entire bay stretching out before her. The island lighthouse, sturdy as ever. The high cliffs beyond. And the blue horizon that will later ignite in a spectrum of wild colours that have to be seen to be believed. She takes a long deep breath.

'Thank you,' she says. And she's saying it to so many people for so many things.

To this place, too. This home.

Thank you.

As if in reply, a lone gull swoops and lands on the fence. It's a kittiwake, a smaller and gentler seabird than the herring gulls that pester tourists for chips. For a moment they look directly at one another, the kittiwake and Ally. The bird tips its head, as if in enquiry. And she smiles, as if in response. Then it spreads its ink-tipped wings and takes flight. Up and over The Shell House. Into all that blue.

Acknowledgements

I loved returning to Porthpella for the third book in the Shell House series, and I hope you did too. I'm very grateful to a number of people for making it all possible.

Thanks, as always, to my wonderful agent Rowan Lawton at The Soho Agency: I'm so appreciative of all you do, along with the brilliant Eleanor Lawlor and Helen Mumby.

At Thomas & Mercer, Vic Haslam and Laura Gerrard continue to be the editorial dream team: I'm so lucky to work with you both. While writing *The Rockpool Murder* I joyfully signed a contract for three more Shell House books – Vic, your passion and commitment means the world to me. Big thanks, too, to the wider team at Thomas & Mercer, including Sadie Mayne, Gemma Wain, Kasim Mohammed and Rebecca Hills. I'm ever grateful to Deborah Balogun for the very much valued cultural read, and to the super-talented Marianna Tomaselli for the cover illustration to die for.

A big thank you to dear friends Lucy Clarke and Emma Stonex for reading the first draft and offering such wise and thoughtful feedback. And to my husband, Robin Etherington, for doing the same, then suggesting that I change the murderer . . . Robin, thank you for pushing me to make this book better (even though my initial response was to, erm, carry out a non-cosy crime of my own).

Thank you to my brilliant police constable friend Oli, for telling me how things are done in the real world. Any inaccuracies of procedure are mine alone.

Thank you to my dad, Alwyn Hall, for giving me the rock star's name, Baz Carson – and all the guitar music down the years: Baz's Northamptonshire boyhood is a hat tip to you. Mum and Dad, you've always filled our house with love and creativity, and for that I'm extraordinarily grateful.

Thank you to my treasured friends for always bringing such joy, inspiration, camaraderie and soul.

This book is dedicated to my family – Bobby and Calvin, the Halls, the Green-Halls, and the Etheringtons – I'm so very lucky to have you all.

Lastly, thanks to you, the reader, for being with me on this Shell House adventure. I hope you join me for the next.

About the Author

Photo © 2022 Victoria Walker

Emylia Hall lives with her husband and son in Bristol, where she writes from a hut in the garden and dreams of the sea. The Shell House Detectives Mystery Series is inspired by her love of Cornwall's wild landscape. The first, *The Shell House Detectives*, was published in summer 2023, followed by *The Harbour Lights Mystery*. Emylia has also published four other novels, including Richard and Judy Book Club pick *The Book of Summers* and *The Thousand Lights Hotel*. Her work has been translated into ten languages and broadcast on BBC Radio 6 Music. She is the founder of Mothership Writers and is a writing coach at The Novelry.

You can find Emylia on Instagram at @emyliahall_author and Twitter at @emyliahall.

Follow the Author on Amazon

If you enjoyed this book, follow Emylia Hall on Amazon to be notified when the author releases a new book!
To do this, please follow these instructions:

Desktop:

1) Search for the author's name on Amazon or in the Amazon App.
2) Click on the author's name to arrive on their Amazon page.
3) Click the 'Follow' button.

Mobile and Tablet:

1) Search for the author's name on Amazon or in the Amazon App.
2) Click on one of the author's books.
3) Click on the author's name to arrive on their Amazon page.
4) Click the 'Follow' button.

Kindle eReader and Kindle App:

If you enjoyed this book on a Kindle eReader or in the Kindle App, you will find the author 'Follow' button after the last page.